THE LACUNA

THE LACUNA

A Novel

Barbara Kingsolver

HARPER

An Imprint of HarperCollins*Publishers*

HarperCollins books may be purchased for educational, business, or sales promotional use. For information, please write: Special Markets Department, HarperCollins Publishers, 10 East 53rd Street, New York, NY 10022.

FIRST EDITION

Library of Congress Cataloging-in-Publication Data

Kingsolver, Barbara.
   The lacuna: a novel / by Barbara Kingsolver—1st ed.
      p. cm.
   Summary: "The story of Harrison William Shepherd, a man caught between two worlds—Mexico and the United States in the 1930s, '40s, and '50s—and whose search for identity takes readers to the heart of the twentieth century's most tumultuous events"—Provided by publisher.
   ISBN 978-0-06-085257-3 (hardback)
   ISBN 978-0-06-194455-0 (International Edition)
   1. Americans—Mexico—Fiction. 2. Identity (Psychology)—Fiction. 3. Subversive activities—Fiction. 4. Mexico—History—1910–1946—Fiction. 5. North Carolina—History—20th century—Fiction. I. Title.
   PS3561.I496L33 2009
   813'.54—dc22

09 10 11 12 13 OV/RRD 10 9 8 7 6 5 4 3 2 1

A Note on Historical References

All articles and excerpts from the *New York Times* used in this text appear as originally published, reprinted with permission.

Diego Rivera, "Rivera Still Admires Trotsky; Regrets Their Views Clashed," April 15, 1939.

"U.S. Forbids Entry of Trotsky's Body; Soviet Calls Him Traitor," August 25, 1940.

"2,541 Axis Aliens Now in Custody," December 13, 1941.

Samuel A. Tower, "79 in Hollywood Found Subversive, Inquiry Head Says," October 23, 1947.

"Truman Is Linked By Scott to Reds," September 26, 1948.

The following article excerpts are also used with permission.

Anthony Standen, "Japanese Beetle: Voracious, Libidinous, Prolific, He Is Eating His Way across the US," *Life*, July 17, 1944.

"Peekskill Battle Lines," *Life*, September 19, 1949.

Frank Desmond, "M'Carthy Charges Reds Hold U.S. Jobs," *Wheeling Intelligencer*, February 10, 1950.

All other newspaper articles in the novel are fictional. Historical persons are portrayed and quoted from the historical record, but their conversations with the character Harrison Shepherd are entirely invented. This is a work of fiction.

❋

The author gratefully acknowledges the usefulness of Alain Dugrand, *Trotsky in Mexico, 1937–1940* (Manchester, England: Carcanet, 1992); Leon Trotsky, *My Life: An Attempt at an Autobiography* (New York: Pathfinder Press, 1970); *The Diary of Frida Kahlo: An Intimate Self-Portrait* (New York: Harry N. Abrams, 2005); Malka Drucker, *Frida Kahlo: Torment and Triumph* (Albuquerque: University of New

Mexico Press, 1995); Hayden Herrera, *Frida: A Biography of Frida Kahlo* (New York: Harper & Row, 1983); Walter Bernstein, *Inside Out: A Memoir of the Blacklist* (Da Capo, 2000); William Manchester, *The Glory and the Dream* (Boston: Little, Brown, 1973); Martha Norburn Mead, *Asheville: In Land of the Sky* (Richmond, Va.: Dietz Press, 1942); and Hernando Cortés, *Five Letters of Cortés to the Emperor*, trans. J. Bayard Morris (New York: Norton, 1969), as well as the estates of Lev Trotsky, Dolores Olmedo, Frida Kahlo, and Diego Rivera for opening these persons' homes and archives. *Gracias* to the Instituto Nacional de Antropología e Historia (INAH) for its meticulous care of Mexico's historical treasures (notably the Rivera murals) and enduring dedication to public access. Finally, special thanks to Maria Cristina Fontes, Judy Carmichael, Terry Karten, Montserrat Fontes, Sam Stoloff, Ellen Geiger, Frances Goldin, Matt McGowan, Sonya Norman, Jim Malusa, Fenton Johnson, Steven Hopp, Lily Kingsolver, and Camille Kingsolver.

THE LACUNA

PART I

Mexico, 1929–1931

(VB)

Isla Pixol, Mexico, 1929

In the beginning were the howlers. They always commenced their bellowing in the first hour of dawn, just as the hem of the sky began to whiten. It would start with just one: his forced, rhythmic groaning, like a saw blade. That aroused others near him, nudging them to bawl along with his monstrous tune. Soon the maroon-throated howls would echo back from other trees, farther down the beach, until the whole jungle filled with roaring trees. As it was in the beginning, so it is every morning of the world.

The boy and his mother believed it was saucer-eyed devils screaming in those trees, fighting over the territorial right to consume human flesh. The first year after moving to Mexico to stay at Enrique's house, they woke up terrified at every day's dawn to the howling. Sometimes she ran down the tiled hallway to her son's bedroom, appearing in the doorway with her hair loose, her feet like iced fish in the bed, pulling the crocheted bedspread tight as a web around the two of them, listening.

It should have been like a storybook here. That is what she'd promised him, back in the cold little bedroom in Virginia North America: if they ran away to Mexico with Enrique she could be the bride of a wealthy man and her son would be the young squire, in a hacienda surrounded by pineapple fields. The island would be encircled with a shiny band of sea like a wedding ring, and somewhere on the mainland was its gem, the oil fields where Enrique made his fortune.

But the storybook was *The Prisoner of Zenda*. He was not a young squire, and his mother after many months was still no bride. Enrique was their captor, surveying their terror with a cool eye while eating his breakfast. "That howling is the *aullaros*," he would say, as he pulled the white napkin out of its silver ring into his silver-ringed fingers, placing it on his lap and slicing into his breakfast with a fork and knife. "They howl at one another to settle out their territories, before they begin a day of hunting for food."

Their food might be us, mother and son agreed, when they huddled together inside the spiderweb of bedspread, listening to a rising tide of toothsome roars. *You had better write all this in your notebook,* she said, *the story of what happened to us in Mexico. So when nothing is left of us but bones, someone will know where we went.* She said to start this way: In the beginning were the *aullaros*, crying for our blood.

Enrique had lived his whole life in that hacienda, ever since his father built it and flogged the *indios* into planting his pineapple fields. He had been raised to understand the usefulness of fear. So it was nearly a year before he told them the truth: the howling is only monkeys. He didn't even look across the table when he said it, only at the important eggs on his plate. He hid a scornful smile under his moustache, which is not a good hiding place. "Every ignorant Indian in the village knows what they are. You would too, if you went out in the morning instead of hiding in bed like a pair of sloths."

It was true: the creatures were long-tailed monkeys, eating leaves. How could such a howling come from a thing so honestly ordinary? But it did. The boy crept outdoors early and learned to spot them, high in the veil of branches against white sky. Hunched, woolly bodies balanced on swaying limbs, their tails reaching out to stroke the branches like guitar strings. Sometimes the mother monkeys cradled little babes, born to precarious altitudes, clinging for their lives.

So there weren't any tree demons. And Enrique was not really a wicked king, he was only a man. He looked like the tiny man on top of a wedding cake: the same round head with parted, shiny hair, the same small moustache. But the boy's mother was not the tiny bride, and of course there is no place on that cake for a child.

When Enrique wanted to ridicule him after that, he didn't even need to mention devils, he only rolled his eyes up at the trees. "The devil here is a boy with too much imagination," he usually said. That was like a mathematics problem, it gave the boy a headache because he couldn't work out which was the wrong part of the equation: being a Boy, or being Imaginative. Enrique felt a successful man needed no imagination at all.

Here is another way to begin the story, and this one is also true.

The rule of fishes is the same as the rule of people: if the shark comes, they will all escape, and leave you to be eaten. They share a single jumpy heart that drives them to move all together, running away from danger just before it arrives. Somehow they know.

Underneath the ocean is a world without people. The sea-roof rocks overhead as you drift among the purple trees of the coral forest, surrounded by a heavenly body of light made of shining fishes. The sun comes down through the water like flaming arrows, touching the scaly bodies and setting every fin to flame. A thousand fishes make the school, but they always move together: one great, bright, brittle altogetherness.

It's a perfect world down there, except for the one of them who can't breathe water. He holds his nose, dangling from the silver ceiling like a great ugly puppet. Little hairs cover his arms like grass. He is pale, lit up by watery light on prickled boy skin, not the scaled slick silver merman he wants to be. The fish dart all around him and he feels lonely. He knows it is stupid to feel lonely because he isn't a fish, but he does. And yet he stays there anyway, trapped in the below-life, wishing he could dwell in their city with that bright, liquid life flowing all around him. The glittering school pulls in at one side and pushes out the other, a crowd of specks moving in and out like one great breathing creature. When a shadow comes along, the mass of fish darts instantly to its own center, imploding into a dense, safe core, and leaving the boy outside.

How can they know to save themselves, and leave him to be eaten? They have their own God, a puppet master who rules their one-fish mind, holding a thread attached to every heart in their crowded world. All the hearts but one.

The boy discovered the world of the fishes after Leandro gave him a diving goggle. Leandro, the cook, took pity on the flutie boy from America who had nothing to do all day but poke around in the cliffs along the beach, pretending to hunt for something. The goggle had glass lenses, and was made with gum rubber and most of the parts of an airman's goggle. Leandro said his brother used it when he was alive. He showed how to spit in it before putting it on, so it wouldn't go foggy.

"*Andele*. Go on now, get in the water," he said. "You will be surprised."

The pale-skinned boy stood shivering in water up to his waist, thinking these were the most awful words in any language: *You will be surprised*. The moment when everything is about to change. When Mother was leaving Father (loudly, glasses crashing against the wall), taking the child to Mexico, and nothing to do but stand in the corridor of the cold little house, waiting to be told. The exchanges were never good: taking a train, a father and then no father. Don Enrique from the consulate in Washington, then Enrique in Mother's bedroom. Everything changes *now*, while you stand shivering in the corridor waiting to slip through one world into the next.

And now, at the end of everything, this: standing waist-deep in the ocean wearing the diving goggle, with Leandro watching. A pack of village boys had come along too, their dark arms swinging, carrying the long knives they used for collecting oysters. White sand caked the sides of their feet like pale moccasins. They stopped to watch, all the swinging arms stopped, frozen in place, waiting. There was nothing left for him to do but take a breath and dive into that blue place.

And *oh God* there it was, the promise delivered, a world. Fishes mad with color, striped and dotted, golden bodies, blue heads. Societies of fish, a public, suspended in its watery world, poking pointed noses into coral. They pecked at the pair of hairy tree trunks, his legs, these edifices that were nothing to them but more landscape. The boy got a bit of a stiffy, he was that afraid, and that happy. No more empty-headed bobbing in the sea, after this. No more believing in an ocean with nothing inside but blue water.

He refused to come out of the sea all day, until the colors began to go dark. Luckily his mother and Enrique had enough to drink, sitting on the terrace with the men from America turning the air blue with their cigars, discussing the assassination of Obregón, wondering who would now stop the land reforms before the *indios* took everything. If not for so much mezcal and lime, his mother might have grown bored with the man-talk, and thought to wonder whether her son had drowned.

It was only Leandro who wondered. The next morning when the boy walked out to the kitchen pavilion to watch breakfast cooking, Leandro said, "*Pícaro*, you'll pay. A man has to pay for every crime." Leandro had worried all afternoon that the goggle he brought to this house had become an instrument of death. The punishment was waking up with a sun-broilt spot the size of a tortilla, hot as fire. When the criminal pulled up his nightshirt to show the seared skin on his back, Leandro laughed. He was brown as coconuts, and hadn't thought of sun burn. But for once he didn't say *usted pagará*, in the formal language of servants to masters. He said *tú pagarás*, you will pay, in the language of friends.

The criminal was unrepentant: "You gave me the goggle, so it's your fault." And went back into the sea again for most of that day, and burnt his back as crisp as fat rinds in a kettle. Leandro had to rub lard on it that night, saying "*Pícaro*, rascal boy, why do you do such stupid things?" *No seas malo*, he said, the familiar "you," language of friends, or lovers, or adults to children. There is no knowing which.

On Saturday night before Holy Week, Salomé wanted to go into town to hear the music. Her son would have to go too, as she needed an elbow to hang upon while walking around the square. She preferred to call him by his middle name, William or just Will, conditioned as that is on future events: You *will*. Though on her tongue of course it sounded like *wheel*, a thing that serves, but only when in motion. Salomé Huerta was her name. She had run away at a young age to become an American Sally, and then Sally Shepherd for a while, but nothing ever lasted long. American Sally was finished.

This was the year of Salomé pouting, her last one in the hacienda on Isla Pixol, though no one knew it yet. That day she had pouted because Enrique had no intention of walking around with her on the zocalo, just to show off a frock. He had too much work to do. Work meant sitting in his library running both hands through his slick hair, drinking mezcal, and sweating through his collar while working out colonnades of numbers. By this means he learned whether he had money up to his moustache this week, or only up to his bollocks.

Salomé put on the new frock, painted a bow on her mouth, took her son by the arm and walked to town. They smelled the zocalo first: roasted vanilla beans, coconut milk candies, boiled coffee. The square was packed with couples walking entwined, their arms snaking around one another like the vines that strangle tree trunks. The girls wore striped wool skirts, lace blouses, and their narrow-waisted boyfriends. The mood of the fiesta was enclosed in a perfect square: four long lines of electric bulbs strung from posts at the corners, fencing out a bright piece of night just above everyone's heads.

Lit from below, the hotel and other buildings around the square had eyebrow-shaped shadows above their iron balconies. The little cathedral looked taller than it was, and menacing, like a person who comes into the bedroom carrying a candle. The musicians stood in the little round belvedere whose pointed roof and wrought-iron railings were all freshly painted white along with everything else, including the giant old fig trees around the square. Their trunks blazed in the darkness, but only up to a certain point, as if a recent flood of whitewash through town had left a high-water mark.

Salomé seemed happy to float with the moving river of people around the square, even though in her elegant lizard-skin shoes and flapper crepe that showed her legs, she looked like no other person there. The crowd parted for her. Probably it pleased her to be the green-eyed Spaniard among the Indians, or rather, the *Criolla*: Mexican-born but pure nonetheless, with no Indian blood mixed in. Her blue-eyed, half-American son was less pleased with his position, a tall weed growing among the broad-faced townspeople. They would have made a good illustration for a book showing the Castes of the Nation, as the schoolbooks did in those days.

"Next year," Salomé said in English, pinching his elbow with her fierce crab claws of love, "you'll be here with your own girl. This is the last *Noche Palmas* you'll want to walk around here with your old wrinkle." She liked using American slang, especially in crowds. "This is posalutely the berries," she would announce, putting the two of them inside an invisible room with her words, and closing the door.

"I won't have a girlfriend."

"You'll turn fourteen next year. You're already taller than President Portes Gil. Why wouldn't you have a girlfriend?"

"Portes Gil isn't even a real president. He only got in because Obregón was iced."

"And maybe you will likewise ascend to power, after some girl's first *novio* gets the sack. Doesn't matter how you get the job, ducky. She'll still be yours."

"Next year you could have this whole town, if you want it."

"But you'll have a girl. This is all I'm saying. You'll go off and leave me alone." It was a game she played. Very hard to win.

"Or if you don't like it here, Mother, you could go somewhere else. Some smart city where people have better entertainments than walking in circles around the *zocalo*."

"And," she persisted, "you'd still have the girl." Not just a girl but *the* girl, already an enemy.

"What do you care? You have Enrique."

"You make him sound like a case of the pox."

In front of the wrought-iron bandstand, the crowd had cleared a space for dancing. Old men in sandals held stiff arms around their barrel-shaped wives.

"Next year, Mother, no matter what, you won't be old."

She rested her head against his shoulder as they walked. He had won.

Salomé hated that her son was now taller than she was: the first time she noticed, she was furious, then morose. In her formula of life, this meant she was two-thirds dead. "The first part of life is childhood. The second is your child's childhood. And then the third, old age." Another mathematics problem with no practical solution, especially for the child. Growing backward, becoming unborn: that would have been just the thing.

They stopped to watch the mariachis on the platform, handsome men with puckered lips giving long kisses to their brass horns. Trails of silver buttons led down the sides of their tight black trousers. The *zocalo* was jammed now; men and women kept arriving from the pineapple fields with the day's dust still on their feet, shuffling out of the darkness into the square of electric light. In front of the flat stone breast of the church, some of them settled in little encampments on the bare earth, spreading blankets where a mother and father could sit with their backs against the cool stones while babies slept rolled in a pile. These were the vendors who walked here for Holy Week, each woman wearing the particular dress of her village. The ones from the south wore strange skirts like heavy blankets wrapped in pleats, and delicate blouses of ribbon and embroidery. They wore these tonight and on Easter and every other day, whether attending a marriage or feeding pigs.

They had come here carrying bundles of palm leaves and now sat untying them, pulling apart the fronds. All night their hands would move in darkness to weave the straps of leaf into unexpected shapes of resurrection: crosses, garlands of lilies, doves of the Holy Spirit, even Christ himself. These things had to be made by hand in one night, for the forbidden Palm Sunday mass, and burned afterward, because icons were illegal. Priests were illegal, saying the mass was illegal, all banned by the Revolution.

Earlier in the year the *Cristeros* had ridden into town wearing bullets strapped in rows like jewelry across their chests, galloping around the square to protest the law banning priests. The girls cheered and threw flowers as if Pancho Villa himself had risen from the grave and located his horse. Old women rocked on their knees, eyes closed, hugging their crosses and kissing them like babies. Tomorrow these villagers would carry their secret icons into the church without any priest and light the candles themselves, moving together in single-minded grace. Like the school of the fish, so driven to righteousness they could flout the law, declare the safety of their souls, then go home and destroy the evidence.

It was late now, the married couples had begun to surrender dancing space to a younger group: girls with red yarn braided into their hair and wound around their heads into thick crowns. Their white dresses swirled like froth, with skirts so wide they could take the hems in their fingertips and raise them up to make sudden wings, like butterflies, fluttering as they turned. The men's high-heeled boots cut hard at the ground, drumming like penned stallions. When the music paused, they leaned across their partners in the manner of animals preparing to mate. Move away, come back, the girls waggled their shoulders. The men put handkerchiefs under their arms, then waved them beneath the girls' chins.

Salomé decided she wanted to go home immediately.

"We would have to walk, Mother. Natividad won't come for us until eleven, because that's what you told him."

"Then we'll walk," she said.

"Just wait another half hour. Otherwise we'll be walking in the dark. Bandits might murder us."

"Nobody will murder us. The bandits are all in the *zocalo* trying to steal purses." Salomé was practical, even as a hysteric.

"You hate to walk."

"What I hate is watching these primitives showing off. A she-goat in a dress is still a she-goat."

Darkness fell down on everything then, like a curtain. Someone must have shut off the lights. The crowd breathed out. The butterfly girls had set glasses with lighted candles onto their braid-crowned heads. As they danced, their candles floated across an invisible surface like reflections of the moon across a lake.

Salomé was so determined to walk home, she had already started in the wrong direction. It wasn't easy to overtake her. "Indian girls," she spat. "What kind of man would chase after that? A corn-eater will never be any more than she is."

The dancers were butterflies. From a hundred paces Salomé could see the dirt under these girls' fingernails, but not their wings.

Enrique was confident the oil men would come to an agreement. But it could take some time. The oil men had come to Isla Pixol with their wives; they all took rooms in town. Enrique tried to persuade them to stay at the hacienda, since the advantages of his hospitality might work in his favor in the negotiations. "That hotel was built before the flood of Noah. Have you seen the elevator? A birdcage hanging from a watch chain. And the rooms are smaller than a cigar tin."

Salomé shot her eyes at him: How would he know that?

The wives wore bobbed hair and smart frocks, but all had entered the third of what Salomé called the Three Portions of Life. Possibly, they'd entered the fourth. After dinner, while the men smoked Tuxtlan cigars in the library, the women stood outside in point-heeled shoes on the tiled terrace with their little hats pinned against the wind and cheek-curls plastered down. Holding glasses of *vino tinto*, they gazed across the bay, speculating about the silence under the sea. "Seaweeds swaying like palm trees," they all agreed, "quiet as the grave."

The boy who sat on the low wall at the edge of the *terraza* thought: These budgies would be disappointed to know, it's noisy as anything down there. Strange, but not quiet. Like one of the mysterious worlds in Jules Verne's books, filled with its own kinds of things, paying no attention to ours. Often he shook the bubbles from his ears and just listened, drifting along, attending the infinite chorus of tiny clicks and squeaks. Watching one fish at a time as it poked its own way around the coral, he could see it was talking to the others. Or at any rate, making noises at them.

"What is the difference," he asked Leandro the next day, "between talking and making a noise?"

Salomé hadn't yet learned Leandro's name, she called him "the new kitchen boy." The last *galopina* was a pretty girl, Ofelia, too much admired by Enrique, given the sack by Salomé. Leandro took up more space, standing with bare feet set apart, steady as the stuccoed pillars supporting the tile roofs above the walkways of this yellow-ochre house. A row of lime trees in large terra-cotta pots lined the breezeway between the house and kitchen pavilion. And like a tree, Leandro was planted there for most of each day, cutting up chayotes with his machete on the big work table. Or peeling shrimps, or making *sopa de milpa*: corn kernel soup with diced squash blossom and avocado. *Xochitl* soup, with chicken and vegetables in broth. Salads of cactus nopales with avocado and cilantro. The rice he made with a hint of something sweet in it.

Every day he said, *You could pick up that knife and stop being a nuisance.* But smiling, not the way Salomé said "nuisance." Not the way she said, "If you come in here with those sandy feet your name is mud."

Regarding the difference between talk and noise, Leandro said, *"Ca depende."*

"Depends on what?"

"On intention. Whether he wants another fish to understand his meaning." Leandro considered his pile of shrimps solemnly, as if they might have had a last wish prior to execution. "If the fish only wants to show he is there, it's a noise. But maybe the fish-clicks are saying 'Go away,' or 'My food, not yours.'"

"Or, 'Your name is mud.'"

Leandro laughed, because in Spanish it sounds funny: *Su nombre es lodo.*

"Exacto," Leandro said.

"Then to another fish, it's talk," the boy said. "But to me it's only noise."

Leandro needed help—too many mouths to feed in this house, the Americans liked to eat. Also it was Salomé's birthday, and she wanted squid. The oil men's wives' eyes would swing like the pendulum of a clock beneath their cloche hats when they saw squid *a la Veracruzana.* But the men would eat tentacles without noticing, enthralled with their own stories. How their hired guns had put down the rebellion in Sonora and sent Escobar running like a dog. The more mezcal went into their glasses, the faster Escobar ran.

After supper Leandro said *El flojo trabaja doble,* the lazy man has to work double, because the boy tried to carry all the dishes to the kitchen at once. He dropped two white plates on the tile, shattering them all to buttons. So Leandro was right—sweeping up took twice as long as making an extra trip. But Leandro came out and helped pick up the mess, kneeling beneath the Americans' gaze as they commiserated on the clumsiness of servants, here is one thing that's the same in every country.

Afterward Salomé tried to get them all to cut a rug. She cranked up the Victrola and waved the mezcal bottle at the men, but they went to bed, leaving her fluttering around the parlor like a balloon of air, let go. It was her birthday, and not even her son to whom she had given life would cut a rug with her. "For God's sake, William, you're tedious," she diagnosed. Nose in the books, you're nothing but a canceled stamp. *Flutie, green apples, wet blanket*, this is only a small sample of the names that came to mind when Salomé was stewed to the hat. He did try to dance with her after that, but it was too late. She couldn't hold herself up on her own stilts.

Salomé is airtight, the men liked to say. Copacetic, the cat's meow, a snake charmer. Also a fire bell. One of the oil men said that to his wife, when the others were outside. Explaining the situation. *Fire bell* meant still married, to the husband in America. After all this time not divorced, some poor sod in D.C., an administration accountant. She had the affair right under his nose with this Mexican attaché, she couldn't have been more than twenty-five at the time, and with that child already. Left the other fellow flat. Be careful of this fancy Salomé, he warned his wife. She's a disappearing act.

On *Cinco de Mayo* the village celebrated with fireworks, commemorating the victory over Napoleon's invasion in the battle at Puebla. Salomé had a headache, one last gift from the night before, and spent the day in her little bedchamber at the end of the hall. She called it Elba, her place of exile. Lately Enrique had been retiring early and closing the heavy door to his own bedroom. Today she was in no mood for noise. Today, she complained, they were making more explosions in the campo than it probably took to scare off Napoleon's army in the first place.

The boy did not walk into town for the celebration. He knew that in the long run Napoleon's generals still came back and cuffed Santa Ana, and took over Mexico long enough to make everyone speak French and wear tight pants until 1867, or something near it. He was supposed to finish the book on Emperor Maximiliano, from Enrique's library. That was Salomé's program for him, Reading Moldy Books, because there was no school in Isla Pixol suitable for a boy who was already taller than President Portes Gil. But the best place for reading was in the forest, not the house. Under a tree by the estuary, twenty minutes' walk down the trail. And the book on Maximiliano was enormous. So it only made sense to carry *The Mysterious Affair at Styles* instead.

The biggest *amate* tree had buttresses like sails reaching out from the trunk, dividing out little rooms furnished with drapes of fern and patchouli. A rooming house for dragonflies and ant thrushes, and once, a coiled little snake. Many trees in that jungle were as broad around their bases as the huts in Leandro's village, and held their branches too high to see. There was no knowing what lived up there. Once the saucer-eyed devils had howled for blood, but maybe those branches were only the balconies of monkey hotels, and nesting places for *oropéndola* birds, whose gurgling song sounded like water bubbling out of a tin canteen.

In Enrique's library, every wall was covered with wooden cabinets. The room had no windows, only shelves, and all the book cabinets had iron grilles covering their fronts like prisoners' windows, locked over shelves packed with books. The square openings between the welded bars were just large enough for a fine-boned, long-fingered boy to put his hand through, like slipping on an iron bracelet. He could reach in and touch the books' spines, exactly as Count Dantès in *The Count of Monte Cristo* had reached through the bars to touch his bride's face, when she came to see him in prison. Carefully he could slide one book from its place in the packed shelf, and with both hands put through the bars he could turn and examine it, sometimes even open it, if the shelf were deep enough. But not remove it. The grilles had iron padlocks.

Every Sunday Enrique brought out the skeleton key, unlocked the case, and took out four books exactly, which he left in a pile on the table without discussion. Invariably historical, stinking of mold, these were to be a boy's education. A few were all right, *Zozobra*, and also *Romancero Gitano*, poems by a young man who loved gypsies. Cervantes held promise, but had to be puzzled out in some ancient kind of Spanish. One week only with Don Quixote, before turning him in to be locked up again and exchanged for a new week's pile, had felt like a peek through a keyhole.

And anyhow not a single one of those books could hold eight minutes to Agatha Christie or the others he'd brought from before, when they came here on the train. His mother had let him carry two valises: one for books, one for clothes. The clothes were a waste, outgrown instantly. He should have filled both with books. *The Mysterious Affair at Styles, The Count of Monte Cristo, Around the World in Eighty Days, Twenty Thousand Leagues Under the Sea*, books in English that didn't stink of mold. He'd already read most of them now, more than once. The Three Musketeers still called out to him, waving their swords, but he always shoved them back in the valise. Because what would be left, when all these books were in the past? He lay awake nights dreading it.

The program of a real school was vague in Salomé's convictions, and frankly in his own: dank memories of wool coats and rough boys, and *sport*, a terrible thing, daily enforced. One lady in a brown sweater used to give him books to keep, that was the best thing he recalled from home. But that is not what we call home now, Salomé said, "We're here and there isn't a school so you'll just have to read every book in that damned library, if we're allowed to stay." If not, her program became less certain.

The library often stank, from the oil men in there smoking Tuxtlan cigars all night. Salomé hated all of it: cigars, men talking. Also locked-up books, or any other kind it seemed, and flutie boys who read them too much. But even so, she bought him a notebook from the shop by the ferry docks, on the day they'd tried to run away from Enrique and cried because of having absolutely nowhere to go. She sat limp on the iron bench in her silk-crepe dress, shoulders shaking, for such a long time he'd had to wander over to the window of the tobacco stand and leaf through magazines. There he'd found the pasteboard notebook: the most beautiful book ever, it could become anything.

She came up behind him while he was looking at it. Set her chin on top of his shoulder, wiped her cheek with the back of a hand, and said, "We'll take it, then." The man wrapped it carefully in brown paper, tied with a string.

That was the story she had wanted him to begin, to tell what happened in Mexico before the howlers swallowed them down without a trace. Later on, many times, she would change her mind and tell him to stop writing. It made her nervous.

At the end of that day, after running away, buying a notebook, and eating boiled shrimps from a paper cone while standing on the pier watching ferries leave, they'd gone back to Enrique, of course. They were prisoners on an island, like the Count of Monte Cristo. The hacienda had heavy doors and thick walls that stayed cool all day, and windows that let in the sound of the sea all night: *hush, hush*, like a heartbeat. He would grow thin as bones here, and when the books were all finished, he would starve.

But no, now he would not. The notebook from the tobacco stand was the beginning of hope: a prisoner's plan for escape. Its empty pages would be the book of everything, miraculous and unending like the sea at night, a heartbeat that never stops.

Salomé for her part was not worried about running out of books, only of having her clothes go out of fashion. *You can't buy a thing on this island. Unless he wants me to be a she-goat, wear skirts down to the ground.* A trunk with her nicest things had been mailed overland from Washington, D.C., last year, according to the lawyer who was supposed to be taking care of these matters. But both the trunk and the divorce seemed to have lost their way. Enrique said they might see that trunk one day, *ojalá*, if the Lord is willing. Meaning if the Lord is not, the Zapatistas held up the train and took everything. The boy cried, "Oh yes, imagine it! The Zapatistas in their gun belts, reading Miss Agatha Christie by the campfire. Eating off Mother's Limoges and wearing her dressing gowns."

Enrique pinched his moustache and said, "*Imagine it!* Too bad you can't sell daydreams like that for money."

"Revolution in Mexico is a fashion," he announced to the oil men at supper on their last night. "Like the silly hats worn by our wives. I don't care what they told you in Washington, this country will work hard for the foreign dollar." He raised his glass. "The heart of Mexico is like that of a loyal woman, married forever to Porfirio Díaz."

The deal was made, the oil men went away. The next morning Enrique let Salomé sit on his lap at breakfast and give him a kiss like a trumpet player. A sign of progress, she declared, after he'd gone out to inspect a new packing house. "Did you hear him say that, hats worn by *our wives*?" Her first project now was to get herself moved back into his bedroom. Her second one was to fire his maid.

The boy's best plan on any day was to make himself scarce. Walk out the back through the kitchen, down a long lane of *mulata* trees with red skin peeling away from their trunks, exposing smooth black skin underneath. Cut across the sand trail through the pineapple field, over the low rock wall out to the sea, carrying a rucksack with a book and a packet of tortillas for lunch, the diving goggle and a bathing costume. No one would see but Leandro, whose eyes following him down the sand trail could make him feel naked when he was not. Leandro, who came barefoot up the lane every morning carrying the smoky smell of breakfast fires from his village, but wearing a clean shirt laundered by his wife. Salomé said Leandro already had a wife, a child, and a baby. As young as he is, she clucked, happy that someone had wrecked his life even faster than she had wrecked hers. If Leandro was already in the Second Portion of Life (the part with children), it was going to be short.

Out on the reef, the fish came every day for the scraps of tortilla the boy brought from the kitchen and tore into pieces, casting his bread upon the waters. One fish had a mouth like a parrot's beak and a fire-red belly, and was always the first in line to come banging up for the day's handout. So really it wasn't a friend. It was like the men who came to visit for the free eats and their eyes full of Salomé in a V-neck satin dress.   •

Salomé formulated her plan of attack. First, she instructed Leandro, we make only Enrique's favorite foods every day. Starting with breakfast: cinnamon-flavored coffee, tortillas warm from the griddle, pineapple with ham, and what she called Divorced Eggs, two of them crowded onto a plate, one with mild red salsa and one with spicy green. Salomé maintained her own perspective on romance.

The kitchen was connected to the house by the passageway of lime trees. It had low brick walls, planks for work counters, and was open all around to the sea air so smoke could escape from the firebox of the brick stove. Posts in the corners held up the roof, and the brick bread oven hunched in one corner. Natividad, the oldest servant, who was nearly blind, came out every dawn to sweep out the firebox and light it again, feeling his way to the flame, laying the sticks side by side like tucking children to bed.

When Leandro came he would push the fire to the sides, keeping the heat away from the center of the heavy iron griddle. He mopped the griddle with a rag dipped in the lard jar so the tortillas wouldn't stick. Next to the lard jar he kept a big bowl of sticky corn dough, pinching up balls of it and pressing them flat by hand. The heat made a necklace of black pearls on each white tortilla as it cooked. In the thick ones, the *gorditas*, he cut ridges as they cooked, for holding the bean paste. But for empanadas he made them thin, folding the tortilla over the filling and sliding it into a pan of hot grease.

Most of all, Enrique cared for *pan dulces* made with wheat-flour dough. Puffy and soft with a grit of coarse sugar on top, filled with pineapple, sweet and tart from the oven's wood smoke. Many a cook had been fired by Enrique, before this Leandro arrived from heaven. *Pan dulce* is no easy trick. The vanilla has to be from Papantla. The flour is ground in a stone metate. Not like masa for tortillas, corn soaked in lime water that's ground up coarse and wet. Any Mexican can do that, Leandro said. Dry flour for European bread is a different matter. It has to be ground so fine it comes up into the air in clouds. The hard part was mixing in the water, going too fast. Dumping water on the flour in a cold gush, causing a catastrophe of lumps.

"*Dios mio*, what have you done there?"

The boy's excuse: the bucket was too heavy.

"*Flojo*, you're as tall as I am, you can lift the bucket."

The dough had to be thrown away, and everything started over. Leandro from heaven, angel of patience, paused to rinse his hands in the wash bucket and dry them on his white trousers. Let me show you how to do this. Begin with two kilos of the flour. Make a mountain on the counter. Into this mound, with your fingers, crumble the flakes of butter, the salt and soda. Then pull it out like a ring of volcanic mountains around a crater. Pour a lake of cold water in the center. Little by little, pull the mountains into the lake, water and shore together, into a marsh. Gradually. No islands. The paste swells until there are no mountains left, and no lake, only a great blob of lava.

"There. Not just any Mexican can do that, *muchacho*."

Leandro flopped the dough over gently on the counter until it was smooth, fluid and solid at the same time. It would sleep overnight in a covered bowl. In the morning he would roll it flat, cut it with a machete into squares, spoon a dot of pineapple filling on each one, and fold it in a triangle, sprinkled with sugar grains soaked in vanilla. "Now you know the secret for making the boss happy," Leandro said. "Cooking in this house is like war. I am the *capitan* of bread and you are my *sergente mayor.* If he throws out your mother you might still have a job, if you can make *pan dulce* and *blandas.*"

"Which are the *blandas?*"

"*Sergente,* you can't make this kind of mistake. *Blandas* are the big soft ones he's crazy for. Tortillas big enough to wrap a baby in, soft as an angel's wings."

"*Si, señor!*" The tall boy saluted. "Big enough to wrap angels in, soft as a baby's crupper."

Leandro laughed. "*Small* angels," he said. "Only baby ones."

On the twenty-first of June, 1929, a giant iguana climbed up the mango by the patio, causing Salomé to stand up from her lunch and scream. And on that day the Three Years Silence ended, though the iguana had nothing to do with it.

It was a declaration signed by the president, ending the three-year ban on saying the mass. The war with the Cristeros ended. The church bells rang all day on Sunday, calling back the priests with their gold rings, landholdings, and sovereignty intact. Enrique took it as proof: Mexico falls on her knees at the altar, ready to return to the days of Porfirio Díaz. True Mexicans will always understand the virtues of humility, piety, and patriotism. "And decent women," he added pointedly to Salomé, quoting Díaz: "Only in her home, like a butterfly in a glass jar, can woman progress to her highest level of decency." He expected her to take herself and her son to town for the Reconciliation Mass.

"If he wants a butterfly, he should let me stay home in his damn glass jar," she fumed in the carriage on the way to church. Salomé was all for the Three Years Silence. In her opinion the mass could only be more tedious if they made you wear cotton stockings. She too had lived under the reign of Porfirio, ruled by a dark supremacy of nuns who showed no mercy to a businessman's cheeky daughter who came to school with her ankles showing. Salomé had maneuvered a miraculous escape, like the Count of Monte Cristo: a study tour in America, where she enlisted a claims accountant in her father's firm who was helpless before her charms. She'd solved the mathematical problem of age sixteen by saying she was twenty. At twenty-four she'd said the same thing again, balancing the equation. She became Sally, confirmed in the church of expediency. Even now, as they approached the cathedral in town, she rolled her eyes and said, "Opium of the masses," parroting the men in government who'd tried to rout the priests. But she didn't say it in Spanish, for the driver to hear.

The cathedral was packed with solemn children, farmers, and old women on tree-trunk legs. Some worked their way through the Stations of the Cross, orbiting around the crowd's periphery as deliberately as planets. A long line of townspeople waited to receive communion, but Salomé walked to the head of the line, accepting the host on her tongue as if this were a bakery line and she had plenty of other errands.

The priest wore gold brocades and a pointed hat. He had managed to keep his clothes very nice, during his three years hiding out. All eyes followed him like plants facing light, except for those of Salomé. She left as soon as possible and walked straight for the carriage, snapping at Natividad to get going, fiercely digging in her beaded bag for her aspirins. Everything about Salomé came from a jar or a bottle: first, the powder and perfume, the pomade for her marcel wave. Next, the headache, from a bottle of mezcal. Then the cure, from a bottle of Bellans Hot-Water-Relief. Maybe some other bottle gave her the flapper-dancing, crank-up-the-Victrola Twenty-Three Skidoo. Stashed under a table drape in her room, something to help her keep it up.

If Enrique didn't love her, she now announced in the carriage, it was not her fault. She didn't see how God was going to help any of this. Enrique's mother didn't approve of a divorcée, so that was one person to blame. And the servants, who did everything wrong. She would like to blame Leandro but couldn't. The white-flour dough he made for the pastries was perfect, as silky as Salomé's white dress that could be poured out of a pitcher, in which she still hoped to be married one more time.

The problem must be this long-legged son, bouncing with the bumps in the road, brushing hair out of his eyes, staring off at the ocean. No place on the top of the wedding cake for a boy already as tall as the president, who was not, himself, elected.

To get to the oil fields in the Huasteca, Enrique had to take the ferry to shore, then the *panga* to Veracruz, then the train. If he had to be gone one day, he'd be gone a week, or better yet a month. Salomé wanted to go with him to Veracruz, but he said she would only want to buy things. Instead, he allowed them to come in the carriage to the pier in town, to watch him leave on the ferry. In the flattering morning light she waved her handkerchief from the dock, elbowing the son to wave as well. They both had roles in the play called *Enrique Makes Up His Mind*. "Pretty soon he'll say the word, and then we can let our hair down, kiddo. Then we'll think what to do about you." Enrique had mentioned a boarding school in the Distrito Federal.

The pasteboard notebook was running out of pages, the book called *What Happened to Us in Mexico*. He asked to purchase a new one at the tobacco stand. But Salomé said, "First we'll have to see if there's more to the story."

When the ferry was gone, they ate lunch on the *malecón* across from the shrimp jetty, watching seabirds wheel in circles trying to steal food. Out on the water, men in small wooden boats pulled in their nets, crumpling up mounds of gray netting that rose like storm clouds from each hull. By late morning the trawlers were already docked with their rusted hulls all listing the same direction along the dock, double masts leaning like married couples, equally drunken. The air smelled of fish and salt. The palm trees waved their arms wildly in the sea wind, a gesture of desperation ignored by all. The boy said, "There is always more to the story. This lunch will be the next part." But Salomé said what she always said now: *You need to stop doing that, put the book away. It makes me nervous.*

On the way home she directed the driver to stop at a little village near the lagoon. "Drop us off here and come back at six, never mind for what," she said. The horse knew how to go everywhere, and it was a good thing, because old Natividad was nearly blind. That was a good thing also, as far as Salomé was concerned. She wanted no witnesses.

The village was too small even to have a market, only an immense stone head in the town square, left over from a century when the Indians had huge ambitions. Salomé stepped down from the coach and strode past the great head with the beard of grass under its chin. At the end of the lane she said, "It's this way, come on," and turned up a path into the forest, walking fast in her sling-back shoes, her lips pursed, chin tilted down so the marcel wave hung forward like a closed curtain. They came to a plank footbridge suspended on ropes over a ravine. Slipping off the pointed white shoes and dangling them from a hooked finger, she stepped out in her stockings onto the bridge over crashing water, then paused to look back. "Don't come," she said. "You should wait here."

She was gone hours. He sat at the end of the plank bridge with his notebook on his lap. An enormous spider with a fire-red belly came along lifting one foot at a time, slowly pulling its entire body into a tiny hole in one of the planks. What a terrible thing to know: every small hole could have something like that inside. A flock of parrots shuffled in the leaves. A toucan looked down its long nose, shrieking: *a mi, a mi!* Squatting by the chasm, he believed again in the tree-devils. And so at dusk, howling, they arrived.

When Salomé returned, she took off her shoes again to cross the bridge, put them back on, and strode toward the village. Natividad was already waiting, a stone head himself, letting the horse graze. She climbed in the carriage and never spoke at all.

※

It was a form of revenge to steal the pocket watch. Something he could keep from his mother, for refusing to tell why she'd gone into the jungle. He did it on the day the tailor rode out from town, eager for Salomé's opinion about fabrics for Enrique's new suit. Enrique was away. It was only good manners for the tailor to take a glass of *chinguirito* with Salomé, and then another one. There was plenty of time for a boy to creep into her room to look at the Father Box. It was covered with dust, shoved underneath the cabinet where she kept her toilet pot. She hated the man that much.

No use crying over a spilt father, she always said. Only once had she let him look at the things in this box: a photograph of a man who had been his father somehow. A bunch of old coins, fobs, jeweled cuff links, and the pocket watch. He craved the watch. That first time, when she'd let him sit on the floor and touch everything in the box while she lay on her bed, propped on one elbow watching him, he'd dangled it on its chain in front of her eyes, making it swing, like a hypnotist: *You are getting very sleepy.*

She said, "*El tiempo cura y nos mata.*" Time cures you first, and then it kills you.

Strictly speaking, these things are yours, she'd told him. But strictly speaking they were not even hers, she'd scooped them up in a hurry without asking, when she left and ran off to Mexico. "In case we needed something to sell later on, if we fell on hard times." If they fell on something harder than Enrique, she must have meant.

Now the watch she'd stolen was stolen again: a double-cross. He'd crept in her room and taken it while she was in the parlor laughing at the tailor's jokes, lolling her head back on the silk sofa. Among all the treasures in the box, he'd only needed that one. The time that cures you first, and later stops everything that's happening in your heart.

The blue fog of Tuxtlan cigars came out of the library and filled the whole house. Two Americans had come back with Enrique this time, to fumigate the southern shores of Mexico with their smoke and end-less talk: the election campaign, Ortíz Rubio, that disaster Vasconce-los. Gringos always made Enrique nervous, and Salomé excited. She poured cognac in their glasses and let them see her chest when she leaned over. One looked, the other never did. Both were said to have wives. At midnight they went out for a walk on the beach, in their fedoras and leather shoes. Salomé collapsed in a chair, all the flapper draining out of her.

"You should go to bed," she announced.

"I'm not a child. *You* should go to bed."

"No bunk, mister. If he gets any more cross, we'll both be hoofing it out of here."

"Where would we go? Hoofs can't walk on water."

One of the men was Mr. Morrow, the ambassador, and the other was an oil man like Enrique. According to Salomé, that second one was high-hatty, but she could make him produce the cash if she wanted to. "He's richer than God," she said.

"Then he must have sunrise in his pocket. And mercy in his shoes."

She stared. "Is that from one of your books?"

"Not completely."

"What do you mean, not completely?"

"I don't know. It sounds like it would be in *Romancero Gitano*. But it isn't."

Her eyes grew wide. She had put her hair in a shellacked wave, hours ago, but now it was coming apart, the short curls across her forehead coming loose from the rest. She looked like a girl who had just come in from playing.

"You made that up, sunrise in his pocket and mercy in his shoes. It's a poem." Her eyes clear as water, the points of her hair just touch-ing her brows. The candlelight found long, narrow lines of satin in the cloth of her dress, a pattern that would never show up in ordinary daylight. He wondered how it would be to have a mother, really. A lovely, surprised woman like this, who looked at you. At least once, every day.

"You do need another book, don't you? To write down your poems."

But already he was on the last page. The scene of his mother in the candlelight filled most of it, and the ending wasn't good. When the men came back, they cranked up the Victrola, and the one called "I Could Make Him Produce the Cash" tried to dance the Charleston with Salomé, but his shoes had no mercy in them at all. You could tell they pinched his feet.

ARCHIVIST'S NOTE

These pages record the early life of Harrison William Shepherd, a citizen of the United States born in 1916 (Lychgate, Virginia), taken by his mother to Mexico at a young age. The words are those of H. W. Shepherd, vouchsafed. But the pages preceding are plainly not from the hand of a boy. He came to his powers early, that is well known and many have remarked on it, but not so young as thirteen. He did acquire a notebook that year for making a journal, a habit kept on through life. The endeavor of it has passed unexpectedly from the author to myself, and all here collected.

In January 1947 he began a memoir that was to be made of the early diaries. The pages here previous came to me from his hand, to be typed and filed as "Chapter One." I took it for a book's beginning. There was no call to doubt it, for he had written other books by then. He'd made what he could of that first pasteboard notebook mentioned, purchased on a dock in Isla Pixol, and probably disposed of it afterward. It was his habit, when he rewrote anything, to shed himself of all earlier versions. He kept a clean house.

A few months afterward, he left off all intention of writing his memoir. Many were the reasons. One that he gave was: the next little notebook in the line had gone missing, his second boyhood diary, and he became discouraged of recalling what it contained.

I believe he did remember a good deal of it, but I'll comment no further on it. He had concerns.

There is a peculiar thing to tell about that second diary. He said he couldn't find it, and that was a fact. It only came to light in 1954. It turned up in a trunk of his things that had been stored many years in the home of an acquaintance in Mexico City. They found it after her death caused the household to be shuffled around. The diary is leather-bound, smaller than a sandwich (approx. 3 x 5 in.), easy to overlook. It was inside a trouser pocket, wrapped in a handkerchief. So it was never kept with all his later diaries, lying there lost a long while. He never did lay eyes on it again. It had no name inside it, only a date and heading on the first page as will be shown. It was only by luck and a certain letter of instruction that the trunk was recognized as his, and sent here to me. He was of course by that time gone. Without its surprising resurrection, that missing piece of the tale, there would be none to tell. Yet here it is. The writing is his for certain, the hand, style, and heading. He wrote similar things at the start of his notebooks even when much older.

The difference in style, from the writer's memoir to the child's diary, the reader will shortly encounter. A man of thirty wrote the previous pages, a boy fourteen wrote the diary herein to follow. All the diaries after it show the normal progress of age. In all, he showed a habit that claimed him for life: his manner of scarcely mentioning himself. Anyone else would say in a diary, "I had this kind of a supper," but to his mind, if supper lay on the table it had reasons of its own. He wrote as if he'd been the one to carry the camera to each and every one of his life's events, and thus was unseen in all the pictures. Many were the reasons, again not mine to say.

The little leather-bound booklet lost and found, then, was a diary he kept from 1929 until summer of 1930, when he left Isla Pixol. That one was a toil to transcribe, the nuisance being its size: small. He penciled it in the empty portions of a household accounts book. It was evidently a common type of booklet they had in the 1920s, stolen from a housekeeper, he plainly states. He hadn't yet the strong habit of putting a date to his entries.

The third diary runs from June 1930 until November 12, 1931. He took more faith with dating the entries after enrolling in school. That one he kept in a hardbound tablet of a type used by schoolchildren of the time, purchased in a Mexico City bookshop.

The rest follow in order, many notebooks in all, an odd lot for shape and size but all one gloss within. No man ever set a greater store in words, his own or others. I have taken pains to do the same. His penmanship was fair to good, and I was no stranger to his hand. I believe these texts to be loyal and stanch to his, apart from some small favors to a boy's spelling and grammars. And small is the need, for a boy that took his lessons from *The Mysterious Affair at Styles* and so forth. I took some reliable help with translating the Spanish, which he used now and again, probably without full understanding of the difference when young. He spoke both languages as a routine. English with the mother, Spanish with most others until his return to the United States. But sometimes he twixed the two, and I've had to guess on some.

The common custom is to place a note such as this at a book's beginning. Instead, I let his own Chapter One stand to the fore. He plainly meant it to be the start of a book. I stand behind the man, with ample reason in this instance. I had good years to learn the wisdom of it. My small explanations here are meant to introduce the remainder. I have set upon the whole of it certain headings, for organizing purposes. These I marked with my initials. My only hope is to be of use.

—VB

Private journal Mexico North America

Do not read this. El delito acusa.

2 November, Dead People's Day

Leandro is at the cemetery to put flowers on his dead people: his mother and father, grandmothers, a baby son that died when it was one minute old, and his brother who died last year. Leandro said it's wrong to say you don't have a family. Even if they are dead, you still have them. That isn't nice to think about, ghost people standing in rows outside the windows, waiting to get acquainted.

Leandro, wife, and dead people are having their party at the grave-yard behind the rock beach on the other side. Tamales in banana leaves, *atole*, and *pollo pipian*. Leandro said those are the only foods that could attract his brother away from a lady. He meant Lady of the Dead, who is called Mictec-something—Leandro couldn't spell it. He can't read. He didn't cook the tamales this time. At his house, the wife is Captain of Tortillas, and the *sergentes* are his nieces. When he leaves here, he goes home to a mud thatch house and women who cook for him. Maybe he sits in a chair and complains about us. No one comes to take off his boots. None to take off.

All the maids went off also for *Día de los Muertos*, and Mother had to warm the *caldo* for lunch herself. She complained about Mexican servants running off for every excuse. In Washington, D.C., who ever heard of the kitchen help having to go throw marigolds on a grave? She says the *indios* have so many gods they have an excuse to stilt out of work every day of the year. *These Mexican girls.* But

Mother is one herself. A good thing to remind her, if you want a slap on the kisser.

This morning she said, *I am no mestizo, mister, and don't you forget it.* Don Enrique is proud of no *indios* mixed up in his blood, Pure Spanish only, so now Mother is proud of that too. But she has nothing to celebrate, because of no Indian gods. Not even the God of Pure Spaniards, she doesn't like him either. She said *chingado* when she burned her hand after the maids went to their party. *Pinche, malinche.* Mother is a museum of bad words.

Don Enrique brought back the accounts books from a shop in Veracruz so we can keep track of the truth around here. He told Mother, *Desconfía de tu mejor amigo como de tu peor enemigo.* Trust your loved ones as you trust your worst enemy. Write. Everything. Down. He slapped the little books on her dressing table, making her jump and the sleeves of her dressing gown tremble. He calls them Truth Books.

Here is the truth. One booklet was pinched by the household thief. Mother was finished with it anyway. She started, but then Cruz took over the job of writing down which days Mother pays them. Otherwise Mother says she paid but really didn't, because she was juiced. Don Enrique told Cruz to keep tabs whilst he is away in the Huasteca. He says money runs out of this house like blood from a wound.

7 November
Seventy-two seconds, longest time ever. If Mother could hold her breath that long she could be divorced. But that time does not really count, it is on land only. On a bed *cercado de tierra*, locked by land. Kneeling by the pillow with a pinched nose, holding the watch up to the candle to see the seconds. It's harder to go that long in the water, because of cold. One way is to breathe a lot first, very fast, then take in one large breath and hold it. Leandro says *in the name of God don't try that when you're diving, it's a good way to faint and drown.*

Leandro used to dive for lobster and sponge for his living, before he was a cooking boy.

That is some slide down the stairs, from a soldier's life out there diving to a *galopino. Cookie! That's as dangerous as sucking on a nurse's tit!* It was a very rude thing to say this morning to Leandro, who isn't allowed to be angry. He came back from the Day of the Dead with his hair tied in a special way, the horse-tail in back wound with henequen string. Probably his wife did that.

Leandro said his brother who made the diving goggle was drowned last year whilst diving for sponge. He was thirteen, *younger than you and already supporting his mother.* Leandro said that without looking up, hitting the knife hard against the board, chopping onions.

Natividad came in then with the tomatoes and epazote from market, so there was no chance to say *No lo supe.* Usually there is something terrible you don't know.

Or for Leandro to say, *You don't know anything.*

From the exciting life of diving, his brother got to be dead. *That is the truth about soldiering, in case you want to know something,* Leandro said. *Cooking won't kill you.*

This morning low tide was early. The village boys collecting oysters came into the cove and said this beach belonged to them. They screamed *Vete rubio,* go away blond boy, scramble away like a crab over the coral rocks. The path by the lagoon makes a dark tunnel through mangrove trees to the other side of the point. The beach over there is only a thin strip of rocks, and disappears when the tide comes up. This morning the tide was lowest ever. Knobs of the reef cropped out of the water, like heads of sea animals watching. That side is too rocky for boats. No one goes there. No oyster boys to scream at a *rubio* who is not rubio, with hair as Mexican black as Mother's. When they look, do they see anything at all?

Floating on the sea is like flying: looking down on the city of fishes, watching them do their shopping. Flying away *como el pez volador.* Like a flying fish. The bottom falls, and in deep water you can soar, slipping away from the crowded coral-head shallows to the quiet dark blue. Shadows of hunters move along the bottom.

At the back of the cove on that side, a rock ledge rises up from the water. You can see that cliff from the ferry. It has long white stripes of guano, banners marking the roost holes where seabirds think they are hiding. At the base of that cliff, something lay under the water that can't be seen from a boat. A dark something, or really a dark nothing, a great deep hole in the rock. It was a cave, big enough to dive down and crawl into. Or feel around the edges and go a little way inside. It was very deep. A water-path tunneling into the rock, like the path through the mangroves.

An unexpected visit from Mr. Produce the Cash. Mother was in a mood when he left. His fancy shoes must have pinched her also. She started a spat with Don Enrique.

24 *November*

Today the cave was gone. Saturday last, it was there. Searching the whole rock face below the cliff did not turn it up. Then the tide came higher and waves crashed too hard to keep looking. How could a tunnel open in the rock, then close again? The tide must have been much higher today, and put it too far below the surface to find. Leandro says the tides are complicated and the rocks on that side are dangerous, to stay over here in the shallow reef. He wasn't pleased to hear about the cave. He already knew about it, it is called something already, *la lacuna*. So, not a true discovery.

Laguna? The lagoon?

No, lacuna. He said it means a different thing from lagoon. Not a cave exactly but an opening, like a mouth, that swallows things. He opened his mouth to show. It goes into the belly of the world. He says Isla Pixol is full of them. In ancient times God made the rocks melt and flow like water.

It wasn't God, it was volcanoes. Don Enrique has a book on them.

Leandro said some of the holes are so deep they go to the center of the earth and you'll see the devil at the bottom. But some only go through the island to the other side.

How can you know which is which?

It doesn't matter, because either one can drown a boy who thinks he knows more than God because he reads books. Leandro was very angry. He said stay away from that place, or God will show you who made those holes.

🔀 The Tragic Tale of Señor Pez 🔀

Once there was a small yellow fish with a blue stripe down his back, Señor Pez by name, who lived in the reef. One unfortunate day he was caught by the bare hands of a monstrous boy, the God of Land. Sr. Pez wanted to eat the tortilla offered by the Hands of God, and so the beggar earns his fate. He was carried to the house in a diving goggle and put in a brandy glass of seawater on the windowsill in the Bedchamber of God. For two days Sr. Pez circled the glass with trembling fins, grieving for the sea.

One night Señor Pez wished himself dead. In the morning his wish was granted.

He was to be given a Christian burial under the mango at the end of the garden, but the plan was spoilt by the cleaning girl. The maid Mother hired this time is named Cruz, which means Cross, which she is, most of the time. She came into the Bedchamber of God to pick up the God's Foul Stockings whilst he was outside reading. She must have found the floating body, and decided to throw him out. God returned to his room to find no corpse, no brandy glass, and Señor Pez gone to the garbage jar with the kitchen scraps for the pigs. Leandro said it was true. He saw Cruz throw it in there.

Leandro helped dig through the scraps to find Señor Pez. The Boy God had to hold his nose for the stink, and felt stupid and flutie because he almost cried when they couldn't find it. Thirteen years old, crying for a dead fish. Not for that really, but its being buried in a slop of onion peels and slimy seeds of a calabaza. Our meals are made from the other part of these rotten things. The food inside us must also rot in the same way, and nothing is truly good or stays here because every living thing goes to rot. A stupid reason for crying.

But Leandro said, There now, *no te preocupes,* we know Señor Pez is in here somewhere. Then he had an idea that was very good: why don't we dig a big hole in the garden and bury everything together? And they did. Together the two friends made a noble burial as in times of old for the Azteca kings, the slop bowl providing the departed Señor Pez with everything needed for his journey into the second world, and a little more.

25 December

The village wakes up in a hurry, whilst the sun seems to struggle with the job as Mother does. Last night was the party for Christmas Eve. Today she will sleep until noon, then wake up with one hand across her forehead, the frilled elbows of her dressing gown shuddering. Her voice like a Browning machine rifle sending the house girls running for her headache powders. And everyone else out of the house.

On the road walking to the village for Christmas mass, a lot of people passed by, nuggets of family in brown shells. A man leading his pregnant wife on a burro, like Joseph and Mary. Three long-legged girls in dresses straddling one gray mare, their legs hanging down like a giant insect. A peevish rooster that ought to have been in a better mood, because look here my friend: at the roadside butcher stand, all your comrades hang upside-down ready for roasting. Sausages also were slung over the line like stockings, and a whole white pig skin just hanging, as if the pig went off and left his overcoat. His wife the sow was alive, tied to a papaya tree in the yard with her piglets rooting all round. They could be free to run away, but don't, because of their mother chained on the spot.

The little church in the village has no bell, only copal-tree incense floating out the open windows to mix with the fish-rot smell of ocean. Leandro was there with his family, resting one hand on each of his children's heads, like grapefruits. Later at the fiesta he didn't ever say *Feliz Navidad* or *Hello friend I come to your house every day.* He only clapped together his small son's hands for the piñata strung from the fig tree. There were firecrackers for the holy babe snapping blue smoke in the road, and amongst all the nut-brown families, one invisible boy.

1 January 1930: First day of the year and decade.
Every *cabeza* in the house is full of headache powders. Shattered glasses in twinkling pools on the terraza. No word is heard from the turkey that chased children from the yard all December. He greets the New Year from the kitchen, a carcass of bones attended by his audience of flies.

A fine day to go out looking for a tunnel to another world. Perhaps to meet the devil. Mother called out *Callete malinche dios mio don't slam the door!* Not even the usual warning about sharks, let them have boy-flesh if they want. Clear sky, empty beach, and the water like a cool pair of hands, begging. Even the reef fishes didn't speak today.

The lacuna was there again, a dark mouth in the rock. This time the opening was deeper below the surface, but it was still possible to dive down and feel between the lips of rock into a gullet that broadened in darkness. It was the last day of the world then, time to swim inside, thinking of Leandro's dead brother. Stroking through cold water, counting the pounding heartbeats: thirty, forty, forty-five, one half of ninety. Waiting that long before turning around, feeling the way back toward the entrance, swimming with aching lungs back to the light.

Sun and air. Breathing. Alive, after all. The hand of the watch returned to the top for one more year of life, stolen back.

5 January
Tomorrow is Feast of the Kings. Only here it will be the Feast of Don Enrique's Sisters and Mother, who came over on the ferry. Leandro has to cook for them all. Cruz and the others went to their villages for the fiesta, but Mother is determined to have a feast for the guests, with or without servants. She pretends she and Don Enrique are married, and the señora is to be called *abuela*. The so-called grandmother in her chic frock lights a cigarette, crosses her legs, blows smoke out the window.

Mother wants green and red *chalupas*, and scrambled egg *torta* with sugar. Leandro would like to be with his family. He's put out with Mother for making him stay, so he made fun of the señora. A scandal. But he knows he won't be caught. The *capitan* and his *sergente* have a conspiracy.

The *rosca de reyes* is hardest to make: the cake called Ring of the Kings, using white-flour dough, the same as for Baby's Crupper tortillas. A blob of dough fit for a king, rolled out on the table, as long and fat as a sea slug. *Como pene.* Poking it and laughing: *Como bato.* Leandro is normally much more pious.

Weiner! Jaker!
Pachango!
Thing! *Thing of the King!*

Leandro had tears in his eyes and said Mother would kill us. He crossed himself and prayed for both souls. He made the cake into a ring by putting the thing-of-the-king in a circle and pressing the ends together. The token goes inside, a small clay baby Jesus that looks like a pig. Leandro said really it's not even Jesus, it's the boy-god

Pilzintecutli. He dies when the days grow dark in December, then rises again on February 2, which is Candlemas. The ancients were concerned with light and darkness. We are in the dark days now, he said. Whoever finds the token in the cake will have good luck, when the light returns.

All the rest of the year, the clay token sits in a jar in the cabinet waiting to go into this cake. Leandro took the little pig Jesus out of the jar and kissed it before putting it in the *rosca*. Round jellied fruits go on top, but he put a square piece where the token was inside, his secret way of marking it. Reach for that one, he said, when the dish of cake is passed around.

Is it still lucky if you cheat, instead of getting the token by chance?

Mi'jo, Leandro said. Your mother can't even remember the day she gave you birth. If an orphan boy is going to have any luck, he will have to make it himself.

What kind of orphan has two living parents? You said everyone has family even if they are ghosts. Or forget your *cumpleaños*.

Leandro took the orphan's cheeks in his hands and kissed him on the mouth, and then spanked his crupper like a child, not a boy as tall as a man. A boy with terrible thoughts of kissing a man as a man. Leandro meant nothing by it. A *beso* for a child.

Leandro went home after the feast. All servants have fled, leaving kitchen scraps, bad moods, and dust. What is the use of good luck in an empty house?

2 February, Candlemas

Leandro was gone nineteen days, now back. He has to make a hundred tamales for Candlemas, without his *sergente*. It's better to hide in the *amate* tree all day reading, a book won't run off to its family any time it wants. Leandro can't even read. Let him make tamales all day.

Today begins a year of perfect luck protected by Pilzintecutli, the clay-pig Jesus.

13 February

Today the lacuna appeared, a little below the surface. It's near the center of the cliff below a knob where a hummock of grass grows out. It should be easy to find again but best to look early, with sun just up and the tide low. Inside the tunnel it was very cold and dark again. But a blue light showed up faintly like a fogged window, farther back. It must be the other end, no devil back there but a place to come up on the other side, a passage. But too far to swim, and too frightening.

One day Pilzintecutli will say, *Go ahead lucky boy. Vete, rubio,* swim toward that light. Go find the other side of the world where you belong.

The strangest thing. Mother believes in magic. She went back to the village of the giant stone head. After sending Natividad away with the carriage, she said, "This time we both go." She took off her shoes again to cross the footbridge, then followed a path through the forest right around the edge of a lake. Yellow-winged *jacanas* flapped up from the water and an alligator rested at the edge, covered with waterweed up to its bulging eyes. Then back into the jungle, under giant trees. We were going to see a *brujo,* she said finally, because someone has put a bad eye on us both, and that's why she can't get another baby. Probably it was Don Enrique's mother.

The *brujo*'s bamboo hut stood in a clearing, inside a circle of stones. It might have been made a thousand years ago. The door was a curtain of snail shells strung together that made a wooden tinkling sound when his hand pulled it aside. Inside was an altar covered with little clay figures, and branches with leaves standing in jars, and cockleshells of burning copal gum, the same incense as in the church. He said to take off our shirts, which Mother did immediately, down to her silk underthings. The *brujo* didn't look at her, his eyes went to the roof of the hut and he began to sing, so he truly was a *brujo*, not just a man.

He seemed as old as a person could be, and still living. His chant was quiet and fast, *Echate, echate.* He walked all around Mother first, swatting her body gently with a branch of leaves dipped in a jar of leaf-water, shaking drops of it on her hair, breasts, and belly, then everything else, son included. Then he blew smoke over her, from the cockleshell of burning gum. With his knotted old hands he held up a figure cut from thin paper, a small catlike man-shaped thing, and burned it in the flame of a candle. Some of the carved figures on his altar looked like a man's thing, his organ. Stone *pachangos*.

When he finished Mother paid him in coins. She didn't speak until after crossing the bridge back to the village. The square was deserted, except for the great stone head. Natividad hadn't come back. "En-rique can't be told about this," she said. "You know that, of course."

"Does he want you to get a baby?"

She straightened her dress and pulled at the back of her stocking. "Well. It would change things, wouldn't it?"

Leandro's baby girl died in January after Feast of the Kings, and no one here knew. Cruz told Mother today. He was gone three weeks, not because he was angry with his *sergente*, but to bury a child. The two small grapefruit heads in church: only one now. Cruz had a fight with Mother because what Don Enrique pays is not enough for feed-ing a chicken. She said Leandro's wife couldn't get her milk, and the baby died.

How can he go home to a family with nothing to eat, then come to this house to make one hundred tamales? He behaves as if he had no dead children. The real Leandro never comes here. He only pretends.

9 March

Today the lacuna is gone. Directly below the knob in the cliff, nothing. If it is there, then buried below too much ocean. The grass hummock on the cliff face is very low to the water now. Or rather, the sea is higher.

Don Enrique is away in the Huasteca, and Mother has taken up kitchen knives. She waved one around this morning. Not to chop onions but to show she means business about keeping her secrets. Not just the *brujo*, but also Mr. P. T. Cash. So, no mention here about another surprising visit from him, while the master was away. Anyway Mother is too lazy to lift up a mattress and find this little book.

13 March

The lacuna came back. In the afternoon the rock opened its mouth and swallowed the boy down its gullet. But it was hard to swim, the water was rushing out. It was the same as before, lungs bursting, turning back too soon. Leandro's brother whispering, *Come live with me here*, but a brain hungry for oxygen loses courage and wants air.

Tomorrow will be the day.

Last Will and Testament

Let it be known. If HWS drowns in the cave, he leaves nothing to anyone. His earthly possessions are stolen things: pocket watch. This book. One year of good luck.
He leaves his body for the fishes to eat.
He leaves Leandro to wonder where he has gone.
He leaves Mother and Mr. Produce the Cash to enjoy the company of the devil.
Dios habla por el que calla.

14 March

The cave has bones inside. Bones of humans! Things on the other side.

This is how it feels when you are nearly drowned: the brain pounds like a pulse in red and black. The salt water burns your eyes, and you nearly go blind following the light until you come to the air, breathing.

At the end of the tunnel the cave opens up to light, a small saltwater pool in the jungle. Almost perfectly round, as big across as this bedchamber, with sky straight up, dappled and bright through the branches. *Amate* trees stood in a circle around the water hole like curious men, gaping because a boy from another world had suddenly arrived in their pool. The *pombo* trees squatted for a close look, with their knobbly wooden knees poking up out of the water. A tiger heron stood one-legged on a rock, cocking an unfriendly eye at the intruder. San Juan Pescadero the kingfisher zipped back and forth between two perches, crying, "Kill him kill him kill him!"

Piles of stone blocks lay in a jumble around the edges of the pool, a broken-down something made of coral rock. Vines scrambled all over the ruin, their roots curling down through it like fingers in sand. It was a temple or something else very ancient.

The light through the trees was shadowy at midday, but the water was clear. Belly-dragged up on a flat stone, sitting at the edge looking back in, it was plain to see the bottom of the cave dropped down to make a sort of room down there, huge and deep. Stones were piled like a sand castle underwater, with bits of shining things mixed into the pile. Maybe yellow leaves, or gold coins. It was like coming up inside a storybook. An ancient temple in the forest, and a pirate's treasure below. The treasure was mostly shells and broken pottery covered with sea moss, mostly too deep to dive down and reach.

It took hours to explore everything. Some of the broken blocks of the ruin had designs carved on them, a script of lines and circles or perhaps the portraits of gods. One looked like a skeleton, its arms flung open, the skull smiling wide. A water snake slipped off a rock and made a sliding S shape across the top of the water. The jungle vines were tangled like fishing nets. It was the type of forest with a watery floor, and no good way to walk out of there. And no good way to swim back out of that cave, either. No way back from this story, it seemed. Nothing left to do but slide like a turtle into the pool, sink down, and sit on slime-covered rocks and the treasure of ancient times.

That is where the bones were! Leg bones, wedged in the rocks. It made for such a shock, it was hard to breathe after seeing them. Floating in the pool was also not very easy because now the tide pulled downward, dropping lower and sucking against the stones around the edge of the hole, hissing a song of drowning: *ahogarse, ahogarse*. The ocean pulled hard, dragging a coward explorer back from the secret place, sucking him out through the tunnel and spitting him into the open sea.

Out there again gasping, it was plain that the tide had turned and gone out. Now it was extremely low. Coral knobs poked out like heads. A great round moon hung on the eastern horizon, just coming out of the sea, white as an oyster.

Then it seemed the bones and temple could not have been real, and this cave would vanish again. Only the moon was real, as big and whole as breathing.

A book in Don Enrique's library says the pagans of old built their castles on this island. Not as tall as the great pyramids of the Azteca, but small stepped temples with platforms for sacrifice. They carved pictures of their gods, which were many in number. The book said the same things Leandro says, that the ancients watched light and signs to tell them when to plant corn, when to get married. But it also told more terrible things: they made sacrifices by throwing gold and sometimes girls (alive) into water holes in the forest. The cave must be that kind of hole, a *cenote*. Because of the bones.

The book was written by a priest, not very good, but interesting at some parts. Hernán Cortés sent an expeditionary force to destroy the pagan city here and build the cathedral in town. If the ruin in the jungle is really part of that ancient city, then for certain the cenote has gold and treasure in its depths, along with the bones of unlucky girls. Leandro might know something about it, but can't be asked. There is no trusting his allegiance, he might tell Mother. So he will never know about going inside the lacuna.

24 March

First, the cave wasn't there today. Or so it seemed. But really it was, nearly two meters down from the surface, buried by tide, with a strong current flowing out of it.

The last time, it was morning when the current inside the cave pulled inward toward the jungle-hole. During the hours of exploring the tide must have turned, so at evening it was easy to swim out. The moon was just rising then. The tides are the cause. The time to go in is just before the tide turns. Otherwise, more bones on that pile.

25 March

The tide was wrong completely, the current flowed out of the cave all day. On the day of the full moon, everything was right.

Don Enrique says a full moon pulls up the highest tides of the month, at midday and midnight. And it pulls them down to their lowest ebb when it is rising or setting. So says a man in a frock coat and breeches who, if he tried to row a boat, would fall out instantly and drown. But Leandro said the same thing about the moon and high tide, so it might be true.

How can you know if the moon is going toward full, or disappearing?

This evening the moon was half, and Leandro said it's dying away. You can tell because it's shaped like the letter C, not curved forward like D. He says when the moon is D like Dios, it is growing to fill God's sky. When dying away it is C, like Cristo on the cross. So, no good tides again for many days.

12 April

Today was the full moon, perfect tide, and the bad luck of slicing the end of a finger with the kitchen knife. Blood everywhere, even in the masa, turning it pink. It had to be thrown out. *Oh no, let's serve it to Don Enrique and Mother! A* clayuda *of her son's blood, like the Azteca sacrifices to their gods.*

Leandro said, Pray God forgives you for such talk. Get busy and make more masa.

Tonight the moon rose, the beach was quiet, and no one swam into the lacuna. The three Musketeers would have done it, diving in with scabbards in their teeth, not bandages on their fingers. But they were three, all for one and one for all.

Tonight a shadow passed across the moon. Don Enrique says an eclipse. But Leandro says it is El Dios and El Cristo putting their heads together, crying over everything that happens down here.

2 May

Birthday of Santa Rita de Casia. Mother needed cigarettes, but there wasn't any market today because of the fiesta. All the women went to the procession in long ruffled skirts, their hair braided with ribbons and flowers. Boys carrying beeswax candles as tall as men. The old woman who sells nopal in the market was at the front, dressed like a wrinkled bride. Her old groom shuffled beside, holding her arm.

Leandro says they couldn't have this fiesta last year because of the Silence against the church. But that Santa Rita de Casia is not really a saint, but a woman-god. Nothing is ever what they say, and no one holy one hundred percent.

12 May

Perfect tide today. Into the cave and back out. The water pushed, all the way in, to touch those bones again. Tomorrow the tide should be almost perfect again. But only a few more days this month, to look for the treasure hidden from Hernán Cortés.

13 May

Mother says tonight. In just a few hours we leave on the ferry. It isn't possible just to go away from here, but she said, Oh yes it is. Leave everything.

Tell no one, she said: Don Enrique will be furious. Not even Cruz can know, don't pack anything from your room yet because she would notice. Wait till it's almost time. Take only what fits in one rucksack. Two books, only. Not those huaraches, don't be ridiculous, your good shoes.

She said: *Bueno.* Very fine. If you want to stay here, stay. On this stupid island so far from everything, you have to yell three times before even Jesus Cristo can hear you. I will happily go without you, and light a candle for you in the Catedral Nacional when I get there. Because when Enrique finds out, he'll kill you instead of me.

Mr. Produce the Cash is meeting us on the mainland.

You will not say one word to Leandro. Not one word, mister.

Dear Leandro, here is the note you won't read because you can't read. The pocket watch is in the jar in the cabinet, with the clay Pilzintecutli. It's a gift to find next year when you have to make the *rosca* with no *sergente* to help mix the flour. The watch is gold, maybe you can take it to monte de piedad and get money for your family. Or keep it to remind you of the pest who is gone.

Mexico City, 1930 (vb)

11 June

La luna de junio, first full moon in June, a day to dive for treasure. But the nearest thing to ocean here is the rot-fish smell on Saturdays after all the wives on the alley cooked fish the day before, and their garbage is waiting for the slop-cart man. The ocean is the last dream in the morning before noise from the street comes in. Motorcars, police on horses, the tide goes out, the prisoner awakes on a new island. An apartment above a bakery shop.

Mother says a *casa chica* means probably his wife knows about her but doesn't mind, because a Small House doesn't cost too much. The maid doesn't even sleep here, no room. The water closet and gas cooking eye are in the same room. The main kitchen is downstairs in the bakery, passed through from the street, with a key. No library and no garden here, in a city that stinks of buses. Mother thinks it is all wonderful and reminds her of childhood, even though that was a long time ago and not this city. And if it was so wonderful, why did she never go back to see her father and mother until dead?

"Quit your moping, mister, finally we're off that island where nothing was ever going to happen. Here you don't have to yell three times before Jesus Cristo can hear you." Probably because after the second yell, Jesus would look down in time to see you get coshed by a trolley.

But, she says. God has a swell house here, the biggest cathedral in the world. One of the high marks of the Distrito Federal. So far we've seen only one high mark, La Flor, the shop where Mr. Produce the Cash and his friends go for coffee. We went there alone, in defiance of orders. His businessman friends don't yet know about his new enterprise, the secret kept in a small box, the *casa chica*. The lid of the box is mother's hush money, which she says is not very much. So probably she will not be very quiet.

She needed to go to La Flor to have a look-see at how they dress here, so she won't be a low-lid dumbdora like people on that island. On the streets you can see which men are farmers who've come to the city for the day: white trousers, rolled to the knees. The men taking coffee at La Flor were all black-trouser men. The ladies wore cloche hats and smart, short dresses like Mother's, but with black stockings for modesty. The waitresses had white aprons and eyes wide with fright. This city is like Washington, and it isn't. It's difficult to remember real places from the book places. The patio had giant fern trees like the forest in *Journey to the Center of the Earth*, and very good chocolate. Cookies called cat's tongues. The cat's meow, Mother said, but really the cat's not-meow. Our alley has so many, with a slingshot you could get a good supply of tongues.

Mother was in a jolly mood, and finally agreed to stop at the stationer's on the way home, for a new notebook. She pouted: You love that little book more than me, you'll go in your room and forget me.

But just now she came in and said, You poor thing. You're like a fish that needed water. I didn't even know.

Today the cathedral. It took all morning to reach the central plaza, the Zócalo, two buses and then a trolley to get there from the outside edge of the Distrito Federal. The *casa chica* is located in an unfashionable neighborhood south of the bullfighting plaza on a dirt alley that runs into Insurgentes. According to Mother, we reside halfway between the Capitol of Mexico and Tierra del Fuego, South America.

The Zócalo is a huge square with palm trees like parasols. Facing one side is the long Palacio Nacional of pink stone, with small windows all the way down it like holes in a flute. The brick streets leading into the Zócalo are narrow as animal burrows in tall grass, the buildings close on both sides, as far as you can see. Downstairs are shops and people live above, you can see the women leaning on their elbows on the iron balconies watching everything below. Bicycle carts, horses, and automobiles, lines of them, sometimes going both ways in the same street.

The cathedral is immense as promised, with gigantic wooden doors that look as if they could shut you out for good. The front is all warbly with carvings: the Ship of the Church sailing over one door looked like a Spanish galleon, and over the other, Jesus is handing over the keys to the kingdom. He has the same worried look the bakery-shop man had when giving Mother the key to come through his shop to our apartment upstairs. Mr. Produce the Cash owns the building.

Inside the cathedral you have to pass the great Altar of Perdón, all golden with angels flying about. The black Christ of the Venom hangs there dead in his black skirt, surrounded by little balconies, maybe for the angels to land on when they get tired. It was such a monument of accusation, even Mother had to bow her head a little as she crept past it, sins dripping from her shoes as we walked around the nave, leaving invisible puddles on the clean tiles. Perhaps God said her name was mud. He would have to yell that more than three times, for her to hear.

Around the back outside the church was a little museum. A man there told us the cathedral was built by Spaniards right on top of the great temple of the Azteca. They did it on purpose, so the Azteca would give up hope of being saved by their own gods. Just a few pieces of temple left. The man said the Azteca came to this place in ancient times after wandering many hundred years looking for a true home. When they got here they saw an eagle sitting on a cactus, eating a snake, and that was their sign. A good enough reason to call a place home, better than all of Mother's up to now.

The best artifact was the calendar of the ancients, a great carved piece of stone as big as a kitchen, circular, bolted to the wall like a giant clock. In the center was an angry face looking out, as if he'd come through that stone from some other place to have a look at us, and not very pleased about it. He stuck out his sharp tongue, and in taloned hands he held up two human hearts. Around him smiling jaguars danced in a circle of endless time. It might be the calendar Leandro knew about. He would be happy to know the Spaniards decided to keep it when they bashed up everything else. But Leandro can't read a letter, so there is no use writing him anything about it.

Mr. P. T. Cash is to come on Mondays, Thursdays, and Saturdays. Mother could put a sign on her door like the bakery shop downstairs.

They discuss The Boy's Future: P. T. says the Preparatoria in September, but Mother says no, he can't get in there. It's supposed to be difficult, with Latin, physics, and things of that kind. What will they make of a boy who has only attended the school of Jules Verne and the Three Musketeers for five years? Her idea is a little school organized by nuns, but P. T. Cash says she is a dreamer, the Revolution did away with those when the priests fled Mexico. If they know what's good for them, he said, those schoolteacher nuns got married. Mother insists she saw a school on Avenida Puig south of here. But Preparatoria is free, and a *católica* school would cost money, if one could be found. We will see who wins: Mr. Produce the Cash or Miss No Cash Whatever.

24 June

St. John's Day, all the church bells ringing on a Tuesday. The maid says it's a signal for the lepers to bathe. Today is the only day of the year they are allowed to touch water. No wonder they smell as they do.

On the way back from the Colonia Roma dress shop today, it started to rain like pitchforks, and we bought paper hats from the newspaper boys. When it rains, they give up on shouting about the New Bureaucratic Plan and fold it up into something useful. Then we lost the way home and Mother laughed, her hair stuck like little black ribbons to her face, for once happy. For no reason.

Standing under an awning to hide from the rain, we noticed it was a shop of books, and went inside. It was fantastic, every sort of book including medical ones, the human eye drawn in cross-section and reproductive organs. Mother sighed for the slim chances of gaining entrance to the no-cost Preparatoria. She told the shopkeeper she needed something to put her boy on the Right Track, and he showed her the section of very old, worn-out ones. Then took pity on Mother and said if we brought them back later, he would return most of the price. Huzzah, something new to read. For your birthday, she said, because it passed almost a week ago and she was sorry for not celebrating. So pick out something for turning fourteen, she said. But still no adventure novels. Pick something serious, history for example. And no Pancho Villa, mister. According to her, if he hasn't been dead twenty years, he isn't history.

The Azteca are dead for hundreds, so we got two books about them. One is all of the letters written by Hernán Cortés to Queen Juana of Spain, who sent him off to conquer Mexico. He sent back plenty of reports, starting each one with "Most Lofty Powerful and Very Catholic Empress." The other one is by a bishop who lived among the pagans and drew pictures of them, even naked.

More rain, a good day for reading. The great pyramid under the cathedral was built by King Ahuitzotl. Luckily the Spaniards wrote buckets about the Azteca civilization before they blew it to buttons and used its stones for their churches. The pagans had priests and temple virgins and temples of limestone blocks ornamented on every face with stone serpents. They had gods for Water, Earth, Night,

Fire, Death, Flowers, and Corn. Also many for War, their favorite enterprise. The war god Mejitli was born from a Holy Virgin who lived at the temple. The bishop wrote how curious it was that just like our Holy Virgin, when she turned up expecting a baby, the Azteca priests wanted to stone her but heard a voice saying: "Fear not Mother, thy honor is saved." Then the war god was born with green feathers on his head, and a blue face. The mother must have had quite a fright that day, all round.

Because of all that, they gave her a temple with a garden for birds. And for her son, a temple for human sacrifice. Its door was a serpent's mouth, a lacuna leading deep into the temple where a surprise waited for visitors. Towers were built from all their skulls. The priests walked about with their bodies blackened with the ashes of burnt scorpions. If only Mother had brought us here five hundred years sooner.

Every day it rains buckets, the alley is a river. Women do their washing in it. Then it dries up, flotsam everywhere. The maid says it's a law that everyone has to clean a section of the street, so we should pay her husband for that. Mother says no dice, if we have to huddle like pigeons upstairs we aren't paying any damn street cleaner.

Mother's room has a tiny balcony facing outward to the alley, and this room is opposite, facing a courtyard inside the block of buildings. The family across keeps a garden there, hidden from the street. The grandfather wears white cotton trousers rolled to his knees, tending squash vines and his pigeon house, a round brick tower with cubbyholes around the top where his pigeons roost. The old man uses a broom to chase away parrots eating his flowers. When the moon is *D como Dios*, his pigeons cry all night.

Cortés is an adventure story, better than the Three Musketeers. He was the first Spaniard to find this city, which was Tenochtitlan then, capital of the Azteca empire. Somehow it was in a lake at that time. They had causeways crossing the water, wide enough for Cortés and his horsemen to ride abreast. He heard of the great city and sent messages first so the Azteca wouldn't kill him the minute he arrived. A good plan. King Moteczuma met him with two hundred nobles all dressed in nice capes, and gave Cortés a necklace made of gold prawns. Then they sat down to discuss the circumstances. Moteczuma explained that long ago their ancient lord went back to his native land where the sun rises, so they were expecting one of his descendants to come back any time and subject the people as his rightful vassals. Cortés had sent messages about being sent hither by a great king, so they thought he must be their natural lord. That was good luck for Cortés, who rejoiced and took leisure from the fatigues of his journey. Moteczuma gave him more gold things, and one of his daughters.

The Azteca in other cities were not so friendly to the Spaniards, and killed them. One was a big troublemaker, Qualpopoca. Cortés demanded him brought in for punishment, and to be safe decided to put Moteczuma in chains, but on a friendly basis. Qualpopoca arrived fuming, insisting he was a vassal of no Great King from anywhere, and hated all Spaniards. So he was burned alive in the public square.

Mother is tired of hearing bits of the story. She says she is not the damned queen of Spain, put the candle out before it falls on the bed and burns you alive.

She says we can't keep the book even if it is the best adventure ever. And a birthday present. It is too long to copy the whole story out, only the main parts. Cortés let Moteczuma go free again and they were still friends, which seems strange. He showed Cortés the buildings and marketplaces, fine as any in Spain, and stone temples higher than the great church of Seville. Inside some, the walls were covered with the blood of human sacrifice. But the people had great culture and politeness of manners, with good government everywhere maintained, and stone pipes to bring water down from the mountains.

Moteczuma had a grand palace and lattice houses where he kept every manner of bird, waterfowl to eagle. It took three hundred men to look after them all.

But really Cortés wanted a tour of the gold mines. Playing dumb-dora, he told Moteczuma the land looked very fertile, so the Great King should like to have a farm there (over the gold mine). They fixed it up with maize fields, a big house for His Majesty, even a pond with ducks. Crafty Cortés.

Next, the Governor of Honduras grew very jealous and sent eighty musketeers over to Mexico, declaring he had the true authority of Spain to conquer and suborn the natives. Just when Cortés was having such a grand time, he had to go with all haste back to the port of Veracruz to defend his position, then rush straight back to save the men he'd left at Tenochtitlan. For the people there finally got wise to Cortés, and his name was mud. The populace advanced upon his garrison, and they fought for their lives. King Moteczuma climbed a tower and shouted for everyone to stop, but he was struck in the head by a rock and died three days later. Cortés got out of that place by the skin of his neck. He had to leave behind almost all his golden shields, crests, and other such marvellous things as could not be described nor comprehended. That is what he wrote, but probably he was too embarrassed to describe or comprehend them because one-fifth share of the booty was supposed to go to her Extremely Catholic Majesty the Queen.

Almost the whole night reading and copying, until the candle burned out. This morning Mother said stop being lazy and run to the market. We need coffee, corn meal, and fruit, but really cigarettes. Mother could go for one year without food, but not one day without her lip sticks.

The Piedad market had no cigarettes. The old women there were smoking cigarettes but said they didn't have any because it's Friday. They said, Try the one south of here, the Melchor Ocampo market. Just walk south on Insurgentes to the next little town from here, Coyoacán. Take the lane called Francia. That market has everything.

Mother is right about the city ending just south of where we live. It isn't South America, but the streets turn to dirt lanes and it's like a village, with families living in wattle huts around dirt courtyards, children squatting in the mud, mothers making fires to cook tortillas. Grandmothers sit on blankets weaving more blankets for other grandmothers to sit on. Between the houses, gardens of maize and beans. From the last bus stop after two maize fields is Coyoacán as the women said, a market with everything. Cigarettes, piles of squash blossoms, green chiles, sugarcane, beans. Green parrots in bamboo cages. A band of *leprosos* walking north toward the city for their morning begging, like skeletons with skin stretched over the bones, and tatters of clothes hanging like flags of surrender. Begging with whatever parts of hands they still had attached.

The next thing to come along was an iguana as big as an alligator, strolling with a frown on its face and a collar on its neck. Attached to the collar a long rope, and holding the rope, a man with no teeth singing.

Señor, is it for sale?

What isn't, young friend? Even I could be yours, for a price.

Your lizard. Is it food or a pet?

Mas vale ser comida de rico que perro de pobre, he said. Better to be the food of a rich boy than the dog of a poor one. But today there was only enough money for fruit and cigarettes. Anyway the maid cries enough already, without having to cook a lizard for lunch. It took a long time to walk back, but Mother wasn't angry. She'd found a couple of dinchers in the pocket of her yellow dress.

Sunday is the worst day. Everyone else has family and a place to go. Even the bells from the churches have a conversation, all ringing at once. Our house is like an empty cigarette packet, lying around reminding you what's not in it. The maid, gone to mass. Mr. Produce the Cash, to the wife and children. Mother rinses her girdles and step-ins, flings them on the rails of the balcony to dry, and finds herself with nothing left to live for. Sometimes when there isn't anything in the house to eat, she says, "Okay, kiddo, it's dincher dinner." That means sharing her cigarettes so we won't be hungry.

Today she pinched the Cortés book and hid it because she was lonely. "You just read your books and go a hundred miles away. You ignore me."

"Well, you ignore me whenever Produce the Cash is here. Go find him."

The door to her bedroom slammed, rattling its glass panes. Then opened again, she can't stay cooped. "A person could go blind from reading so much."

"Your eyes must be good, then."

"You slaughter me, cheeky Charlie. And that notebook is giving me the heebie-jeebies. Stop it. Stop writing down everything I say."

E-v-e-r-y-t-h-i-n-g. S-h-e. S-a-y-s.

Finally tonight she had to give up Cortés in exchange for the cigarettes, because she was going to die without them.

The market in Coyoacán is not like the Zócalo downtown, where everything comes ready-made. The girls in blue shawls sit on blankets with stacks of maize they just broke from the field an hour before. While waiting for people to come, they shell off the kernels. If more time passes they soak the corn in lime water, then grind it into wet *nixtamal* and pat it out. By day's end, all the corn is tortillas. *Nixtamal* is the only kind of flour they use here. Even our maid doesn't know how to make white-flour bread.

While the girls make tortillas, the boys cut bamboo from marshes by the road and weave it into birdcages. If no one comes to buy a cage, they will climb up trees and steal birds from their nests, to put in the cages. You have to come before ten in the morning if you want whole maize ears or an empty birdcage. By the end of the week they will have made a world. And on the seventh day rest, like God.

The old lizard man comes every day. He and his creature look the same, with whitish scaly skin and wrinkled eyes. The man is called Cienfuegos, and his beast is named Manjar Blanco: creamed chicken.

On the plaza near the Melchor market the palace of Cortés still stands. He ruled from there after conquering the Azteca. First it was the garrison where he gathered his musketeers and schemed to take over Tenochtitlan; a plaque on the square tells about it. This very place Cortés described in his third letter to the Queen. How strange to read of a place in a book, and then stand on it, listen to the birds sing, and spit on the cobbles if you want. Only it was on the shore of the lake then. The great city had dikes to hold back the waters, and sometimes the Aztecas removed stones from the dikes, causing floods to rush over Cortés and his men as they slept. They had to swim for their lives.

21 July

The question of school lurks. Exams for entering the Preparatoria are a few weeks away, tomorrow we will go back to the bookshop for more Improving Texts. The letters of Cortés will be traded for something else, and it's no use tearing a fit to keep it. Tonight is the last chance to finish and copy out the good bits.

The last siege of Tenochtitlan: Cortés tried to block the causeways across the lake and starve them out. But the people threw maize cakes at him and said: We are in no want of food, and later, if we are, we shall eat you!

He made his men build thirteen ships in the desert and dig a canal to move them to the lake, so he could attack both by land and water: the final assault. He bore his ship straight into a fleet of canoes hurling darts and arrows. "We chased them for three leagues, killing and drowning the enemy, the most extraordinary sight in the whole world," he told the Queen, and mentioned how it pleased God to raise up their spirits and weaken those of the enemy. Also the Spaniards had muskets.

The people fought him as the bitterest of foes, including women. Cortés was dismayed by their refusal to submit. "I was at pains to think in what way I could terrify them so as to bring them to knowledge of their sins, and the damage we were in a position to do them." So he set fire to everything, even the wooden temples where Moteczuma kept his birds. He was much grieved to burn up the birds, he said. "But since it was still more grievous to them, I determined to do it."

The people uttered such yells and shrieks that it seemed as if the world was coming to an end.

22 July

The new book is nowhere near as good: *Geographical Atlas of Mexico.* The City of Mexico is two and a half kilometers above sea level. In ancient times it was different islands built on stone foundations in a salt lake, connected by causeways. The Spaniards drained the lake with canals, but it is still a swamp, the old buildings all tilt. Some streets still run like canals when it rains. The motorcars are like ancient canoes, and the people flow from one island to another. And rulers still make grand buildings with paintings on the outside. The newspapers call them Temples of the Revolution. Modern people are just like ancient ones, only more numerous.

4 August

A victory for Mother: being seen in the daylight with Mr. P. T. Cash. He took us in his automobile to have lunch at Sanborn's, downtown near the cathedral in the Casa Azulejos. The grand lunch room at the center of the building has a glass ceiling so high that birds fluttered under it, indoors by accident. One wall was covered with a painting of a garden, peacocks and white columns. Mother said it portrayed

Europe. Her cheeks were pink, because of meeting the important friends.

Waitresses in long, striped skirts brought carts of rainbow-colored juices: pomegranate, pineapple, guayabana. The Important Friends paid no attention to the pretty juices, discussing the federal investment plan and why the Revolution will fail. Mother wore her smartest silk chiffon, a blue helmet hat, and ear drops. Her son wore a dress coat too tight and short. Mr. P. T. Cash wore his Glenurquhart plaid suit and nervous expression, introducing Mother as his niece visiting for the year. The friends were oil men with oiled hair and one old doctor named Villaseñor. His wife, a Rock of Ages in high lace collar and pince-nez. All gringos except the doctor and wife.

The oil men said the sooner the Mexican oil industry collapses, the better, so they can take it over and make it run straight. One told his theory about why America is forward and Mexico is backward: when the English arrived in the New World, they saw no good use for Indians, and killed them. But the Spaniards discovered a native populace long accustomed to serving masters (Azteca), so the empire yoked these willing servants to its plows to create New Spain. He said that was their mistake, allowing native blood to mingle with their own to make a contaminated race. The doctor agreed, saying the mixed-race mestizos have made a mess of the government because they are smoldering cauldrons of conflicting heritages. "The mestizo is torn by his opposing racial impulses. His intellect dreams of high-minded social reforms, but his brute desires make him tear apart every advance his country manages to build. Do you understand this, young man?"

Yes, only, which half of the mestizo brain is the selfish brute: the Indian or the Spanish?

Mother said her son intends to be a lawyer, causing everyone to laugh.

But it wasn't a joke. Cortés and the Governor of Honduras were tearing one another apart before they'd even got started. Cortés burned people and birds alive, to be terrifying. The Azteca priests smeared their churches with blood, also to be terrifying.

The oil man named Thompson told Mother she should make a military man of that one, not some snake of a lawyer. President Ortiz Rubio sends his two sons to the Gettysburg Academy in America, just the ticket.

Mother asked the doctor's wife if there were any little schools left, run by the Catholic Sisters. The Rock of Ages nearly started to cry, saying they are all gone due to the Revolution. But they still have a place for the ones who aren't clever enough for the Preparatoria. The government has let Acción Catolica take over the schools for the deaf mutes, cretins, and children of bad character.

Mrs. Doctor said the Revolution has wrecked everyone's morals and turned the churches into newspaper offices or moving-picture theatres. She told Mother they used to have laws to restrict things like gambling, concerts, divorce, and somersaulters. In the time of Porfirio a person didn't have to see all that.

Mother might quite like to see some somersaulters and divorce. Her favorite song is "Anything Goes." But she put her hand on Mrs. Doctor's lace sleeve. As a helpless mother trying to raise a young boy alone, she needed advice.

13 August

Feast of St. Hippolitus, and entrance exams at the Preparatoria. It was a scorching: most terrible of all, the maths. Latin was a guessing game. Outside the window, noisy green parrots came all afternoon to tear apart a patch of yellow tube-shaped flowers.

25 August

Today begins the year of all suffering at the School of Cretins, Deaf-Mutes, and Boys of Bad Character on Avenida Puig. The classroom is like a prison hall full of writhing convicts, its iron-barred windows set high along one wall. Small boys and monkeys for pupils. No one else there could be fourteen or anything near it, they're the size of baboons. The Holy Virgin feels very sorry but remains outside, on her cement pedestal in the small tidy garden. She has sent her son Jesus in with the other wretches, and he can't flee either. He is pegged to his cross on the wall, dying all the day, rolling his eyes behind the back of Señora Bartolome, even He can't stand the look of her clay-pipe legs and those shoes.

She teaches one subject only: "Extricta Moralidad!" The tropical climate inclines young persons of Mexican heritage to moral laxity, she says.

Señora Bartolome, *perdon*: We are at an elevation of 2,300 meters above sea level here, so it isn't tropical, strictly speaking. The average monthly temperature ranges from twelve to eighteen degrees Centigrade. It's from the *Geographical Atlas*.

Punished for insolence. Bad Character accomplished, the first day of term. Tomorrow perhaps Deaf-Mute. After that, one could aspire to Cretin.

1 September

No reading in class. Señora Bartolome says a book will distract from her lessons of hygiene, morality, and self-control. *You'll sing a different song in the administrator's office.* She hints it may contain iron maidens and the wresting rack.

After lunch the older boys fall into sword fights, and smaller ones play at Hawks and Hens. If one pupil stilts out for the afternoon, subtracting from the bedlam, the señora could only be the happier. Mother doesn't notice either. Too busy fuming about P. T.'s big house with nineteen maids in Colonia Juárez, which we will probably never see because of P. T.'s wife. Mother's big plans, washed out. Like flotsam in the alley after it rains.

Saturday is the best day at the Melchor Ocampo market. One old cigarette seller named La Perla is boss of that place, telling the girls to

tidy their flower stalls. *Guapo, ven aqui*, take this money and go buy
me a *pulque*. I see you here every day, *novio*, are you too good-looking
for the schoolroom?

Handsome! To an old woman with the face of a lizard.

13 September

P. T. Cash came today to the *casa chica*, but left early. Everyone in a
foul mood, God included. The rain kept pouring until it seemed the
whole sky would drain like a tide. First Mother cried, then drank tea
like a foreigner, trying to drown her Mexican passions. He shouted
that her head is in the clouds, he is a man, not a fountain of money,
the PNR is falling apart and everything he worked to build is running away like the water out in the streets. The American businesses
will run across the border like Vasconcelos did. Mother knows this
small house could fall at any moment. And we shall be beggars looking for scraps at the market. Bathing on St. John's Day.

15 September

Independence Day, the town boiling with parades for the Revolution. At school the cretins performed in costume: traditional dances,
impaired by the absence of girls. The teachers made a Patriotism
Banquet: rice in the colors of the flag, red and green salsa. Cups of
rice water, sugared almonds, a little of everything, and of nothing
quite enough. At the head of the table by the bowl of pomegranates,
Señora Bartolome had put a note: Take only one, our Lord Jesus is
watching!

A second note appeared at the foot of the table beside the sugared
almonds: Take all you want, Jesus is looking at the pomegranates.
The other boys laughed and spit rice water. The prank earned great
approval and a whipping. But the administrator has a weak arm.
Halfway through, he had to sit and rest, saying, *this squalid school, is
there no better place for you?*

16 September

Stilted out of school before morning roll call. North on Avenida Puig and straight on, past the Hospital for Lepers. Past the Plaza Santo Domingo, where the scribes write letters for the people who can't. Many blocks of *multifamiliares* with tiny balconies like ours, each building painted pink, blue, or ochre. The wooden trolleys run in straight lines: north to south, east to west. The Azteca built it this way, with the Templo Mayor the center of everything. The Spaniards couldn't change what's underneath.

The Zócalo was crowded with men selling ices, women in long braids selling vegetables, charlatans selling miracles. The scent of copal. Music from the organ grinders. A man selling *carnitas*, the hungry boys following him like dogs. Some Preparatoria students put on a play in the street about Ortíz Rubio and Calles: the president was a puppet on strings, and old dictator Calles was his puppet master. The Preparatoria students had also stilted out from school.

The shortest way home was to walk by the Viga canal, filled with floating newspaper pages and one dead dog, swelled up like a yellow melon.

29 September

Today at the Melchor market, a fantastical sight. A servant girl with a birdcage on her back, full of birds. She wore her blue shawl wrapped around the cage and tied in front to hold it. The willow cage must have been very light because she was not bent over, yet it towered over her head, with turrets like a Japanese pagoda. And full of birds: green and yellow, flapping about like dreams trying to escape from a skull. She looked like an angel moving down the rows following her mistress, looking at no one.

The mistress had stopped to haggle with a man and buy another bird. She was so tiny, from the back she also looked like a servant girl. But when she turned, her skirts and silver earrings whirled and her face was very startling, an Azteca queen with ferocious black eyes.

Her hair was braided in a heavy crown like the Isla Pixol girls, and her posture very regal, though she wore the same ruffled skirts as her maid. She gave the vendor his money and took two green parrots, slipping them neatly into the cage on the girl's back. Then moved off quickly toward the street.

The old market woman La Perla said, "Don't fall in love with that one, *guapo*, she's taken. And her man carries a gun."

Which one is married? The servant girl, or the queen?

La Perla laughed, and so did her friend Cienfuegos the lizard-man. "That's no queen there," she said. More like a *puta*, was La Perla's opinion.

But Cienfuegos didn't agree. "It's her husband who chases women, not the other way around." The two of them argued about whether the tiny Azteca queen was a harlot. The lizard found and consumed a scrap of tortilla in the street. Finally Cienfuegos and La Perla agreed on one thing: the regal little woman is married to the *discutido pintador*. The much-discussed painter.

Who discusses him so much?

Cienfuegos said: "The newspapers." La Perla said: "Everyone, *guapo*, because he is a Communist. Also the ugliest man you ever saw."

Cienfuegos asked how she knew what he looked like, did he come around courting her? La Perla said she saw him once at the Plaza Caballito, down there with the troublemakers when the workers had their strike. He was as fat as a giant and horribly ugly, with the face of a frog and the teeth of a Communist. They say he eats the flesh of young girls, wrapped in a tortilla. "He's a cannibal. And from the look of her, I would say his little bride there might also eat children for lunch."

"From the look of things today, they're having parrot stew."

"No, *guapo*," La Perla said. "Not to eat! Those birds are for his paintings. He paints pictures of the strangest things. If he gets up in the morning and wants to paint the hat of an Englishman, his wife has to go find him the hat of an Englishman. Small or big, if he wants to paint it, *eso*. She has to run to the market and buy it."

"She must be carrying a lot of money in her purse then," said Cienfuegos, "because the newspaper says right now he's painting the National Palace."

6 October

Mother reached a diplomatic compromise with P. T. Cash. She gets to visit his house in Cuernavaca next week, and maybe some parties. Mother wants to learn the new dances. The Charleston is for dead hoofers, she says, only the meatballs are doing that now. In this city the smooth girls put on long skirts to do the *sandunga* and *jarabe*.

Suddenly the butterfly girls with long skirts and braided hair are in fashion. Mr. Cash does not agree; he says only nationalists and outlaws let their girls do those dances. But Mother bought a phonograph record for practicing the *sandunga*. Finally the Victrola is unpacked from its box, finding its outlaw voice.

15 October

Mother in Cuernavaca all week with P. T. Cash. She has agreed to the theory that looking for some jobs is better than staying at the school of cretins. Because of the oil men's money running over the border like water. None yet, except running errands for La Perla, which is work but no job. Trying to hire as a scribe to write letters for people in Plaza Santo Domingo was a bad idea. The men with stalls there howled like monkeys, defending their territories. Even though lines are long, and people wait all day. For two days the baker downstairs needed help with mixing the dough, while his wife was away. But now she is back, and he says Run away, we don't need a beggar boy here.

18 October

Mother is back in fine feather, with extra hush money. She bought one of the newspapers that carries the long adventure of Pancho Villa. The story is told a little each Saturday, so you'll have to buy another paper. But when people finish, you can pick it up from the sidewalk for free. Yesterday's heroes fall beneath the shoes of the city.

On Saturdays the university students have their *carpas* in the street, like a Poncho and Judas play, only with Vasconcelos and the president. Vasconcelos is always saving Mexico for the Mexican people: in a country school he takes down the cross from the wall, routs the nuns, and teaches the peasant children to read. He should come to Avenida Puig. President Ortíz Rubio gets to play more various roles: a puppet of gringos, or a baby in a basket, or a hairless *escuincle* dog. Everything but an iguana on a leash. Some newspapers agree with the students that the president is a villain, and others say he saved us from Vasconcelos, the foreigners, and the Russians. The newspapers only agree on the much-discussed painter: he covers the walls of our buildings with colors like a tree produces flowers. One newspaper showed a picture of him. La Perla was right: ugly!

They say he's making a huge painting on the stairwell of the National Palace, the long red building on the Zócalo with windows like holes in a flute. Cienfuegos and La Perla disagree whether you can walk in and have a look. The old lizard man says they have to let you, because it's courts and public offices. "Tell them you're getting married."

La Perla said, "Stupid old man, that won't work. Where is his wife?"

"All right," Cienfuegos said. "Tell them you're getting a divorce."

24 October

Dios mio. The paintings pull you right up the walls. Cienfuegos was right, they're inside, but you can walk through the main door into the courtyard with a flying-horse fountain and a portico all the way around. In all the little offices, men stand in shirtsleeves recording marriages and tax accounts. Outside their doors on the hallway walls, Mexico bleeds and laughs, telling its whole story. The people in the paintings are larger than the men in the offices. Dark brown women among jungle trees. Men cutting stone, weaving cloth, playing drums, carrying flowers as big as brooms. Quetzalcoatl sits at the center of one mural in his grand green-feathered headdress. Everyone is there: Indians with gold bracelets on brown arms, Porfirio Díaz with his tall white hair and French sword. In one corner sketch, a native *escuincle* dog growls at the European sheep and cattle that have just arrived, as if he knows the trouble ahead. Cortés is there too, in the hallway outside Property Assessment. The painter has made him look like a white-faced monkey in his crested helmet. Moteczuma kneels, while the Spaniards make their mischief: fat monks stealing bags of gold, the Indians enslaved.

But Cortés was not the beginning of Mexico or its end, as the books say. These paintings say Mexico is an ancient thing that will still go on forever, telling its own story in slabs of color, leaves and fruits and proud naked Indians in a history without shame. Their great city of Tenochtitlan is still here beneath our shoes, and history was always just like today, full of markets and wanting. A beautiful lady lifts her skirt, showing her tattooed ankle. Maybe she is a *puta*, or a goddess. Or just someone like Mother who needs an admirer. The Painter makes you see that those three kinds of women might all be the same, because all the different ancestors are still inside us and don't really die. Imagine being able to tell such stories, whispering miracles into people's brains! To live by imagination alone, and get paid for it. Don Enrique was wrong.

Where was the Much-Discussed Painter? The guard said usually he's here day and night, any hour he can get his plaster mixers and pigmentists to show up. Every day but not today.

The mural on the wall behind the grand staircase was enormous. And not even half finished. Ladders and platforms covered most of the wall, so he could reach the highest parts. The guard looked up there at the planks for a while, as though he expected to find the Painter sleeping there. But today, no.

"Maybe he shot someone," the guard said. "Come back tomorrow. He has a lot of friends here at the ministry. He always gets out of prison."

25 October

Today the Painter came to work. He was already on the scaffolds at nine o'clock. High up on the planks, hard to see, but plainly he was there because workers swarmed around him like his own hive of bees. The assistant boys were running all over the courtyard with water and plaster, planks and ladders. They mix plaster in buckets and haul it up to him on a rope. It's not just a painting, these boys explained with proper scorn. A *mural*. Hard to say that in English: a wall-made. Not wall or painting but both combined, made at the same time so the picture will never fall off unless the wall itself tumbles. A Plaster Captain up on the scaffold works continuously at the Painter's side, spreading the last thin coat of white paste. Not too quickly or too slow, so the Painter can put his pigments in the plaster as it dries.

"Those two have worked together since God was sucking his mother's tit," the boys said. They seemed more afraid of the Plaster Captain than the Painter, though both men shouted down like God sending commandments: too much water in the plaster, or not enough. Today every boy was stupid.

The problem was the man in charge of plaster mixing, named Santiago but today named mud, because absent. They said he broke his head in a fight over a woman. And according to the Painter, without Santiago none of these boys could mix plaster any better than his grandmother's dog.

I can mix plaster.

Go ahead, then.

It was like mixing the flour for *pan dulce*: how could it be so different? The powder they called *cal* has the same fine grind, floating up in white clouds around the boys when they dumped bags of it into the mixing buckets. Their eyelashes and the backs of their hands were white, and the edges of their nostrils, from breathing it. They were dumping powder into the water, not the other way around.

Wait. Spread a canvas on the floor, make a mountain of the powder. Pour water in the center, a lake in the volcano. Mix the lagoons with your fingers into marshes, making the paste thick. Gradually, or there will be lumps.

Even the old Plaster Captain up on the platform stopped working to watch. It was terrifying. "Where did you learn that?"

"It's like making dough for *pan dulce*."

That caused the plaster boys to laugh. Boys don't make bread. But they were in trouble, so got quiet again. One asked, "Like *nixtamal* for tortillas?"

"No, the white flour dough. You use it for European bread and sweet buns."

Ha ha ha, Sweet Buns! So the new job has a new name to go with it. But the Plaster Captain and Painter both remarked on the plaster. The plaster captain is Señor Alva, the painter is Señor Rivera. He is even more fat than he looked in the newspaper, and feared by the boys, so it might be true he eats flesh. But when he climbed down from the scaffold to go make his water, he said, "Hey, Sweet Buns, come over here! Let me have a look at the boy who's mixing this good plaster."

He said, "Come back tomorrow. We may need you again."

29 October

The Painter keeps boys running as late as the last trolley runs. Sometimes you mix, or tie ropes, or carry things up the scaffolds. The Palacio has spiked iron lanterns hanging from the ceiling, you have to watch your head or could crown yourself. The stairwell mural is the size of two walls, one above the other. It is meant to be finished before the end of the year.

A coarse plaster full of sand goes on first, to cover ridges and bumps in the brick wall. Next, three more layers, each smoother and whiter, more marble dust and less sand. The bumps are erased, like forgetting, and the painter begins the story new. Each day he leaves more history on the wall, and boys leave with more pesos in their pockets.

Today Señor Alva came down from the scaffold as fast as a monkey to fight with one of the guards. They are rude about the paintings. Four boys in *tejano* hats came in and said they would throw tar on the wall after the Painter goes home, to defend Mexico and save her national symbols from insult. Señor Alva shouted at the guards to keep those boys away. But the Painter seems not to care what they say. He keeps painting.

10 November

Señor Rivera is gone. And the wall only half painted. Indians and horsemen ride above white air. The mountains have no ground beneath them. The coal sketches on the rough white wall remain half alive, waiting. This can't be the end, but Señor Alva says for sure he's gone. To San Francisco to paint for the gringos. The only work now is to take apart the scaffold and clean the splatters of plaster off the floor. That's it, boys, he said. The pesos have gone to San Francisco too.

18 January 1931, Feast of San Antonio

The priest did the blessing of animals. The society ladies brought parrots and canaries to church, clutching the cages against brocaded bosoms, baby-speaking to their birds with bird-pursed lips. Or holding cats that wriggled violently, hopeful of eating a parrot. Or hairless *escuincles* that watched with big disapproving eyes popping out of their dog skulls. At the back of the church, villagers waited with goats and burros on ropes. After dogs and parrots were satisfactorily blessed, the farm women were allowed to lead their beasts down the aisle, all eyes upon the burro blessings dropped on the floor.

One old man brought a sack of dirt over his shoulder that was crawling with ants and caterpillars. When he marched to the altar, all the women in smart hats leaned away from the aisle, their long strands of pearls all swaying to one side as if the deck of a ship listed beneath them. The priest in his clean hems backed away from the altar as the farmer heaved his sack onto it and black ants swarmed all over. "Go on, make these pests into Christians!" the farmer shouted. "I'll take them home to convert the others, so they'll stop chewing on my crops and leave me a living."

Cienfuegos came with Manjar Blanco on his leash. The ladies did not know how to pray for a Christian lizard. Their little dogs are probably still barking about it.

31 March
School or a job is the only choice, Mother says. So it's school again, murderous. Today there was a body! Draped in black cloth, lying across four wooden chairs lined up side by side in the administrator's office. The administrator was still out having his lunch when the Penitent was sent in for a minor infraction involving spittle, and had to wait there a long time, examining The Body. Its feet stuck out from beneath the drape, plainly the feet of a dead person. Man or woman, it was impossible to tell, but nothing was breathing under that cloth. No scent of corpse gas either. Detective novels often mention that. But perhaps it was recently dead and hadn't had time to decay. Or perhaps there was corpse gas, the whole school smelled of piss, and it might be similar. The hour passed horribly, measured in held breaths.

Twenty minutes. It couldn't be Señora Bartolome under that black drape. Too slim. And not the administrator—everyone saw him leave for his lunch. What kind of school punishes boys by making them sit in a room with a corpse?

Fifty minutes. Outside in the sun the Holy Mother stood on her pedestal in the garden, sorry but unsympathetic. The usual position of mothers.

Fifty-eight minutes: the administrator returned in a high mood, smelling a little of pulque. At the sight of the Penitent he fell into his chair, abruptly depressed. Lately he can summon little courage for the beatings. "Oh, it's Shepherd, our troublesome foreigner. What is it today?"

"Reading in the class again, sir. And participating in a contest of sorts."

"Of what sort?"

"Of spitting to hit a mark on the floor, sir."

"Anything that might improve your character? The reading, I mean."

"No, sir. Booth Tarkington."

The administrator leaned so far back in his chair, it appeared he might fall out of it, or else begin a nap. He made no mention of the draped form. Who could it be? It seemed taller than the stunted type of boy inclined to this school. But hard to judge, lying down.

"Sir. Is it possible to ask, has any of the teachers been ill?"

Sitting near enough the body that he could reach over to box its ears, the administrator replied, "All as hale as can be expected for women of their age and temperament." He sighed. "Which is to say, probably immortal. Why do you ask?"

"One of the students, then? Has any boy turned up, well, dead?"

The administrator now seemed unlikely to nap. *"Dead?"*

"Perhaps subjected to an overly long punishment by accident, and perished?"

The administrator now sat up. "You are an imaginative boy. Are you also a suspicious one?"

A glance at the feet that poked from under that drape. "No, sir."

"You should write stories, boy. You have the disposition for a romantic novelist."

"Sir, is that a good or bad disposition to have?"

The administrator smiled and looked sad, both at once. "I am not certain. But I'm sure of one thing, you don't belong in this school."

"No, sir. That seems certain to me also."

"I've spoken of it to Señora Bartolome. She says your competence at learning the Latin lessons has surpassed her competence to teach them. It isn't fair to the others, for her to teach so much. They struggle with conjugating their shoes and stockings."

A long pause.

"We discussed a transfer to the Preparatoria next year."

"Sir, the entrance examinations are murder. At least, for anyone who's missed learning everything they teach after the sixth-grade primary."

"Indeed. How did that happen to you?"

"A drastic home life, sir. Something like a novel."

"Well, then. One can only hope you are writing it all down."

"No, sir, only some of it. On the interesting days. On most of the days it's along the lines of a bad novel with no character learning any moral."

The administrator placed his elbows on the desk and touched his fingers together, making his hands into a flower bud. The unanswered question of the corpse still lay beside him. This was more of an interesting day.

"Back to the classroom with you then, young Shepherd," he said, finally. "I will tell Señora Bartolome you have my permission to read adventure novels as much as you like, in preparation for your writing career. But I'll advise you to pay attention during the maths. They could turn out more useful than they seem."

"Yes, sir."

"One thing more. We are aware your attendance is casual."

"I had a bit of work, sir. But lost it again."

"Well, I expect there is little I can do about keeping you here. But please come on Friday. Before we dismiss for Easter week, our school will be leading the processional down the street to St. Agnes. We need six of our older boys for carrying the Santo Cristo. You may be the only one who can remember which way to walk."

"For carrying the what?"

The administrator leaned out from his desk and yanked the silk drape from the corpse, exposing a bloody head and naked shoulders. "Our crucifixion figure. We've just had it cleaned and varnished, ready to carry into the chapel."

"Oh. Indeed sir, *corpus Deum*. He lives."

School is closed for Holy Week, but Mother is in an unholy frame of mind, due to the predicted collapse of the Mexican oil industry. According to P. T., production has fallen to less than a quarter what it was when the Americans first came in. They thought they were tapping a deeper vein, he said.

"So did I," Mother says.

In a jam, she asked the doctor's wife for guidance. As usual, it was suggested that God might provide, so Palm Sunday mass at the cathedral is part of the plan. The place was a forest of palm leaves standing upright, swaying in the windless air, held up by villagers with pleading eyes and hungry children. Mrs. Doctor was dressed up in a silver fox stole like Dolores del Rio. She pulled Mother toward the front pews, away from the odors of poverty. The kneeling lasted hours, but Mother wrestled through.

The streets outside afterward were like a festival. People pouring in from the provinces, maybe some even from Isla Pixol. All eyes turn to the Virgin as she is conveyed about town in many different processions, dressed in her jeweled diadem and many new frocks at once.

Uninteresting days without number. A *National Geographic* pinched from the bookshop. It had a photograph of a Hindu with six hundred pins inserted in his body. Two skewers through his abdomen, one through the tongue. Dressing each morning takes him one hour and a half. For overcoming life's catastrophes, he walks through fire.

8 May

The administrator called Mother in for a talk before school ends. She would sooner walk through fire, yet she put on her worst dress and went. The administrator told Mother it was in the boy's interest that he should attend a different school next year. There were choices—technical, professional—but his advice was the Preparatoria. He lectured Mother using many conjugations of the verb "to prepare." Preparation for Preparatoria. But Mother prepares for nothing. She informed him it was none of his business, but her son was going to the United States to live with his father, and she was certain the schools there were of higher caliber.

Is it true? On the angry walk home, she refused to say.

10 June

The angel servant girl of the birdcage reappeared at the Melchor market. This time she was without the birdcage, but again followed hastily behind the Azteca queen, accepting every form of purchase that dark little woman could shove in her arms. Clay bowls, sacks of beans, a devil's head made of papier-mâché. The mistress limped slightly but otherwise was exactly the same, snapping her fingers at the servant girl and everyone else as she moved down the rows. Measuring every object with fearsome black eyes.

La Perla recognized them too: *That scandal, the painter's wife,* she called her. "They went away, but see, they're back, probably kicked out by the gringos. It will be in the newspapers. The Communists always make trouble so they can get in the papers."

24 June, St. John's Day

The lepers bathe again.

La Perla was right, the Painter is in the newspapers. The president wants him to finish what he started on the Palacio stair wall. All the top-level men want this Painter now, Ambassador Morrow hired him to paint his palace in Cuernavaca. Mother claims she saw it when she was there, and the ambassador also, who is now a senator of the United States. She says she spoke to him on the street, and why not, they're acquainted. Ambassador Morrow came to visit Don Enrique, it was the time she made P. T. Cash dance with her in his black-and-white shoes. Now she thinks Morrow would have been the better bet.

6 July, cumpleaños. *Fifteen years of age.*
No birthday fiesta, but Mother said to take some extra coins from her purse and buy some *carne asada* or something nice at the market. Only, no coins.

The Painter's wife was there today buying buckets of food, getting ready for a fiesta at her house from the looks of it. But no servant! The little queen looked like a burro under all her baskets. Two bananas fell on the street behind her as she walked. Down at the end of the market, men were unloading a wagon of green-tamale corn in the husk, stacking the ears in tall pyramids. The queen pointed through her bundles, making a man fill a big sack for her.

La Perla said, "Stop staring, *guapo.* Just because it's your birthday, you don't get any girl you want. Your eyes will roll in the street behind her like those bananas."

"How is she going to carry that corn? She'll collapse for sure."

"So, go talk to her. Tell her for ten pesos you'll carry it. She'll pay you, she's rich. Go on, *go.*" La Perla pushed with her little hands like knives. Crossing the street was like walking through water.

Señora Rivera. Would you like some help carrying something?

She set down her two baskets, picked up the great bulging sack, and handed it over with a thump. "Go ahead. Anybody has the right to make a kite from his pants."

There was no further discussion. Following behind her was a whole conversation by itself: her swirling skirts, her short legs walking as fast as a little dog's, her proud head crowned with its circle of braids. Make way for the queen, pulling a boy behind like a kite on a string. Her house was down four streets and over one, on Londres at the corner of Allende. She walked through the tall front door without saying "Follow" or "Stop here" or anything, sweeping past an old woman with her apron bunched up in one hand, who took the sack of corn and went away. But the Queen stood where she was, framed in the entry by bright sunlight beyond. The high wall enclosed a beautiful courtyard inside, with the rooms of the house all around it.

It was impossible to turn away from the sight of her strange little figure there, the palms and fig trees waving behind her like fans. The courtyard was a dream. Birds in cages, fountains, plants sprawling from their pots, vines climbing the trunks of the trees. And in that jungle, the Painter! Sprawled in a chair in the sun, wearing the wrecked clothes of a beggar and the glasses of a professor. He was smoking a cigar and reading a newspaper.

"Oh! Good morning, sir."

"Who is it?" He barely glanced up. His wife gave a warning look.

"Sir, the nation rejoices in your return."

"The nation considers me to be worth approximately two peanuts, at most."

"Nevertheless, sir. Do you need a plaster mixer?"

Now the paper dropped onto the round belly and he looked up, taking off his glasses, his bulging eyes like two boiled eggs in that enormous head. He glared for a moment, then brightened: "Sweet Buns! How I've missed you. Those other boys are hopeless."

The Queen stood staring with such a fierce frown, her dark eyebrows joined in a handshake over the bridge of her nose. But her mouth remained amused as she watched her husband get up to clap this strange boy on the back, hiring him on the spot.

❊

The great mural grows down the staircase day by day, like a root into the ground. Presidents and soldiers and Indians, all coming alive. The sun opens its eyes, a landscape grows like grass, and today fire came out of the volcano. Señor Alva says the Painter is working his way toward the beginning of time, at the mural's center, where the eagle will sit on a cactus and eat the serpent, home at last.

Señor Rivera makes charcoal sketches over the wall, and every day begins a new section. He frames the scene with long lines sloping to a point on the distant horizon, the Vanishing Point. Then holds the picture in his head as he works to paint in shadows, then color, finishing a panel as fast as we can mix plaster for the next one. The slake-lime paste burns our hands, white marble dust becomes the air we breathe. Today he scolded the pigmentist because the blue paste was too blue. But the plaster was perfect.

14 October

Ambassador Senator Morrow died in his sleep while his wife was playing golf. All the newspapers are about him, Best friend of Mexico. His daughter's husband is Charles Lindbergh, so he only has to wave his cap at the crowd and everyone cheers, or mourns. Mother says she had that ambassador pegged from the start: the type to love his wife and die young. She's sore because P. T. did not produce the cash after all.

26 October, luna de octubre

Some of the boys at work say the Painter is going away again. Señor Alva says they want to make a big show of his paintings in a museum in New York. But his paintings are on the walls of Mexico. How could they leave here?

12 November

He's gone. He took Señor Alva with him. In the forgotten white land at the bottom of our wall, the eagle has no cactus, no snake for his lunch, he can't find home. The story of Mexico waits for its beginning.

PART 2

Washington, D.C.

1932–1934

(VB)

1 January 1932
For a son on the wrong track, Mother has found a different set of rails
and packed him off on them. *Lock, stock, and barrel,* she said with a
raised glass. Describing a firearm in its entirety.

This train runs north from the city. At the little struggling desert
towns, children run alongside, reaching toward the windows. Then
come the rocky flatlands where the towns give up altogether. Spiked
maguey plants reach out of the ground like hands. A great clawed
creature trapped underground. At evening, the light drained and the
land went from brown to umber, then dried blood, then ink. In the
morning the pigments reversed, the same colors rising out of a broad,
flat land that looks like a mural.

This compartment has one other person, an American named
Green who got on at Huichapan. Not old, but he stares out the window like an old person, rocking in rhythm with the suitcases over
his head and water in a glass in his hand. He sips a little every hour,
as if it's the last water on earth. Overnight some flames appeared in
the distance, each standing alone like a candle. Oil wells, burning to
remove the gases.

Last night the conductor came through to say we were three hours
from the border and it was twelve o'clock; his privilege was to wish us
a prosperous New Year. He moved down the car repeating the same
news and the same privileged wish.

Happy new year, Mr. Green.

Just before the border were pecan orchards, dark blocks of trees
with their boughs half bright and half shadowed, lit by the electric

lights of the shelleries. People working there in the dead of night, New Year's morning. The train sighed and stopped at the border, waiting for the customs agents to arrive at their offices. The whitening sky showed a thin stretch of river with dogs skulking along its shores, their up-curved tails reflected on the gray surface. The riverbank is a dumping ground: planks and metal, flaps of tarred paper. At daybreak children began walking from the scrap piles, not a dumping ground after all but a terrible kind of city. Women came out of the shacks too, and last the men, straightening to unfold themselves, placing both hands against their backs, shifting their trousers and pissing in the ditches. Squatting to splash their faces at the river's edge.

Old men thin as bones walked along the stopped train, looking in the windows. They lingered at the rear until police came with sticks to beat them away from the iron-sided cars. These people look as poor as could ever be, worse than the beggars and *borrachos* of Mexico City, who at least always have a ballad of the Revolution to sing into their shirt collars as they lean on a doorway. Here is the end of Mexico, end of the world and Chapter One. This train ride is like the long, narrow cave in the sea. With luck it might open on the other side into someplace new. But not here.

6 January

Five days and the train has passed through many underworlds. Grass hills, dark swamps of standing trees. And now, almost nothing but fields of dead sticks, immense as the sea. Not a green leaf anywhere. The gringos read magazines, failing to notice their world has nothing left alive in it. Only the Mexicans look out the windows and worry. A woman and four children are the only others who have come this same unimaginable distance, from Mexico City. Today when the train crossed a bridge over a high river gorge, she made the children sing for the Feast of the Kings so they wouldn't cry. She took a *rosca* cake from her bag, crumbling out of its paper wrappings into the worn velvet seats. The family huddled together, locking their small holiday from the inside.

7 January: Federal District of North America

Lock, stock, and barrel the human cargo arrived today at Union Station, delivered into such fierce cold, stepping off the train felt like being thrown into water and commanded to breathe it. The Mexican mother reached her little foot down from the doorway like the feeler of a snail. The freezing air set her to panic, rolling her children up in shawls like tamales, pushing them ahead of her into the station, *adios*.

Would he be here? And if not? Mother had suggested no other plan, if the father should fail to arrive and claim his baggage. But now here he was: a painful clap on the shoulder, the blue eyes measuring, how strange, a relative with pale eyes. Who could have picked *that* one, from just the one tinted photograph? Of course, he must have been experiencing similar disappointments in the son. "Your train was an hour late."

"Sorry, sir." Ragtag boys rushed past like pigeons flushed from the bush, coshing people's suitcases into their knees.

"A bunch of little tramps on the rods," he said.

"On the rods?"

"They ride into town on the outside of the train."

The cold was killing, every breath prickling into needles of nostril-ice. And clothes itching like mange after so many days. People in long coats, the howling steam engines. Finally it dawned, what he'd said: these ragged boys rode *outside* the train. *Dios mio.* "Where will they go now?"

"Bunk on their ears in some hobo jungle. Or else they'll go listen to the Christers. Accept the Lord for one night in exchange for a mulligan."

"Is mulligan a kind of money?"

His laugh was a loud burst, like notes exploding from a mariachi trumpet. He was amused by this empty bank of bewilderment, his son. The inside of the station was like the cathedral: so much space overhead, a great dome rising toward heaven, but not enough room down here for all the people jammed in. A grand marble doorway opened to the street, but outdoors the sun was cold, shining without heat, like an electric bulb. Crowds hurried along, unconcerned their star had no fire.

"Where is everybody going?"

"Home, son! Time for a two-bit square and a working man's nap. This is nothing. You should see it Monday morning."

Could a street hold more people? Inside the station the trains were still shrieking, the sound of digestion in the belly of that monument. Like an Aztec temple drinking blood. Mother's parting advice: Try to put a positive face on things, the man hates whining, let me tell you.

"Union Station looks like a temple."

"A temple." Father gave a sideways look. "How old are you now, fourteen?"

"Fifteen. Sixteen this summer."

"Right. Temples. Built with government money by Hoover's swindlers." He scowled at the trolley stop, as if the city had slyly shifted around behind his back while he was in the station. A freckled, pinkish man, the pale moustache discolored along its bottom edge. The photograph hadn't recorded the unheroic complexion—that skin would broil to a crisp in Mexico. One mystery solved.

He dodged into the crowd and moved fast, leaving no choice but to tuck-chin like a boxer and watch out for horse droppings, tugging the behemoth trunk. Mother's driver had put it on the train; porters carried it after that. No more help now, America was help-yourself.

"They're planning to put up a whole string of your *temples* here on the south side of Pennsylvania. See that eye-popper? Washington's Monument." He pointed into a leafless park, the pale stone rising above the trees. A memory rose with it: the long, narrow box of hallway rising like a dark mouse tunnel. An echoing argument in the stairwell, Mother's hand pulling downward, back to safety.

"We went in there, didn't we? One time with Mother?"

"You remember that? Small fry. You got the screaming heebies on the stairs."

He'd stopped at a corner, panting, emitting breath in bursts of steam like a kettle. "They've put an elevator to the top now. One more temple to Hoover's swindlers, if you ask me." He chuckled, tasting his clever remark again after the fact, like a belch. People were gathering here, a trolley stop. An officer clopped past on a huge bay horse.

"Mother said *you* worked for President Hoover."

"Who says I don't?" A hint of ire, suggesting he might not. Or not in any capacity Mr. Hoover would know about. A bean counter in a government office, Mother said, but one of the last men in America with a steady job, so it serves him right to get his boy sent him on the train.

"President Hoover is the greatest man ever lived," he said, overly loud. People looked. "They've just had a telephone put in on his desk, for calling his chief of staff. He can get MacArthur quick as snapping his fingers. You think your president of Mexico has a telephone on his desk?"

Mexico will be held as a grudge, then. Probably for reasons to do with Mother. Ortíz Rubio does have a telephone; the newspapers say he can't make a move without ringing up Calles first, at his house on the Street of Forty Thieves in Cuernavaca. But Father didn't want to hear about that. People ask without wanting to know. He boarded the trolley through the brew of people, shouldering his way toward the seats. The trunk wouldn't fit under the wooden bench, but hunched in the aisle: an embarrassment. People coming on the trolley flowed around it like a river over a boulder.

The ride was long. He stared out the window. It was impossible to imagine this man in the same room with Mother, the same bed. She would swat him like a fly. Then call a maid to wipe up the residue.

The men here wear suits like businessmen in Mexico City, but with more layers due to the cold. The women have complicated stuff, long scarves and things to put their hands in, hard to name. One had a shawl around her neck made from a whole fox with its head still on, biting its tail. If Cortés came here, he could write the Queen a whole chapter about the ladies' clothes.

After many stops, Father said: "We are going out to the school. They said it's the best to start right away, in your situation." He spoke slowly, as if "situation" meant a boy with a damaged brain. "It's bread and board. You'll bunk there with your pals, Harry."

"Yes, sir." (*Harry.* It will be Harry now?)

"That'll be a barrel of laughs." He bit his moustache, then added, "It better be."

Meaning, it is costing some money. *Harry. Harry Shepherd looked out the window.* Whoever pays the bill, names the boy.

Scenes passed by: marble edifices, parks of skeletal trees, boarded warehouses. Pale white men in black suits and hats. And then the opposite: dark-colored men in pale shirts and trousers, no hats at all. They were digging a long trench with pickaxes, their muscled arms bare even in this cold. In all Mexico there is not one Indian so black as those men. Their arms had a shine, like the rubbed wood of black piano keys.

At the end of the trolley ride, a motorbus. The great trunk occupied its own seat, with a window for viewing the scenery of mansions strung along a river. Father took long fishing expeditions into his pocket to find his watch, pull it out, and frown at its face. Did he remember the other watch, the one Mother took, later on pinched again from her jewelry case? The memory of it feels like a sickness now, not for the sin of thievery but for the dreadful longing pinned to it. For this man. This father.

17 January

Most Lofty Excellent Empress, the place called Potomac Academy is marvellous bad. A prison camp in brick buildings built to look like mansions, where native leaders called Officers rule over the captives. The Dormitory is a long house of beds like a hospital, with every patient required to go dead at Twenty One Hours. Lights Out means no more reading or else. In the morning the corpses rise again on command.

The strangest thing: the captive boys don't seem to wish for escape. In class they take their orders and knuckle under, but the minute the officer leaves the room, they commence to rapping heads with inkwells and aping the language of radio men named Amos and Andy. In the dormitory they gawk at someone's eight-pager with a girl called Sally Rand in it, naked with feathery fans. She looks like a cold baby bird.

The captives are released Saturday afternoon, no classes or exercises for once, and the dormitory empties out. Boys go to homes if they have them. The morning is Chapel first, then Mess Hall, then Freedom.

All the other boys in form nine are younger. But taller than the cretins anyway, and less spittle. Form nine was a compromise, because of being too tall to go all the way back to form six. The officers teach Latin, maths, and other things. Drill and psychomotricity. Best is literature. The officer recommended a pass to the form-eleven literature class, Samuel Butler, Daniel Defoe, and Jonathan Swift. Who gives a fig if they are Restoration or neoclassicists? New books in endless supply.

Drill is cleaning and display of firearms, not so different from cleaning dishes.

Mathematics: the worst. Nothing past the *tablas de multiplicar* will ever fit in this calabash. Algebra, a language spoken on the moon. For a boy with no plans to go there.

Sunday, January 24

Notes on how to speak in America:

1. Do not say "Pardon me." People in books say it constantly. Here, they ask who sent you to prison.
2. Shouting "Go fry asparagus!" won't make them leave you alone, as it would in Spanish.
3. "Beat it" means Go fry asparagus.
4. "Punk" means fluter. Also: chump, ratso, and "sure it ain't the YMCA."
5. "Mexico" is not a country, but a name. Hey Mexico, comeer.

The United States is the land of the square deal and the working stiff. Even though the newspapers say nobody has a job, and deals are not very geometric.

The boys move in cloudish groups, like schools of fish on the reef. In the hallways the groups approach, pass by, and join up again behind, as if you were a rock, not a sentient being. A splay-legged thing dangling in the wrong world.

February 21

So many people are sore at President Hoover, he had to chain up the gates to the White House and lock himself in. According to the boy named Bull's Eye. Yesterday a one-armed vet tried to break through the gate, got his ass beat up, and was hauled off to the hoosegow, where the one-armed man received his first square in a fortnight.

6. A square is a meal.

Bull's Eye pinches newspapers and cigarettes from the Officers' Mess. When he pulls the papers out of his jacket in the lavatory, the boys crowd around. They can't wait for him to read his made-up headlines in the loud voice of a news hawker: EXTREY, HEXTREY! CHICKEN LIVER HOOVER CRAWLS UNDER PRESIDENTIAL BED! MRS. HOOVER TO GET SOME PEACE AT LAST!

The real name of Bull's Eye is Billy Boorzai. He isn't a regular student. He was, until his pop lost his job at a radio shop and his mam lost her marbles. Now he takes classes only half the day, then works in the kitchen and mops the lavs. At night he reads what he has swiped from teachers' desks, getting his education on the lam, he says.

Bull's Eye has admirers but no friends in here, he says, his friends are all on the outside. He gets to leave the grounds because of his job in the kitchen (*the mess*). The cooks send him to the butcher's, the canvas man's, even the gunsmith's sometimes. He says the cooks need firearms for self-defense, the food is that bad.

February 28

A logic problem: is the tedium of maths class better or worse than the tedium of maths detention? Being held prisoner in the library with an algebra book is not improving. But, that great hall full of books is not punishment, either. For certain it is safer than outdoors with boys shoulder-banging at American football, screaming in the language of Gee Whiz and Your Old Man.

March 13

Every morning Bull's Eye stands naked in the lav, shaving his face. He looks twenty. He says he's only the same age as everybody else here, plus a few hard knocks. He says you grow up fast when the South Sea Bubble bursts and your dad gets the boot. He doesn't go home either. We have that in common: dads who won't look a son in the eye. He says it's good as any reason for friendship.

It's the only one so far. The boy called Pencil in the next bed will talk if no one else is around. The Greek boy named Damos says, "Hey Mexico, comeer," but he also says, "Hey Brush Ape." Bull's Eye told them to watch out, the kid from Mexico is ace at firearms, maybe he used to ride with Pancho Villa.

Now they use that name: Pancho Villa. It took a while to recognize it because they pronounce it something like Pants Ville: *Hey, Pantsville, comeer!* It sounds like a location, one of the hanging-laundry neighborhoods you see from the train to Huichapan.

March 14
Lucky Lindy's baby is kidnapped, and everyone is afraid, even boys locked up in a brick school. For the hero who flew across the ocean, a terrible crash. The newspapers say any child is in danger if Lindbergh could be that unlucky. But this country already had bad-luck people everywhere, sleeping in the parks, wearing newspapers for coats. The people who have good cloth coats look out the trolley windows and say, *Those bums need to buck up.* Unlucky Lindy makes them afraid because it happened to a hero.

March 20
Bull's Eye smells like peeled potatoes, cigarettes, and the mop bucket. When the others go home on Saturday, he says, "Hey-Pancho-Villa, you are cor-di-ally invited to assist me with my labors." These include scrubbing the lunch mess, running with the wet mop in the commissary, jumping on it, and sliding across the floor between the long tables. And so forth. The assistant receives no pay except getting his head squeezed inside Bull's Eye's elbow and his hair scrubbed with knuckles. That is how boys touch here, Bull's Eye especially.

March 27
Military strategy is interesting. Running an army is similar to running a household of servants. Mother is good at that kind of warfare, she has instincts for reconnaissance and the surprise attack. Officer Ostrain says the United States has the sixteenth largest army in the world, ranking leagues behind Great Britain, Spain, Turkey,

Czechoslovakia, Poland, Romania, and many others. (Mexico was not mentioned.) Our poorly equipped military seems to offend Officer Ostrain to the limits of his brass-buttoned endurance. He says it's a disgrace that General MacArthur and Major Eisenhower have to stand on Pennsylvania Avenue waiting like common citizens for the Mt. Pleasant trolley car, to get to the Senate chambers.

The boys say they have seen them and Major Patton also, playing polo on Saturdays at Myer Field. They want to grow up to have ponies like the generals, and sport them around polo fields on Saturdays with Sally Rand riding behind, her breasts bouncing like footballs. That is why they never plot an escape from the academy.

April 10

The K Street market is like a piece of Mexico. The fish hawkers sing the same as on the *malecón*, but in a kind of English: *four-bits a mack-rel, la-yay-dies!* Old women with teas and herbs promise to cure any ailment. The air smells like home: charred meat, salt fish, horse dung. Going there today was like bursting through the surface of water and finally breathing. After being in a tunnel of dark, for thirteen Sundays.

The outer part of the market has stalls selling leather goods, teakettles, every earthly thing for anyone that still has a nickel to rub against a dime. Inedibles are sold on the outside of the market, comestibles in the interior. The knife grinders with big naked arms stand at the entrance to the butchers' avenue. Oystermen in white aprons wheel full carts up from the wharves. The *cilindro* man has one missing ear, and a monkey in a blue cap to dance to his organ music. Women sell figs and roses, eggs and sausages, chickens and cheese, racks of dressed rabbits, even live birds in cages like the market in Coyoacán. One woman sells *conejillos de Indias*. Bull's Eye says they are not called Indian rabbits here, but Guinean pigs. He has no good explanation for it, and agrees they are probably more rabbit than pig.

This morning he told the head cook he needed an assistant for his errands at the market. Have a heart, Bull's Eye told her, you're asking for more than one poor sod can carry. His first destination is the Atlantic and Pacific Tea Company, which he calls the A and P, and which sells more than tea. The week's supply of rice, beef, flour, coffee, and fifty more things for the Potomac Academy go into crates from there onto a horse-truck every Saturday. The week's changes to the list have to be brought in person, the shop men want a boy to help with the boxing up. Other things are purchased from the rest of the market. The boy for the errand is Bull's Eye, and now his assistant Pancho Villa.

It took hours to get to the A and P. With so many swell things to look at on the way, dogs to be fed, friends to cuff on the shoulder. Blue-black workmen to be stared at as they pick open a trench as long as Pennsylvania Avenue. Where do they come from?

"Africa acourse," was Bull's Eye's reply.

"From Africa, all that way, just for the job of digging ditches?"

"No, you lob. They were slaves first. Before they all got put free by Abe Lincoln. Didn't you ever hear of the slaves?"

"Maybe. But not like these. Mexico didn't have them."

A lob is a *pendejo*. But Bull's Eye will answer questions that can't be asked of other boys. Those dark men and their wives can't shop here or ride the trolleys, he said, it's against the law. Even to get lunch in a restaurant. If one of them needs to make water whilst digging the ditch on Pennsylvania Avenue, or get a drink, he has to walk two miles out Seventh Street to find a restaurant that will let him touch a glass or use the lav.

It's a strange way. Being a servant, making a bad wage, that is no puzzle. All the richest men in Mexico were once lifted from the cradle by servants. But they all drink from the same water jar that fills the master's glass, and they use the same chamber pot, still warm from the piss of the *patrón*. In Mexico nobody ever thought to keep those streams flowing separately.

April 17

School is closing two weeks for Easter holiday. Then comes the end of the term soon, and summer. Most of the boys will go home, but not all. Some have to stay for remedial maths and repeating Virginia history in the sweat of July. Living here in the sock-stinking dormitory, and not with Father. He clearly explained that, in his letter about coming to visit while school is closed for Easter holiday. That will be swell, he says, a visit with old Dad. Swell enough for two weeks, not the whole summer.

Nothing here counts for anything now but Saturdays. Going to the market with Billy Boorzai. The rest is just coasting with half-closed eyes through another week.

May 3

Father's explanations made no mention of a lady. She must have cleared out of his apartment in a hurry, to make way for the Easter visitor. On the Q.T., Father is putting on the feedbag with a dame. Dust-colored stockings hang like cobwebs on the bathroom radiator, a lipstick winks like gossip on the bureau. Why would he hide her? Does he not know about Mother and her swains? He should listen through her wall some night, if he thinks his son is unacquainted with bedroom jolly-ups and pig fights.

Or he would lose some bargaining score if the Dame is reported back to Mexico. He and Mother are still not divorced because of the Mexican paperwork. "Divorce," he pronounces like a taste of soup with too much salt. Her name, he says like the Lord's taken in vain. Sometimes he says "Mexico," and the word has nothing in it at all. A wall with no colors painted on it.

May 5

A Trip to the Museum with the Father Figure. The weather has gone from freezing to broiling, with some talk of cherry blossoms in between. People on the trolley press against you in a crush, men in white linen suits, girls in sailor dresses and felt turbans. The smell of perspiration is different here. Cortés could write about that also: Most Excellent Empress, the sweat of the Northern People has a redolent stench. Maybe because of so many layers of clothes. Father's white suit hangs limp from his shoulders, wilting by the minute, like the moonflowers in the garden in Isla Pixol.

Smith Sonian is the name of the museum, a brick castle containing the stuffed, dead skins of every species but our own. Why not a few humans too? Father laughed at that one, like a man in some kind of a show, with an audience. His mood has shifted. Now he seems to take his son as a joke, rather than a serious offense. The museum had rooms of things from Tenochtitlan and other ancient sites of Mexico, fabulous artworks in gold that Cortés did not manage to carry off. Now in Washington, instead.

On the ride back to Father's apartment the trolley passed a long park, a row of warehouses, and then the most amazing spectacle: a city of tents and shacks roiling with people. Cooking fires, children, laundry hanging on lines, like a Mexican village of the very poorest kind set down in the middle of Washington City, surrounded by office buildings. A hand-lettered sign said: BONUS EXPEDITIONARY ENCAMPMENT. The American flag hung about in multiples over the shacks like laundry, blending in with the laundry really. The flags were as sun-faded as the upside-down trousers on the lines. The size of the camp was astonishing, a whole nation of beggars arrived in the capital. "That lot," Father spat through his moustache. "They've run their hobo jungle all the way down Pennsylvania. I have to pass through all that to get to work every morning."

A woman in a headscarf held up a naked baby toward our trolley. The baby waved its arms. A hobo jungle is unlike other jungles, where monkeys howl through the leafy air. "What do they all want?"

"What does anybody want? Something for nothing acourse." In that moment Father sounded like Bull's Eye.

"But why so many of them? And all the flags?"

"They're war veterans. Or so they say, because vets are entitled to a soldier's bonus. They want their bonus."

Ragged men stood at military attention every few meters, like fence posts all along the edge of the camp facing the street. Veteran soldiers, you could tell it from the placement of feet and shoulders. But their eyes searched the passing trolley with a terrifying hunger. "They've been here all week? What do the families live on?"

"Shoe leather soup, I'd say."

"Those men fought in France, with mustard gas and everything?"

Father nodded.

"We studied the Argonne. In Military Strategy. It was very bad."

Another nod.

"So, can't they get their money now, if they fought in the war?"

"I'd have been there too, in the Argonne," he said, suddenly turning pinkish, "if I could have been. Did your mother tell you I wouldn't fight in the war?"

A subject to steer around. "What's the soldier's bonus supposed to be?"

Surprisingly, Father knew the answer: $500 a man. He is a bean counter for the government. Five hundred bucks for risking a life in the war, so they could begin a new one here. Congress turned them down, decided to pay out the bonus later when these men are old. So they've come here from everywhere, wishing to take the matter up with the president.

"Does Mr. Hoover mean to meet with them?"

"Not on your life. If they want to talk to him, they better use the telephone."

May 14

Going with Bull's Eye to the market, that first time, was like Mother's first cigarette in the morning. Now every minute is a long piece of waiting, fidgeting out the minutes, pecking the desk, trying to think of something else until Saturday. Living in dread of not being asked again. On Friday nights the boys raise a cloud of stink in the barracks, throwing dirty drawers in satchels to get ready for the weekend, and then they fall down asleep. Leaving only the sound of one cricket ratcheting, a slant of puny moonlight. An hour or two for thinking: Billy Boorzai. Will he ask tomorrow? Or not?

Who cares. A person could prowl the library instead, in peace for once. Find some book that's better than noisy K Street. Keeping up with that big rough-elbowed dodger is worse than American football. It takes forever to get anywhere, Bull's Eye knows every third fellow he sees, not just boys but men of all sorts. And then has to renew the acquaintance with shoulder jabs and insults while the tagalong stands watching, like a pet dog. What does it matter if he asks or not?

June 17

The barracks have emptied; almost all the boys went home for summer, collected by servants in fancy carriages or mothers in horse-drawn taxis. It was entertaining to see which ones were rich or not. They all act like imperial kings when the parents aren't here.

Tomorrow begins a real job, for pay. Pearl diving, Bull's Eye calls it. Washing dishes in the mess hall. Father arranged it to cover board over the summer. But this afternoon, nothing yet to do in the empty barracks but take out every pair of pants from the foot locker and fold it up again. Or sit on the bed with *The Odyssey*. Until the head of Bull's Eye appears around the door. All ears and smile, the half-bit haircut. "Heya bookworm. Too busy lollygagging, then?"

"Too busy for what?" The book claps shut.

"Noodle juice and cookies with Mrs. Hoover. Whatcha think, for what? An ankle excursion."

"K Street?"

The smile disappears because the whole boy disappears. *The Odyssey* can be reopened to any page, it doesn't matter which. And then he is back, that grin. The scion of a ruined family, delighted with himself. This hurts, an ache in the groin, wanting so badly to see that smile and follow it somewhere. It keens like Mother waiting for the next cigarette. That is how she loves men, too. It must be. But in this case, can't be.

"What doesn't kill you," Bull's Eye likes to observe while scrubbing pots in the mess, "will make you piss on your shoes."

June 28
President Hoover asked the treasury secretary for a nickel to telephone a friend.

Secretary Mellon said, "Here's a dime. Phone both of them."

According to Bull's Eye, two million Americans are on the road. Half are probably just boys, not lucky enough to scrub pots for three squares and a plunk. Or farmers. Radio repairmen, teachers, nurses, or they finished school and no job anywhere. "It gripes my soul, truly it does," says Bull's Eye. He is steamed about the relief bill passed by the Congress, then knocked right down by the president because it's an Unexampled Raid on the Public Treasury. That was the news headline. Hoover says it's no crisis, only depression, everyone down in the dumps feeling sorry for themselves. If the gloomy people would buck up and smile, this mess will go away.

July 16
Only twenty-two boys are taking summer classes, most of them living at home. In the long, echoing barracks it's only Bull's Eye and Pancho Villa in the two end beds, and all the others empty. It feels like a hospital at the conclusion of a plague.

Bull's Eye has a friend living in the Bonus Army encampment. Nickie Angelino, a cousin of his mother's from Pennsylvania. Sometimes Nickie can be tracked down in the tent village, sometimes not. There are so many there now, acres of humankind, and people living under tarpaper tend to move around a good deal. Everyone at the camp knows Nick Angelino though. Famously, he scaled the White

House fence without arrest and left a gift on Hoover's doorstep: his medals from the Argonne, and a picture of his family. Angelino has a girl he calls his wife, but she looks too young, in her thin, short dress. To cover her breasts she wears a green nobbled sweater, even in the heat. Their baby wears old shirts torn up for nappers. He was born last month, here in the encampment. The girl won't talk about it.

The smell of the Bonus Expeditionary Force always comes first: cooking smells, latrine smells. *Phew*. A clock on the head from Bull's Eye, for saying that.

"What? It stinks!"

"Nothing." Bull's Eye gets angry easily, at the camp.

"What *nothing*? You hit me."

"*Phew*, says you. Here's a hundred thousand men that served your country."

"My country is Mexico."

"Damn you."

"Okay, they served our country."

"And here's their girls and kids with nothing and no place. All they want is what the government says they got coming. And you say *phew*."

"Well, crap stinks. Even if it came from a hero's ass."

"You know what it said in the paper? The bonus marchers are not content with the pensions already received, although seven or eight times those of other countries. The *New York* goddamn *Times*."

"What pensions already received?"

"None. They got no red cent so far, after discharge."

"How could the newspaper say that if it's a lie?"

"Lob. If the president lies, why wouldn't they?" Bull's Eye frowned, scanning the crowd for Nickie.

"How can the government refuse to pay, if they served?"

"They got VFW certificates they're supposed to cash in. But now they have to wait ten more years, because of the bank crisis. That wasn't the deal when they shipped out. If Congress can't pay the soldiers, they shouldn't be declaring war on the Krauts."

"Gee whiz."

"See those two behind the bread truck? They're the men from the VA, checking papers on the people waiting for the free bread. They won't turn a guy away anyhow. But they said it's running ninety-four percent."

"Ninety-four percent what? Certain your old man's your dad?"

"Lob. I talked to them yesterday. That many have got Army or Navy discharge papers. Or wives of men with records. One in five disabled."

Bull's Eye decided to look in the warehouse district. Men with families are starting to move their broods up there now, into the old brick hulks on Pennsylvania, camping out in condemned buildings. Blue and white flags of laundry hung out of almost every warehouse window. Kids ran out of the big open doors, and so did smells: cooking, cabbage, the inside of a shoe. Bull's Eye followed the bread wagon up Pennsylvania, hoping to spot Nickie in the crowd that pressed around the truck.

The bread comes from a bakery in New York, he says, a bunch of vets with jobs who got together and send it here for free. Even though the papers say these men are "rioters." Unpatriotic to help rioters. If a reporter came down here, he might notice there isn't any riot. Only Nick Angelino climbing the fence to leave a picture of his baby.

Angelino was located at last, carrying a loaf of bread and his wrapped-up son of about the same size. He tried to wave, looking as if he might drop one or the other. Bull's Eye went loping to catch him. He loves Nick's stories of riflemen and trenches and gas and men going blind in the war. The Argonne is a fantastic story these men all marched through together, and in the end it led here.

July 22

Summer more than half gone. Soon the Boy Army will return to take the place over again, making it loud. But for now the dormitory is still a camp for two tramps on the rods. Bull's Eye pretends he's a hobo, pulling out his Hoover flags, empty pockets turned inside out. Sometimes for a joke he covers himself with Hoover blankets, his newspapers. When it's hot he sits on his bed with nothing on at all, pumping his muscles like a wrestler, talking half the night, smoking fags he's pinched from the officers' mess.

Tonight the moon is five days past full, bleeding white blood into the sky, C *como* Cristo. Nobody else, only Bull's Eye, sitting there naked as Sally Rand, behaving as if he thinks he's quite worth looking at, too. Eye to eye, holding that stare as he leans back against the wall. The moon lighting up the smoke over his head like storm clouds. Every place the light touches his skin, he is a statue made of marble. All but the hairs on his chest.

"Whaddayou staring at?"

"Nothing."

"Go back to Mexico then."

"All right, sure. It's going to happen."

Bull's Eye stared. "When?"

"What do you care?"

He came over and sat on this bed, took the lit fag out of his mouth. "Smoke this. It makes you dizzy, but then you feel good."

"Okay."

But the dizziness was there already. Dizziness and ache. From seeing everything the moon was allowed to touch.

July 25

Staying on for fall term is contingent on passing the summer classes. Bull's Eye says they should pay us more for pearl diving.

"We should go and march with the Bonus Army."

Bull's Eye laughs. "Tell it to Sweeney."

July 28

Today was terrible. The end of summer term should be a fine day, and instead, people killed. If you ever think a day is fine, you weren't paying attention. Probably somebody was getting clapped bloody while you ate your breakfast. It happened right in front of us. The heat was bad on K Street, but Bull's Eye kept yelling to hurry up, into the thick of the encampment. Men standing on the back gate of the bread truck were passing out loaves into all those hands, like in the Bible. Loaves floating from hand to hand.

The encampment has changed shape all summer, it started at the riverbank but grew and swelled up into the warehouses on Pennsylvania, where the whole thing started today. With Bull's Eye scooting right toward the fight, *acourse*, a moth to the candle, and there is no keeping up with him. But the moth at the candle dies. He survives every time. Yelling his head off that it was going to be a real sockdolager. It was the police superintendent on his blue motorcycle, sent down to kick the Bonus Army families out of the warehouses. They're supposed to be tearing those down, to build more temples.

Bull's Eye said Glassford's in a jam. The superintendent. Hoover is on his neck for letting people get in the warehouses in the first place, and wants them kicked out today. Some people who'd been watching since early morning said two companies of marines in their helmets had already come to do the job, sent down there by Vice President Curtis—on trolley cars! And Glassford sent them back, ready to spit, because the vice president has no authority over military troops.

"Is that true?"

"Asking me? You seen me in government class?"

Now the superintendent was sweating in his brass-buttoned uniform, taking off his helmet and wiping his forehead a lot as he talked with the Bonus Army men. His job on the line. But those families, on a worse line surely. The crowd of gawkers was growing. Two men in white suits arrived in a limousine, also sweating, and had words with Glassford, gesturing at the building. Bull's Eye pushed to get closer, nearly tipping an old man with a shopping basket on his arm. The old man was mad as bugs, shouting at the police. *Where was you in the Argonne, buddy?* You wouldn't have guessed the fellow had so much air in him.

Other people picked it up, shouting things too. "They risked life and limb in France! You're running them out like dogs!" But mostly the crowd was quiet, waiting to see how it would go. A banner painted on a bedsheet furled out a second-story window: God Bless Our Home.

"All right then, we're off to K Street," said Bull's Eye suddenly, and off he headed toward the A and P. For once, his magnet for trouble failed him, and he was putting sacks of corn grits in a crate at the back of the store when the showdown started. A woman came running in the front door screaming that Officer Glassford had been shot. Bull's Eye took off at a lope. The story changed many times before we could get to the scene: Glassford was dead, or else he wasn't. He'd finally ordered the area cleared, and got hit with a brick thrown out a window of the warehouse. That was how it went, people talking and running for the scene, and at the warehouse it was bedlam. Women streaming out the door carrying cookpots and children, a lot of crying and screaming. Some Bonus Army men lay bloody in the street. Shot, maybe dead.

Bull's Eye looked ready to murder. More men were roaring up from the main encampment by the river, they'd gotten wind and come running with bricks to defend their women and kids, and Glassford's men returned fire with bullets. They weren't even ashamed, scads of people saw them do it, the whole crowd was screaming. Like Cortés and the Aztecs: one side always better armed.

An ambulance sounded from far away, probably stuck. The mob was like an ocean now, shifting from side to side. Nothing could get through, the only thing running fast was rumors: Hoover had called up MacArthur to put on his whipcord britches, get down here with troops, and rout the Bonus Army. Half the city stood jammed together on the hottest day of the year; offices were letting out, all eyes watching to see what would happen to these women and men. They stood on the step of a wrecked building, clutching what was left of their lives in a wad at their bellies, and every shopper and business-man, idler and schoolboy felt a horror rise, wondering the same thing: Where can they go?

A grumbling sound like thunder seemed to come out of the street.

An out-of-breath newsboy grabbed the corner of a building as he came round it and flung himself against the wall, gasping. "It's a tank!" he shouted. "The treads are turning the pavement into gravy!"

It seemed a fair time to leave, but escape was impossible. The front of the crowd began backing up from the street, shoving the rest of us against the window of a telegraph office, jammed between men in straw boaters and secretaries in point-heeled shoes. Two girls in cloche hats, one white hat and one black, stepped out of the door of the telegraph office and said, "Gee, what's the story?" People were pouring out of buildings with nowhere to go, milling in the street across from the Bonus Marchers.

The cavalry arrived just then, clopping up the street. It was Ma-jor Patton. Probably he'd arrived ahead of MacArthur's tanks be-cause the horses could dodge around the stalled motorcars choking up Pennsylvania Avenue. The horses reared and pranced sideways, spooked by the crowd. Their riders had long sabers, held high in their right hands. Behind them came a machine gun detachment, audibly marching in step.

"Gee *whiz*," said the white-hat girl again. Bayonets appeared, bristling above the heads of the crowd. People pressed back harder against the buildings as the tanks rolled up, their treads chewing the road as they came. The Bonus Marchers were lined up across the street, standing steady. Women struggled to hold babies, but all the men stood at attention, like the soldiers they are. They saluted the cavalry's color guard, and one small ragged boy on a man's shoulders pumped his own little flag in the air. A lady in the crowd of onlookers raised up a high shout and the whole throng took it up: *Three cheers for our men who served, hurrah! Hurrah! Hurrah!*

Patton's horsemen wheeled and charged the crowd.

Everyone ducked and shoved, the white-hat girl screaming, stepping sideways with her pointed white shoe, stabbing like a knife, and everyone tumbled. "Pull her up quick!" Bull's Eye said, helping from his side to drag her up by the elbows, but she seemed to be swooning. A man fell against her, someone else against the man, and then it was a whole smash-up of secretaries and bean counters. With flat hands pressed against the stone wall of the telegraph office, it was possible to inch back up to standing. Bull's Eye began to swim with his elbows *toward* the street, while everyone else pressed back, and that was a good time to say so long to Bull's Eye. Between the stone wall and the crush of shoulders, it was hard to breathe. Over the sea of heads and hats you could catch sight of cavalrymen leaning down from the waist, on their horses, flailing their saber blades against whatever was below them.

Against *people*. That hit with a shock. They were beating at the Bonus Army men and women with the razor-sharp blades of sabers.

Someone pushed into the near crowd with a bloody face, the meat of his cheek sliced back and bone shining. Roar after roar rose from the crowd in front, leaving those at the rear to guess and dread the cause of it. The cavalry men kept shouting to clear out, but the crowd shouted "Shame! Shame!" until it became a chant. The Bonus Army had linked arms to form a colonnade across the street, and the cavalry flung their horses through the line, snapping bones. The crowd howled, screams erupting with every charge of horsemen into flesh.

Bull's Eye suddenly reappeared: "Come on!"

"We can't get through. I'm smashed potatoes."

Bull's Eye swung open the door of the telegraph office and, like a magician pulling a scarf through a ring, yanked us both through the knot of people into the office. The people trapped inside all looked up, the same shocked face.

"Back to the alley," Bull's Eye yelled, but no one else made for it as he threaded through the desks and clerks to the washroom, climbed onto the radiator, and popped open the window. Outside, the alleyway was surprisingly empty. Trash heaps and crates of sodden lettuce, it must be a restaurant next door—it was a stench to beat the band. Not one other person had thought to escape from the melee by this route. Bull's Eye turned south at a hard trot.

"School's the other way."

"Right!" he said, without slowing up.

A burning stench began to choke out the restaurant smell. "God," Bull's Eye croaked. "It's gas. Come on, this way or we're cooked."

People came into the alley with hands over their faces, coming from the direction of the river. What followed was the sight of blindness itself coming on, and a feeling exactly like trying to breathe saltwater. Like swimming into the cave, the longest possible held breath. Every gulp of air tasted like poison. People were stumbling over trash heaps and people heaps. A newsboy curled like a fetus on his big stack of papers; suddenly the whole pile was old news.

"Come on," Bull's Eye said, "he's not dead. You don't die of gas."

Bull's Eye's face was purple as liver, his eyes streaming tears, but he still moved at a clip that wasn't easy to follow. An ambulance entered the alley, and people mobbed it. Between two buildings a tableau of the riot appeared: an infantryman pulling a blue bottle from his belt, uncorking it, and hurling it into the haze.

July 29

It's all in the newspapers today. Bull's Eye sat reading on his bed without a word, handing the papers over when he finished reading each part.

Gallinger Hospital filled to overflowing with the casualties. Any Bonus Marchers who made it to the Eleventh Street bridge joined the ones at the riverbank encampment. Mr. Hoover sent orders for troops to stop at the bridge, but MacArthur "couldn't be bothered with new orders," so he mounted machine guns on the bridge and led a column of infantry across the Potomac into the encampment. They set flaming torches to the canvas and pasteboard homes. Exactly as Cortés said it: Much grieved to burn up the people, but since it was still more grievous to them, he determined to do it.

It was shameful to read those newspapers, to feel any eagerness for knowing each awful detail of the massacre. How the artillery marched right over the camp on the riverbank, destroying the hobo jungle of fruit crates, chicken coops, tarpaper shacks, and dirt-colored tents. God Bless Our Home. Families must have been kneeling in there, praying for any miracle a tightfisted God might have left for them.

The Bonus Army families had crops planted in their camp. Every Saturday this summer Bull's Eye had pointed those out—how we cheered for the measly corn rows sprouting by the Potomac. They made the encampment look like Mexico. A real village, where people might live and eat. Hungry kids were waiting for those almost-ready ears—after months of porridge, sweet corn roasted in the coals. To think of MacArthur's horses trampling it on purpose: somehow that small part of the story made tears come.

Bull's Eye never came to bed after lights-out. He turned up hiding in the infirmary, sitting hunched on the side of a bed, smoking. With more newspapers.

"Look at this." He threw it.

The penalty for prowling around after lights-out is severe, but the infirmary was deserted. The late extra: After sunset yesterday the flames in the Anacostia encampment rose fifty feet in the air and spread to the surrounding woods. Six companies of firemen were required to defend adjacent property. The president observed from the White House windows an unusual glow in the eastern sky, and conceded MacArthur was right to proceed with the routing. In his opinion the Bonus Army consists of Communists and persons with criminal records.

The editorial writer applauded MacArthur for sparing the public treasury: The nation is being bled dry by persons like these who offend the common decency.

"Why would the paper say they're criminals?"

"They were treated like criminals," Bull's Eye replied. "So people want to think it. The paper says whatever they want."

It was no use reading more, but hard to stop. The late extra had photos. A society page. While soldiers poured gasoline on the shacks, the upper crust were cruising the river on their yachts, watching MacArthur spare the public treasury. A Mrs. Harcourt required medical attention after she saw a small boy receive a bayonet through his lower body. Senator Hiram Bingham of Connecticut was badly jostled on the street in front of the warehouse while attempting to leave his office. His injuries were not mortal, but earned as many newspaper inches as all the others together, including a woman in the Anacostia camp who lost her sight to flaming gasoline thrown in her face, and the vets from the Argonne shot dead in their own country. A dozen kids got shattered limbs or broken skulls. Two infants died of inhaling gas.

"Was one of them Nick's baby, do you think?"

Bull's Eye kept his head turned away. "For Christ's sake," he said. "A gas bomb costs more than a hundred loaves of bread."

ARCHIVIST'S NOTE

The next journal after this one will not appear to the reader, for it was destroyed in 1947. This note presents an intrusion, and I beg pardon for it. The notebook was burned in a metal tar bucket outdoors on a September evening, at the start of a rain. Mr. Shepherd watched through an upstairs window. The one doing the burning was myself.

It was a slim book of lined paper and cotton-duck binding with "Potomac Academy" stamped on it, a type of thing issued to the boys there, probably in great number. But this one in particular he had used for a diary, in 1933. It isn't my place to give an opinion about the burning. I'm a typist. But he made it plain he didn't want that little book to reach the public view. Nor any of these personal writings, truth be told. He was averse to making himself known. Even when greatly misunderstood. He liked to say, *"Dios habla por el que calla,"* meaning God speaks for the silent man. If he believed that, after all that happened, I am not sure how.

So, any regrets over the missing "Potomac Academy" 1933 would not be his. Evidently the notebook had something in it to disturb him, and he decided to destroy it. Later he would make the same judgment about all the rest of his diaries. But that particular one he plucked out first from among all the notebooks and pages he kept in portmanteau bindings on a shelf in his study. I won't try to say why a man would write pages he meant no one to see, let alone keep them nice in bindings. The sole place he let his words be seen was in the books published with his name on their spines. Harrison Shepherd. You might think of him as your friend, when closing one of these books. Many did. But he never let any photograph of himself go on the dust jacket, to encourage that kind of feeling. Even though he was a good-looking man, well groomed with dark hair and Roman features, about six feet and five inches in height. He did not have physical deformities, as has been said. The height alone was unusual.

But maybe you'll not have heard of him at all, nor have any idea why you should have. Until reading all this here.

The notebook that burned, then. People who make a study of old documents have a name for this very kind of thing, a missing piece. A lacuna, it's called. The hole in the story, and this one truly missing still, I know it is gone and won't turn up later in any trunk, as that first little leather-bound one finally did. The burned book from the Potomac Academy probably described his friendships and so forth until his leaving the school in 1934, midway through the graduation year. I didn't read it, before putting it to the flame. I am not concealing any scandal. Mr. Shepherd spoke of having made a disaster of his schooling, but said little else of it. He went back to Mexico then to live with his mother, who had abandoned her liaison with the American and found work as a seamstress in a Coyoacán dress shop. Mr. Shepherd and his mother accumulated some disagreements. He took a position again with the painter Diego Rivera, as a plaster-mixer to start. By late in the year 1935 he was paid as a member of their household staff.

Some writings did survive from his time at the Potomac Academy, sheafs of typewritten pages describing battle scenes and dialogues he later used in his novel *Vassals of Majesty* (1945). But as to the journal, his express wish was to see it removed from this earth. In time, with full voice and sound mind, he expressed that same wish for the other journals too: all these now collected in a volume.

I didn't make this plain at the beginning. I do so now. If you're of the mind to honor a dead man's wishes, always and regardless, be now fairly warned. If you feel it is best or kindest, then put these pages down and read no more.

—V B

PART 3

San Angel and Coyoacán

1935–1941

(VB)

Directions for making empanadas dulces

They can be triangular, or curled like snails with the filling inside. The dough is the same, either way: white flour with lard and a little salt rubbed in. Beat egg yolks into a little cold water (as many eggs as Olunda will spare), then mix the liquid lake into the volcano of flour. Exactly like mixing plaster.

Roll the dough in a rectangle as wide as the whole counter in this kitchen, which is so small, if two ants are in the sugar it's already too crowded in here. Next, with a clean machete cut the dough into squares like little handkerchiefs. Spoon some filling on each one and fold it diagonally to make a triangle. The square of the *hipotenusa* can go to hell. The filling can be custard or pineapple. For the custard, heat a liter of milk and some sugar with pieces of cinnamon. Beat seven egg yolks with some corn starch and pour it in a thin stream into the boiling milk. Stir until your arm is falling off. The *lechecilla* will be yellow and very thick.

For pineapple filling, cook the fruit with brown-sugar syrup and star anise.

The other way to make them is to spread the filling over the whole rectangle of dough and roll it into a log, then cut off round pieces, each one like a snail. For that, use the pineapple filling. The custard will make a devil of a mess.

Bake the pastries in the oven, if you live in a normal house. If you live in a supermodern house dreamed up by an idiot, go next door to the San Angel Inn. One of the cooks there, Montserrat, will meet you at the back door and take your trays to bake in the kitchen. She'll send one of the hotel girls to tell you when they're done.

Those are the instructions. If your boss has the appetite of an elephant and a kitchen the size of an insect, this is how to keep your job. Do it exactly this way, because he said, "Write out the recipe, *mi'ijo*, in case you ever leave me the way she did. You're the only person who knows how to cook like my wife."

What he doesn't know is the servants did the cooking, not her, right from the beginning when they still lived with her parents. After they moved here, secretly she had most of the meals picked up from the San Angel next door.

The girl Candelaria is the angel of the birdcage, sighted years ago in the Melchor market hurrying behind her mistress. It took a few days of working here to be sure she is the same servant. It's not a face you forget. Smooth skin, the countenance of a village girl, hair that reaches her knees. Olunda makes her tie her braids in loops, for safety and hygiene. Her mistress the Azteca Queen is gone. But Candelaria remains.

Could there be an uglier house in all Mexico than this one? *Functionalismo*, architecture as ugly as a fence made of dung. Except the fence here is the nicest part: a row of organ cactus surrounding the courtyard, planted so close together you can only see cracks of light between them. From upstairs you can look over it to the inn across the road, and a field where some cattle graze. San Angel is only two bus stops from the edge of the city, just one from Coyoacán, yet here is a farmer working in his field with an iron-bladed hoe that looks like it was forged during the reign of Moteczuma. When he stops to rest, that poor old man has to raise his eyes to this modern mess of glass and painted cement that looks like a mistake. It looks like a baby giant was playing with his blocks when his mother called him, so he ran away and left his toys lying in Calle Altavista.

Two blocks: the big pink one and small blue one standing separately, each with rooms stacked one above the other, screwed together by a curved cement staircase. The big pink block is the Painter's domain, and his studio on the second floor is not so bad. That window is the size of a lake, a whole wall of glass looking down at the neighbor's trees. The planks of the floor are yellow, like sun on your face. That room feels like someone could be happy in it. Everything else feels like being shut up inside a crate.

The small blue block is meant to be for the small wife. Servants are only allowed up the staircase as far as the kitchen (which is not worth the trip). Her rooms above it are sealed like a crypt since the Queen moved out. Good riddance, says Olunda. "She won't be back, I promise you. I'll eat a live dog if she ever shows up here again. After she caught master with his pants down as usual, but this time, humping her own sister!"

What a strange couple. Why would a man and wife live in separate houses? With only a little bridge between them, red pipe railings connecting one roof to the other. You can see it from the inn across the street. Functionalist *tonteria*. *He* is the one who eats, but the kitchen is on *her* side. If you manage to cook anything, you have to carry it down the staircase, which is like the inside of someone's ear, outside into the blazing sun to cross the gravel courtyard, then up the other cement ear to the studio where the master stands with his pants belted high on his giant dumpling belly, waiting to be fed.

And now he says she's coming back, he wants her greeted with empanadas and *budines* and *enchiladas tapatías*. He has never put his two giant feet in this tiny kitchen or he would know, you might as well try to make enchiladas in a peanut shell. Mixing plaster was easier. But living with Mother was not. So he'll have his enchiladas.

November 30
Live dogs beware of Olunda. The mistress has come back after all. Moved back in with her furniture and strange collections packed into

the rooms above the kitchen. It was like a surgery to carry her bed up the stair and through the narrow cement doorways without breaking out a glass-block wall. Candelaria and Olunda went up to help, and came back with hair standing on end. She has a pet monkey, they swear. He hides and leaps on your back when you carry food into her studio. Olunda moved her cot out of the little salon below the kitchen, because the mistress wants that space for a dining room. Olunda would rather sleep in the laundry closet under the house, anyway. The monkey is the least of it. The little queen has a temper like Mother's.

This servant's quarter out in the courtyard is probably the safest place to be, even with César the Flatulent for a roommate. He says this little block house wasn't meant to be a servant's quarter: they put it in the corner of the courtyard for keeping the motorcar, but the Painter decided to let the motorcar reside on Altavista Street, to make room for its driver in here. He says the architect planned for no driver or servant's quarters because he was a Communist, like the Painter. Olunda agrees. They said it was to be a revolutionary house, free of class struggle, no servants' rooms because they didn't believe in laundry maids or cooks.

Nobody does, really. Why should they? Only in having clean clothes, clean floors, and *enchiladas tapatías*.

4 December 1935: The Queen Takes Notice

She was on her throne, the chair at the head of the mahogany dining table. It's a wonder of the world she has fit her parents' furniture into that room, including a cupboard for dishes. The old carved chairs are so enormous she looks like a child, feet swinging below her ruffled skirts and not quite reaching the floor. She was in a foul mood, sneezing, wrapped in a red shawl and scribbling away, putting names in the ledger book where she means to keep better track of expenses and sales of her husband's paintings. One more thing she has taken over from Olunda, since moving in. All the names go in the book now, including the new kitchen boy, and what he is paid.

"*Xarrizzon Chepxairt!*" She grasped her throat when she said it, like choking on a chicken bone. "Is that really what people call you?"

"Not many people, señora. It sounds better in English."

"I was saying it in English!"

"Sorry, señora."

18 December: Second Audience with the Queen

She's sick in bed still; Olunda says she's twenty-five with the ailments of ninety. Kidneys and leg at the moment. Nevertheless she was propped up on pillows and dressed like an Indian bride: ruffled blouse, lip rouge, earrings, at least one ring on every finger, a crown of ribbons braided around her head. But she still looked half dead, staring up at the little windows at the top of the wall. Her bedroom is like a cement box, only slightly larger than the bed.

"Señora, sorry to disturb. Olunda sent me to get your plates from lunch."

"No wonder she won't come fetch the dishes herself, she's ashamed of that *jocoque*." She glanced up. "Olunda la Rotunda. Do they still call her that?"

"Not if they're still alive, señora."

"How does she get so fat on her own cooking? Look at me, I'm vanishing."

"Fried bread with syrup is her secret."

She made a little puzzled scowl. "And you, skinny creature. What's your name?"

"It didn't please you much the first time. When you wrote it in the ledger."

"Oh shit, that's right, you're that one. The unpronounceable." She seemed to wake up, sitting up straighter. When she looks at you, her eyes are like lit coals inside the hearth of those shocking eyebrows. "What does Diego call you?"

"*Muchacho, mix some more plaster! Muchacho, bring me my lunch!*"

She laughed. It was a good impersonation: it's all in his eyes, the way he opens them wide and leans forward when he bellows.

"So, you make plaster for Diego's lunch?"

"Never, señora. On my honor. He hired me first as a plaster boy, and a few months ago he moved me in here, to work in the kitchen."

"Why?" She cocked her head, like a beautiful doll propped on the pillows. One among many, in fact. The bookshelf behind her bed was full of porcelain and cloth dolls. All of them, like her, look dressed up for some party that will be noisy for certain.

"He likes my *pan dulce* and *blandas*, señora. I'm good at soft dough, in general. On the plaster crew they used to call me Sweet Buns."

"You can make *blandas* in this house? In that stupid little kitchen with the *fuego electrico*? You must be the Son of God. Tell Olunda to put you in charge of *everything*."

"She wouldn't take that kindly."

"What do you think of that kitchen?"

A pause, for guessing the right answer. It's well known that the Painter likes the house; a wrong answer in this interrogation could prove deadly. It felt like being back at the academy, but with a different category of officer.

"Everyone says it's an outstanding house, señora."

"Everyone will say horse shit smells like flowers," she stated, "if they want to be popular with a horse's ass."

"And your opinion, señora, if I may ask?"

She frowned at the white wall, the metal-cased window. "Bauhaus," she said, like a dog barking twice. "It's a monstrosity, isn't it? How do you even fit in that kitchen?"

"The same way you fit in your water closet. It's the same size room, directly underneath."

"But you're twice my size!"

"Standing in the center of the kitchen, it's possible to touch all four walls, exactly."

"It's that *pendejo* Juan O'Gorman showing off his modern ass. I don't know what he and Diego were thinking, it's like a hospital." She gestured with the back of her ring-ring hand. "And stairs! To get up to that stupid bridge and go across to Diego, I'm supposed to go out the window and climb little steps up the side of the house like an acrobat. What shit. He's not even worth it, I would kill myself, *chulito*. Who are you? Say it again, I swear I'll try to remember."

"Harrison. Shepherd."

"Christ, I'm not going to call you that. Diego calls you what, again?"

"Sweet Buns."

"The crew is very unkind to the plaster boys. As you know. But honestly, XARrizZON! It sounds like strangling. What kind of a name is that?"

"It was a president, señora."

"Of what? Some place where they don't have any oxygen?"

"Of the United States."

"As I said."

One more country is now to be held as a grudge, then. The mother country, the fatherland, two is all you get. Best to keep quiet, and stack the lunch dishes onto the tray. In two minutes César and Olunda would be fighting over everything left on those plates.

"You're from Gringolandia, then," she pressed.

"Born there, yes, señora. A half-citizen on my father's side. My mother sent me back there to be educated, but it didn't work."

"Why not?"

With the examination ending now, a quick last grasp at redemption: "The school kicked me out."

"*Really.*"

It was a good guess: now even the ribbons in her hair curled forward to hear more. All the dolls stared. "Kicked out for what, *chulito*?"

"For a scandal."

"Involving?"

"Another student."

"Another student *and?*" Her hair practically standing on end.

"*Conducta insólita*. Irregular conduct. Señora, no more can be said. You would have to put me out on the street if you knew the rest."

She crossed her arms and smiled. "That's what I'm going to call you: Insólito."

The examination: passed, with highest honors. The prize: a possible ally in this impossible house.

5 January 1936

After weeks lying in bed existing on air and pink bananas, the Queen has risen. She came down the stairs, ribboned and ruffled like a Oaxacan saint's day, to reclaim her rightful place in this house and terrorize the staff. She announced a hundred people are coming for the Feast of the Kings tomorrow. Later she said, "Really only sixteen are coming, but cook for one hundred in case." Chalupas, flautas, tacos, *gaznates*, and macaroons. The dining room is the only place Candelaria and Olunda can sit to cut up vegetables without poking out one another's eyes. And the *rosca*: the mistress started screaming when she remembered that, "Tell César to get the car and take you into the city to find a *rosca*, they'll all be gone already from the bakeries here in San Angel." But Candelaria told her we have one already: "This boy knows how to make it."

Señora gawked as if a fish had arrived in her home, wearing an apron. "Insólito. It's just as I said. You're the oddest egg. A boy who makes *rosca*."

"Odd egg, go upstairs and get me a bowl," commanded Olunda, rolling her eyes. She had argued against making a *rosca* in the first place. (Too much trouble. Not enough space.) Then she insisted there was no Pilzintecutli to hide in the cake. When Candelaria retrieved the porcelain figure from a storage chest, Olunda stomped out. Now the Christ Child himself was contradicting her.

It's a new year in a house turned upside down. The mistress hangs bright, fluttery paper banderas over the Bauhaus windows, making the house embarrassed, like a plain girl in too much makeup. On the heads of her husband's Azteca idols she puts red carnations, turning them into altars, and she sets the table the way a priest prepares the tabernacle: white lace tablecloth from Aguascalientes reverently unfolded from the cupboard, blue or yellow plates set out, each one blessed by her fingertips, then the Kahlo grandmother's silverware. Finally, the flowers and fruit piled in the center of the table like a sculpture: pomegranates, bananas, *pitahaya*, everything chosen for color and shape. She was finishing the arrangement this morning when the monkey scuttered in and snatched out the bananas. The mistress bellowed, tiny as she is, and chased him out into the courtyard with a mimosa branch she was using in the centerpiece: "*Wicked child!*"

The diagnosis of Olunda is that this hairy child is the best the señora can hope for. Only twice pregnant in six years of marriage and both times the baby bled out, one at a gringo hospital, the other one here. They say it's because of a trolley accident years ago that ruined her woman parts and is "too horrible to discuss," though Olunda and Candelaria still manage to do so. By their accounting, in the last two years she's had two miscarriages, four surgeries, thirty doctor visits, and a giant fit over her husband's affair: she broke a lot of the *talavera* crockery before she moved out. It took her all of last year to forgive him. "And that was only the affair with her sister Cristina, we're not even counting women outside the family. Listen, how do you make the dough shiny like that?"

"You brush it with softened butter and then the white of one egg."

"Mmph." Olunda folded her arms across the mountain range of her bosom.

"Where did the señora live? Before she moved back in here?"

"An apartment on Insurgentes. Candelaria had to go clean it

sometimes. Give me those dried figs, *mi'ija*. Tell him about the mess, Candi, it was even harder to clean up over there than here."

"It was because of the paintings," Candelaria explained.

"He painted, in her apartment?"

"No, she did."

"The Mistress Rivera is also a painter?"

"If you can call it that." Olunda was shredding chicken breasts for the chalupas, grunting as she worked, settling an old grudge with those hens.

Candelaria said once she went to the señora's apartment and found a sheet of metal covered with blood. "I thought she had cut herself while setting it up on the easel, or else murdered someone. Probably her husband, considering. But then the mistress sat down with her red pigments, whistling, and happily applied more blood on the picture."

"Enough gossip," said Olunda, who was clearly jealous not to have seen this sight herself. "Candi, you have to peel every tomato in that bucket, and you, Odd Egg, I want to see you chopping onions until tears come out of your ass."

2 February

Eight kinds of tamales for the feast of Candlemas. Even César was ordered to help. He threatened all day to quit, as he is "a chauffeur, not a peon for women's work." He's been angry since October because of having to share his room with an Odd Egg, and now he even has to put on an apron, the world may end soon. The Painter says he's sorry, but that's how it is, Frida rules the house. "And besides, old comrade, you're getting too old for driving, so you better get used to peonage." It's true, yesterday César got lost four times on the way to the pharmacist's. The mistress calls him General Wrong Turn.

Even more than aprons he despises this notebook. He calls it "the espionage." He is adamant, shutting off the lights on pen and paper. But most nights, by the time every dish in the house has been scraped, cleaned, and put away, he's already snoring like a whale. The spy may do his work here unless the whale is roused from stupor. It is like being in a *casa chica* again with Mother, *Put out the damn candle before you burn us all.*

19 February

Candelaria doesn't remember that day when she carried the parrot cage on her back through the Melchor market. She says she must have just come from the village then, the Painter and Mistress hired her when they were newlyweds, living at the Allende Street house with the señora's parents. Candelaria doesn't remember the parrots, or why they were purchased, or how long the couple lived in that place with the fantastic courtyard, before building this house. She couldn't say if she liked it better there. She seems to forget almost everything. The secret to surviving the storms of Rivera service.

2 March

The señora is making a painting in the little studio next to her bedroom. It's not such a mess, she uses a cloth under her chair. At the end of the day, it looks like it rained blue, red, and yellow. She cleans her own brushes and knives, a hundred times tidier than the Painter, who throws everything on the floor and stomps out in his cowboy boots. But Candelaria and Olunda refuse to carry her lunch upstairs, saying her temper is even worse when she's painting. She never says *gracias* because life is made of survival not grace, she says, and servants are paid to bring what they're asked. Today she demanded stuffed chiles, more blue pigment, and surprisingly, advice.

"The painting looks good so far, señora." When people ask for advice, this is what they want. "Good progress too. We'll see that finished by the end of the month."

"We will?" She gave a fierce, quick smile like a cat showing itself to another cat. "As the fly said, sitting on the back of the ox, 'We are plowing this field!'"

128 * Barbara Kingsolver

"Sorry."

"It's okay, Insólito. If anybody says it's ugly, I'll tell them 'we' painted it."

The painting has people floating in the air, connected by ribbons. She asked, "Do you like art? I mean, do you understand it?"

"Not really. Words, though. Those are nice. Poems and things like that."

"What did you study in school?"

"Awful things, señora. Drill and psychomotricity. It was a military school."

"*Dios mio*, you poor skinny dog. But they didn't succeed in enslaving you, did they? I notice sometimes you still piss on the shoes of the master."

"Excuse me, señora?"

"I've seen you reading the newspaper to the girls down in the dining room. Changing the headlines to make them laugh. Your little insurrections." She still faced the painting, speaking without turning around. Was this going to be a dismissal?

"It's just to pass the time, señora. We still do our work."

"Don't worry, I'm a revolutionist. I approve of insurrections. Where did they send you to school, Chicago or something? One of those freezing places?"

"Washington, D.C."

"Ah. Throne of the kingdom of Gringolandia."

"More or less. The cornfields outside the throne of the kingdom. The school was in the middle of farms and polo fields."

"Polo? That's some kind of crop?"

"A game. Rich people play baseball riding ponies."

She put down her paintbrush and turned around. "Isn't it crazy? Rich people in the United States don't even know how to use money properly." She peeked at her lunch plates now, inspecting the *rellenos*. "They don't mind throwing big parties while people stand outside in the street with nothing. But then they serve puny little foods at the party! And live in houses stacked on top of one another like chicken crates. The women look like turnips. When they dress up, they look like turnips in dresses."

"You're right, señora. Mexico is the better place."

"Oh, Mexico's going to the devil too. The gringos steal a little more of it every week, replacing the beauty of our campos and our Indios with the latest fashion in ugliness. Probably they'll turn our maguey into fields for pony-*beisbol*. It can't be helped, I suppose. The big fish always eats the little one."

"Yes, señora."

"Little dog, don't give me this '*si señora.*' I'm sick of that."

"Sorry. But it's right, what you said. My mother is Mexican, but all she's ever wanted to do is dress like an American lady and marry American men."

The eyebrow went up. "A *lot* of them?"

"Well, one at a time. And really she only succeeded once, with my father. The other slippery fish all got away."

She laughed, shaking her head full of ribbons like a flag in the wind. She would never be converted to a turnip. "Insólito, you should come out and piss more often."

"Olunda keeps my rope tied very short, señora."

"You have to stop calling me señora. How old are you?"

"Twenty this summer."

"Look, I'm practically the same as you, twenty-five. It's Frida, only. César calls me that so you can too, it's not a crime against the state."

"César is like your grandfather."

She tilted her head. "You're not afraid of me, are you? Just shy, right?"

"Maybe."

"You don't have a lot of heat in your blood, is the problem. You're not completely Mexican, and not all gringo either. You're like this house, Insólito. A double person made of two different boxes."

"That might be true, señora, Frida."

"In the house of your mother, a taste for beauty and poetry. Secret passions, I suspect. And in the gringo side, a head that's always thinking and surviving."

"True, maybe. Except my house is only a kitchen, it seems. And very small indeed."

"The kitchen of your house is ruled by Mexico, thank God."

4 March

Our Lord Jesus has not yet risen. How do we know this? Olunda grumbles about another day of Lenten meals. But they can be some of the best: lima bean soup, potatoes in green sauce, fried beans. At supper this evening the Painter hinted he needs more boys on the plaster crew, and the mistress scolded him: "*Sapo-rana!* The way you eat, you should know we need your plaster boy here." Toad-frog, she calls him, then gets up, walks over to him, and kisses his toad-frog face. They are the strangest couple. And why do these Communists observe Lent, in any case?

The Painter's new mural in the Palacio Bellas Artes has the newspaper reports flying so fast, their pages might combust. He's copying the mural he did in the United States that created a scandal and had to be torn down before completion. It frightened the gringos that badly. Scaring gringos can make a hero of any Mexican. Other artists now come to the house every night, crowding around the Riveras' dining table with two colors of paint still in their hair. Writers, sculptors, bold women in makeup who want the vote, and students who are evidently waiting for San Juan Bautista to bathe, along with the lepers. Some are too old to be students, so who knows what they do. (If anything.) One is a Japanese in gringo clothes, arrived here to make a mural in the new Mercado.

The only place big enough for washing that many dishes is in the laundry closet under the stair. Down in the courtyard you can still hear them up there drinking their way to an agreement, sometimes all night, like the men who used to visit Don Enrique. But this crowd wants to kick out all the American oil men. The señora shouts: "Save Mexico for the Mexicans! Save the Mexicans for Mexico! The two commandments of our revolution!" Then they all jerk back their heads, swallowing tequila for Mexico.

Tonight the Painter explained, for the benefit of servants trying to slide behind the guests' chairs to clear the dinner plates, that this was a famous quote from Moses.

"Señor Rivera, Mexico is in the Bible?" Poor Candelaria, the Painter sometimes makes a sport of her. Possibly in more ways than one.

A different Moses, he told her. Moisés Sáenz, in 1926. "Ten years of revolution may not have saved all the Mexican children, but at least we've saved them from the pope and the Italian Renaissance."

"The Renaissance had its good points," his wife maintained.

"Honestly, Friducha. Who needs all those fat little cherubs flying around?"

As a matter of fact she is painting one with cherubs now. They look like unruly children with wings. She never seems happy with what she's painting, and talks to herself: "Oh boy, that won't work. What a lot of shit. That looks like it came out of the ass of a dog." Candelaria won't go near her. Next to Mother's Museum of Bad Words, Señora Frida could construct a pyramid.

But in her husband she has perfect confidence. She always says to the guests: "Damn all other artists to hell, Diego *is* the cultural revolution!" Even when some of her guests are among the damned. One time in her studio she said, "He's very great. Don't forget that, if you think you're looking at a fat frog who won't pick up his pants from the floor. His work is the whole thing. He's doing what nobody could do before." Maybe she heard Olunda complaining about him. Voices carry in this strange cement house.

She says Mexicans have trouble making friends with their history because we're many different nations: Toltec, Aztec, Mayan, Oaxacan, Sonoran, all fighting each other from the very beginning. That's why the Europeans and gringos could come in and walk over every-thing. "But Diego can take all those different people and make them into one Mexicanized *patria*," she said. He paints that on the wall, so big you won't forget.

It explains a lot, what she said. Why he is much-discussed. And why some people want him torn down, not just gringos but also the Mexican boys in *tejano* hats who don't want anyone saying they were born from between the legs of an Indian woman. He makes people feel things. How thrilling it must be, to tell the story of La Raza in bold colors and no apology: Indians walking out of history into the present, all in a line with their L-shaped noses, marching past Cortés into the vanishing point of their future.

9 April

President Cárdenas agrees with the Rivera dinner guests, it's time to kick out the oil men. Mexican oil for the Mexican people now. The newspaper says the workers will only have to work eight hours a day from now on, and get a share of profits. Cárdenas even kicked out Big Chief Calles, boss of every Mexican president since the rocks of the earth were still warm. Now he can enjoy the company of his gringo business friends more than ever, because the president had him ar-rested and put on a plane to New York. "What a Boy Scout, that Cárdenas," Olunda said. "Usually they just assassinate their rivals."

It was also a day of liberation for the peons of the Kitchen of Mi-croscopia. The señora wants a huge Easter party, and decided to have it at a regular house with a real kitchen: her father's house on Allende Street. It's where they lived before, near the Melchor mar-ket, with the jungle courtyard. She had César drive the staff there to get started cooking for Saturday, assisted by that house's ancient housekeeper and two girls. The dining table was piled with newspa-pers; the Painter still gets a lot of mail there. The others begged to be entertained with dramatic readings while cutting up one thousand tomatoes. Candelaria is tender-hearted, but Olunda only wants the motorcar plunges into the canyons of Orizaba, so the kitchen readings always involve some compromise. The Allende Street house staff were an easier audience: old Perpetua seems deaf, and the two girls laughed at anything: *Upon arrival in New York City, Calles told reporters . . . "I was thrown out of Mexico because I forgot my pants and wallet in the bedroom of a* puta *on Avenida Colón."* Candelaria and the girls shrieked and giggled.

Mistress Frida appeared in the doorway, completely unexpectedly. Olunda threw down the fork she was using to mash avocados and cupped her hands over her fleshy ears. The house girls ardently peeled the nopales without looking up.

"My concern is for your ignorance," the señora snapped. "This is a historic day. Read it to them correctly."

"Yes, señora."

She stood, waiting.

"Upon arrival in New York City, the former Jefe Maximo told reporters, 'I was exiled because I opposed the attempts to create a dictatorship of the proletariat.'"

"Very good. Keep going." She swirled and walked out to attend to her father, leaving the kitchen proletariat to absorb the real news of the day. The State Department of Chiapas, responding to the Syndicate of Indigenous Workers, has voted to raise the wages of all coffee workers throughout the state. In a formal declaration to the Congress, President Cárdenas stated, "In the new democracy, organized laborers exert a genuine influence on the political and economic leadership of our country."

Olunda's eyes darted from her avocados to the doorway, to the newspaper, and back to her bowl. Dreaming, perhaps, of a Syndicate of Avocado Mashers.

19 April

The mistress is having a relapse of difficulties with her back, an infection of her eyes, kidney stones, and an affair with the Japanese sculptor. So says Olunda, but it hardly seems possible: when would she have time? But Candelaria has evidence: the last time she let the Japonés through the gate, the Painter came barreling down the spiral stair with his pistol out. The sculptor is no longer welcome in either half of the double house.

22 April

The señora packed herself off to the hospital, taking paintbrushes and some dolls. Today she sent word she also needed chiles rellenos, so the master dispatched the male servants to the hospital with her lunch. Possibly to see if the Japonés is lurking there, attempting sexual liaisons with a woman in a plaster spinal corset. César got lost twice on the way, then remained in the car to nap and recover himself for the voyage home.

"Insólito!" she cried from her hospital bed. "Look at your poor Friducha, falling all to pieces and dying. Let me have that basket." She wore only half the usual pirate's chest of jewelry today, but her hair was pinned up the usual way. She must have nurses and stretcher-bearers at her command at the Hospital Inglés.

"Did you stop by my father's house to give him some of this?"

"Of course. Señor Guillermo sends you his heart."

"He's going to starve, with Mother gone. She's the only one who ever ordered those servants to get up off their *nalgas*." She pulled out the napkins and silver, arranging her bed for dining as carefully as she sets the table at home.

"With respect, señora, his housekeeper is the same one who managed to keep you alive through your childhood."

"My point exactly. She's ancient. It's like an archaeological ruin over there."

"Everything is fine at Allende Street, you shouldn't worry. Perpetua hired two new housegirls. Belén and something. Today they were planting lilies in the courtyard."

"Lilies! The whole house needs repairs and a good coat of paint. I would make it plumbago blue. With red trim. What's the news from home?" she asked, tearing into the rellenos. She had an excellent appetite for a dying woman.

"You don't want to know."

"*Meaning?* Has Diego replaced me already?"

"Oh, no, nothing like that. It's all the same people coming over in the evenings."

"The painters?"

"Mostly the writers and the theater ones."

"The Contemporáneos. Oh boy, you're right, I don't want to know about them. Villaurrutia with his *Nostalgia for Death*! Just go ahead and drink the poison, *muchacho*, get it over with. I think he and Novo are having an affair with each other, they're both impervious to flirtation. And Azuela is just gloomy."

"Mariano Azuela? That's him? The author of *Los de abajo?*"

"The one. Don't you find him gloomy?"

"He's a very great writer."

"But very cynical, don't you think? Look, that character Demetrio in *Los de abajo*: What kind of hero is he? Fighting in the Revolution without a single idea in his head about *why*. Remember the scene where his wife asks him why he's fighting?"

"Of course. He throws a rock into the canyon."

"And the two of them just stand like a pair of dummies, watching the rock roll all the way down the hill."

"It's a moving scene, Señora Frida. Isn't it?"

"Maybe if you're a rock. I'd like to think I'm being pulled through history by something more than the force of gravity."

"But gravity is winning. Look how short you are."

"This is no joke, I'm warning you, Sóli. Be careful of your heart going cold. The Mexican writers are cynics. Our painters are the idealists. Take my advice, if you ever need a party to cheer yourself up, invite the painters, not the writers."

She cocked her head, like a cat inspecting a mouse prior to

consumption. "But . . . you are a writer, aren't you? You write at night."

How could she know that? Now they will make it stop.

"Pages and pages. César told me that. He said it's like you're possessed."

No confession.

"I also believe you find it *most* interesting that Novo and Villaurrutia are sleeping with boys instead of girls? Don't you."

None.

"I'm not charging you with crimes, you know."

"No. No secrets, Señora Frida."

"What a lot of *mierda*. You always call me señora when you're lying. So tell me, how are things in the soap opera of Los de Kitchen?"

"The same, Frida. We're just tedious little servants."

"Sóli, you are neither small nor tedious. Sooner or later you're going to have to confide in me, one pierced soul to another. Sleep on it, Sóli. Consult your pillow."

4 May

A visit with Mother, to take her to La Flor for her birthday. She was dazzling as always in a violet frock and dyed-to-match wool cloche. Her new plan is to win the heart of an American engineer contracting for the government. She describes him as "plenty rugged." Also plenty married: they met when he came in the dress shop to buy a gift, not for his wife but his mistress. "Former mistress," Mother calls her hopefully.

"It's inspiring, Mother. You never shrink from competition."

"What about you? That girl came in the shop again last week. This is the Rebeca I told you about, the friend of that little jelly bean you took to the Posadas last winter, and if you ask me, this Rebeca is ten times prettier. If the other one is a wet sock, that's your good luck. She was a half-portion, if you ask me. But the friend is really swell."

"I didn't ask you."

"Rebeca, this one is. Write it down, *mi'ijo*, at least pretend you're interested. Or am I going to have to hire a *puta* to get a woman in your little *pinche* life?"

"A *pinche* life full of women, thanks all the same. One more and it might split open like a pomegranate."

"I mean a woman in *bed*."

"That house is ruled by a woman in a bed. Completely."

"*Mi'ijo*, you exasperate me. This Rebeca, look, she's a smart one like you. She wants to go to university, but right now she's a seamstress. Did she stop in? I told her where you're working. I didn't tell her the kitchen, of course, I said you were some kind of a secretary. Intending to become a lawyer. It isn't a lie to say you're *intending*."

"Let's go back to your love life. It's more interesting."

"It had better get that way soon, let me tell you. Forty! Look at me, I'm a rock of ages." She covered her face with her hands. Then peeked through, because the watermelon salad arrived. "And you, almost twenty! It's unbelievable."

"Half a rock of ages."

"And what will you be doing on your twentieth birthday, mister?"

"Cooking, probably. The señora has the same birthday. She doesn't know it."

"Listen, if we go anywhere together now, you are not to say you're my son, do you hear me. Look at you, a *man*! How could you do that to me? That's it, mister. The men nowadays want fillies and pips and sweet patooties and no-o-o dotie brodies."

She has moved on from oil men, there was no future in that stock. Don Enrique has lost everything in the nationalization. Mother reports that the hacienda on Isla Pixol has been appropriated, turned over to the people of the village as a communal farm. They turned the house into a school.

"Well, good. One provincial school will have some books in it, anyway."

"You would be on their side, wouldn't you? Houseboy for the pinkos."

"The point of the appropriation law is restitution, Mother. Meaning Don Enrique or his family must have taken that land from the villagers in the first place."

"But look, were they really using it? Your Leandro is probably the president of the collective now, trying to work out how to put on a pair of shoes."

"*My* Leandro? He had a wife. The only man in that house who did."

"Ooh, you slay me. Poor old Enrique, he got his sock chorus, didn't he? Can you imagine the scrow, when they put him off his own place? And his mother! Holy moly, that must have taken the army." Mother took a nibble of her watermelon salad.

"Consorting with Americans has improved your English."

"As far as I care, Enrique and his relatives can go chase themselves, and you can put that in your hat. There's some jazz talk."

"And you can put this in your hat, Mother. Washing the dishes of pinkos doesn't make someone a pinko. It's not like an influenza."

"I'm just razzing you. I'd take up with a pinko in two toots, if he was famous and had a wad of tin. That artist's little girlfriend is one lucky duck."

"The little girlfriend is actually his wife."

"Like I said. But what a piece of calico, all spuzzed up like an Indian. She's no Garbo. How'd she get lucky?"

"He's fond of the way she dresses. They're nationalists."

"No soap!" She shook her head. "To me she looks like a corn-eater."

"You used to ask, What kind of man would chase after that? In Isla Pixol, remember? Now you know."

"Hey, you got a gasper?" She took a cigarette and lit it, pushing away her unfinished lunch. Poor Mother, still living from one gasp

THE LACUNA ❋ 139

to the next. She removed a piece of tobacco from her tongue, and announced: "A corn-eater will never be any more than she is."

It was no use reminding Mother of her temporary craze for learning the *sandunga*. If corn-eaters are now having their day in nationalist Mexico, in Mother's estimate they will soon lose the race to fillies and sweet patooties. The afternoon crowd at La Flor had waned, but she kept glancing around the patio, always on the alert.

"What's become of Don Enrique, then? Is he begging on the streets?"

"Oh golly no. He's living in one of his other places. Up in the oil fields somewhere in the Huasteca. Enrique could always pull more money out of his *nalgas*. No matter how much he complained to us about our spending."

She leaned forward and looked up with big eyes under the brim of her cloche hat, and suddenly there she was: the other Mother. The mischievous girl, drawing another child into her conspiracy. "Don't worry about Don Enrique, *mi'ijo. Dios les da el dinero a los ricos, porque si no lo tuvieran, se morirían de hambre.*"

God gives money to the rich because if they didn't have it, they would starve.

1 July
The Riveras' wad of tin must not be as big as Mother thinks. Señora Frida had to make a strategy for financing her birthday party: she painted a portrait of the lawyer's wife and sold it to him. The party will be at the Allende Street house to hold all the people, as she has invited three quarters of the Republic, including mariachis. The painters and the gloomy writers are coming. Olunda is in a frenzy. Chicken *escabeche*, pork and nopales in *pipián* sauce, *mole poblano*. Sweet potatoes mashed with pineapple. Tomato and watercress salad. The pork-rib and tomato stew she calls "the tablecloth stainer." At last report she also wants shrimps and marinated pigs'

feet. The señora might have to paint portraits of the guests as they come in, and sell them on the way out, to pay the butcher after this fiesta. A wearying twentieth birthday expected for the cook.

14 July

Housecleaning. Eight paintings moved from Señora Frida's cramped studio into the storage room on the Painter's side. The nice painting of her grandparents, the odd one of herself and the monkey, and the bloody one that Candelaria talks about, from when she lived in the apartment on Insurgentes. Each title has to go in the ledger before it's moved upstairs: the bloody portrait of the stabbed girl is called *A Few Little Pokes.* She painted it after a man in the Zona Rosa stabbed his girlfriend twenty-six times, and when the police came and found her dead, the boyfriend said, "What's the problem? I only gave her a few little pokes." The story was in all the newspapers. Señora said, "Insólito, you'd be amazed what people will buy."

Did she mean the painting, or the man's story?

5 August

The people who come to dinner with paint in their hair now have a name for themselves: the Syndicate of Technical Workers, Painters, and Sculptors. After the plates are cleared they bring the typewriter from the Painter's office and make a newspaper right on the dining table. The writer in charge, Señor Buerrero, was the pigmentist on the mural crew. They argue about everything: Which is better, art or philosophy? Easel art for the bourgeoisie, or murals for the public? Which is the more nationalist, pulque or tequila? The servants get an earful, better than any school yet. Tonight they argued about how to defeat fascism in Spain. Mexico opposes the Fascists, even though the gringos and British think a stern fellow like Franco is just the thing to straighten up Spain. The Riveras' old friend Siqueiros is there now, fighting alongside the Spaniards.

But he was strange, Alfaro Siqueiros. The type to find a fight anywhere, war or no war. When he used to come to supper, Olunda would pull out her crucifix and say, "*Dios mio*, don't use the good *talavera*, it will be in pieces before the pastry." Rivera calls him a bang-bang artist, making murals with a spray gun and airplane paints. Siqueiros called Rivera a high-flying Communist, getting commissions from gringos and robber barons. Then Rivera would say, Look at your friend Stalin if you want to see the robber baron *maximo*, and usually that was when the *talavera* became endangered.

Really, those two have only one fight: Who is a better painter, Siqueiros or Rivera?

19 August

The señora in the hospital all week; it seems very serious. They moved her again to the Inglés. It's a long drive to take her lunch. On the way back today we brought food to the Painter in the Palacio Bellas Artes, where he's touching up that mural after they put some electric wires in the wall behind. It's the re-creation of the one that frightened people in New York so badly. Last summer the plaster boys made bets it would show monsters with devils' heads, or worse. Seeing it now, it's hard to guess which part is frightening. No monsters. Maybe the white and dark-skinned workers side by side. In the United States they require different bathrooms. But the Painter says no, it was only the face of Lenin, leader of the Russian Revolution.

The boys on the plaster crew are all different ones from last summer, so no one there today remembered Sweet Buns. That name is gone. Sometimes the past can vanish.

25 August

Señora Frida is still in the hospital. The house is both dull and chaotic, the blue side ruled by the monkey lurking on the stairs, awaiting the return of his mistress. He hangs by one hand from the stair rail, scratching his *nalgas*. The Painter, on his side of the house, is doing approximately the same. She is the center of everything.

29 August

The Painter is working like a madman in his studio. Candelaria refuses to take him his food or clean the studio while he's in there, for reasons she won't disclose. An acceptable reason would be: it looks as if a giant dog, after a large lunch of food, socks, paints, trousers, and pencils, walked into that room and vomited everywhere.

It's no easy trick to clean up around him. The man takes up a lot of space. He seems to be painting landscapes. Unlike his wife, he does not ask for a servant's opinion on his work. He interrogates. Yesterday: "How long have you been in this house?"

"All day, señor. My bed is in the little carriage house, shared with César."

"I know that. And you used to be on the plaster crew. Sweet Buns, they called you. I'm asking how long you've been with us here in San Angel."

"Living here, since last October, sir. Before that, two times in the summer when you had those gatherings and needed an extra cook. You hired me full-time after a girl left. Olunda recommended me to your service. Probably she regrets it now."

"Why is that?"

A pause. "Modesty should prevent my saying it, but my bread is better than hers. Beyond that, Olunda views life in general as a regrettable contract."

"I see your point. That's enough for now."

But today he launched a second interrogation, even more blunt. Beginning with: "Your name is Shepherd, and you're a foreigner. Is that right?"

"Only one-half foreign, sir. Mexican mother, gringo father."

"He lives in the United States? Doing what?"

"Keeping track of money in a government office. Building and road repairs."

"I see. And are you trustworthy?"

"It's a hard question to answer, sir. Saying 'yes' could prove either case."

He seemed to like that answer, smiling a little.

"Half American does not mean half loyal, Señor Rivera. Your household is generous and inspiring. A worker could not ask for much more."

"But workers do, every minute. I understand you're a writer."

"Señor, what on earth gives you that understanding?"

"One person. By name, César."

"He does?"

"He says you scribble every night. Are you reporting on us to someone?"

César is a perseverant snitch. "It's nothing like that. Just a diary of kitchen nonsense and little stories. Romantic adventures set in other times. Nothing of consequence, meant for no one else's eyes."

"César says you write in English. Why is that?"

"With respect to your old comrade driver. How does he know it's English?"

The Painter considered this. "Meant for no one else's eyes, including César's."

"You could understand the need for privacy."

His toad-frog face broadened helplessly. "You're talking to a man who smears his soul on the walls of public buildings. How would I understand?"

"Well, no sir. But consider how your wife views her art, something she does for herself. It's more like that. But of course it isn't art, these little notebooks, there's no comparison. What she does is very good."

"Don't panic, I'm not going to fire you. But we have to start being careful about security. We can't have a spy in our midst."

"Of course not." A long pause. Clearly it is important not to ask why. Does he want more reassurance, something personal? "About the English, sir. It's a habit from school. They taught us to use typewriters, which are very handy, I have to say. But they didn't have the Spanish characters. So a story begun in English keeps going in English."

"You know how to use a typewriter?" He seemed quite surprised.

"Yes, señor. When the question of Spanish characters came up, the officer at school said no typewriter anywhere has characters beyond those needed for English. But it isn't true. The one you sometimes leave on the dining-room table has them."

"Those gringos. What jingoists."

"That was the problem at school. You can't get far on a story without the accents and *eñe*. You begin with Señor Villaseñor in the bath, reflecting on the experience of his years, but instead he is *'en el bano, reflexionando en las experiencias de sus anos.'*"

The Painter laughed, throwing a streak of blue across his big belly. Olunda will offer up some curses over those trousers. The big toad has a wonderful laugh. That must be what women like about him, besides the wad of tin. Not his face, for sure. But his joy, the way he gives himself up entirely. As he said, a soul smeared on walls.

The suspect was then released, carrying a pile of dirty plates from the room of interrogations. If César can read his name here, let him worry. Let him fret all day over Senor Villasenor in the bath, reflecting on the experiences of his anuses.

3 September

Señora Frida is back from the hospital, but not well. Both master and mistress are in the house now, requiring service day and night. Candelaria, forced to choose between devil and dragon, has chosen the one that needs her hair combed. Just as well, because the other devil needs a typist. The Communist Party has thrown him out over the never-ending argument of who is better, Stalin or Stotsky or Potsky or what. The other Communists won't come over for supper and do his typing anymore. And the mistress seems angry with him over some private matter. Olunda has plenty of theories. Poor toad-frog Diego, losing people faster than he can paint new ones on a wall.

14 September
Today General Wrong Turn got lost on the way to the house in Coyoacán where he lived for forty-one years. The errand was the usual, taking food to Señor Kahlo. When César first began driving Guillermo Kahlo around for making his photographs, it was in a carriage. Not a motor coach in all Mexico City, he says, and those were the good days. It's true that horses have certain advantages: namely, knowing the way home.

It's strange every time, returning to the Allende Street house where Señora Frida marched home from the Melchor market that birthday long ago, a stranger, with a shy boy carrying her bags because Every Man has the Right to make a Kite from his Pants. And in the courtyard inside, the Painter sat under the trees reading his newspaper, waiting to be found, all on a chance. How strange that a boy could make a kite of his pants, fly them around the world, and somehow arrive back at the house where everything began.

1 October
A tiresome day. Being the Painter's typist is harder than mixing his plaster. The worst of it isn't the typing but his interrogations. He says cleverness in a servant is not always a good thing. Candelaria, for example, could straighten all the papers on his desk and come away with no more idea of what's written there than Fulang Chang the monkey. And the master doesn't hold Fulang Chang entirely above suspicion. Only the illiterate, wide-eyed Candelaria. "How about you?" he needled. "What did you see just now, while you were typing the invoice letters?"

"Nothing, Señor Rivera."

"Nothing, including the official letterhead of the President of the Republic? You didn't notice a letter from Cárdenas?"

"Señor, I have to admit, that did catch my eye. The seals are outstanding. But you're an important person. Commissions from the government are nothing exceptional. I didn't care enough to read the letter, that's the truth. I'm uncurious about politics."

He closed his newspaper, took the glasses off his nose, and stared across the room from the armchair where he likes to sit while reading and dictating. "*Uncurious?*"

"Señor Rivera, you stand for the people, anyone can see the good of that. But leaders all seem the same, no matter what they promise. In the end they'll let the poor people go to the dogs."

"A cynic! A rarity, in revolutionary Mexico. In your age group, anyway."

"I didn't go to university. Perhaps that's helped me maintain my position."

"A severe young man. You allow for no exceptions?"

"Exceptions haven't presented themselves. I read the newspapers a little. Which I take from your studio when you're finished, señor. I offer that confession."

"Here, take this one too, it's nothing but junk." He folded it and tossed it at the desk. "Did you ever hear of a man named Trotsky?"

"No, sir. Is he a Pole?"

"A Russian. There's a letter from him over there as well. In the same stack with the president's."

"That one I did not see, Señor Rivera. I swear it's the truth."

"I'm not accusing. The point I want to make is that you're wrong, idealism does exist. Have you heard of the Russian Revolution at least?"

"Yes, sir. Lenin. He got you in trouble with the gringos on your mural."

"That one. Leader of the Bolsheviks. He sent the monarchs packing, along with all the rich bloodsuckers living off the workers and peasants. He put the workers and peasants in charge. What do you say about that?"

"With no disrespect, señor, I would say, how long did he last?"

"Through the revolution and seven years after. He did what was best for his people, until death. All the while living in a rather cold little apartment in Moscow."

"It's admirable, señor. And then he was murdered?"

"He died of a stroke. With two men poised to succeed him: one with scruples, the other with cunning. I suppose you'll say it's predictable, the cunning one took power."

"Did he?"

"He did. Stalin. A selfish, power-mad bureaucrat, everything you seem to require in a leader of men."

"I'm sorry, sir. It's not that I want to be right about this."

"But I contend you are not. The other one, with scruples, could just as easily be in charge now. He was Lenin's right hand and best friend. Elected president of the Petrograd Soviet, a populist, certain to succeed Lenin. Different in every way from Stalin, who was infatuated with party bureaucracy. How could the people fail to support the populist over the bureaucrat?"

"And yet they failed to do so?"

"Only thanks to an accident of history."

"Ah. The populist with scruples was murdered."

"No, to Stalin's frustration, he remains alive in exile. Writing strategic theory, organizing support for a democratic People's Republic. And avoiding Stalin's ant colony of assassins, who are crawling over the earth right now looking for him."

"It's a good story, señor. Strictly from the point of view of plot. May I ask, what was the accident of history?"

"You can ask the man himself. He'll be here in a few months."

"Here?"

"Here. It's the Trotsky I mentioned, the letter lying over there on the desk under Cárdenas. I've asked the president to grant him political asylum under my custody."

So. For this, all the questions and mystery. The Painter stood grinning, his hair in an unruly halo around his head, or perhaps it was a devil's horns. His smile underlined by double chins. "Well, my young friend. Do you remain *uncurious?*"

"Señor, I confess, I maintain that position with increasing difficulty."

8 October

Sometimes when the Painter is reading over the day's typing, there's time to look at the books in his library. The whole wall is shelves. On the bottom are Frida's wooden-spined box folders where she files the household papers. Each one she has identified with a picture drawn on its spine: a naked woman, for Diego's personal letters. The Evil Eye, for hers. The one for accounting has only a dollar sign.

The rest is books, a wall of them about everything: political theory, mathematical theory, European art, Hinduism. One shelf the length of the room is devoted to Mexico's ancient people: archaeology, mythology. Scientific journals on the antiquities, which look tedious. But others are fascinating. The Painter took one down to show it off: a codex. Made a hundred years ago by monks, who labored to make exact replicas of the ancient books the Mexica people made on thick tree-bark paper. It didn't have pages exactly, but was one long folded panel like an accordion. The ancient language is pictures, little figures. Here, a man cut in half. There, men standing in boats, rowing.

He said it was the Codex Boturini, about the peregrinations of the Azteca. On the advice of gods they left Aztlán in search of their new home, and took 214 years to find it. The long page was divided into two hundred fourteen small boxes, each one recording the main thing that happened in that year. Not good, mostly. A head hanging on a rotisserie over a fire! A man with eyeballs falling out! But most of the years showed simply their search for home. Anyone could feel the anguish of this book—what longing is keener? Pictographs of weary people walking, carrying babies or weapons. Small, inked footprints trailed down the full length of the book, the sad black tracks of heartache. When completely unfolded, the codex stretched almost the whole length of the studio. That is how long it is possible to walk, looking for home.

November 2

Day of the Dead. The señora made altars all over the house to recall her beloved dead: ancients, half-born children. "Who are your dead, Insólito?" she keeps asking.

They request a suspension of all writing, this notebook put away. César will enforce the ruling. They set their trap and pounced in the Painter's study at lunchtime, husband and wife in one room for once, for this purpose. *For security. No more of your little notes. We've promised extraordinary measures for the Visitor, you can't imagine how frightened he is.* Devil and dragon in one lair, the Painter sitting at his desk, and she pacing the yellow floorboards with rippling skirts, a tiny tempest. *Not even a market list.* They claim César is becoming agitated, convinced he's sleeping in the same room with an agent of the GPU. "Poor old General Wrong Turn, I know he's confused," she said. This woman who has said many times: *Sóli, to stop painting would feel like being dead.* She understands what she's asking. To stop writing and be dead.

"It's for safety," he added. A man who throws paint in the face of safety.

Where are your dead, Sóli? Here, and the devil take it, a notebook for the altar of the dead in this lonely house. Dead and gone, the companionship of words.

Report from Coyoacán

This record of events will be submitted to Señora Frida for weekly inspections, or at any other time she requires, for purposes of security. According to her authorized instruction it is to harbor no opinions, confessions, or fictions. Its purpose is: "To record for history the important things that happen." The señora's sympathy for record-keeping is noted with gratitude—HWS, 4 January, 1937.

9 January: Arrival of the Visitor
The petrol tanker *Ruth* arrived from Oslo at dawn this morning to discharge its only passengers at the Tampico docks. The landing party were brought from the ship by a small launch, under the watch of Norwegian guards, and welcomed onto Mexican soil by the following persons: Sra. Frida, Mr. Novack (American), and General Beltrán representing the government of Mexico. Diego R. still hospitalized with an infection of the kidneys. The Visitor and party were taken by government train to the capital.

11 January: Arrival of the Visitors in the House at Coyoacán
He is to be known here as "Lev Davidovich." His wife: "Natalya." Because of the danger of assassination, a welcoming party assembled at the San Angel house to distract attention while Lev and Natalya were secretly brought here to Coyoacán. Their secretary of many years is expected to arrive here in the coming week. He did not travel together with them, but through New York.

12 January

The visitors are settled in the house, the former dining room serving as their bedroom with Lev's study in the adjacent small room. Lev in extraordinary spirits, despite his years of travails fleeing from Stalin and recent twenty-one days at sea. He steps through the glass doors of his study into the sunny courtyard and stretches himself, flexing his arms: a compact, muscular man, truly the Russian peasant to lead a revolution of peasants. He seems built for a life of work rather than confinement. When he's working at his desk, his broad hand clasps a pen as if it were an ax handle. When he smiles, his eyes shine and his cheeks dimple above the little white beard. Delight appears to be his natural state. Does a man become a revolutionary out of the belief he's entitled to joy rather than submission? This surprising man looks up at the bright Mexican sky, remarking that with only one country on earth that will have him now, he's glad this is the one.

He could leave this house for a stroll if he liked, though of course he would have to be guarded. In Norway they were indoors under house arrest since last September, Natalya said. Stalin threatened trade sanctions against Norway unless the government rescinded his asylum. And we can be sure, Stalin already knows he is here.

14 January

Arrival of the secretary: to be known in this record as "Van." Tall, blond, broad-shouldered as a footballer, it's good he traveled separately. Such a d'Artagnan as this fellow could hardly walk down a street without attracting attention, as the señora will shortly see for herself.

Lev's study and bedroom are the most secure part of the house, as they form an interior wing jutting into the courtyard. Good light from the portico doors facing the courtyard and magnolia tree. Van is keeping very busy there today, unpacking books.

16 January

Sra. Frida will be shocked to see her childhood house so transformed. It was a good choice to move her father to San Angel, all Sr. Guillermo's things are packed away. The exterior walls have been painted plumbago as requested, so it is the Blue House she wanted. But really, a Blue Fortress. The courtyard wall is raised to a height of seven meters, and the masons are moving their scaffolds now to begin bricking up the windows. The men agree these security measures are needed. From the tall wooden doors on Londres Street, visitors now enter through a guarded vestibule into the courtyard garden.

The courtyard is still the jungle it was; the masons haven't trampled the flowers completely. The house retains its original U shape, with the long front room facing Londres Street (fireplace and leaded-glass windows intact) to be used for dining and political meetings. Lev's bedroom and study make the other long wing. The string of tiny rooms across the back, connecting the two main legs, will house everyone else: Perpetua, the house girls Belén and Carmen Alba, the secretary Van, the cook HS, bodyguards Octavio and Felix. The windows in these small rooms face the exterior on the Allende Street side, so all are being closed by the brickmasons, making them dark little cupboards. One guard is posted out on Londres at all times. Sr. Diego is now feeling well enough that he brought over his Thompson machine gun.

The kitchen retains good light and air, extending outward as it does on the Allende Street side to enclose the back of the courtyard. The masons agreed to leave windows open for ventilating the wood fires in the stoves, after voluble argument from Perpetua, who warned of *cocineras ahumados*, the kitchen girls smoked like hams. Perpetua is confused and worn out from the changes, and resigned to her new position as assistant to a male head cook, HS, who vows to do his best by this duty. This kitchen is a wonder, with its extravagance of blue and yellow tile, woodstoves as long as divans, and the welcome sight of large wooden tables for rolling out dough. It will be a pleasure preparing the daily repast here for the visitors, and any feasts required for evening gatherings.

Household directives noted here: No food from unknown sources to be served, under any conditions. No unknown person to enter the house. HS is to assist the Visitor with typing and correspondence (recommended by Diego R.) and to retain this written record of events (requested by Sra. Frida). The first report from Coyoacán is here complete for the week Jan. 9–16, submitted for inspection.

19 January

The Coyoacán house is proving a good accommodation. Old houses have their wisdom. Despite the bricked-up exterior, the main rooms are comfortably lit by the courtyard. That jungle enclosed by high blue walls is a comforting world for visitors who are not at great liberty to roam elsewhere. Perpetua is taking care with her lilies and figs; it remains a cheerful world, in no way resembling a prison. Perpetua said Guillermo had this house built for his family more than thirty years ago, and through all those years no one saw a need for turning it upside down, until now. (Her resentment of the current upheaval is understandable.) The deep adobe walls keep a good temperature all day. The contrasts between this house and the modern one built by the Riveras in San Angel are many, most particularly their *kitchens*. But on that subject no opinion is given here.

Sra. Frida's choice of blue walls is greatly approved by all here.

A note on meal preparations: The visitors prefer tea over coffee. Another exceptional preference is unsweetened bread cut into thin slabs, toasted in the oven until somewhat hard, as if stale. Otherwise they are generally agreeable to normal foods. Natalya made plain their disinterest in pickled fish, after a long Norwegian winter of almost nothing else. They request mashed turnips and a green vegetable unknown to these parts, translated by Van as "the Sprouts of Belgium." Tomorrow Perpetua will be driven into the city on a search, as the Melchor market here has neither tea nor turnip. But they are adapting well to customary foods: sugared fritters, baked guava, and fermented cream are all favored. This morning they took enchiladas with eggs, and tea.

On days when no special meals are scheduled, all hands go to helping Lev unpack and arrange his study. He is curious about Mexico: the altitude of mountains, population of the city, its history, and so forth. Perpetua on her trip to town is to fetch the *Geographic Atlas* owned by HS, from his mother's apartment. It is outdated but will serve for now; Pico de Orizaba has not changed its height in a decade.

Lev communicates with help from the secretary Van, since Lev's Spanish and English are rudimentary, and clever Van seems to speak everything possible: French, Norwegian, Russian. He claims both French and Dutch as native tongues. He makes a point of moving the largest crates, insisting no extra help is needed in Lev's office. It can't be argued really; Van is tall and strong as an ox. (Though more handsome.) He complains sometimes in English about the "native typist," apparently not realizing HS also has two native tongues. But Lev is agreeable to having an extra fellow to help him. Plainly, Van has a habit of protecting his chief from outsiders, which is natural. He first became Lev's assistant in France, where they lived from 1933 until 1935. That was before Norway. Prior to that, Lev and Natalya were hiding in Istanbul, and before that, Kazakhstan. Lev Davidovich has been living in exile under threat of death since 1927. "I am a man in a very large world," he said slowly today, "with a very small place to be."

Mexico is fairly good sized, sir. You'll see.

Van said, "He's speaking metaphorically. He means that he lives in the planet without a passport."

21 January

A telegraphed message came this morning, delivered by Diego wearing his holster and gun. The message was in a code. Lev spent many hours in his study working it out, rejecting even Van's offers of help, with Natalya the whole time walking between the study and the kitchen, pulling on her fingers, making Perpetua burn the milk. The message concerns the son in Paris. Van says there are two sons; the younger was taken to prison camp three years ago, almost certainly dead. Two daughters are also dead.

Lev is not very sure of the message except for one important part: the telegram is definitely from Lyova, so he is alive. They have a code for his identity that is known to no one else on earth, not even Natalya. Lev speculates that GPU killers in France have tried to assassinate Lyova, and we can expect the newspapers to report him killed. To spare distress, he wanted his parents to know he is alive, in hiding.

They seem little spared from distress, though. If her son escaped murder this time, Natalya asks, what about the next? Lev rages that his children have done nothing to earn a death sentence from Stalin. The younger one, Sergei, only ever cared for books, sport, and girls, but ended in a concentration camp. "And now Lyova. His crime is to be the son of his father. Who can change the things that brought him into the world?"

23 January

Diego arrived early, upset, with the bundle of newspapers he receives by special post. Two report the death of Lyova, as predicted, but they know this is false. There is worse news yet: headlines declaring L. D. Trotsky found guilty of crimes against the Soviet Union. His trial in Moscow has been going on for weeks, with the accused in absentia. Van says Lev petitioned to go there and stand trial, for the chance to defend himself, but Stalin wouldn't lift the exile order. The aim of the trial is to discredit anyone who ever spoke against Stalin. Some of Lev's friends are also declared guilty: men named Radek, Piatakov, and Muralov, all three imprisoned now in Moscow.

The charges are strange and diverse: derailing trains, collaborating with Rudolf Hess and the Nazis, acting as agents of the Japanese emperor, stealing bread. Attempting to assassinate Stalin by poisoning his shoes, and his hair cream.

Stalin uses hair cream?

"Careful, lad," said Lev. "That knowledge alone could get you the firing squad."

The penalty for the charges against Lev is death. Yet he seems in good spirits, despite the newspapers from France and the United States calling him a villain, and the Mexican ones calling him a "villain in our midst." The editorials speculate on why he betrayed his principles. These newspaper men have never met Lev, yet confidently they discuss his innermost feelings and motives! They take it on faith that the treacheries were all committed. They don't even wonder how a man could derail so many Russian trains after he was put on a cargo boat for Prinkipo Island.

The security regimes here are strictly maintained, as the news makes clear Stalin intends to have Lev assassinated. The guard in the street changes hourly. Lorenzo organizes drills in which Lev and Natalya must be hidden very quickly. When Diego comes in the car, Lev has to move to one of the inner rooms before the court gates are opened to let the car drive in. Snipers could be in Allende Street, waiting for a line of fire into the courtyard. And if any unknown person comes to the door, even a grocer's boy delivering eggs and flour, the intruder is patted down, relieved of belt and shoes, and made to open all packages for inspection. The GPU will certainly strike, and no one knows how they will do it. (Though entering in the guise of a grocer seems unlikely.)

Lev says he has been a revolutionary from the age of seventeen, with a gallows waiting for him somewhere for forty years. His friends will know these new charges against him are invented. "And my enemies know it also. Which of these has written anything new?" He threw the newspapers aside and made Natalya come and sit on his knee. She obeyed him, but with a frown on her bottom lip, like the little dogs that have long wool in their eyes and a flattened nose. Lev took off his round-rimmed spectacles and sang to her in Russian. He asked to hear some songs of the Mexican revolution. Perpetua knew a surprising number. For such an old cook, her voice is steady.

24 January
Lev and Natalya went for a stroll in the Melchor market, their first venture outside the house since arrival. Between all the guards and Diego's machine gun, Coyoacán village must have entertained a commotion. But the so-called Villain in Our Midst means to hold his bearded chin up to the world without shame.

With Lev and Natalya out strolling and all the guards escorting, the house was quiet. A slow afternoon passed, helping Van file cartons of Lev's letters and published writings. It's hard to believe such an outpouring of words could come from one man—"the Commissar," Van calls him. He works each day as if the calendar on his desk were on its last page, which it could well be. Today while he was out, Van took the opportunity to ask many questions, not friendly. Place of birth, education, and so forth.

He revealed some scraps of his own life: a difficult childhood, the French mother losing her citizenship for marrying a Dutch husband, who died soon after Van's birth. Van has a weakness for what he calls Nederland licorices. They look like black glass beads, in a packet he keeps in the desk drawer, guarded rather anxiously, as he is sure they can't be bought in Mexico.

Here are two fatherless boys, then, eager to be anything for Lev, with his own two sons so far gone from him, and the man so kind. Already Lev remembers which assistant takes sugar in his tea. He puts everyone through stretching exercises so they won't get backaches while typing what he himself stayed up all night to write. But Van will always be the favored son, of course. He has served Lev so long.

Van was surprised to learn the "native typist" is also of hybrid origin, half gringo. He changed to speaking English after that. His Spanish is very imperfect. He needs help with interpreting at the political meetings, especially when the talk flies around the table like a flock of crows. Last evening it flew from Russian to English (for Mr. Novack), then Spanish (for the Riveras' colleagues), then back to Russian, with some French thrown in by Van, just for show, it seemed. Excuse this opinion, if it is one, but as Sra. Frida can plainly recall, no one at that meeting needed French.

All papers filed today were letters from the past four years, most in French but some typed in Russian, pages of characters in that strange alphabet lined up like rows of little men doing bending exercises. So it's untrue that typewriters are restricted to characters of the English language. Van cracked his composure and smiled at the story of Officer Gringo and the Potomac Academy typewriters. He understands Spanish well enough to laugh at the joke about Señor Villanueva and his *anos* in the *bano*. Or he pretended. He seems fearful of losing his position as his commissar's sole interpreter.

With apologies here to Sra. Frida, because the last paragraph undoubtedly contains at least one opinion. But not a fiction. The second weekly household report from Coyoacán is herein submitted for her inspection.

30 January

A wire came from Paris: Radek, Piatakov, and Muralov were executed in Moscow. Lev's spirits flag—more of his friends are dead—but he stays absorbed in work. What the newspapers say about Lev is shocking, charges more improbable every day. Lev said that when the public nerve is aroused, the most impressive capacity of man is his skill for lying. Van said, "It's good to hear you indignant, Commissar."

But Lev maintained he was not at all indignant. He was holding a Russian newspaper with such ink-stained fingers he could be a printing press. "I'm speaking as a naturalist, stating fact. The urge to lie is produced by the contradictions in our lives. We are made to declare love for our country, while it tramples our rights and dignity."

"But newspapers have a duty to truth," Van said.

Lev clucked his tongue. "They tell the truth only as the exception. Zola wrote that the mendacity of the press could be divided into two groups: the yellow press lies every day without hesitating. But others, like the *Times*, speak the truth on all inconsequential occasions, so they can deceive the public with the requisite authority when it becomes necessary."

Van got up from his chair to gather the cast-off newspapers. Lev took off his glasses and rubbed his eyes. "I don't mean to offend the journalists; they aren't any different from other people. They're merely the megaphones of the other people."

"It's true, sir. The newspapers are like the howlers on Isla Pixol."

Lev seemed interested in the comparison, and changed from English to Spanish. "What are these howlers?" he asked.

"A kind of monkey, very terrifying. They howl every morning: first one starts, then a neighbor hears it and starts his own howl, as if he can't help it. Soon the whole forest is bellowing, loud as thunder. It's their nature, probably they have to do it, to hold their place in the forest. To tell the others no one has gotten the best of them."

"You are a naturalist also," Lev said. He struggled but was determined to continue the conversation in Spanish. Van left the office. "Where are these creatures?"

"Isla Pixol. It's a coastal island, south of Veracruz."

"A monkey does not swim. How did they become isolated?"

En isla, he said. Probably he meant, *en una isla*, on an island.

"It wasn't always an island, an isthmus of rocks connected it with the mainland, but they dredged it for a shipping channel. It was during Maximilian, I think. The monkeys that had gone out there couldn't get back."

22 February

The jacaranda in the courtyard has put on its bloom. This purple can't be ignored, it's like a tree singing. The walk down Londres Street to the market is a concert: the small jacaranda on the corner hums the tuning note, then all others in the lane join in. Even Perpetua has a light in her eye, holding one hand to her flat old bosom as she takes the cucumbers out of the market basket, one by one.

From Lev's study, the view from the end window is a solid blaze of purple. Van sits there to take dictation from the Ediphone, with his square profile framed against the window like Poseidon in a purple sea. Or some Teutonic god who causes all he touches, and the air itself, to burst into purple flames. It is not a fiction or opinion to report that he is breathtaking. Perpetua is not the only one in this house thinking of cucumbers.

1 March

Octavio apprehended a man with a repeater, in the alley. After every fresh newspaper rant on the villain residing in Coyoacán, these men show up. So far it's only citizen-desperados vowing to protect their wives. Lev fears more sophisticated men, Communist Party operatives working under command of Stalin's GPU. But a bullet from a barefoot soldier is no less deadly than from a well-paid one. Lorenzo sleeps in the front dining room now. Those lovely windows will have to be closed with brick. The masons have made a mess, and Van had to move into the tiny cupboard with HS, close quarters for two. Though he left his multitude of serge jackets in a trunk in the other room.

This week is too hot for early spring. And this week the household staff are banned from the front of the house due to the government officials negotiating there, late into the night. The heat in this bricked-up cloister is unbearable. Van is dismayed at being held out of the meetings, but Diego says it's sensitive. President Cárdenas is expected here himself, to help arrange the Commission of Inquiry for Lev.

After cooking and serving supper, washing up, tidying, and sweeping, nothing is left for the staff but to sit on cots in these tiny rooms in undershorts and gob shirts, smoking panatelas, telling exaggerated stories to pass the time. It's like being at school. These are not brotherly feelings Van inspires. Mother would say: Van is plenty rugged.

March 3

The guards spend every long evening all in one small room, breathing the same exhaled air and drinking one another's spit from one warm jug of pulque. Playing cards for pesos, boredom games. Earlier this evening, the usual one: name your one wish if you could have it, then die tomorrow. Boys at school played this, reliably coming round to getting hands on some celebrated pair of *tetas*. Van from his high place added to the earnest list, "success of the Commissar's revolution." He was on the cot and everyone else on the floor, passing the cigarette packet. "You, Shepherd. Name yours."

"To make something beautiful, that people would find very moving."

"*Pendejo*, you do that every day in the kitchen."

"I mean a work of art that isn't in the toilet pot by the next day. A story, or something like that."

"Like the murals of Rivera, commanding men to rise from their knees and fight!" Lorenzo said. Stewed or not, loyal to the cause.

"Or smaller, like the paintings she does. Something people would find . . . dear."

"*Querido*. That's all you want, sheepdog!"

"Our shepherd," Van said, leaning out to pat a shaggy head as if it belonged to his dog. In front of the other men. The small dog panted.

10 March

A wire from Mr. Novack, now back in New York: he has persuaded Professor John Dewey to chair the commission of inquiry. Some

American journalists will follow the story to Mexico. Diego and Lev are extremely happy, as it will give Lev opportunity to answer Stalin's charges, for the world to hear.

Noted: That Sra. Frida, after inspecting last week's record of events, repeats her request that it remain objective, especially with regard to the secretary Van.

April 6

Professor John Dewey of Columbia University arrived today by train from New York. He will preside over the joint Commission of Inquiry into the Charges Made Against Lev Davidovich Trotsky in the Moscow Trials. He and seven journalists will reside for the month at the San Angel Inn. The opening press conference will be there, honoring Professor Dewey's wish for fairness and no contact with the defendant prior to hearings.

The proceedings will be held here, because of special needs for Lev's security. The attorney for Lev's defense, Mr. Goldman from Chicago, arrives by train tomorrow. Sandbags are being laid across Londres to close the neighborhood to traffic. Extreme publicity is expected during the trial. The Mexico City newspapers are already having a run of extras on the subject of the Villain in Our Midst.

April 10: First Session of the Joint Commission of Inquiry

Professor Dewey opened. Thanked Mexican government for its political democracy, stated no man should be condemned without a chance to defend himself. "I have devoted my life to the business of enlightening minds, in the interest of society. I accept my responsibilities in this commission for one reason: to do otherwise would be false to my life's work." The responsibility is to investigate charges of sabotage and sedition brought by Stalin against the defendant.

Defendant is Lev Davidovich Trotsky, b. 1879. Fought as anti-tsarist from age seventeen, led the Bolshevik Revolution, elected president of the Petrograd Soviet in 1917. Author of the manifesto of the Third

International Comintern, 1919. Expelled from the Soviet Communist Party in 1927. Forced into exile in Kazakhstan at that time.

At the table with the defendant are his wife, his lawyer, and Van, who has the job of producing requested documents. At a table near it, two Americans and HS, who are to translate and record all questions posed to Lev, and his answers. A man named Glotzer (American) is official court reporter and knows a language (shorthand) that allows writing everything very fast, but only if he understands the words. So all proceedings go to English for his sake, and of course for Professor Dewey's. Therefore HS has the duty to record and translate any questions asked or answered in Spanish.

None today, only testimony. Cross-examination begins tomorrow.

12 April

One question in Spanish today, from Sr. Pontón of the Sociedad de Naciones, translated as follows: "Sir, for our Mexican correspondents I beg you the trouble of answering: your persistent charge against Stalin is a lack of democracy. Is that correct?"

Lev answered: "Correct. A rank of party workers has been created who enter the government and renounce their own opinions. Or at least any open expression of them. Every page on their desks comes from above. They behave as if the hierarchy had already created all party opinion and decisions. From this hierarchy, every decision affecting the country stands in the form of a command."

When Lev isn't speaking he puts his feet on the table and leans back in his chair. Today he reached such an extreme backward angle, it seemed the GPU might not be needed to crack the man's head. But he was still listening. He looks down his Russian nose and his whole lower face crumples into his collar when he concentrates. He has no consciousness of how he must look to others, only aiming his mind with such a ferocious focus that it could set all those bureaucrats' papers to flames. This must be the countenance of a revolutionary.

This daily record complete and submitted: 4/12/37.

13 April

Sr. Pontón's question and Lev's answer have gone on the front page of today's *Washington Post*! Exactly as translated by HS, and quoted again on the editor's page, in a discussion of the Moscow Trials and the commission. The article even used the description of Mr. Trotsky leaning in his chair, and the headline in very bold letters was: THE COUNTENANCE OF A REVOLUTIONARY.

These were only some notes and doodles submitted with the translation transcript, Sra. Frida. This is a shock, and a terror. The very first try at translation, and some notes jotted on a whim, now on display for the world to read? It was hard to think about breakfast this morning. Perpetua said, "Sit down and stop shaking, *mi'ijo*. It's a bad start to the week for a man who's hanged on Monday."

Hanging is what it feels like! A twenty-year-old *galopino* who knows nothing about politics could have mistaken yes for no, a *renunciar* for a *renacer*, and then what? History could hang on it. Lives could be lost, for the sake of a wrong word. No wonder writers are pessimistic. Better to be a cook, where a mistake will only send someone away hungry, or at worst, to the WC.

But Van complimented the translation. He read the article to Lev and Natalya at breakfast, translating it back to Russian as he went. They listened to the words of a cook, while eating toasted bread for which the same nervous cook had already burned his knuckles.

14 April

After the day's hearings closed today, Lev went to the front door to see the huge crowd gathered there. Not only newsmen but workers of all sorts, even laundrywomen. No barefoot soldiers want to kill him anymore, after hearing his fiery defense of the worker and peasant reported in the news. Now he's afraid they'll want to knock Jesus off the pallets of the Holy Week processions this week and put Trotsky up there instead. A group from the miners' syndicate walked here all the way from Michoacán.

He spoke to the crowd in Spanish, slowly but well. "I am here because your country believes with me in democratic government and the worker-control of industry. Our efforts cannot succeed in an empty space." (Probably he meant "a vacuum.") "True change will come from an international organization of workers for world revolution." The crowd has been quiet all day, but at those words they roared.

Nearly every day he takes small pauses from his writing to practice Spanish with the native typist. Van doesn't like the distraction, pointing out that translators are always at the ready. And Lev says, "Trust an old revolutionary to trust no one completely." He was teasing, it seemed. But today as he spoke directly to the crowd, his purpose was clear.

15 April

A long day of hearings. Mr. Dewey says it's nearly concluded, but the crowd still grows, both the number of foreigners inside and the Mexicans outside. Lev has such a passion for this hearing, he wouldn't mind if it went on until the sun burned cold. Van seems content beside his chief, undaunted by the army of observers: Mexican and foreign reporters in fedoras and rolled-up shirtsleeves, magazine writers, even some novelists, watching Van's every move as he fishes into the paper caverns of the files with his long fingers, retrieving whatever obscure page Lev might need, indicated only by a word, a date, or a person's name. They are like father and son. Lev and Van.

Very few questions in Spanish today. Sr. Pontón of the Sociedad de Naciones has the most. Today he had two. The first: "Sir, is it your position that a worker's state could genuinely honor suffrage and all democratic rights, as in a social democracy?"

Lev's reply: "Why should it not be so? Even now, in all the capitalist countries, Communists take part in the parliamentary struggle. When we achieve a worker's state, there is no difference in principle in the way we will use suffrage, freedom of the press, assembly, and so forth."

Second question: "Sir, you say the Soviet Union under Stalin is a degenerated workers' state, controlled by an undemocratic bureaucracy. You predict this corruption will be overthrown by a political revolution, establishing a democracy of the working class. Or that it will continue to degenerate under world pressure into a purely capitalist state. In either case, can you rationalize the costs to society?"

Lev answered: "Young man, you make a point. Humanity has never succeeded in rationalizing its history. Much harm comes from leaders who insist that for every advance, someone else must slide backward. The dictatorship of the Soviet Secretariat came about because of the backwardness and isolation of the country, for so long imposed on us by the tsar. We were accustomed to the rationalizing of a despot. People accept what they have already known. When mankind is exhausted, he creates new enemies, new religions. Our best task is to move forward without seeking to do so."

April 17

The commission has ended its work after thirteen sessions. If it went another day, the dining room of this house would crack like an egg. Lev closed with his usual vigor: "The experience of my life has not destroyed my faith in the clear, bright future of mankind. At age eighteen I entered the workers' quarters of Nikolayev with nothing but a boy's belief in reason, truth, and human solidarity. My faith since then has become more mature, but no less ardent."

Every hand stopped; the reporters looked as if they might need handkerchiefs. Mr. Dewey said, "Sirs, anything I could say after that would be a waste of breath."

Mr. Dewey and colleagues will consider the evidence and find the defendant guilty or not guilty. They will take many weeks before releasing their written verdict. But Lev is jubilant. Before the world, he has answered the charges.

28 April

The house is calming to the previous routines. If "calm" describes a man who works like three, signaling the typist to finish a letter and bring a book while he dictates political theories into the microphone of the wax-cylinder recording machine. It's very warm, even working in shirtsleeves. Van is always last to remove his tweed jacket. An unexpected brush of his hand, when he reaches for a book, feels like boiling water. Van and Lev are both men of northern temperaments, yet Van seems agitated by Mexico's vivid sun and landscapes, while Lev seems enlivened. He even loves the cactus.

1 May

Sra. Frida has continued her daily visits here since the hearings ended, making sure Lev is content. Let it be noted here: bringing Fulang Chang "to cheer the place up" may not be helpful. Natalya despises the monkey and yesterday, while Sra. Frida was in the kitchen, gave him a whack on the skull with a Conservative Party newspaper.

Lev is energized by the news of the workers' uprising in Barcelona, citing it as a sign that the Third International agreement between Stalin and the world's other communist parties has collapsed. Lev has been asked to write a fourth set of Internationalist agreements, hence his frenetic rush of words congealed into wax cylinders from his Ediphone. The alternative to Stalin's Comintern now sits in jars on the desk, waiting to be transformed into typewritten words, and then the actions of men.

To celebrate, the household staff is complying with Sra. Frida's requests to prepare for her "Fourth International party." Sr. Rivera is more worried about security than table decoration.

2 May: The Dance

Lev was already in his study when Sra. Frida arrived this morning to take over the dining room, before Natalya had eaten her breakfast.

So she ate in the kitchen. Begging pardon, but please let it be noted: this is Natalya's only home. Lately she has mentioned feeling like an unwanted guest.

Begging a second pardon, señora, but it was impossible not to laugh at the sight of you standing there at the table, decorating it for the party, with red carnations in both hands and one in your mouth. You looked like Carmen.

What are you laughing at? You think it's so simple to create history? Long skirt sweeping the floor like a broom, moving around the table, carefully laying out the long-stemmed carnations on the white tablecloth. The pattern looked like a huge eye, the long stems as eyelashes radiating outward like rays of the sun.

It's true, dining tables are part of history. The Painter's walls and Lev's wax cylinders are not the whole story. The Sra. frowned, already picking up the flowers again before the design was finished. Commanding: *Fetch the scissors!* without even looking up. Snipping the heads of the carnations from their stems, working so quickly that trails of blood might have begun flowing from her fingertips, like one of her paintings.

Then she put a hand on her hip and held up the scissors, menacing the air. "We're going to have dancing tonight. A lot of handsome artists. Belén and Carmen Alba told me you dance the *sandunga* and *jarabe*, perfectly. I will not even ask how they know this. But how did you learn?"

"From my mother."

"Your mother, a nationalist? I had a different impression."

"She would deny it now. She had a flirtation with it when we first came to the city. But now she's moved on to the age of swing, and well-paid engineers."

"And do you renounce us also? Or would you dance with an Indian girl?" She held out her hand and moved like liquid, rolling herself up into the arm that received her, making a flirtatious snip with her scissor like a flamenca dancer with her castanet.

Señora Frida is a confusion of terms: sometimes like a stern little man, then suddenly a woman or a child, but in every form demanding that you remain in love with her. Commanding even her giant of a husband, until he runs off to be rescued by softer, pillowy women. This is the truth and not an opinion: her cat smile, those hands, the paintbrushes. Any one of them can be like a slap across the chest.

After an hour's work she was satisfied with the arrangement of red flowers on white linen. "Here will be Lev's place," she said quietly, "and here. Natalya's." Uttering that second name as if her place at the table were a concession.

Jealous, of Natalya? Frida, is it possible?

It's a lot of work to use flowers as paints. By the time the party ends, they'll be a mess of wilted petals. Stains on your white tablecloth that could have been prevented. But you whirled around at that suggestion, looking fierce: lips pursed, the hand on your red rebozo, those silver earrings caressing your shoulders like hands.

"Unnecessary stains and dead flowers! Sóli, excuse me but what else do I have for making my marks on life, if not *lo absurdo y lo fugar*."

You wanted to know how to say that in English. "The absurd" is easy. The other is more difficult. *Fugar* means things that run away with time. What would we do without the absurd and the running away?

That was the moment when the door flew open *bang!* and of course it was Diego. Carrying books and jacket, dropping things as he went, his boots hitting the tiles like cracks from a rifle as he crossed the room, kissed you, took the flowers away, and began to rearrange everything. All your work, you, everyone in the room—it all vanishes in the presence of Diego. Always right, because he is always riveting. For La Frida there is El Diego and nothing else.

A long time ago at school there was a boy like that, Bull's Eye, always right even when he was wrong. Once you said it would be necessary to confide in you, Frida, sooner or later, one pierced soul to another. That maybe you could help. Since you are the only one reading this report each week, here is the confession you requested: the scandal of irregular conduct. For the Insólito there was Bull's Eye and nothing else. *Insólito* means ridiculous. It means all those things you said, absurd and running away. Where would you be without *lo absurdo y lo fugar.* Maybe you're also lonely in this house, and you were asking: My friend, what would I do without you?

16 May

The press reports that Mr. Browder of the American Communist Party has come here to warn Mexican Communists against any communication with Trotsky. He says "unity at all costs" means supporting Stalin. Lombardo Toledano and many other Mexican party leaders have dined at the Riveras' table, eaten the food of this kitchen. But Diego's membership in their party is now revoked. They all ignore his invitations to come here and meet with Lev.

The heat is unbearable. Van goes out to a bar at night, the Golden Earring, just to get some air, he says. Lorenzo goes along, hoping to meet girls. *Do you want to come too?* Van asked. But probably the bar would be just another airless place.

1 June

The commander in chief of the Red Army, executed for treason. Tukhachevsky had expressed support of Trotsky's position, and for this reason only he is dead. Lev dreads there will be a purge, thousands of officers affected. Nothing else here to report.

4 June

A telegram this morning from Lyova, as always in code. The purges in the Soviet Union are terrible. The chief of the Soviet Secret Service has resigned his post in protest of the killings, and announced his loyalty to Trotsky and the Fourth International.

Lev fears for the safety of Chief Reiss, but is cheered by news he has broken from Stalin. A congenial day in the office, despite sweltering heat. Lev had the big red worktable from his office carried outside to the courtyard. The commissar was quite a sight, working in his big straw hat and old-fashioned balbriggans. Even Van has finally stripped from gob shirts to Vee Lines, and over the course of the day his great Dutch shoulders began to glow. Tonight they are nearly the same maroon color as the desk.

This afternoon he knocked over the ink bottle and laughed about it, for a change. His sympathies are improving. He gratefully accepted help with changing the typewriter ribbon, and later with a repair of the electrical cord of the Ediphone. He complimented a small correction in a translation, saying we make a fine team. Who knows where else the pair of us might work, outside of these walls, if such a day should come.

5 June
Señora Frida's wish this evening was to dine intimately with the Visitors. Natalya is not well and remained in bed. Van went out for the evening.

8 June
Let it be noted: Every time Sra. Frida brings out a tray of tea, the commissar lights up like the sun. He used to bear interruptions with polite tolerance. Now he glances up often to see if it's time yet for another. Listening for the jingle of bracelets. Van agrees, Lev's behavior is strange. Today Lev and the señora went in the automobile to Sra. Cristina's house on an undisclosed mission, and stayed several hours, not for the first time. The lack of security is extremely worrisome. Frida, this is not an opinion.

10 June

Today while Lev was out for the afternoon, he instructed the office should be well cleaned and the table moved back indoors. Rains are expected.

Evidently the commissar didn't expect such a thorough tidying-up. Van found a box of letters that worry him greatly. The nature of these letters may be known to Sra. Frida. *The new workers need not only your husband's murals, but also what you offer: beauty, truth, passion. True art and revolution are joined at the lips and the heart.* Some letters, even more explicit, had been placed inside books he's borrowed from Sra. Frida. He means to return these later, evidently. The letters remain in place.

Tonight Van paces like a prisoner around his cot in this tiny cupboard of a room. He sucks on licorice pastilles when he is anxious, after first laying out the evening's ration end-to-end as Mother used to do with her cigarettes.

"Can we say anything about this, to anyone?"

"How could we?"

Van is desperate for his chief's safety. And feels loyalty to Natalya as well; he has lived with them so many years. He wants this behavior explained. But not the explanation.

"For the sake of heaven," he keeps saying, alternately pacing and slumping onto his cot. His broad shoulders and white V-shirt glow in the darkness of this bedroom with its closed-up windows. "I thought she looked up to him as a father. For the sake of heaven, she calls him El Viejo."

"The *old man* is only five years older than Diego. Maybe she says that to disguise her feelings."

Bricked into this tiny cell: two men wrapped in heat like a blanket, whipped into two entirely separate frenzies. At the root of each man's distress, although from entirely separate quarters: the damages wrought by love, the cruelties of sexual attraction.

He hasn't any notion. In a moment he will be naked, it happens every night. Innocently he lays out his body, piece by piece like a banquet. His long, flat belly like a white-flour tortilla. His beautiful feet extended beyond the wildest hopes of his little cot.

"How can they be so foolish?" he keeps asking.

"Love can be like a sickness, Van. They didn't want it to happen."

11 June

Four of Sra. Frida's paintings will be included in an exhibition at the National University. Likely she is happy about it, though she has not mentioned this, or anything else of a personal nature, since the last inspection of this journal. She comes to the house almost daily to see Lev, but avoids the staff. Most especially she avoids Van.

The personal confidences of her cook, for which she has earnestly asked on several occasions, have gone unnoticed here, or at any rate passed without comment.

12 June

An unforgettable outing: strange and wondrous, but in the end, bitter humiliation. The confidences of this report have been used against their author. Fact, not opinion.

The workings of a household are like those of the world. The Russians tolerate Stalin's tyranny, Lev says, only because they know nothing else, from centuries of isolation under the Tsar. So it may be here, as well. So it may be with a mistress whose cruelty merely contains her past. Cruelties imposed on her by a husband, or life itself.

Yet, as Lev said at his trial: our best task is to move forward without insisting others slide backward.

The authorized reporting of history, then: Sra. Frida proposed the outing as a kindness to all, "to escape this insufferable heat." But Natalya of course is still unwell, and Diego too busy even to be told about the outing. The escapees included only herself, Lev, and his two secretaries—two pairs, like playing cards in her hand. She arranged it with more than the usual secrecy and drove the motorcar herself because César can't keep his mouth shut, she said. And that much is true.

A long drive to the dusty edge of the city, out to the embarcadero. Xochimilco is a strange village, farm fields that appear to float on the water. Really they are built-up islands, farmed since the time of the Azteca, when this city still stood in a lake. The canals and square farm-islands are the last evidence of what lies beneath all this history and claptrap called Mexico City. Sra. Frida lectured with great flair during the drive, sometimes letting go of the steering wheel to wave her hands, telling how the ancients supplemented their diet of frogs by making these islands for growing vegetables. How the layers of water lily leaves and fertile mud are built up inside a fence of inter-laced reeds, until the island gets above water level and the farmer can plant his crop.

Now it is a mad maze of colors and cool water. Squash and corn-fields, floral explosions, with waterways running on a perfect grid between the island fields. Angel's trumpets dangle their pink bell-flowers over the water, and white herons stand one-legged among the reeds. Giant old poplars tower along the borders of each field, shading the watery lanes. You can see how it's all constructed; they begin by planting these poplar saplings in a rectangle under the wa-ter, for anchoring the interlaced reeds and poles that will become the island's perimeter. Now the saplings planted long ago are ancient, leafy giants, with coral beans crowding in thickets between them. Some islands have the farmers' reed-thatched huts built right upon them, with children running and swimming from one to the next, naked as fish. Women cast lines into the water or hawk jugs of pul-que to the boaters passing by. Every side channel offers another thrill-ing glimpse, a long ribbon of shining green water overarched with a tunnel of trees.

The passenger boats made for the canals are broad, flat-bottomed *trajineras*. Gaudy ducklike things, every one is painted up in red, blue, and yellow, with an arch across the front of each one spelling out a woman's name in flowers. Made to order with each hire. Frida and Lev had a dispute when they hired the boat: she wanted to call it *Revolución*. Not the best (Van pointed out) for the security of our comrade guest. Lev prevailed, and the boatman spelled out *Carmen*, Sra. Frida's first name. She snuggled up happily with the "old man" on the bench on their side, with Van and HS on the other bench, two pairs facing one another across the plank-table. All the boats have one, a long, narrow table for picnicking bolted right in, running from prow to stern. Ours was painted the brightest yellow, which seemed to suit Frida's mood. She would know a name for this color. The canals were jammed with these boats, all painted with similarly violent imagination, bobbing with couples and families escaping the city's heat, pushed along by boatmen with poles. The farmers in canoes full of vegetables had some trouble poling between the traffic jams, making their way out to the marketplaces of the city.

A canoe swept by carrying marimba players, two men in white shirts standing side by side at their long instrument of wooden blocks, rolling their hands over the rippling wooden notes. Frida tossed the marimba men a few pesos to play "The Internationale." Other boatloads of musicians bobbed past also; the place was filled with them, even a whole mariachi band standing up in their canoe, entirely precarious, balancing the enthusiasm of song with their will to keep dry.

It was a wild, floating marketplace. Men selling flowers, women with giant aluminum pots balanced in tiny boats, pulling up alongside to sell you a lunch: roasted corn, *pollo mole*, *carne asada* and tortillas, handed up into your boat on crockery that would be washed afterward in the canal. Lev bought a bunch of red roses and tucked them one by one into Frida's crown of braids. He poured glasses of red wine for all of us, and then refilled them. He paid a band to play "Cielito Lindo" and then twelve or fourteen other songs, all about the heart and not one concerned with the Revolution. When he leaned out over the water to pay the musicians, he forgot to let go her hand, which he was holding under the table. The lovers were quite on display, cuddling all the afternoon, her little elbow folded neatly against his.

Van looked away, listing various sights as we passed by them in a childish way that was very unlike him, thanks to his discomfort. It would have been just as well to stare at these two; they make a better physical match than the little dove and the toad-frog. A more pleasing alignment: the Indian girl and her compact Russian peasant. Across from them, the Nordic god and native typist were shoved so close together on the bench, every turn of the boat pressed some part of a leg or shoulder against another. The air was breathlessly still, a cottony hot roar that swallowed everything: heat and music, a pounding pulse. Van close enough to touch his cheek, or clasp his knee. It took everything not to do it.

Then suddenly, loud screaming split the quiet. Our sleepy boatman raised his pole in alarm, but it was only a boatload of schoolgirls. They came alongside, waving wildly, with another boat following behind in right pursuit. That one, of course, filled with schoolboys, splashing and hurling flowers at their victims.

"It's a war of flowers!" the girls shrieked, launching back long-stemmed arrows across the water. They fell short every time, like the Azteca warriors uselessly slinging arrows at Cortés, just before their hearts were blown apart with cannon fire.

"*En garde!*" cried Frida, arming herself from the bower encircling her head, tossing roses in every direction. Lev also threw some flowers: a probable first in his long career as a militant. Frida reached into the water to catch a long-stemmed carnation and pointed it like a sword, swiping Lev's cheek and then his chest.

"I am hit!" he cried, clasping his chest in mock drama, falling back against the bench. "Struck in the breast by a posey. What do you call this one?"

"*Encarnado,*" she said.

"*Descargado por encarnado,*" he said. Carnal wounds. Injury may be mortal.

She kissed his cheek. Van looked carefully at the trees. The two boatloads of warriors moved away down a side canal, leaving the water behind them clotted with their colorful ammunition. Another canoe approached, and a man selling toys climbed aboard our boat, his pockets filled with trinkets of woven palm leaves. "Any children here?"

"No," Frida said, and Lev said "Yes" at the same time. Van explained, "I'm afraid the children have all gotten away."

"Well, this one is indispensable for people of any age." The man pulled from his pocket a long, woven tube. "A *trapanovio*. You had better try it, señorita." He held it toward Frida, who obligingly put her finger in the end of the tube and then made a show of not being able to escape. Everyone knows this trick. The weave of the tube holds tighter, the harder one pulls away.

"Señor, you'll have to buy it now, and hold on to the other end yourself," the man told Lev, extracting from him five pesos. "Otherwise she'll have this dangerous device for catching boyfriends, entirely at her disposal. Who else here needs to trap a few *novias*? You, young men?"

"That one maybe," said Frida laughing, pointing across the table. "He's desperate to trap a particular *novio*."

There was no need to say it like that. *Novio*, the masculine form.

"But forget about the other one." She tugged her trapped finger free of Lev's grip, its long prosthesis still attached, and shook it at Van as if he were a naughty child. "He needs no devices for trapping girls, apparently he has his own equipment. What time is it now, four o'clock? They're already lined up waiting for him at the Golden Earring."

"What is this?" Lev sat forward. "You go to that bar at night?"

"Not every night. And the girls don't make a queue."

"Oh, I've heard some stories!" Frida said. She seemed quite intoxicated, but maybe it was an act. She can seem that way at any time, for her own reasons. The toy man sensed that he had stepped in the pie, and scurried back to his canoe.

"What is this, Van?" Lev asked again, seeming interested but not disapproving. "You didn't tell me about any girls."

Van blushed acutely. "Not *girls*. One girl. Her name is Maria del Carmen."

"Maria del *Carmen*," Frida sang. "So this boat named Carmen carries more than one torch. Tell me about this young lady. Is she a bar girl?"

"A waitress. But educated at university. She tutors me in Spanish sometimes in the evening."

"Oh, very good, very good," Frida said, smiling ferociously, a cat with the mouse beneath its paw. "University educated and pretty, I have no doubt. Tutoring you in Spanish! Have you learned this one yet, *esternón*?" She touched her breastbone, leaning forward, and then cupped her own breasts in her hands. "What about *pezónes*?"

Van's complexion gave over completely to his blush. His ears and even the back of his neck. "I know the words. If that's what you are asking."

She stood up and leaned across the table, close to his face: *"Y besos suaves?"*

Lev pulled her back by the hand. "Frida, he's a man, not a child. If he has a lover in the town, it's not your concern."

"Everything is my concern, *mi viejo*. Lovers, most of all." The looks she gave to Van were smoldering. She worked the woven boyfriend trap gently off of her finger and studied it for a moment, before tossing it across the table to the object of no one's desire.

"Insólito, you're the one who needs this. Better go trap yourself a different fish."

14 June

The household has exploded. Diego and Natalya learned of their spouses' affair, leading to the unpleasantness one could reasonably expect. Lev left this morning for a house in the desert at San Miguel Regla, loaned on short notice by trusted friends of Diego. When Sra.

Frida came to the house today, Natalya made a very painful spectacle of her anger. Poor Belén was so frightened she dropped a plate of fritters.

Of course Van went with him, and Lorenzo also, but not the other bodyguards. Lev says he can't impose an army on the hospitality of the Riveras' friends, even if they support the Fourth International. Diego fears the place can't properly be guarded. And to complicate the arrangement, Diego may count himself among those lined up to assassinate his comrade guest.

Frida seems both disconsolate and unrepentant. A strange mix. Surely, señora, you don't blame anyone but yourself? You wanted to be discovered, that was obvious. Remember what you asked for in these pages: a history without deceit.

17 June

In the kitchen, the stories burn hotter than the stove. Perpetua says Señora Frida went up to San Miguel Regla yesterday, on the excuse that she needed to give some money to the Landeros family for taking Lev in their house. Perpetua clucked her tongue. "What business could she have up there except monkey business? But once you're on the horse you have to hold on, I suppose. Even if he bucks."

"That old man must have spice in his sauce yet," said Carmen Alba.

"*Old?*" Perpetua spat. "He's not even sixty. You girls are children, you don't know. The longer the sauce cooks, the spicier it gets."

Belén kept a nervous eye on the kitchen door, fearing the wife of the sauce in question.

30 August

A telegram came yesterday: Lev's former secretary Erwin Wolf, murdered in Spain by the GPU. Natalya felt someone should take the sad message to Lev. It was a quiet drive to San Miguel; César seems more than ever suspicious, even though he no longer has to share his room with a notebook-keeping spy.

The road to Regla passes near the great pyramids of Teotihuacán. Then through little mountain towns, steep streets filled with taverns, donkeys and dust, and pink colonial mansions from an earlier time, before it was shameful in Mexico to be rich. Now the mansions are all apartments, displaying laundry from their balconies.

Lev's place at San Miguel Regla is a small apartment at the back of a large hacienda. It seems safe enough, a high wall and Lorenzo posted at the window, in a desert outpost visited mostly by vultures. The Landeros are rarely in residence, the family and servants in any case asked not to approach the rear of the house. With no women around, the rooms shared by Van, Lev, and Lorenzo look like drawers in a giant cabinet, the beds swimming among notebooks, pistols, shoes, and inkwells. If Lev stays much longer, he may drown in his river of paper.

Lev finds the desert air invigorating and takes long walks each morning on the empty roads. He has fallen in love with cactus, finding a hundred varieties populating the dry ravines. To Van's dismay he digs them up, wraps them in burlap coats, and carries them home on his shoulder. Somehow, he plans to make a garden of these bizarre, prickled creatures. Van seems prickled also. Maybe missing life at the Golden Earring.

The return trip was even slower due to César's somnambulant driving and the anticipation of Natalya's poor eager face, the small bulldog sniffing for her absent master. She'll have to be told; Lev indicated no plans for returning soon. He doesn't mean to neglect her; it's only his pure fascination with life as it is, however it is. For any homeless wanderer he is a miracle of instruction: now that he is exiled from every place on earth except a desert wilderness, he declares a passion for cactus.

Here, very little is to be done. Cooking for unemployed bodyguards and Natalya, who hardly eats. She has survived six weeks now on lemon-juice tonics and Phanodorm. Every afternoon at two o'clock she parks her black shoes like two tiny automobiles beside her bed and lies down, fully dressed, to survive the remainder of the day.

One of the messages carried to Lev concerned a visit from Joseph Hansen, a comrade from the Trotskyist Party of the United States. Natalya sees hope in it: Lev's true appetite, she says, is for his work. The arrival of Hansen will bring him back.

8 September

Lev returns, as predicted, and with him the flood tides of paper. Idle days gone. Van works all day transcribing the wax cylinders, while Lev generates more. The typing is endless, interrupted only by the security drills.

Our menage is stirred like a soup: Diego wants Mr. Hansen and his wife Reba to have one of the connecting rooms. So all the guards will now share one tiny room, unless one would share a bed with old Perpetua, who snores like a boar pig. The house girls made a pallet under the fig in the courtyard so they can get some peace.

Members of the staff feel more than ever like inmates, because of the crowding and extreme security measures. The threats are real—this is understood, but not easy. Belén and Carmen Alba can't visit their mothers. The door is rarely opened; even a trip to the market has to coincide with the change of guards, so as to interfere less with Lev's work schedule. Van has ceased his nocturnal visits to the tavern. The bodyguards sleep with pistols in their belts, the possibility of death waiting behind every knock. The heat of summer has abated, and nothing is as it was.

12 September

Arrival of Joseph Hansen and his wife Reba. Lev and Joe are so happy to meet, they stayed up all the night talking. Reba helped make up extra beds, stuffed mattresses on the floor of a tiny room where now five men will sleep when not on duty. Reba apologized terribly and offered to share Perpetua's bed. Diego didn't forewarn her about the number of people already living here, probably because he neglected to notice it himself. She nearly wept. "And tomorrow you'll have to feed us all. You must be tired of salvaging these men who are saving the world."

Hansen means to write a biography of Lev. In that case, this recording of events may no longer be necessary. Mr. Hansen understands politics far more perfectly, and can record conversations objectively, not laced with an ignorant cook's prejudices for sweet and salt. History can fall into more capable hands.

In any case, a record maintained to another person's standard is no real comfort to the spirit. Let it here be said, the writer understands this assignment was intended as a kindness, for which he is grateful. But the task has no freedom in it. A record meant for another's eyes is not recording, but spying.

September 16
Frida.

Carmen Frida Kahlo de Rivera, to be precise. And Van.

Were discovered sleeping on the pallet under the fig tree, where the house girls usually sleep but were tonight sent home to their families for the national holidays.

Recorded here for history: the couple lay with limbs entwined, his great white arm sheltering her small, curved body. Her black hair surrounded both of them, rooting them to the bed as if they were growing there, a single plant. They seemed consoled by sleep, unaware of an observer who had consumed some beer, earlier in the evening during the Independence fiesta, and hoped to deposit a secret piss in the geranium bed. The pair did not know they had been discovered. Apparently they still do not. The observation is here reported. Some madness of penned dogs infects this camp.

November 7
The Dewey Commission formally acquitted Lev of every accusation from the Moscow Trials. After months of deliberation they have re-

leased their written verdict to every nation. Of course Stalin still wants him murdered, more than ever. And the American and European newspapers that made him guilty in the first place have barely reported the Dewey Commission. Diego says the gringos are watching Hitler with a nervous eye, especially now with the Anschluss and the Rome-Berlin axis. He says Britain and the United States will want Russia on their side, if there is a war. So they can't let Trotsky be right about Stalin being a monster. They are going to need that monster.

Still a cloud has lifted, in time to celebrate Lev's birthday and the October Revolution. The Riveras made the largest-ever fiesta, hired marimbas, the patio and house filled entirely. The security men nearly exploded from nerves. The guests are not artistic Communists any more but peasants, white-trousered men in huaraches, unionists who support Lev. The women entered shyly with their heads down, braids nearly sweeping the courtyard stones. A few brought live chickens as gifts, their feet tied nicely with henequen ribbon. But the cooking for this fiesta started a week ago.

Señora Frida was especially extravagant in a gold Tehuana blouse, green skirt, and blue shawl. She arrived with a large parcel wrapped up in paper: a portrait of herself, a birthday gift for Lev. Somehow it did not get presented, in the middle of so much celebration. People were already sleeping on chairs and window ledges, and it was half-way to morning when she came in the kitchen demanding, "For the love of Petrograd, can anybody tell me why we celebrate the October Revolution on the seventh goddamned day of November?"

"Belén asked Van the same question. Apparently it took more than a month for the Russian proletariat to overthrow seven centuries' worth of oppression."

"Well, according to Diego you should go to bed now. He says it's inappropriate to have the servants spend more than one day making so much food to honor the ten million starving peasants."

"Don't worry, all the other oppressed cooks have already gone to bed. I was just cleaning the chocolate pots. And I'm sorry to report it, but the cooking for today started a week ago. What does Diego expect? For you to do that kind of work yourself?"

She sank delicately into one of the wooden chairs at the yellow table, perched like a canary. "Oh, Sóli. You know that frog and me. We can fight about any stupid thing."

"Not to mention the things he doesn't know about."

You looked up then with a child's dread, clutching your shawl as if it might protect you from bullets or ghosts. How interesting, to discover the power to frighten you. *When mankind is exhausted, he creates new enemies*, Lev says. The qualities of cruelty are spontaneous. *Our best task is to move forward.*

"Frida, forget it. Nobody will tell Diego about you and Van. It only went in the book so you would know you've been seen. You can tear out that page. But as the wife of a man who keeps a Luger next to his dentifrice? You could be more careful."

"I thought you would be furious. Because of Van."

"Fury demands a fire. For Van and me, no hope of a fire. As you pointed out that day on our boat outing. Had you already been with both of them, back then?"

"You make me sound like an animal. 'A madness of penned dogs,' that's cruel."

"It wasn't you who surprised me, only Van. And Lev too, they seem such moral fellows. Forgive me for putting it that way."

For once your eyes stayed steady, trained on the question, not looking for the door. "What do you know about love?"

"Nothing, apparently. That it winks on and off like an electric bulb."

You seemed to be excavating your soul to locate some kindness. "People want to be consoled. You're so young. You still have a lot of time for being moral."

"You're only a few years older. As you've said."

"But old anyway, with all my patched-up parts. I'm as doomed as all these men, for lesser reasons of course."

The pots were all shining now. Nothing more to do.

"Sóli, there's an ache in this house. Tomorrow anybody could get a bullet in the head. Men like Diego and Lev have to make their vows of sacrifice. 'Better to live on your fucking feet than die on your knees,' and all that. But under all that fatalism, they want life."

"Who doesn't want life?"

"But they do, more than most. They want it so badly they shake the world until its teeth fall out. It's why they're the men they are."

"And Frida can help them to be alive. When she feels like it."

"It was only that one night, with Van. I think he had a lot to drink. But you can never tell with the big, quiet ones. He's dying of loneliness."

"Who is, Van?"

"Yes. Did you know he had a wife?"

"Van is married?"

"He was. To a girl in France. They were very young when they met, I gather, both working for the Party. They had a little boy. The wife's name is Gabrielle. She wanted to come here but Natalya wouldn't have it—apparently they had quite a row. You know how protective Natalya is, she thinks of Van as her son."

"It's understandable. After all they've been through. Her losses."

"You're right. Forget about Diego, I think Natalya would kill me if she found out about Van and me."

A wife. Van had a wife named Gabrielle. He has a son. This is what it means to be alone: everyone is connected to everyone else, their bodies are a bright liquid life flowing around you, sharing a single heart that drives them to move all together. If the shark comes they will all escape, and leave you to be eaten.

This is the last report. November 7, 1937.

Coyoacán notebook

25 April 1938

Mother is gone. Dear God in whom she never could believe, please let her not be alone in some drear heaven without men or music. Salomé, motherless mother, never more than a child herself. Dead, with her heart in the wrong place.

In the beginning were the howlers, mother and son joined in terror of the devils stalking from above. No matter how many times men told her, "It's nothing. It's a practical matter." *Write down the story of what happened to us*, she said. *Promise me. So when nothing is left but bones and scraps of clothes, someone will know where we went.* She said to begin this way: They are crying for our blood. But how can the story end so soon, and so bitterly? Salomé in a shattered sedan with her heart dislocated one last time. Nothing left but bones and scraps of clothes. Who can say where she went?

The new beau was a foreign-news correspondent. They were dashing to the airfield to catch a glimpse of a daredevil pilot said to be landing there for just a few hours. A stunt flyer, planning later this year to circle the world. These men with their great plans. The correspondent is an Englishman, Lewis. Probably he promised Mother the chance to meet famous people at the airfield. Instead they met head-on with a truck coming from Puebla, carrying cattle to market. Some cattle escaped. Lewis suffered a broken collarbone and lacerations from flying windshield glass. But it was on Mother's lap that the engine of his Studebaker came to rest, causing what the doctor called a spontaneous pneumothorax. It means that a hole ripped in one lung suddenly let out all the air, pulling the heart into the right half of her chest. Tearing it thus from the position it held for forty-two years, without ever settling in completely. Maybe for those last few shivering beats it was at rights. Maybe her heart stopped yearning to be somewhere else.

Lewis told what he remembered of it, offering condolences from a bed in the English hospital. His head was bandaged like a mummy from the films. "You're the son," the mummy observed. "She said you were planning on university, to be a solicitor." He had only known her a short while. Didn't feel entitled, really, to say anything at a funeral. Diego, with usual generosity, paid for the casket and a special mass despite his atheism. And despite Mother's. The mistake passed unnoticed among the few friends gathered, none of whom had known her in life. Just the one son, bearing up the weight of his own bones and damp unmanly grief. What a raging, salted wound, that sad little passage, what arrogance the world holds against women like Salomé. So many salons she has entered on the arm of a beau, always ready to charm the necessary bureaucrats of this world. Yet in the end, not one proved willing to escort her out of it.

How could a life of such large hopes be so small in the end? Her last apartment: one room above a lace-and-girdle shop. One trunk of frocks and phonograph records, donated to a coworker. Every *casa chica* was smaller than the one before. Were the beaux less generous over time? Her assets less marketable? If she had lived to be old, would she have resided in a teacup, to be sipped at intervals beneath some gray moustache?

At least she made the papers, departing as she did. A small note in the big News Extra about a daredevil flyer called Howard Hughes: "Among the press mobs, a foreign correspondent was injured and female acquaintance killed in a collision while speeding to the site on the Viaducto Alemán." Her mark on history: the female acquaintance.

26 April

Lev couldn't attend the mass of course, for safety, but continues to say he was sorry for that. His whole body winced the morning of the news. He and Natalya are raw at every edge since Lyova's murder in February. In a Paris hospital, where in heaven's name any person should be safe. They have no children left now, only the grandchild Seva from the eldest daughter. Lev's supporters are falling to a pogrom, everyone in the Vorkuta labor camp executed on the same day. And yet the United States claims Stalin as an ally, *still*. They have offered to help extradite Lev, for the purpose of execution.

Ever since Cárdenas expropriated the American oil, the news promises sanctions will come, and maybe war. Francia Street last week filled up with students shouting: "Let the gringos come. We already turned back Napoleon!"

Natalya takes Phanodorm morning and night, and cups of tea one after another: drowning her sorrows, as Frida would say, until the damn things learn to swim. But maybe some sorrows can't be borne. When Lev pauses in his work to stare out the window, his eyes are as cold as his children's bodies. The clear, bright future he once saw so plainly must now be charcoal lines, drawn down to a vanishing point.

Last night he came out to the courtyard to smoke a pipe and talk, just memories, not necessarily ordered. He told about a dinner he had with Stalin many years ago, when no one yet saw the man as anything more than an ambitious, irritating young bureaucrat. They were sharing a bottle of wine with Kamenev and Dzerzhinsky, talking nonsense as young men do, and the question came up: What did each like best in life?

Lev said the question exhilarated Stalin. "He leaned forward on the table gripping his knife like a pistol, leveling it at each one of us, and said: 'To choose your victim, to prepare everything, to revenge yourself pitilessly. And then to go to sleep.'"

11 August

Teotihuacán is the place where gods live. Xipe Totec, who rules over lust and birth. Round-eyed Tlaloc who brings the rain. Even in the times of the Azteca this mysterious city of pyramids was already ancient, lying in ruins northwest of the lake when Cortés arrived. The priests showed him the gigantic temples and told him it was where the gods had lived while creating the world. It was only logical, to assume they had needed a central office.

The Avenue of the Dead runs down the center of the ancient city, with the Pyramid of the Moon standing mighty against the sky, and the Pyramid of the Sun opposite, even taller. Temples flank the central avenue all the way down its length, some with great carved snakes undulating across their facades. Coral bean trees sprout from between the huge pavement stones, reaching for the sky with their blood-red fingers of blossom. Really, no one knows who lived and died in Teotihuacán, to what end. Walking wide-eyed and human among the great temples, though, it was easy to imagine blood and flesh, hearts ripped out to appease a terrible destiny.

Going there with Frida made it seem an especially likely setting for human sacrifice: her usual custom for picnics. Strangely, it was the opposite. A day for the history books. She showed up at the Blue House after breakfast, leaning her head into the kitchen doorway and motioning to come outside quickly, as if hiding something.

"You have to come with me to Teotihuacán," she announced. "Right now. For the day." She looked ready for any possibility, dressed in a gabardine overall rolled to the knees, and the usual full-body armor of jewelry.

"I have a lot of work to do, Frida."

"Sóli, this is important. You call yourself a Mexican, and you've never seen the pyramids of Teotihuacán."

"I haven't had affairs with all Mexico's elite, either. Poor citizenship, I suppose."

"Look, you and I have things to talk about."

"We do. And it seems we won't."

"I have the Roadster out on Allende Street. It's just you and me—I'm driving, not César. Are you going to be a big prick about this?"

"Sorry, Frida. I have a very large snapper in here, and he's a good joe but he refuses to shed his scales and bathe himself in tomatoes and capers without supervision. There's a dinner tonight. Twelve people coming to hear Diego and Lev and Mr. Breton present their paper. In case you've forgotten."

"They can use their big paper to collect bird defecations for all I care. And Perpetua can cook that snapper—you're not as important here as you think."

"Are you firing me?"

"If that's what it takes to get some goddamn company for the day. Okay. I'm going to smoke while you make up your mind."

She leaned against the wall and lit a cigarette, in plain sight of the men if they bothered to look out the window of Lev's study. Lev is adamantly old-fashioned about a few things. One of them: women shouldn't smoke. Another: he doesn't like women in trousers. Frida was diving from the steeple today.

"So. Here's the story." She slid her eyes toward the office window, exhaling a long plume. "Do you remember Gamio? He's that friend of Diego's, the Professor of Ancient Shit who excavated the pyramids. According to himself, he's discovered something astonishing."

"What a mood you're in. A person would be crazy to get in a car with you."

"Fine, stay here with Diego and the Old Man and Monsieur Lion-Maned Poet so full of himself he makes me want to piss in his wineglass. I'm certain you will be dazzled by their Manifesto on Revolutionary Art for the *pindonga Partisan Review.*"

"Well, I already know what it says. I typed it."

"And?" Suddenly she was interested. Maybe she hadn't been allowed to read it. But flying on a trapeze between Diego and Frida could end in a smashup. It would pay to be cautious.

"Mostly it condemns the restrictions Stalin imposed on artists in the revolutionary state. No surprise there. I thought Diego discussed everything with you."

"Mrs. Breton, Mrs. Trotsky, and Mrs. Rivera are not a part of this historic conversation. Ever since that bedbug poet showed up here, it's a boy's club."

"You're not exaggerating about that. It's noticeable."

She pursed her lips. "At least Jacqueline likes to smoke and gossip. Otherwise we would have died of boredom up at Lake Pátzcuaro. While our husbands spent every damn minute working on their *chingado* paper."

"You could have written it yourself, Frida, it's no big manifesto. 'The artistic imagination requires freedom from coercion. Artists have an inalienable right to choose their own subjects.' That kind of thing."

She whistled. "What genius. Fulang Chang could have written that."

"There's also a bit about surrealism. How Mexico is destined to become the true place of surrealist-revolutionary art, because of its flora and dynamism and all that. The mix of races. So what's the astonishing discovery from the professor?"

"Okay, listen. He said they were putting back a wall of a temple that fell down or something. And accidentally uncovered a mass grave. This is *old*, Sóli. Diego adores all that ancient crap, Gamio knows it, so he invited us to come up and have a look before they have to move the bones and everything. But Diego has this meeting. So I'm going, as soon as this cigarette is finished. You have twenty more seconds to decide."

It was a lively trip in the Roadster. Frida had more than her ordinary jittery energy, tugging at her necklaces and offering a steady stream of half-invented history lessons mixed with urgent personal advice. "Sóli," she declared suddenly, "I have to teach you to drive this car. César isn't going to live forever. You know, I've been thinking maybe he died already. He's been looking mummified all this year."

The car was headed northwest at a fairly breakneck pace. The city's outskirts trailed out into villages like the ones on the southern edge, tucked between lime orchards and stony stretches of desert. Hens picked through the roadside litter, and here and there a rooster stood in the center of the road with the authority of the police. Mangoes spread their leaves like umbrellas. The car shuddered when Frida abruptly veered to avoid a boy chasing an emaciated cow in the road. Mother's death loomed large, an apparition.

"I'm serious," Frida said, after relocating the road with the majority of the Roadster's tires. "You have to learn to drive. I'm commanding you, as your boss."

"Promoted! From secretarial assistant of the world's leading political theorist, to Señora Rivera's driver."

"I'm trying to do you a favor. You could have more freedom."

"A knowledge of driving, with no hope of ever owning a car. An interesting formulation of freedom. Maybe you should present a paper."

"When did you become such a big *sangrón*? You used to be nice."

She kept her mouth closed for several kilometers, which improved her driving. Running through the speeds in the Roadster with the gear-shifter on the floor looked simple, compared to the Model T with its hand-grip levers for running the accelerator and clutch. Even so, Frida grinds the gears like a butcher. The Chevrolet even has a gauge showing the gasoline level, so you don't have to guess when it's running out. Sometimes César forgets and lets the Model T run so low he has to back it up a hill, to drain out the last of the fuel from the tank under the seat. That would be Frida's style as well.

Eventually she pulled over in a village, asked directions, and came back determined to get in on the passenger's side. The driving lesson that followed was successful, until too successful.

"You can't go this fast," she admonished, though we moved at a fraction of her former speed. "You have to move the shifting thing across to the other side first."

"We're in the highest gear."

"Well, you must not be doing it right. It's supposed to make a sound when you put it into high."

"Not if you double-punch the clutch. Watch this, you stop the shifter in neutral, that's the cross-part of the H, and let the clutch all the way out, then put it back in again to match the gear speed."

"Bastard. How did you know that?"

"I've spent a thousand hours in the car with César, trying to keep him from wandering off the end of the earth. I learned the gears. What else was there to do? Listen for the one-millionth time to the story of Pancho Villa in Sanborn's?"

Frida laughed. "Poor old Cesár. Drinking a citrate of magnesia in the presence of Pancho Villa. And that's the best war story he'll ever have."

"At least with his slow-motion driving you can see how everything works. He treats the transmission like a woman. He'd rather cut off his fingers than grind the gears the way you do, Frida."

"Screw yourself."

Pupil and teacher were relieved when the tops of the pyramids rose into sight, looming over the tile roofs and palm trees of San Juan Teotihuacán. The archaeological site was closed because of the excavations, and the crew had vacated for a long lunch. Their trowels and notebooks lay about every which way. While awaiting Gamio's return, Frida decided to climb to the top of the Pyramid of the Sun, to get a perspective on the place. It took half an hour because of the steepness and number of steps: two hundred twenty-eight. She dragged her bad leg up every one, counting them with a hail of obscenities: cuarenta-y-*dos*-chingada, cuarenta-y-*tres*-chingada. Sometimes the steps were so steep she had to climb "on all four paws," but she never accepted a hand. "I might be a damn cripple but I'm not dead yet," she spat. "If my heart stops, fine, you can carry me back down." Still angry from the driving lesson.

The view from the pinnacle could stop any heart: the complex geometric forms of the ancient city revealed themselves below, and beyond them, a landscape of black volcanic mountains. The pyramids of lava rock seemed to rise straight from the land, rather than having conquered it. And in fact, a half hour later when we stood on a platform in the ancient city's central plaza looking back at the Pyramid of the Sun, you could plainly see what she called "the joke of the ancient guys." The profile of the Sun Pyramid—its staircases, balustrades, and rounded top—perfectly follows the shape of the volcanic mountain rising behind it. A giant monument playing copycat to a mountain.

"They were laughing. The joke is on God," she said, and sat down on the dusty plaza to make a sketch of the pyramid and mountain.

"If you say so. But it's a joke with years of planning behind it, and terrible labors. Probably people died building it. Why throw away life to play a joke on God?"

She held a spare pencil in her mouth, and didn't look up from her drawing.

When Dr. Gamio arrived, he had plenty of theories on the subject. The people wanted greatness. They worked hard to be remembered by eternity. Alignment was a sacred matter, as important as water and bread. He escorted Frida to the excavation site holding her arm, warning her against tripping over every pebble. His first words were to say how sorry he was that Diego couldn't come, but he was not sorry. He was enamored of her, like everyone else.

The excavation lay open: a mass grave, protected under a temporary tin roof set on posts. Down a few dirt steps, there they were, skeletons of men lying in a row like fish in a box, their narrow, dust-colored bones only faintly lighter than the reddish dirt in which they were embedded. Oddly, the skeletons were perfectly flattened, as if all these humans had been pressed under a hot iron. It took a moment for the eye to adjust to the increments of dust, discerning the human from nonhuman elements. The dead wore jewelry that had survived where flesh did not, bracelets loosely encircling bones. Most peculiar of all: around each neck, a sort of cravat or necklace made of human lower jaws, with the teeth still in place! It was a riveting sight, these bizarre, scalloped strands of mandibles strung together, looping low across the former chests, a fashion beyond anything even Frida might wear. The professor pointed out cut marks here and there on the bones, butchery marks, which he claimed as proof that these unfortunates were sacrificed.

A cool breeze whistled past our ankles, causing the tin roof to tremble. A storm was rising in the distance, but this cool air seemed to come from beneath the ground. The professor said in fact, it did. The place has lava tubes, long caves where the molten earth once ran as rivers. The ground beneath the whole ancient city is laced with them.

"Tunnels, you mean? Like the water caves out on the coast?"

He said it's different rock but a similar formation. The ancients were directed by their gods to look for a doorway from the earth, and here they found them.

The professor talked and talked without releasing Frida's elbow. She shot a few trapped glances before the final escape, a quick getaway down the Avenue of the Dead while Gamio was distracted by a student volunteer. To avoid the dazzling heat, Frida suggested leaving the ancient stone pavement and climbing down the bank of the little San Juan River. It was nearly dry, a trickle in the bottom of a grassy ravine. She flung out a tablecloth in a grove of old pepper trees with gnarled trunks and birds singing from their drooping fernlike boughs. She collapsed on the ground, panting, "Help, we're saved! I thought I would be a human sacrifice. Bored to death by Theories of Antiquity." Then set about unpacking the heavy picknick basket she'd brought from home.

"Why do you think they made necklaces like that, of human mandibles?"

She fingered her own necklace, huge jade stones, a wedding present from Diego.

"Fashion," she said. "Diego showed me pictures of that before. Most of the people weren't important enough to collect real human teeth, you know, the regular low-class citizens. So they made fake ones, flint teeth stuck into clay jawbones." She pulled a bottle of wine from the basket and uncorked it, pouring it into two good crystal glasses that probably shouldn't have risked the journey. But that is Frida, using her best, the devil can take the shards.

"Isn't it awfully sad to think that's all history amounts to, just following the next stupid fashion?"

"Fashion isn't stupid," she said, handing over a glass, spilling a dark red splash on the knee of her overall.

"It's worse than stupid. There's damage in it. Mother lived and died in dread of wearing last year's frock. And look at what Lev loses, every time the newspapers jump in line to call him a villain. When one says it they all have to say it, for fear of being left behind. It's all the same thing more or less. Following fashion."

"*Fashion* is not the same as *idiocy*."

She produced an impressive meal from her basket: pork tamales in banana leaves, stuffed chayotes, prickly pear fruits fried in batter.

"Don't tell your professor boyfriend, but I agree with you about the pyramid copying the shape of the mountain. It's a joke. They were just people. We come here to be dazzled by sculptures of giant snakes, imagining the ancients labored for us, so we will remember them for all time. But maybe they just liked the look of snakes."

"When did you have this big revelation?"

"Today."

"I told you, every Mexican has to come here."

"Look, Frida. I'm going to tell you something, and it doesn't even matter if you make fun of me. Ever since I was fourteen and read Cortés, I've been writing a story about the Azteca. Mostly in my head, but a lot is on paper. And now I can see I've had the story wrong, all this time. I've spent years writing something really stupid."

She nodded, biting into a tamale. "Tell me in what way it's stupid."

"My impression was from books. The ancients seemed to be . . . what the professor said. Locked in the struggle for greatness. Heroes and battles, mythic kings."

"Well, nobody knows how they were, so you can make up anything you want." She pawed through the basket for napkins. She brought the blue-and-yellow ones. "A story is like a painting, Sóli. It doesn't have to look like what you see out the window."

"Well, the ancients might not have been very heroic. Most of them were probably like Mother, crouched somewhere trying to work out how to make fake jawbone jewelry that would look like the real thing."

"That's a better story, to tell you the truth," she said. "Greatness is very boring."

The prickly pear fruit was delicious: thick slices, lightly fried with sugar and anise. "Did you cook all this today, this morning?"

"Montserrat, at the San Angel Inn," she said with her mouth full. She chewed thoughtfully. "I mean it. Your idea for the story sounds good."

"Well, it doesn't matter because I can't be a writer."

"Dumb kid, you *are* a writer. Cesár tried to get you fired for always writing in your notebooks, and Diego tried to make you stop, too. It killed me to see him try. Now these men want to make you an efficient secretary. But you keep writing about soft hearts and scandal. The question is, why do you think you can't be a writer?"

"To be a writer, you need readers."

"I'm no painter, then. Who ever looks at my dumb little pieces of shit?"

"An American movie star, to name one. Diego told me that fellow looked at all your paintings and bought a couple."

She was pouring more wine but glanced up, under her dark brows. "Edward G. Robinson. He bought four of them, if you want to know. Two hundred dollars each."

"*Dios mio*. You see?"

"I see nothing. I see a boy who chews off the ends of his fingers and bleeds ink."

"A dumb kid, is what you said."

"Let's get back to the topic of your story. What do you think people want, if it's not greatness and to be remembered for all time?"

There was hardly anything left of that huge lunch but greasy fingers and a crackle of anise between the teeth. The wine bottle was empty. "Mostly? I believe people want to eat a good lunch, and then take a good piss."

She was digging in that basket again, and unbelievably, produced another half-bottle of wine, recorked from some previous adventure. "And love, Sóli, don't forget that. We are bodies, sometimes with dreams and always with desires."

"Love. But the pure kind of love, what Lev has for humanity, I don't think that comes very often. Most of us are ordinary. If we do anything great, it's only so we'll be loved ourselves. Maybe just for ten minutes."

"Love is love, Sóli. We give greatly to receive. Don't spit yourself out like a seed all the time. When Lev was your age, he was probably more like you than you think."

"All right. People are ruled by love, and our kidneys. That's my opinion, and now I really do have to take a piss. Don't watch, please."

"Hey, you could have found a bigger tree," she called out. "A skinny guy like you, and you're not even halfway hidden."

"You could allow a gentleman the privacy of his piss."

Frida in her dungarees lay back against the bank, looking through her black eyelashes. It's impossible to explain how or why, but she had completely transformed. From venomous snake to friend. "If you want to write romantic novels about the Azteca," she said, "I mean, if that's what moves you, then you should do it."

It was a true conversation. About whether our ancestors had more important lives than we do. And how they've managed to trick us, if they did not. Frida felt it helped them not to put anything in writing. The people at Teotihuacán had no written language, according to Dr. Gamio. "So we can't read their diaries," she pointed out, "or the angry letters they sent their unfaithful lovers. They died without telling us their complaints."

She is right about that. No regrets or petty jealousies. Only stone gods and magnificent buildings. We only get to see their perfect architecture, not their imperfect lives. But it's a strange point to argue for an artist whose paintings are rants and confessions. Without regrets and jealousies, she would have blank canvas.

"You'd better burn all your paintings then, Frida. If you want people in the future to think you were heroic."

She fingered her beads and knit her eyebrows. Raised her glass up to the light and rolled the red liquid around, studying it. "I think an artist has to tell the truth," she said finally. "You have to use the craft very well and have a lot of discipline for it, but mostly to be a good artist you have to know something that's true. These kids who come to Diego wanting to learn, I'll tell you. They can paint a perfect tree, a perfect face, whatever you ask. But they don't know enough about life to fill a thimble. And *that's* what has to go in the painting. Otherwise, why look at it?"

"How does an artist learn enough about life to fill a thimble?"

"Sóli, I'm going to tell you. He needs to go rub his soul against life. Go work in a copper mine for a few months, or a shirt factory. Eat some terrible greasy tacos, just for the experience. Have sex with some Mexican boys."

"Thank you for the advice. You seem to favor foreigners."

"Never mind about me. I've done everything already—nothing is left for these bones but the grave." She drained her glass. "You've been so angry with me. Why?"

"Good God, Frida. Because you treat me like a child."

She looked truly startled.

"I understand. I'm not an important person like you. Or Van, for that matter. But working for you and Diego, sometimes I don't even feel human. I'm a mouse creeping around the shoes of giant people, trying not to get stepped on."

"Look, if I don't flirt with you, you should take that as a compliment. I don't always respect myself, but I almost never respect men. They're like flowers, all showy, a lot of color and lust. You pick them and throw them on the ground. But you I respect. I always did. From the first day I saw you."

"You don't even remember the first time you saw me. It was before I ever came to work in the house, years before. On your birthday."

"In the Melchor market." She tilted her head, but without the coy smile. "You asked if you could help me carry a bag of corn. I told you any man has the right to make a kite from his pants."

She is a marvel or a trickster, a brilliant, terrifying friend. She divines the unknown. There will never be another Frida.

"I approve of your program, Sóli."

"What program is that?"

"Cortés and the Azteca. Writing a true history of Mexico. I think you're right, you should crack open the mute culture, give those boring heroes some sweat and piss."

"Do you think?"

"Look, there's no sense pretending history is a goddamn Homeric Odyssey."

A brilliant red bird landed overhead, the same color as the coral-bean blossoms, resting briefly on the swaying branch before it flew away. Frida packed up the last of the meal. "It's good we talked today. We don't have a lot of time."

"What do you mean?"

"I have to get ready for a show. I'm having a real show, my own paintings entirely. Can you imagine?"

"That's wonderful."

"Sóli, it's terrifying. It feels like I've been lying in the bathtub all this time admiring my own curly *pendejos*. And now a hundred people are looking in through the curtain, applauding."

"Oh. When is the show?"

"When is not the question. *Where* is the question. New York. I'm going at the end of summer. The show opens in October, and after that I'm going to do another one in Paris. It was Mr. Lion-Maned Poet who set up the show in Paris, to tell you the truth. André. I should try to be nicer to him. Anyway." She seemed out of breath.

"Are you all right?"

"A little afraid, I guess. I'm leaving Diego for a long time. Leaving everybody, but in a different sense, leaving Diego."

"I don't believe that. You and that frog can't breathe without each other."

"Well, we'll see. Anyway, I wanted to repair some damages, before I go."

She lay back and closed her eyes. After a minute she asked, "How do you know it was my birthday, the day we met in the Melchor market?"

"Because it was mine too."

She sat up and her eyes opened wide, like a doll. "We have the same birthday?"

"Yes."

"All this time?"

"Every year, in fact."

She stared, recalculating history. "All those parties and birthday fiestas. You've been working like a slave on your own *cumpleaños*."

So after all, she cannot divine everything.

She lay back again and closed her eyes. "*Mi vida*, don't keep secrets from me. You shouldn't even try, you see how we're connected? It will always be the case. We came into life through the same passage."

With damages repaired to her satisfaction, she fell asleep almost immediately, leaving one strange landscape for another, her dreams. Soon she would leave this place altogether—Diego, Mexico, the house and everyone in it.

The bones of the ancient city radiated heat, but the little river ran a cool thread through its belly. A lizard moved in the grass of the bank, running into the shade of a ledge, coming to rest near a stone that seemed rounded and glossy, even in shadow. That stone was smooth to the touch, and when turned over, revealed itself not as an ordinary pebble but a small, carved figurine. A little man made of jade or obsidian, something ancient, small enough to hide inside a closed hand. A remarkable artifact. It should be turned over to the professor. Obviously it would be wrong to take it from this place.

Every detail of the little figure was perfect: his rounded belly with indented navel, his short legs and fierce face. A headdress that resembled a neat pile of biscuits. Eyes deeply indented under arched brows. And inside his rounded lips, a hole for a mouth, like a tunnel from another time, speaking. *I am looking for the door to another world. I've waited thousands of years. Take me.*

The New York Times, *April 15, 1939*

Rivera Still Admires Trotsky; Regrets Their Views Clashed

Artist Explains He Quit Fourth International So as Not to Embarrass Leader—Reveals Letter Caused Their Rift

By Diego Rivera

MEXICO CITY, April 14—The incident between Trotsky and myself is not a quarrel. It is a lamentable misunderstanding which, going too far, brought about the irreparable. That compelled me to break my relations with a great man for whom I always had, and I continue having, the greatest admiration and respect. I am very far from harboring the silly presumption of engaging in a polemic with Trotsky, whom I consider the center and the visible head of the revolutionary movement that is the Fourth International.

The Mexican proverb says, "He who does not block the way helps a lot." In the future, my personal actions and opinions, should I have any, will block neither Trotsky's nor the Fourth International's path.

The incident between Trotsky and myself had its origin in a letter addressed by me to my friend, the French Poet André Breton. That letter was typed in French for me by one of Trotsky's secretaries. Trotsky happened to see a copy that had been left on the secretary's desk, according to the written declaration that he sent me, and the concepts I expressed in my letter, in reference to the general situation of the Leftist forces in the world, to the social role of artists and to their position and rights within the revolutionary movement, besides some personal allusions to him, so displeased Trotsky that he expressed opinions against me which I found unacceptable and which compelled me to split with him.

Trotsky toils without respite, helping continually with his mental effort the slow and difficult work in preparation for the liberation of the workers of the entire world. About him he has a general staff of young secretaries, volunteers come from the four corners of the earth, to help in this work. Meanwhile, other voluntary workers watch day and night over the safety of the man who, together with Lenin, gave its victory to the proletariat of Russia. These and all the other thousands of heroes of October now, from the exile imposed upon them by Stalin's counter-revolution, continue to labor for the future victory of the workers of the entire world.

The enemies, the "organizers of defeat," Stalin and his GPU, persecute the man of October. Everywhere they have tried to hurt him, to annihilate him psychologically through the extermination of his family. . . . Meanwhile his closest collaborators, persecuted and threatened, are murdered, one after another. It is natural that this state of things and the accumulation of sufferings it produces have had their effect upon the man of October, despite his enormous will power and self-assurance. It is natural that Trotsky's disposition should have become more and more difficult, despite his huge reserve of goodness and generosity.

I regret that fate should have decreed that I should collide against that difficult side of his nature. But my dignity as a man precluded my doing anything to avoid it.

❋

Casa Trotsky, 1939–1940 (VB)

On the morning Lev and Natalya moved out of the Blue House, an egret came down from the sky, its broad white wings spread like a parachute, and landed in the courtyard. It extended the S-curve of its long neck until nearly as tall as a man, turning its long-beaked head this way and that, peering at each person present. Then it strode across the bricks to the front gate, lifting its long legs at the knee like a man riding a bicycle. The chief guard shoved the gate open, just a crack, and four men with pistols in their belts stood watching an egret cross Allende Street, disappearing around the corner.

Frida would have claimed it as an omen on Lev's departure. But she is not here, she's in Paris where everyone is an idiot, according to her reports. Natalya, unprepared to trust in signs, was swaddled in the same woolen suit and hat she wore the day they arrived on the ship from Norway. Lev was less armored, in a white shirt open at the collar. Each carried one small suitcase. Van, who has been inattentive since falling in love again (this time she's American), kept his eyes down and stayed busy moving crates of papers into the car sent by Diego. Diego himself was not present.

Every person may have felt some accusation in the heron's glare, for which member of the household was blameless? Frida went away, leaving Diego and Lev with only their needles of irritability to fill a space evacuated of desire. And Diego, poor man, can only be the person he is. An organizer who can't get to meetings on time, a secretary who forgets to answer letters. He has the heart of an anarchist, not a party functionary.

Some blame of course goes to Stalin: his threats hanging over this house, the murders of Trotsky's children, peers, and collaborators, the annihilation of his whole generation in Russia. Stalin's cruelties have pressed the souls of this household flat as ancient skeletons in the dust.

But most to be blamed: the careless secretary who unraveled everything.

Diego wrote the newspapers about his split from Trotsky, reporting his desire to stand out of the way of a great man. "An accumulation of sufferings have had their effect," he wrote, without naming them all: the affair with Frida, for example, though that's said to be forgiven. The note he dashed off to Breton complained, "The bearded old goat is serious every minute. For God's sake, can't he let the Revolution rest for a night and get drunk with a friend who risked everything? Who's housed and fed his entourage for two damn years? How can any mortal tolerate these overcast Russian temperaments?"

He scribbled the note in Lev's own office and gave it over to be typed, a hasty act of bravado, while Lev was elsewhere. The letter should have been posted to France immediately. Instead, the preoccupied secretary, in his haste to get the evening's cooking started, left it lying on the Ediphone table, where Lev later found it. The old man came in the kitchen later with his glasses off, rubbing his eyes, too tired, he said, for supper. Just a piece of toast, perhaps. Bed early, plans to make tomorrow.

What a knot of history one mistake can become. Trotsky was meant to succeed Lenin as president of the Soviet, but a small accident caused the job to fall to Stalin instead. Diego never told what the accident was. Only that small caprices alter fate. One letter, left out by accident. If Diego and Lev had kept their alliance, they might have forged a movement to overthrow Stalin. The peasant armies of Mexico worship Diego, but they need Lev's strategic intelligence.

From Michoacan, blazing through the brigades of Spain into all of Europe, the world might yet take up Lev's dream of socialist democracy. But a careless mistake has torn this league asunder.

Why did Diego call his friend a goat? He expected the word to vanish with the afternoon post, that's why. Bitter words normally evaporate with the moisture of breath, after a quarrel. In order to become permanent, they require transcribers, reporters, complicit black hearts. Diego meant nothing by that letter; his respect for Lev is undying. He had an eye infection that week, a cramp in his stomach after a lunch of too many pork sandwiches. From somewhere in that roil, a few poisonous sentences erupted. Now the world has them.

And the secretary? Was his sin sloth, or pride? The letter was in French, but why couldn't he have asked for Van's help to change the words, and type a tactful version? And why didn't he post it at once, as requested? A remembrance of last year's jacaranda in the window, the sound of something breaking in the kitchen—for no good reason he forgot, and left the letter on the table.

The mistake has left him panting like the victim in a crash: his loyalty to Lev bent like pieces of metal around his chest. The wrecked engine of Rivera spewing petrol, threatening flames. He must extricate himself by making a choice. Diego says stay, as typist-cook and errand boy, for the same coins that have rained down steadily since the first bewildered day of mixing plaster on the floor of the Palacio Nacional. But Lev also asks for continued service. He needs a trusted secretary more than ever, because of the perilous relocation, and Van's increasing distractions. Lev offers a room and cot in a house of clear, bright dreams, which could all be murdered tomorrow. The Painter offers money, asking only to be worshipped.

At seven this morning, after a brief rainstorm, Lev Trotsky lifted his suitcase, stepped across the puddles in the brick walk, and left the Blue House for the last time. He and his wife climbed into the back of the car with Lorenzo the guard, his rifle lying across their knees,

208 * Barbara Kingsolver

and Van in the front passenger's seat, also armed. The driver sat very straight, as if his body were pierced like a Hindu's with a thousand nails of guilt.

"We are ready, my son. Drive," Lev said, and together the small party traveled six blocks to a wrecked, vacant house on Calle Viena, rented from a family called Turati, where they will make their new home.

If any brokenhearted man ever made a better show of good cheer, it could only have been in the moving pictures. Lev's efforts to make the best of the new arrangement have buoyed everyone. Natalya has put away Phanodorm and taken up housecleaning: sweeping cobwebs from the high, pale green ceilings of this Porfirian mansion, washing its leaded-glass windows and arranging furniture. Sometimes she ties on an apron and makes Lev's breakfast. Today she painted chair rails and all the wooden cabinets in the dining room, a nice combination of yellow and brown that Frida would have called boring. What a relief, that she is no longer reading these pages.

The Americans, Joe and Reba Hansen, have come here from the apartment where they had retreated from Rivera hospitality and Rivera complications. A new couple has arrived also, Mr. O'Rourke and his off-beat girl friend Miss Reed. Everyone seems relieved to gather over simple suppers in the main room here, with an old yellow-checked tablecloth on the long table and no one worrying about wine spills. Debating the day's news instead, under no secret storm clouds of household intrigue. Van plays music programs on the wireless and whistles along while typing, when no one else is in the office. His happiness, as always, seems to be linked to a girl.

Only Lorenzo is cheerless, but that's nothing new. He frets, whether on or off duty, a worried monument pulling on his huge black moustache, his face burned to red leather from the hours spent staring out at the menacing world. His forehead, a startling white above the line made by his hat, when he removes it for supper. Protecting Lev has been a terrifying charge since the day they walked off the planks at Tampico. Lorenzo has apprehended dozens of threats, not only the barefoot vigilantes but also the cool plots of Mexican Stalinists. Lately Toledano has been going to unionists' meetings, offering cash to any man willing to put a bullet in Trotsky. Most men these days need the money.

Everything is reported to Lev but not Natalya. She only learns the worst of it when the police are forced to arrest someone and the story makes the newspapers, wedged between the usual confabulations about the "Russian Traitor in Our Midst." Lorenzo and the three young guards take six-hour shifts on the roof, around the clock, walking the perimeter on the brick parapet. The black rock wall around the courtyard was three meters tall to begin with, but the masons have raised it higher still, with brick turrets and notches for rifle bores. It will be good if Lev can purchase the house, because of the need for these alterations. Joe Hansen says money is coming from the Trotskyist party in the United States. The Socialist Workers.

The kitchen here is very adequate: a gas stove with four eyes, a plank counter and icebox. And within the high walls, the courtyard offers a bright relief of trees, shaped as a triangle between the main house and the long, narrow brick guard house running opposite at an angle. Here at last, guards and secretaries may have some privacy, the guard house has four rooms in a row downstairs and four above. The garden is shaded by an old jacaranda and some figs. Lev wants to retrieve the cactus specimens he collected in San Miguel Regla, which stand potted in some forsaken corner at the Blue House, so he can make a cactus garden. Today after lunch he pointed out where he intends to plant each one, with stone paths for roaming between the bits of garden, a park in miniature. It's an impossibly small space for such an elaborate plan. But this tiny plot, measured in meters, is Lev's last remaining homeland.

It seems an airy enough estate, from inside. The strange spectre of confinement becomes striking only from the outside, when one

walks home to it from the market, for example. The compound oc-
cupies a flat-iron shaped lot in Coyoacán where Calle Viena and Rio
Churubusco meet at an angle. The high, dark walls enclosing it come
together at a point, looking exactly like the dark prow of an ocean
liner: the great, slow ship of Trotsky's fate setting sail down Churubusco, as if it were still a canal in the city on a lake, as Cortés found
it. As if one could still build a ship in the desert, and set one's sights
on a new world.

Lorenzo's mother came this week from the country, bringing one
more pair of eager eyes for guard duty: her daughter's boy, Alejandro.
Also, two pairs of rabbits and some checkered hens. Lev is as happy
as a lad with his new livestock. The rabbits now have hutches near
the entry gate, but Lev says the chickens are "emancipated travelers,"
free to roam the courtyard. Natalya objected on grounds of sanita-
tion, and the hens' safety.

"Nataloschka," her husband said, "no wolves live here. The chickens are the only ones without the worry of a predator. Let them have
an open visa." Of course she conceded. In Lev's new study, he sets
his chair so he can see out the window into the courtyard where they
scuttle around, cocking their heads at beetles in the dust.

Perpetua has walked down the street from the Blue House twice this
week, to deliver some pottery Natalya liked especially. Her favorite
is the white glazed platter with fish leaping over it, a gift from Frida
when they first arrived. Natalya thanked Perpetua and put it away in
a cabinet, but today she has brought it out and set it against the wall.
In the years with Lev her world has been so constrained, with so few
objects of beauty in it. She is not a bulldog, only a woman pressed
into the shape of a small jar, possibly attempting to dance in there. It
shows in the way she places a seashell on a window sill, a red-painted
chair in the corner: she is practiced in the art of creating a still life and
taking up residence inside it.

◈

Lorenzo's nephew, Alejandro, is the youngest of the guards, nineteen or twenty perhaps. From a tiny village near Puebla, he's the only one of the guards who is not from the political movement, but Lorenzo guarantees his loyalty. Lev welcomes a new recruit.

Alejandro seems happy just to escape a certain village misery. He has a shy, odd manner, precisely what Frida would call a queer duck. She would say she approved, then make sure everyone watched him like a fish in a bowl. Probably she can't help that, she's been watched that way herself since marrying Diego.

In New York and Paris when she flew high, the newspaper stories tried to shoot her down. Now that she is coming home, apparently washed up, what they say about her is worse. Like Natalya, she must feel the need to retreat into a small space, making still-life creations and painting herself inside. She doesn't have to hide from assassins, but being Much-Discussed appears to be its own kind of prison.

The chickens are not the only emancipated ones here. Lev allows writing of any kind. While he himself works tirelessly on Lenin's biography and a dozen political articles at once, he confessed that really no book can beat a good novel. He wishes he could write one himself.

What a strange discovery. He came in the office late this evening to look for a dictionary, surprised to find one of his assistants still banging at a typewriter.

"Young Shepherd! What business could keep you so late in headquarters?" Headquarters of the Fourth International is his name for the big office next to the dining room. Natalya moved in all three typewriter tables and her roll-top desk, the telephone, bookshelves, file cabinets, and all. It was her idea to make a separate office so all can work here—herself, Van, the Americans who've come to study with Lev—without driving the commissar out of his mind. Lev keeps to his little study in the other wing by their bedroom, writing in peace until he needs someone to come and take a dictation.

"I'm sorry, sir." *Gather up the pages quick, put them in a folder. No confession unless forced.* "It's nothing that will liberate the people."

He waited for more, standing wide-eyed at the doorsill in his shirt and tie. His white hair stood on end from a long day's work. He pulls his hair while he thinks.

"Sir, I'm reluctant to say."

"Oh, no. Some secret report to the adversary?"

"Please don't suggest such an awful thing."

"What, then? A love letter?"

"It's more embarrassing than that, sir. A novel."

The muscles of his face collapsed like a dumpling, all dimples and wrinkled eyes behind the beard and round glasses. Lev's smile is like no other. He pulled out Natalya's desk chair and sat in it backward, straddling it like a horse, leaning his elbows on its back and laughing until he nearly wept. "Oh, this is a *mechaieh*!"

There was nothing to do but wait for a more comprehensible verdict.

"I've been worrying where it is you go, my son. When your mind is not here." He clucked his tongue, said some words in Russian. "A novel! Why do you say this won't liberate anyone? Where does any man go to be free, whether he is poor or rich or even in prison? To Dostoyevsky! To Gogol!"

"It surprises me to hear you say it."

His halo of white hair was lit from behind by the blue blaze of the street lamp outside. The windows facing the street are bricked up halfway, but light comes in from above. It looked like a setting for a detective film. He stood and walked to the back bookshelf, making his way between tables and the recording machine cabinet with its cords snaking across the floor. He clicked on the lamp near the bookshelf.

"I want to show you something. My first published book. An account of a young man only twenty-seven years old, imprisoned by the tsar for being a revolutionist, maneuvering a bold and dramatic escape to Europe where he plotted his return with the People's Army." Lev found the book and tapped it thoughtfully with his thumb. "This was a popular sensation among the workers of St. Petersburg. The entire Soviet, eventually. If a Russian can read, he has read this one."

"A novel, sir?"

"Unfortunately, no. Every word of it is true." He opened the book and turned a few pages. "And since then, only theory and strategy. What a bore I've become."

"But your life is still a potboiler. Stalin's assassins lurking, the Communist Party and Toledano scheming to poison your name. I hate to say it, but the newspapers might get on your side if you wrote it that way. They could carry your saga in weekly installments, the way they did for Pancho Villa during the war."

"Getting the newspapers on our side, oh, my boy. That is a career for circus acrobats and worthless politicians."

"Sorry, sir."

He smiled. "Well, it would win the Russians. Our brains have a weakness for morose and thrilling plots." He snapped the book closed. "What is the subject of yours?"

He listened carefully to the idea of a historical adventure about ancient Mexicans, even if it is more adventure than history, and will never be any good. He pulled a pile of books out of his shelf that might inspire a novelist just starting off.

"Do you read Russian? No. Well, Jack London, certainly. And Colette, for the female view. Oh, and this one by Dos Passos, it's called *The Big Money*." He also offered one of his typewriters, the spare one that only needs a little oil to get working again, and a small table for use as a writing desk in the guardhouse room at night. "So you won't again have to creep into headquarters on the sly," he said. "With Lorenzo as nervous as he is, he might shoot you through the window by mistake. A fine potboiler you would make of yourself then, my son. And who would write it?"

❊

Alejandro, the village boy, almost never speaks. Yet claims he wants to learn English. One quiet assertion at a time, he begins: *I am. You are.* His room is the one at the opposite end of the guard house, but he comes to this one every morning at four, after finishing his shift of pacing the roof with his rifle cocked in darkness. This room that has housed no secrets up to now, except for a box of things hidden under the bed: a small stolen idol. A partly written, entirely dreadful novel. The little woven finger toy called a *trapanovio*, souvenir of a remarkable humiliation.

Alejandro is the first one to see the *trapanovio* since that day in Xochimilco, and he didn't laugh when he heard the story. He inhaled sharply, fists on his face, and wept.

At four o'clock while the world sleeps off its judgments, reliably he arrives. *He has, they have.* A strange kind of love it is. Or no kind of love at all. A solace of the soft tissues only, not the first or last of anything, grateful and urgent and terrified by turns. Afterward, in plain sight of his unsettled accomplice, Alejandro prays.

Frida is home a month, and unraveling like a yarn doll. Diego wants a divorce. She suspected it last autumn, but her plan was to stay away so long, he would learn he couldn't live without her. Such plans rarely succeed. She's moved out of the Double House, living in Coyoacán now, and it's odd to see the Blue House filling up with her things. She has layered on more paint, the colors of blood and the depths of the sea. The bedroom that was Lev and Natalya's, spare as a servant's back then with its woven rug and neatly made bed, now is crammed with her dressing table, jewelry, doll shelves, and trunks of clothes. Lev's former study holds her ruckus of easels and paints. It should not seem strange, as it was her house all along, and her father's before she was born.

This morning Perpetua sent Belén running down the block for help because the mistress had gone mad. Frida spends madness the way she spends money; it was all over by the time help could arrive. Perpetua answered the gate, pointed without a word, and returned to the kitchen. Frida sat on a stone bench in the courtyard with her hair all cut off. It lay in thick black parentheses on the bricks, all around her feet.

"Natalya sent me to ask if there's anything you need."

Frida smiled insincerely at the lie, revealing new gold caps on her incisors. It seemed she might have been drinking, even at this early hour.

"What I *need* is to castrate the son of a bitch and be done with it." She made some menacing snips at the air with her scissors, startling the black cat that had been disguised in the nest of hair. It stood and arched its back.

It seemed pointless to mention she has also been having affairs, in New York and Paris. At least, such things were much discussed in the press. A handsome Hungarian photographer. "Sorry, Frida. But with Diego and women it's nothing new, right?"

"Is this the kind of *mierda* you walked over here to tell me? I've been miserable for a long time already, so I should be used to it now? Thank you, my friend."

"Sorry." The cat slunk away into the laurel bushes.

"Sóli, you'll never guess: now I have fungus on my hands. A new ailment! One thousand operations, plaster corsets, medicines that taste like piss, collapsed organs, and there's still something new that can go wrong with me. Maybe I could be a little miserable about this?" She held up her hands, mottled pink, raw and dreadful.

"All right. If you need permission."

Even in her disconsolate state she looked like a peacock, perfectly dressed in a green silk skirt and enough jewelry to sink a boat. Even drowning, Frida would cling to vanity. "Don't forget Paris and New York, Frida. They loved your show. Yesterday Van showed me a fashion magazine with you on the cover."

"The opinion of me in Paris and New York, if you want to know, was the same as for a talking pony. Imagine it, a Mexican girl who dresses funny and curses like a soldier! Every day was, what do you call it? A bowl of fish."

Translating Frida is no easy trick. "A kettle of fish? That means you're in bad trouble. Or else a goldfish bowl, which means people are looking at you all the time."

"Both. I was in a kettle of goldfish. People pointed on the street."

"Because you're famous. People saw your paintings."

"Listen, don't ever become famous. It's killing. You should see what they wrote in the papers, those reviewers. They hardly bothered to look at the paintings, they only wanted to write about the painter herself. 'She should be making nice pictures of nature instead of these nightmares. And always *herself*—she's not even that good looking!'"

"We saw the reviews. A lot of them were good. Diego says Picasso and Kandinsky think you're a bigger talent than both of them combined."

"Okay, but that cockroach André Breton didn't bother to pick up my paintings from the customs house until I got there and screamed at him. And it's true what I'm telling you about the reviews. They write what *they* think you should be painting."

That courtyard seemed more than ever like a fairy-tale house, with tree leaves for its ceiling and an ivy-covered floor. White calla lilies rose up through the ivy carpet, all of them bending their hooded heads toward Frida, like charmed cobras.

"Obviously you had a miserable time. But you can't blame anyone for seeing you as a spectacle."

She looked puzzled. Her earrings today were a pair of heavily embossed golden snakes, but with her newly shorn, glossy head she looked like a sea lion. With gold teeth. "What spectacle?"

Carmen Frida Kahlo de Rivera. Who could explain her to anyone, least of all herself? "You play a certain role. You have to admit that. Mexican peasant, queen of the Azteca or what. You don't dress to blend in."

Her gold incisors flashed. "If I don't choose, they choose for me: Wife of the Much-Discussed Painter. The newspapers would wrap me in gauze and make me a martyred angel, or else a boring jealous wife. Above all, a victim—of Diego and life. Of disease. Look at this leg." She yanked up the green silk to reveal her naked, lame leg. It was a more awful sight than the infected hands: thin as a stick because of the childhood polio, bent and scarred from the accident, years of limping and indignities uncountable.

"You've never seen it, have you?" she asked.

"No."

"How long have you known me?"

"Nearly ten years."

"And in that time, have you thought of me as *this*?"

It was hideous: the leg of a leper, a street beggar, a veteran of wars. Anything but the leg of a beautiful woman. "No."

She tossed the long silk skirt back down, like covering a corpse. "People will always stare at the queer birds like you and me. We only get to choose if they'll stare at a cripple, or a glare of light. The jewelry and everything makes people go blind. The gossips will say a million things, but they never ask, 'That Mexican-Indian-Azteca girl, why does she always wear long dresses?'"

With the points of her naked toes she carefully set about pushing the locks of hair on the ground into a round pile. Everything with her is an artful project, flowers laid out on a table, even her own self-destruction. "So," she said, "how is your wonderful story, the scandals of the ancients? Are you working on it every day?"

It was tempting to tell her about the writing desk in the guard-house room, a newly oiled typewriter, a pile of pages growing higher every night. It would excite Frida to make her an accomplice. But she is no good at secrets. "What do you mean, queer birds like us? Nobody is staring at me."

"So you think."

The cat circled warily near her feet, eyeing the strange black pelt.

"And your dear comrade Van. How is he these days?"

"Not staring at me. That is for sure."

The cat decided the new animal between his mistress's feet was neither predator nor prey, so he crept away over the ivy, lifting his feet as if walking through shallow surf.

"Being a peacock is not the only way to hide yourself, Frida. A pigeon can hide."

"Is that what you are? A pigeon hiding in a little hole in the bricks?"

"I'm a typist. And a cook. Sometimes now I get to clean rabbit cages."

She sighed. "What a waste of time. I thought you had *chispa*. A spark, or some kind of discipline. It turns out you're a little gray pigeon." She smoothed her skirt over her leg and pulled her shawl around her shoulders, composing herself against what she had revealed.

"I'm sorry about your leg. I'd heard different things."

"Sóli, let me tell you. The most important thing about a person is always the thing you don't know."

Twelve people living in this household now, and only one bathroom. Miss Reed calls it The Dance of the Hours. The four Americans always stay up late—the strange, funny Miss Reed (who dresses like a boy) and her husband sleep in one of the guard-house rooms but rarely retire to it until dawn, the same time Lev rises for his morning exercise. Joe and Reba still have their apartment, and take field trips to its bathroom. For everyone else the clock is ruled by quick dashes and rationed cups of coffee. Lorenzo and the other three guards have been known to piss over the side of the roof, declaring that the GPU must be defeated by every known weapon. But some weapons they hold in reserve. The competition of morning is not for the weak-hearted.

The secret hour is seven forty-five. Lev has long finished his ablutions by then, and Natalya as well. The late risers are no threat as yet, and the morning shift are still holding off, respecting Natalya's privacy. It's possible then to slip from the dining room into Lev and Natalya's wing, tiptoe through Lev's study. Lev will soon be in there, as surely as the map of Mexico will be on the wall. But at seven forty-five he's still outside feeding the chickens.

The narrow bathroom runs alongside Lev's study and bedroom under a tin shed roof, added on the house some time between Porfirio Diaz and modern plumbing. Its fixtures stand in a row like soldiers at attention: the bathtub on clawed feet, the lavatory on its pedestal, the cabinet with Lev's medicines and everyone's shaving things in a jumble. The pitcher and bowl on a stand. The dreadful hairy rug someone should throw out. Lev should write a paper: "The Political Challenge of a Commonly Held Bathroom: No One Has the Authority to Throw Out the Rug." And at the end, the captain of this army: the commode. Its tank above, the pull chain awaiting the private's salute.

Rather than exiting by the door into Lev's study (he might be there now), it's less awkward to exit through the empty end room Natalya calls "Seva's room," still hoping their orphan grandson can be brought here from Paris. For now it houses a wooden wardrobe of coats and jackets. This morning it also contained Natalya, standing at the laundry table folding a pile of Lev's striped silk pajamas. Awkwardness sometimes cannot be escaped.

"Good morning."

"Good morning."

It seemed necessary to say something else. "Lev has a lot of pajamas."

"Yes, he does."

"Nice ones. Most people don't dress as well, even during the day."

She said, "Most people don't have to think of dying in their pajamas. And being photographed for the papers."

"Dear God."

"Don't apologize. We're accustomed." She lifted her eyes briefly, a pair of gray stones, then looked back to her work. "I've been wanting to tell someone, and probably rather than Van, I should mention this to you. His blood pressure is higher."

"Lev's blood pressure? How high?"

"Extremely. The doctor yesterday was very worried."

"Is Lev worried?"

She folded the last pajama. "Lev thinks a bullet will find him before the stroke arrives. If that answers your question."

"But you wanted someone else to know. Understandably."

"Probably there's nothing you can do. He gets terrible headaches."

"He seems calm."

"Oh yes, Lev is calm, calm is Lev. What I said about wearing good pajamas when he is murdered. It's not photographs he worries about. I don't mean he is vain. I just cannot think of the word. My English."

"The word is *dignity*, maybe?"

"Dignity, yes."

"He could rest a little more. He's out every morning taking care of the chickens, but any of us could do that."

"Oh, he is crazy for those animals. I haven't seen him so affectionate for something since Benno and Stella. Two dogs we had in France." She grew quiet, visiting memories of dogs, and maybe living children. "I think the animals relieve him," she said finally. "Something in the world he can keep safe."

"But maybe it wouldn't hurt to offer some help?"

"Yes. To you, he might listen. He calls you 'son.' You notice it, of course."

"Of course. Lev has a large heart. He's father to the whole world, it seems."

"He said he finds you steadying."

"He does?"

"In your manner you resemble Sergei. He wouldn't have mentioned that, but it's true. Sergei was quiet. Always paying attention. He was for the good of other people."

"You must miss him. All of them."

She shook her head side to side, looking out the window, her lips tightly closed.

Outside, the morning was cool, with puddles still standing from a rain in the night. In the far corner of the courtyard against a blaze of red bougainvilleas covering the wall, Lev stood in a circle of hens. He tossed out grain and clucked softly in some form of gallinaceous Russian, apparently engrossed. He looked up, startled.

"Oh! Have you come asking my friends for proof of their dedication?"

"No eggs needed just now. Breakfast is nearly ready."

"Now you see, I was thinking, the hens make only a collective contribution. But the rabbits are fully dedicated, when called to serve. We may have two factions here."

"Like the Mensheviks and Bolsheviks."

He pursed his lips and nodded. "The Omelletscheviks. And the Hassenpfefferviks."

"Natalya thought you might need help with the animals."

"No, no." The flat shovel was out of the tool rack, leaning against the rabbit hutch beside a filled manure bucket. He had cleaned the little shed where the hens roost at night. Later he would take the manure and bury it around the garden.

"You're a very great thinker, sir. You shouldn't be doing farm work."

"You're wrong about that, my son. Everyone should do farm work. Your name is Shepherd. Did you ever tend sheep?"

"No, sir."

He took the shovel in hand, watching the hens make their excursionary expeditions into the garden. "Do you know that Stalin is murdering farmers now?"

"Why?"

"His idea for feeding the masses is to create enormous farms. Like factories, with vast machines and armies of unskilled labor. Rather than trust the wisdom of men of the land. He's imprisoning yeoman farmers, trying to destroy their class."

One of the hens caught a lizard, and it writhed wildly in her beak. She ran helter-skelter with all the others in zealous pursuit. Their aptitude for carnivory was impressive.

"That is enough talk of Stalin before breakfast. My young friend Shepherd with no sheep. I meant what I said. Everyone should get dirt on his hands each day. Doctors, intellectuals. Politicians, most of all. How can we presume to uplift the life of the working man, if we don't respect his work?"

Lev carefully folded the garment he wears to greet the animals each day: an ancient green cardigan with holes at the elbows. Evidently he does not expect to be assassinated while feeding chickens. Or it's his best hope. He took off his glasses and turned his face to the sun for a moment, boots planted wide, the peasant brow facing heaven. He looked the very image of the People's Revolution in one of Diego's murals. Then the former president of the Petrograd Soviet put away the manure shovel and went to his breakfast.

Today Van was married. Who could have imagined it two years ago, this very day, on a painted picnic boat in the canals of Xochimilco? Frida was correct, of course, Van didn't need the *trapanovio* to catch his true love. Nor did Lev, it seems. He holds hands with Natalya, and together they stand on the deck of this ocean liner, a ship with trustworthy friends and cactuses planted in its hold, and they watch the sun set behind the high wall that encloses them. Frida has been less lucky in love or anything else, declining to get out of bed for weeks now. Her body threatens to fold up shop, and good riddance, she says, since Diego no longer wants it.

Van and his American girl Bunny were wed this morning in city hall, in the nuptial office whose door happens to be directly under Diego's mural of the ancient Mayans harvesting cacao, though the lovers probably didn't notice. They plan to move soon to an apartment in New York. Natalya shed a few tears, as tiny and undramatic as her black shoes. She has always known she would lose this son, along with every other.

Lev was more jovial, congratulating the couple with formal toasts and Russian love poems recited from memory. Bunny wore a crown of twined flowers, some old-world notion of Natalya's, and somehow procured a bag of Van's beloved licorice for a wedding present. In the courtyard he stood blue-eyed beside his bride making disheveled toasts, absent his shoes for some reason. When Bunny reached on tiptoe to set her floral crown on Van's head, he smiled so broadly his molars gleamed. So grateful for her affection. He has no idea that everything about him can stop a heart: his shrug, like a little Dutch boy, shoulders raised high and then dropped. His beautiful white feet.

Celebrations are rare in this house, maybe all the more joyful for that reason. And if joy did not fill every quarter, at least no one spent the whole day cooking.

Britain has entered the war. Winston Churchill sent an Expeditionary Force into France, thousands of soldiers to defend the Maginot Line and prevent all of Europe falling to Hitler. Every evening after the plates are cleared, Lev turns on the radio receiver, and everyone goes quiet. All the boisterous opinions that normally fill this room are quashed by one thin voice quivering out of the air from some other world into the yellow-painted dining room. Why should Lev believe the wireless reports, when all others fail him? He struggles with the question himself. But is so hungry for knowledge, he casts his net wide and picks through the catch, hoping he can tell fish from flotsam.

It seemed impossible that this singular man, Hitler, could pull the whole world into the cauldron of his ambitions. Now it's only a question of the order in which nations are pulled. And what unexpected arrangements, as nations find themselves shoulder to shoulder with others, or face to face against: Canadians on the soil of France, Germans in Poland, Russians and Finns on the shores of the Baltic Sea.

Even in the horror of war, Lev is optimistic; he says it will make internationalists of us all. A modernized proletariat will unite, because war so conspicuously benefits rich men and kills the poor ones.

"Surely the French munitions worker can see how his labors fill the pockets of war financiers in the city of London." He says the factory worker and peasant of every nation will discover that their common enemy is the factory owner, exploiting their labor, keeping them poor and powerless.

But this boy in a French or British factory, standing in his leather overall welding the casing on a metal bomb: what can he see? That thing will fly through the air, fall hundreds of miles away, and kill boys in leather overalls in a German factory. The reports will roar victory or defeat, and boys will never know how alike their lives have been.

Seva has arrived from Paris, to put his arms around his grandparents for the first time in his memory. He calls Lev "Monsieur Grandfather," it breaks Natalya's heart. The Rosmers, who brought him, are their oldest friends: Alfred the cartoon Frenchman with his long neck, moustache, and beret, and round Marguerite, clasping everyone to her bosom. Lev says he and Alfred have fought Stalin together since Prinkipo. The Rosmers will stay some months now in Mexico, they are renting a house. France is uncertain, to say the least, and the boy needs time to adjust. He's lived with the Rosmers most of the time since Zinaida died, after Marguerite located him in a religious orphanage. Lev never talks about any of that. Zinaida was his eldest, the story unfolds a little at a time: tuberculosis, leaving the USSR with her baby for treatment in Berlin. Her visa revoked by Stalin, the husband Platon disappearing in a prison camp.

Seva is now thirteen, a tall schoolboy in short pants and leather sandals. He speaks Russian and French and not a word of Spanish, and walks carefully around the courtyard watching the hummingbirds that hover at the red flowers. Marguerite wanted to know what they are called. In France, she said, they don't have such things. It must be true, because Seva dashed in red-faced with excitement over the creature. Marguerite made him slow down so she could translate his desires. A net or a pillowcase, he wanted. Anything in which he could capture it.

Natalya hugged him hard, already torn with remorse over the forces that govern this family. "No, Seva, you won't be allowed to capture it," she said. "Your grandfather believes in freedom."

On Your Leaving

Praise the Vanguard, because it says your name. Van evanescent, servant of the advance, praise any word that could hold you. Praise your jacket that hangs on the peg, still holding one shoulder aloft, slow to forget the comrade it embraced.

Praise all but the vanishing point where we stand now, not quite parted. Already memories fall like blows. But soon they will be treasure, dropped like gold through a miser's fingers as he makes his accounts: the years at a desk, elbow to your elbow. The Flemish lilt of your words, like the shift and drop of a typewriter carriage, every sentence luminous and careful: a library with poppy fields inside. The times our teacups crossed by accident, the shock of tasting your licorice there. The brotherhood of small rooms in locked-up houses, the drift of quiet words while waiting for sleep, a restlessness we cast over blended boyhoods: the captured fish in a glass, the spaniel that ran away in a Paris park. You were always first to escape. The sight of you, falling like rain into your own beatific slumber.

Praise each insomniac hour, kept wide awake by your glow. Sleep would only have robbed more coins from this vandal hoarded store.

—HWS, OCTOBER 1939

Folded into an envelope, it was another letter left lying in the office for someone to see, this time not an accident. With Van's name typed on the outside, and then for good measure the address also, it looked like one of the endless messages delivered in the courier's bag. A memorandum to be filed. A cowardly disguise, yes, but who in this world who ever wrote a love poem wants to stand by blushing while the lover reads it? Such things should be tucked in a coat pocket and read in a different room, or somewhere else altogether. He and Bunny leave tonight on the evening train.

His valises were all packed and his mind too; he seemed halfway in New York when he came into the office looking for his black shoes. He took the jacket off the peg by the door, one last time, and put it on as he always does, shifting it across his shoulders to get it settled. The shoes were located, absurdly, on top of the file cabinet. Probably set there by Natalya when she swept.

"Well, comrade Shepherd. We have had a go at the world together in this little headquarters, have we not?"

"We have. It has been very great, Van. You taught me worlds of things. It's hard to say how much."

He shrugged. Glanced at the envelope on the corner of the desk. "More filing, on a Sunday?"

"I think it's old, maybe from Friday."

"But it's for me, you're sure? Not for the commandant?"

"It's your name on it. Probably just a news clip or something. It couldn't be very important."

He smiled and shook his head, sliding his eyes toward the dining room where Lev plowed his way through the daily quotient of newspapers. "Long live the Revolution and work that never ends. But mine here is done."

He dropped the envelope in the wastepaper basket.

The rains have ended. Soon the migrant birds will come back from the north.

The Trotskyist Party in the United States continues to send migrants too, a small, steady flow of young men eager to work for Lev. They are good boys with plenty of heart and muscle, put to work mostly as rooftop guards and kitchen help. Socialist Workers, they call their party, and most are from what they call the "Downtown Branch" in New York. Jake and Charlie were first to arrive, with a fat, smuggled envelope of cash, support from the worldwide movement that is well put to use in this household. As was the bottle of brandy they produced in time for Van's wedding.

The newest one is Harold, who "bunks" with Jake and Charlie, speaking their same language of *conk* and *dig me* and *togged to the bricks*. Mother would have adored these boys, though she'd probably lose patience with their praise for the common man.

With Van gone, letters and drafts are starting to pile in a backlog inside Lev's brain, but he won't let these boys help much with secretarial work. He says it requires special skill; the best secretary to a writer must be a writer himself. ("Even, perhaps, a novelist," he conspires with a twinkle.) Lev's study table is mounded with papers, ink bottles, boxes of wax cylinders from the Ediphone. The calendar lying open on his desk must be excavated each morning, to turn the page on a new day. The books mount in polyglot piles: Russian, French, Spanish, and English all in one stack, representing different strata in his miraculous brain. A layer for each new country in his journey.

Now he means to add another: the United States. He is invited to travel there as a witness, in a trial before the Congress. A man named Dies wants him to testify against the American Communist Party. Lev is eager to do it. Their devotion to Stalin must be checked, he says. The American Communists still believe all Stalin's charges against Lev, but when they know the truth, he says, they will shift their allegiance to the movement for socialist democracy in Russia. He believes this Dies Committee could be used to engage the world war as a platform for world revolution.

Jake and Charlie say it's a trap, and Novack sent telegrams warning Lev not to cross the border. The United States seems ready to get in the war, most likely on Stalin's side, against Hitler. What a goodwill gift Lev Trotsky would make, delivered to Stalin in chains. Natalya is terrified; the U.S. press uniformly say Lev is a monster. But still he makes plans to go. The Dies Committee has issued his papers and promised police protection for the journey. But won't grant a visa for Natalya, or any Mexican assistant.

Lev can work around any obstacle. He plans to bring a secretary and translator whose legal status is without reproach: who has never belonged to any political party. Who holds a U.S. passport because his father is a citizen, working in a government accounting office. Lev even assumes the father will offer hospitality in Washington during the hearings, which will last several weeks.

If Father even recognized his son at his door, he would likely send him off to go and bunk with the Christers. And if Stalin has offered a bounty on Lev's head, Father would gladly collect it. But Lev won't believe it, this man to whom paternal affections come as naturally as beating to a heart. No dictionary has words that can make Lev understand estrangement between a father and son. Departure is set, November 19.

The bags are all packed, filled with papers. Natalya had to remind Lev to bring some clothes and a coat. It will be cold in the north. Important files have been excavated from the time of the Dewey Commission, in which Lev already worked hard to prove his innocence. His belief in justice still burns so brightly, it's hard to watch.

Lorenzo will drive the car to the train station in the morning. Mexican police will provide bodyguards to the U.S. border. Marguerite Rosmer made a party here this evening for bon voyage, though Natalya finds little to celebrate. But Marguerite always cheers her, and so did the presence of other friends: the Hansens, Frida, and Diego of course. He and Lev get along famously now that they're no longer friends.

And Frida: if anything can get her out of bed, it's a party. She showed up in a wild *tehuana* dress with a bodice of ribbons, and her short hair brushed out in a wave like a motion picture star. She brought her sister's two children, who adore Seva. Diego arrived late, wearing a hat like Pancho Villa's. The children had firecrackers and caused Lorenzo a near collapse, he was so nervous about the possibility of an attack. He stopped the party four times, forcing everyone to clear the courtyard and go into the bunkhouse because the guards on the roof had sighted a strange vehicle in the street. Once, it was the Buick that dropped off the Rosmers. The car belongs to their friend Jacson, a young Belgian they've befriended who sometimes drives them places. Marguerite told a story during the party about how this same young man once chased Frida around Paris. "He won't admit it," Marguerite said. "But his girlfriend Sylvia says he was infatuated. Do you recall him? Apparently he followed you for days, trying to meet you."

"How could I remember which one he was?" Frida asked, tilting her head so one gold earring danced against her black hair. There was no smile or dazzle, she was play-acting at being coy, a habit without feeling.

"On the day your show opened, Jacson apparently waited all afternoon outside the gallery with a bouquet the size of a Dalmatian. When you finally came, you told him to make a kite from his pants, and threw the flowers in the gutter!"

"The poor man," Diego said. "Frida destroys them all."

The look that passed between them held such awful sadness. If either of the two had painted such a thing, it would have to be torn down from the wall.

Marguerite was still in the thrall of her story, imagining this boy on the street with his broken flowers. "That's true! He probably didn't know she was married."

Frida says the divorce will be final before the year's end.

❈

Natalya is ecstatic, Lev is irate, and everyone else holds an intermediate position. There will be no journey, no testimony. Lev didn't even get on the train. Somehow the Dies Committee must have caught wind of his revolutionary intentions, or sensibly guessed them. At the last possible moment the Department of State wired a permanent revocation of his visa. He is *never* to be allowed to enter the United States.

Already the newspapers have their story. They interviewed Toledano and also the artist Siqueiros who is in league with him now, both of whom know less than Lev's chickens about what really happened. But still they had plenty to say: Lev was foiled in a plot against the people, financed by the oil magnates and the American FBI.

Alejandro's English improves, but not his conversation. His shyness suffocates him like a caul. But like any child he fights to be born, to land himself in the tribe of men. With the other guards around, he can piss off the roof with the best of them. He swears loyalty to the Fourth International, and also to Jesus, especially at Christmas and other holy days of obligation.

Lev counsels Lorenzo and the other guards to be lenient, the lad will develop a revolutionary discipline. Give him time. Alejandro is unschooled, afraid of being wrong.

February is the hardest month for Lev. Too many deaths have left their stains on its walls. On some days he drifts into memories, visiting with beloved ghosts of so many he's known—his young first wife, friends, daughters and sons, coworkers and comrades, all murdered by Stalin, many of them for no better reason than Lev's anguish. He and Natalya have frank talks about where she can go, if Lev is the next in that line. Joe and Reba vouch they can get her safely to New York; Van of course is already there. "Take me along for burial," Lev said. "The United States would gladly admit me as a corpse."

What a vast tapestry Lev must have woven in sixty years of living, the meetings of minds and bodies, armies of joined hands and pledged oaths—and now this household is nearly all that's left of it. Only these few could tell a story of him from memory when he is gone. It's such a small measure to stack against the mountain of newsprint fables, the Villain in Our Midst. What will people find in libraries one day, if they go looking? So little hope he will be honestly remembered. No future history in this man.

Today he turned over a handwritten letter to be typed. It seemed more private than public, some sort of will or testament. The heading said only: "February 27, 1940."

"For forty-three years of my thinking life I have been a revolutionary; for forty-two of those years I fought under the banner of Marxism. If I had to start all over again, I would of course try to avoid this or that error, but the general course of my life would remain unchanged. I will die a proletarian revolutionist. My faith in the communist future of mankind is firmer today than it was in the days of my youth.

"Natalya has just come up from the courtyard and opened my window so the air may come in. I can see a wide strip of green grass along the wall, the pale blue sky above, and sunlight on everything. Life is beautiful. Let the future generations cleanse it of all evil, oppression and violence, and enjoy it to the full."

Natalya declared today it was time for a "walk." It's the name she and Lev use for outings, long drives into the country where Lev can scramble through cactus-filled ravines while Natalya spreads a picnic blanket in a grapefruit grove. "He needs to get out of this coffin," she said at breakfast, even though she worries herself sick whenever he leaves the fortress. But she knows his hungers. With every passing month lived outside of Frida's shadow, Natalya seems to be more of a person, a wife. That blue house was a mouth that swallowed her down. Or a dark necessity they passed through together.

Some words that have meaning in this house: Forgiveness. Trust.

As the Commissar of Picnick, she commanded the kitchen troops in the packing of lunch, while the Steering Committee of Outings spread out maps on the dining room table and made a reconnaissance. Keeping to deserted roads would be safe. They decided on Cuernavaca, by a route that would afford good views of the volcanos Popocatapetl and Ixtaccihuatl. It was noted that the American Faction would amuse the Mexican Faction by trying to pronounce these names.

The Rosmers were telephoned, as this adventure would require two automobiles: the old Ford on permanent loan from Diego, and their friend Jacson's Buick. He appears willing to take his friends anywhere on short notice, probably because he likes being inside that immense car. Reba and Joe, Miss Reed, Lorenzo, food, wine, blankets, and one machine gun all fit in the Buick, along with the Rosmers. In the smaller Ford, the bodyguards Alejandro and Melquiades crammed into the front seat with the driver, who contained his displeasure with the cantankerous Ford. (Oh, for Diego's Chevrolet Roadster, its powerful engine and smooth gearshift.) Lev and Natalya sat in back with their excited grandson, and the equally wide-eyed lad Sheldon, newest volunteer from the States.

Lev kept his head down as always, lying across the others' laps in the back seat until the car was well outside the city, climbing a dirt road out of the dusty central valley. Large stretches of land lay uncultivated, studded with spiny plants fiercely defending their territory from no one who wanted it. Stockmen in wide-rimmed hats rode along the roadsides driving their cattle, whose large, down-turned ears gave them a look of hopeless sadness in the inhospitable landscape. Nopal plantations and occasional sugarcane fields gave the only glimpses of green.

"Shepherd, I was thinking," Lev said, after it was deemed safe for him to sit up and look about. "We should always have a second driver in the vehicle. Do you think you could teach Melquiades?"

"Yes, sir." Lev meant: in case the first driver is shot by a sniper.

The passengers would need the protection of escape. It's the kind of horror Lev needs to anticipate and solve daily, like working out the finances or fixing a broken hinge.

In time the road gained purchase on the shoulder of the mountain. Rolling fields of brown grass and oaks gave way to dry pine forest. The plan was to avoid the city of Cuernavaca, taking rugged roads to a gorge near Amecameca. The day was *jueves santo*, the Thursday before Easter, so every village church in the land was cloaked in a purple drape, mourning the dead Christ who was expected to return shortly. Alejandro crossed himself each and every time a church was passed. He did it inconspicuously, probably embarrassed in the present company: just a tiny movement of a curled hand at his chest, the smallest possible gesture that might still be visible to a sharp-eyed God.

At certain bends in the road, the pine forests opened onto breathtaking views of Popocatapetl and Ixtaccihuatl, the dazzling snowy peaks of the twin volcanoes. "Killer!" Sheldon sighed from the back seat. This boy was already known to Jake and Charlie when he arrived, from "the Downtown Branch," and had never traveled outside New York before. Now he remarked on each vista, as unfailingly driven to it as Alejandro was to cross himself at each church. "Popo, po—" Sheldon tried, and gave up, which was just as well. The others were tired of laughing.

"Try Cuernavaca," offered Seva, into whose mouth both Spanish and English have run like water in a faucet, since the day the Rosmers brought him.

"*Cornavaca!* Thanks, pal! And now I think I'm done in for the day."

The little boy is especially fond of Sheldon, quick to come to his defense when the other guards tease. It's no wonder Seva wants to follow him around, Sheldon is such a good joe: first to volunteer for the worst guard shifts, never taking offense at a joke, never taking a second *pan dulce* off the plate until they've gone around. On his first great adventure, Mexico has struck Sheldon star-eyed. Mexico, he says, is *keen*.

"The Aztecs called the city Cuauhnahuac," Lev said. "It means, 'near the woods.'" Who knows where Lev learns such things? He reads everything.

"But Grandfather, Cuernavaca means cow horn, yes?" Seva asked. "Why did the Spaniards change it?"

Melquiades suggested that the Azteca changed it themselves to keep from laughing to death when they heard the Spaniards try to say "Cuauhnahuac."

The destination was a forested ravine with a shaded glen and a cold, rushing stream for swimmers with strong hearts. Lev took his grandson on a hike and they came back triumphant, Lev carrying his burlap-wrapped prize like a stout log over his shoulder. It was his favorite cactus, the *viejito*, "little old man" they call it because it grows long white hair instead of spines. Melquiades and Lorenzo together hefted the cactus into the trunk of the Buick and swear it weighed thirty kilos, at least. Stalin and high blood pressure notwithstanding, Lev may outlive us all.

His happiness, when it comes to him, is so pure. He has a ridiculous old straw hat he wears only for these outings. No one could remember when they'd seen it last, or his smile. Or the camera. For a change, here was a day worth remembering, and Lev wanted to record everything: Natalya and Marguerite on a blanket at the feet of pines, setting out plates of batter-fried chicken. Natalya in her little brimmed hat, seated on a rock by the water, smiling at the camera. The bodyguards clowning. Seva in his swim trunk posing on the cliff for a high dive he did not—under a hail of alarmed Russian from Natalya—actually execute. Sheldon took the camera and made Lev get in most of the photographs. Of the many vicissitudes to be recorded that day, most important was Lev's joy.

An hour before sundown the party elected an Executive Committee of Packing Up, and everything went into the cars. A white egret picked through the minor leavings of lunch strewed on the ground. This bird had spent the afternoon stalking snails along the riverbank, ignoring the acrobatics of bodyguards leaping off rocks, shaking water from their ears, and complaining of frozen *cojones*. It looked like the same bird that strangely appeared in the courtyard of the Blue House, the day Lev left it. That day had felt like a sad, terrible pageant: the Children of God cast from Eden. But it was not Eden; that leavetaking was a good one for Lev and Natalya. And of course the egret today looked like that other one. All egrets look the same.

Of all things, a letter has come from Father. Dated in April but arrived today in May, on Mother's birthday, by strange coincidence. Its arrival at all is a miracle; it was addressed to the house in San Angel, care of Diego, and anything that falls to the care of Diego could well be shoved under the leg of a wobbling table, or put in a sandwich. That address must have been sent him by Mother years ago, when she was still living.

Father didn't have a great deal to say. He was ill last year, and has bought a car. He mustered two paragraphs describing the car, and none of the illness. Synchromesh in the lower gears, floor-mounted shift lever and clutch on the floor. A Chevrolet Roadster like Diego's, apparently, but a later model, and white. He closed with the hope that Mother's passing might provide occasion for a closer rapport between father and son. Rather than use his own address, because he said he intended to be leaving his apartment shortly, he gave the address of his solicitor, located on I Street in Washington, D.C.

"A closer rapport" could mean, for example, one letter in every year divisible by four. It's worth considering.

24 May

They must have parked somewhere down Viena Street and crept toward the house, two hours before dawn. The men wore city police uniforms, Lorenzo swears, so he was confused when they approached in the usual friendly way and then forced his arms behind his back, tying and gagging him. Alejandro was near the gate on the other side, taken at the same time in the same way. They held a pistol to his head and asked about locations of the telephone lines. He told them nothing, but the men still found and cut them quickly, along with the new electric alarm. They knocked on the gate, and Sheldon opened it, not understanding Alejandro's distress when he gave the password at gunpoint, or perhaps failing to ask for it. Alejandro can't clearly remember.

The gunmen rushed through into the courtyard, opening fire on the guardhouse where the thunder of machine guns woke everybody at once. Round after round also went through the windows of the main house into Lev and Natalya's bedroom. The *tat-tat-tat* kept going, for as long as it took to scramble under a bed in the blackness, feel the cold floor, and consider the end of life. Outside in the courtyard was a peculiar glow, not the moon or the streetlight. The air smelled of gunpowder, and then came the scent of riot gas—a bizarre memory. Incendiary bombs, thrown into the house.

Natalya and Lev had rolled onto the floor beside their bed and lay flat. Natalya says she kept her hand on Lev's chest the whole time, to know if his heart was beating. The doorway from their room to Seva's filled with flames. A black silhouette of a man appeared there for a few seconds. They watched him raise a pistol and fire, four times, into the blankets that lay in a jumbled pile on their bed.

Seva, Seva, she said when the phantom had gone, Seva must be dead or they've taken him. It was the most horrible sound, and also a terrible relief, when she heard her grandson scream. She crawled to the doorway and found him bleeding from his foot, under his bed. He was already there, he said, when he'd seen the man's feet come in. The gunman had fired into Seva's bed too. One bullet went through, striking Seva's foot.

One at a time, the bodies in the guard house stood up from the floor, put their hands on their own heartbeats, and struggled to put life back on like a suit of clothes ripped away. Every body alive. We have survived. Only Sheldon is missing. Alejandro believes he might have been shot—he thinks he saw him collapsed by the gate, maybe dragged away by the assailants. Seva won't stop asking where he is. If we are alive, he insists, then Sheldon is alive.

Lorenzo says the man who nearly broke his arms out on the street was a person he recognized. Wearing a false moustache, but it was the muralist, Diego's old friend who became his enemy: Alfaro Siqueiros. No one quite believes it. But Lorenzo is not a fanciful man, and he is sure.

The police came today and used kitchen knives to dig the lead slugs from the walls of Lev's bedroom. Seventy-six bullets. The pocked, crumbling wall, what's left of it, looks like the face of a leper. Bullet holes only centimeters from Lev's pillow. The officers worked all day, collecting evidence. The survivors stood in the ruined court-yard blinking at the light, with eyes unprepared to see the life that is spared into their custody.

Survival, by itself, is not reason enough to rejoice. If life was a suit of clothes momentarily ripped away and put back on, the tearing has ruined it. Today seems harder than yesterday. Night is worse than day, and day is bad. No one has slept. The whistle of a teakettle causes every heart to lurch. Natalya's arms are bandaged, she burned them putting out the fire in Seva's bed. She sits in a chair with tears in her eyes, holding her arms forward as if to embrace a ghost. Lev paces, his thoughts scrambled. With so many others already dead, he must see this assault as a rehearsal for the inevitable. Everyone else in the house must surely harbor secret thoughts of leaving here. Those thoughts layer the misery of guilt upon the misery of terror.

Lorenzo is furious over the breach, and now tediously repeats the security drills everyone knows too well already. "When the horse is gone, it's too late to shut up the barn," Lev warns gloomily. "They won't come by the front gate next time." But Lorenzo can't stop himself, driven by anger or embarrassment at his failure. "When the bell rings for changing the night guard, the man inside is to pull one bolt only. *Are you listening? One bolt only!* The bolt that opens the grille. Ask the pass word. If correct, the entrant may pass *only into the vestibule.*" But the vestibule is controlled by an electric button, and the electricity was cut. Alejandro was blind with panic. And whatever Sheldon's excuse for opening the gate, he can't defend it.

The newspapers have been unspeakable. They say it was a pantomime, mounted by Trotsky himself to gain publicity. The police questioned everyone here, and poor Alejandro they held for two days, probably guessing his vulnerability. Keeping him awake, shoving a rifle butt into his shoulder, the police interrogated him about the so-called fake attack: if it had been real, they asked again and again, how could anyone have survived it? How could seventy bullets fill a room, and every one miss its mark?

In desperate logic, Alejandro pointed out that Seva was actually hit. It was only on the toe, but still. If this were staged, what grandfather would choose a child as victim?

The police reported his words to the press, neatly turned: *The ruthless villain chose his innocent grandchild as the victim in his charade!* In their haste to repeat the scurrilous story, some of the papers even reported Seva dead.

Alejandro is beside himself now, feeling that he caused these vicious reports. He was never quick to come to words, but now he won't ask for coffee at the breakfast table. He is wrung out and sick over his poisoned words, and may not speak again.

28 May

The Rosmers have departed for home, or whatever they find in Europe. Marguerite looked miserable to be leaving her friends at this moment, not so concerned with France's upheaval, as with Natalya's. But the passage is booked and can't be changed. But good news— when they came to the house this morning to say good-bye, they managed to talk Natalya into coming with them as far as the seaport. A small vacation on the coast. Reba went with her, they will come back next week on the train. Natalya's burns are almost healed. She didn't want to part from Lev, but he insisted. This is perfect, they don't even have to take the train to Veracruz: Jacson agreed to drive them in his beautiful Buick, of course.

The good-byes in the courtyard were unmercifully long. Every kiss now between Lev and Natalya is heavy with grief. And Marguerite hugs everyone twice. By the time it all finished they had nearly lost their driver. Jacson was finally located in the house with Seva, playing with a model glider.

25 June

Sheldon Harte has been found, in the village of Tlalminalco, at a house owned by relatives of Siqueiros. Seva hasn't been told yet, but his friend Sheldon will not be back. The police found him under four feet of quicklime in the bottom of a pit.

Thirty people have been arrested, including Siqueiros, though he will probably be allowed to leave the country. The Mexican newspapers are calling him a "half-mad artist" and "irresponsible pirate." Guilt and blame in this story are already established—Trotsky did it himself—and so finding a true culprit creates some awkwardness. In a strange extension of their logic, one newspaper suggested the mad painter had sold himself to Trotsky, who paid him for the simulated attack. "*The* simulated attack," no longer even posed as a speculation, but the fact of the matter. Once a truth is established in newsprint, none other can exist.

Sheldon was a good joe. A *friend*: one more word that has sprouted leaves of meaning in Casa Trotsky.

Diego is gone, already in San Francisco. While the police were busy avoiding any trail that actually led to the Stalinist culprits, they accused Diego of participating in the attack. Now the charge is moot, with Siqueiros in custody, but the presses are locked in their own frenzy: the much-discussed painter a murderer! What reporter could contain his enthusiasm for that particular theory? Diego had to leave without a farewell, and Lev is sad of it. Through all its stages, the camaraderie of these men is remarkable.

Now Lorenzo is behaving like a madman: he installed metal doors three inches thick, on both entrances to Lev and Natalya's bedroom. Lev says going to bed now is like getting in a submarine. Lorenzo also has drawn up plans for a bomb-proof redoubt, three new brick turrets to overlook the streets, and barriers of barbed wire and mesh that will withstand grenade attacks.

Lev is plainly tired of mentioning the barn and the horse already escaped. He says they won't come in the same way again. "Lorenzo, my friend, if they were that foolish, you would have nothing to worry about."

The gloom may yet lift. Natalya has taken out her summer dresses finally, and put away her ancient Russian fur-trimmed coats. Of course, the weather in this city is exactly the same in any month, give or take a chance of rain. Yet Natalya follows the seasons scrupulously, wearing light-colored prints in the spring, dark coats in autumn. Her sense of order is still ruled by the weather of Paris, or Moscow. And because of it, she survives. Lev survives. The past is all we know of the future.

Another good sign: Natalya accepted guests for tea. In the Melchor market Reba ran into the faithful chauffeur Jacson and his girlfriend Sylvia. On a whim she suggested they stop by, so Natalya could thank Jacson for driving them all to Veracruz. Reba worried whether it was right to ask without Lev's permission, but Natalya said of course it was fine, the Rosmers have known Sylvia for years and Jacson has shown a thousand kindnesses in recent months. Natalya seemed to enjoy Sylvia and Jacson. She said they should come again, bringing a little diversion into this fortress.

Lev seems to have his own opinion of the couple. He took an unusually long time to check on the chickens before coming in to join the visitors for tea. Natalya grew a little exasperated and sent a messenger to get him.

"Pardon, sir, but your wife is wondering why it would take forty-five minutes to feed eleven hens."

"Tell Natalya these hens are more interesting company than her guests. No, no, don't tell her that. He's a good sort, this Jacson. But he fancies himself a writer."

"What's he writing?"

"Well, that's the problem. He doesn't know. He showed me a draft. It's supposed to be some sort of analysis, Schachtman's theory of the Third Camp. But really it's a tedious mess. His thinking is very shallow, if he's thinking at all."

"Oh."

"And he'll want me to critique it."

"That's difficult."

"Difficult. Oh, my son. I have faced the GPU and the gulag. But somehow I cannot face a young man who has been very kind to my wife, and say to him, 'Well, my friend, you are a shallow thinker. And tedious.'"

"Would you like me to tell Natalya the hens are extremely hungry today?"

He sighed, rattling the grain scoop. The hens tilted their heads, watching his every move. "Look at this. In 1917 I commanded an army of five million men. Now I command eleven hens. Not even a rooster at my service."

"More often than not, Commissar, it's the roosters that give the trouble."

He chuckled.

"If you'd like a little help with passing the time here, sir, I have a question to ask you. About being commander of the Soviet. I've been wanting to ask for a long time."

"Well, then, don't wait. The doctor says my blood pressure is through the roof. What can this question be?"

"Diego told me you were meant to succeed Lenin. You were his second in command, with the people's support. You would have led the revolution to a democratic Soviet Republic."

"This is the case."

"Then why did Stalin come to power instead of you? The books say 'an unsettled transition,' that kind of thing. But Diego said it differently."

"How did he say it?"

"An accident of history. Like a coin toss, that could have gone either way."

Lev was quiet for an extremely long time. It seemed likely that Jacson and Sylvia would leave before this conversation moved forward at all. It was a bold question, possibly even rude. Van had said many times that Lev hates to talk about this, and won't.

But finally he did. "Vladimir Lenin died in 1924, this you know. He had a stroke, soon after the Thirteenth Party Conference. He was exhausted by that conference, and I was also. I had been ill many weeks and came down with pneumonia during the sessions. Natalya insisted we go to the Caucasus afterward for a rest. She was right, I might have died otherwise. The conference concluded, and I embraced my comrade and friend Vladimir before departing."

He paused, took off his gloves, and wiped his eyes.

"Natalya and I were on the train to the Caucasus. In the dining car, having a cup of tea. The porter came and handed us a telegram: Lenin was dead of a stroke. Stalin had sent the wire. 'Dear comrade Lev,' he said, or some such thing. In friendship and full solidarity he shared my grief, and gave details of a funeral. He said for various reasons, mostly for maintaining calm, the family and secretariat had decided against a large state funeral. They would hold a private burial the very next day. There was no time for me to return, of course, but Stalin assured that I should not worry. The family understood. In due time, they would want me to eulogize Lenin in a state ceremony."

"And so you went to the Caucasus."

"We proceeded to the Caucasus, for a week of rest. And before the end of it, learned that Stalin had lied. The information he sent in the wire was false. The funeral had not been immediate or small. It was a large state funeral, three days after the wire. I could have managed to return in time, had I known. I should have been the one to speak there. To calm people, because it was a frightening time. With Lenin gone so suddenly, it was chaotic. People were very uncertain about the future."

"But instead of you, Stalin spoke at the funeral."

"The newspapers said I had refused to come, declining to be disturbed from my vacation. He told that story openly. But not from the platform, of course. At the funeral he spoke of leadership and reassurance. How he accepted the mantle of the people's trust, when others had shirked it. . . . Everyone knew of whom he spoke."

"You had their loyalty, a few days before. Did that count for nothing?"

"They were so afraid. In that moment their keenest desire was to lean on someone who seemed unfailingly strong."

His eyes fixed on the sky, above the wall that enclosed him. No wound to his flesh could have pained Lev more than this memory. It was cruel to raise the subject, Van had been right about that.

"Sir, you couldn't have known. It was not your mistake."

"The mistake was to believe him. To accept the sympathy of a friend extended in a telegram. I was very ill of course, with a fever, Natalya reminds me of that. And the loss was disorienting, no one expected it so suddenly. But to take Stalin at his word, look what has come of this. A hundred thousand deaths. The whole revolution betrayed."

"How long did it take you to get back to Moscow?"

"Too long. That is the simple truth. Stalin moved so quickly to fill the bureaucracy with men who swore loyalty to him. These were supposed to be neutral positions, men dedicated only to the country. But loyalty to Stalin guaranteed the future of Stalin. It's hard for a nation to retrieve itself from such a change of guard."

"But people desire fair government. You say that constantly."

"They want to believe in heroes, also. And villains. Especially when very frightened. It's less taxing than the truth."

Lev scrutinized the doorway to the dining room. The visitors were leaving. He waved the grain scoop. Jacson and Sylvia waved back. Natalya stood on the patio with a raincoat pulled over her shoulders like a cape. The sky was dark with a threat of rain.

"So that was the accident of history. A false telegram on a train."

"It was no accident."

22 August

This impossible thing cannot be. Something should have stopped this.

In the morning he was in the best spirits. He transplanted four cactus plants in a new garden. He was pleased about devising a new cactus-planting technology involving a canvas hammock, chicken wire, and a counterweight. "From now on *everything* will go faster!" he declared, as if he had invented internal combustion.

By lunchtime he'd finished revising the next-to-last chapter of his book on Stalin. In the afternoon he dictated an article on the American mobilization. From three thirty to four it rained pitchforks, and the day remained overcast. At five he took a break to have tea with Natalya, as always, and afterward asked for help with the rabbits. Two females had given birth to litters, in the same hutch. He needed to move one family lest the mothers cause trouble with one another's young. Cannibalism is always a possibility.

Lev had one of them by her nape, the big spotted one called Minuschka, when Jacson arrived unexpectedly from the gatehouse. Lev handed over the hare with instructions on where to move her kits.

Jacson also appeared to have his hands full: a folder of papers, his hat, a raincoat over his arm. He was leaving for New York shortly, he said. But had finished his first article. Please, could Lev give it an honest critique?

Lev looked back, shooting a certain feckless glance, nearly comic: *Help! I would sooner face the gulag!* But he said, "Of course. Come into my office."

They went in the house, he probably asked Natalya to make a cup of tea for the visitor, and then they must have proceeded to Lev's office. It's easy to picture: Lev sitting down, rooting out a clearing on his desk to set down the pages, collecting the patience to read it and make some tactful comment. The future waits. The world revolution waits, while Trotsky gives his full attention to a shallow-thinking but hopeful fellow, because nothing wondrous can come in this world unless it rests on the shoulders of kindness.

He would have asked Jacson to sit down opposite him in the armchair. But instead he stood, probably a little nervous to have this great man examining his syntax and logic. Fidgeting, annoying Lev to no end. Fingering things on Lev's desk: the glass paperweight, wedding gift from Natalya. Cartridge cases in the pen tray, souvenirs of the Siqueiros raid in May. Jacson laid his raincoat on the table.

And we heard the roar. A scream or a sob but really a roar, indignation.

Joe and Melquiades scrambled down the ladder from the roof, and everyone else from everywhere. Natalya cried out from the kitchen, "Lev?" Two baby rabbits fell to the ground and squirmed in the dust. The strangest sight had appeared in the window of Lev's study: Lev standing with his arms around Jacson—he seemed to be embracing the man—and screaming. There was blood. Joe and Lorenzo and Natalya all were shouting at once. Somehow Joe got there first, on his long legs, and already had Jacson pinned to the floor, and Natalya was white as chalk, collapsed against the door. Lev was seated now at his desk, glasses off, his face and hands covered with blood. On the floor lay a strange small pickax, with its handle cut short. Not a kitchen tool. Some other thing.

"You're going to be all right, old man," Natalya said quietly. Melquiades had his rifle cocked, trained on the writhing man on the floor. Joe was kneeling on Jacson's chest, grappling to control the man's flailing arms.

Lev spoke: "Don't let Seva in. He mustn't see this."

And then Lev said to Joe, or Melquiades, "Don't kill him."

"Lev," Joe said, almost sobbing the word. He had Jacson's wrists pinned now, his own large knuckles white against the stained floor. Lorenzo eased the Colt .38 out of Lev's desk drawer. It was always kept there, with six bullets in the magazine. A .25 automatic had also been lying on the table by the Dictaphone, within easy arm's reach of where Lev had sat reading Jacson's paper. And the security alarm bell is wired under the desk. They don't come the same way again.

Melquiades didn't lower the rifle. Both guns were trained on the man on the floor, aimed at his head. Intermittently he bucked and twisted under Joe's knees.

Lev held his hands away from his face and stared at the blood. There was so much of it. His white cuffs were soaked like bandages. It dripped onto the papers, this morning's typed drafts. Very slowly he repeated, "Don't kill him." It was an impossible spectre, an impossible request.

"It's no time for mercy," Joe said, his voice strange.

Lev closed his eyes, obviously struggling for words. "There is no hope they will . . . tell the truth about this. Unless. You keep that man alive."

When the Green Cross ambulance came, Lev was alive but half paralyzed, his body suddenly seeming terribly thin and strange to the touch, colder on that side when lifted onto the stretcher. Reba, Alejandro, and most of the others stayed at the house with Seva. Natalya rode in the back of the ambulance. It was dark. Streetlights were on.

At the hospital Lev began to speak in French, and later in Russian, just before they took him to surgery. Languages fell away, a long exile peeled from him like the layers of an onion.

The surgeons found that the blade had penetrated through Lev's skull, seven centimeters into the brain itself. He died the next day without waking again. Yesterday.

His last sentence in English had begun, "There is no hope." Natalya remarked later that those words were so strange to hear, from a man who lived decades on nothing but hope. But hope was not the issue, nor was mercy. There is no point discussing it with Natalya or Joe, but that was a clear instruction: No hope they will tell the truth, unless you keep that man alive.

He meant the newspapers. A dead assailant could become anyone, a victim himself. Another mad artist hired by Trotsky in a plot gone wrong, his final practical joke. Lies are infinite in number, and the truth so small and singular.

Lev was right; the man lives, and the world will know what he was. The police have him, already they're starting down the trail that now spools backward through our memories as a terrible thread: Reba running into him in the Melchor market last week, not by chance. Driving Natalya to Veracruz, not a whim but a calculation. The gift he gave Seva that day, the little glider: a chance to get inside the house, memorize the rooms. His attachment to the Rosmers' old friend Sylvia, and then befriending the Rosmers themselves. Driving them everywhere in his elegant Buick. Even his possession of the Buick. Where did he get such money? We didn't think to ask.

In custody he admitted it proudly, right away: he is a trained agent of Stalin, in the pay of the GPU for many years. Jacson is not his only name, or his real one. How many avenues did he have to try, before finding one door ajar? The trail goes back years, even back to Paris, his stalking of Frida, waiting outside her gallery with the bouquet of flowers. So much careful work, for the chance to sink a blade into the brain of Lev Trotsky.

The New York Times, *August 25, 1940*

U.S. Forbids Entry of Trotsky's Body

No Specific Reason Is Cited, but Fear of Demonstration Is Believed Cause

SOVIET CALLS HIM TRAITOR

Press Sees Deserved End for Exile— Accused Says He Had No Accomplices

Special to The New York Times

WASHINGTON, Aug. 25—The State Department announced today that the body of Leon Trotsky would not be permitted to be brought to the United States from Mexico.

There was no reason offered, but it was assumed that the possibility was foreseen of Communist and anti-Communist demonstrations, if the body were brought here.

"In response to an inquiry from American Consul George P. Shaw in Mexico City," the announcement said, "the department has informed him that it perceives no reason for bringing Trotsky's body to the United States and that it would not be appropriate to do so."

Soviet Charges Perfidy

MOSCOW, Aug. 24 (AP)—The Soviet press, giving the Russian people their first word today of the death of Leon Trotsky in Mexico City last Wednesday night, proclaimed it the "inglorious end" of a "murderer, traitor and international spy."

It was the first mention of the attack since a brief dispatch on Thursday reported that an attempt had been made on the life of the exiled Communist leader by one of his followers.

The Communist party organ, *Pravda*, charged Trotsky with sabotaging the Red Army during the civil war, plotting to kill Lenin and Joseph Stalin in 1918, organizing the slaying of Sergei Kiroff and plotting to kill Maxim Gorky, and with having served in the secret service of Britain, France, Germany and Japan.

"Trotsky, having gone to the limits of human debasement, became entangled in his own net and was killed by one of his own disciples," said Pravda. "Thus, a hated man came to his inglorious end, going to his grave with the stamp of murderer and international spy on his forehead."

The Train Station Notebook, August 1940 (VB)

Today is a Saturday, the last of August. This train rocks, sliding north. It's four in the afternoon and the sun is bright on the left side of the train, beaded like a salt crust on the dirty windows, so that much is sure: the train is headed north. The last ten days are like shreds in a bag of scraps. Nothing in memory makes sense. Everything is gone, pockets full of ashes.

Lev was right to the end. The story of Jacson Mornard is so vile, the newspapers have been bound to tell it. President Cárdenas has condemned Russia and the United States as well, a league of foreign powers that dishonored our country with the attack. Three hundred thousand Mexicans walked down Paseo de la Reforma in the funeral procession, after walking here from mines and oil fields, from Michoacán and Puebla. Half made the journey without shoes. A quarter of them might not be able to say the name of Lev Davidovich Trotsky. Only that he was one of the generals in their Century of Revolution, as the president says. A man cut down by outsiders who refuse to believe the people can succeed.

On which day was the funeral? The attack was on a Tuesday, his death on Wednesday, and everything else is gone. Papers, books, clothes, and every memory ever recorded in a notebook. The police took everything from the guard house rooms, confiscated as evidence. The only hope of sorting out anything now is to put it in this little book. Starting with today, working backward: Day Last in Mexico, the train slides north; the train begins to move; the train is boarded at the Colonia Buenavista station; a packet of sandwiches and a small notebook bound with a wire coil are purchased at the new Sanborn's in the downtown station, using pesos out of the little purse from Frida.

Already the rest is a jumble. On which day was that, when Frida handed over the purse with the money and the documents for getting her crates through customs?

It was after the murder, but before the funeral. After the interrogation at the police station. They even questioned Natalya, for two hours. Everyone else they held for two days at least. Frida was ready to bite those men for making her sleep on a cot in that cold, stinking room. She was nowhere near, on the day of the murder. Joe gave the best statement, he remembers the most, even though he was on the roof when Jacson arrived, so didn't see him come into the courtyard.

No one else saw that: his nervous smile when asking the favor, one more critique of this paper he'd written. The raincoat over his arm: the weapon must have been underneath his coat. No one else saw Lev's silent glance back over his shoulder: *I would rather face the gulag!* His plea. A secretary's only work is to protect his commissar— Van would have done it. Any small discouragement could have sent Jacson Mornard away: Sorry, but as you know, Lev is awfully busy. He has to finish his article on the American mobilization. Maybe if you could just leave your paper, he'll have a look at it when he gets the chance. That could have happened. Lev could have been saved.

Now Miss Reed sits on the side of the bed holding Natalya's hand, whether it is Tuesday or Sunday, morning or midnight. Joe and Reba are in Lev's study packing up the papers and files. In that room only, the police left everything in place. They didn't take much from the house, either. But from the guard house: everything. It was astonishing. To be driven home from a blank brick cell at the police station, walk through the gate, and see Lev's cactuses still standing in place as if nothing had happened, the hens waiting to be fed. And then the guard house: the doors to every room standing open and nothing at all inside, only blank brick cells. The metal cots, the mattresses. The floors swept as clean as the day of moving in. The little table loaned from Lev was still there, but nothing on it, not even the typewriter. The books, gone. The trunk and boxes under the bed, gone. Clothes, tooth powders, the few photographs of Mother. And every one of the notebooks from the very beginning, from Isla Pixol. Also the box of typed pages that had grown to weigh as much as a dog, and had been that kind of faithful friend at the close of each day. The stack of pages growing fatter and more certain all the time. It doesn't matter. None of that matters.

Frida says the police are stupid cockroaches, they confiscated anything written in English because they couldn't tell what it was, the idiots couldn't see it's only diaries and stories. The Scandals of the Ancients, evidence of no crime except Mistaken Identity: a young man possessed of the belief he was a writer. So distracted by his dreams, he was a careless secretary, the type to leave letters lying around. Or leave his boss at the mercy of a tedious visitor, one more deadly supplicant with a badly written article.

Joe and Reba will pack up what's left of Lev, his thoughts crammed on paper, so it all can be sent to a library somewhere, sold for enough money to help Natalya get away. Van might arrange the sale, if he can be found. His last letter came from Baltimore; he was teaching French. He may not even know about Lev's death. Unthinkable. All of this is unthinkable, however much Lev and Natalya did think of it, anticipating death with each day's dawn. To think is not always to see.

Natalya will finish out the bottle of Phanodorm day by day, holding tight to Miss Reed's hand until she can open her eyes and walk on a ship and sail away. The United States won't let her come back with Joe and Reba. So Paris, then, to live with the Rosmers. She has to go. Lorenzo believes she's now a target, a highly watched symbol of her husband. She can't sleep for fear of the GPU, the wolves of her dreams.

Frida is going to San Francisco, where Diego is already. As usual she has a plan: her friend Dr. Eloesser will cure all her illnesses, and Diego will want her back. Melquiades plans to go south where he has relatives, Alejandro may go that way too. San Francisco, Paris, Oaxaca, the four winds—everyone scatters. Lev's writings will be kept together somewhere, but what of the secretaries who recorded them, their small contributions to his logic? Or even the contribution of a good breakfast, the satisfied stomach on which the greatest plans were launched, who will remember that? The New York boys versus the Mexicans in courtyard football, Casa Trotsky is gone, as if it never existed. The house will be swept and sold to new owners who will tear down the guard towers, puzzle over Lev's cactus gardens, and give away his chickens, or eat them.

This household is like a pocketful of coins that jingled together for a time, but now have been slapped on a counter to pay a price. The pocket empties out, the coins venture back into the infinite circulations of currency, separate, invisible, and untraceable. That particular handful of coins had no special meaning together, it seems, except to pay a particular price. It might remain real, if someone had written everything in a notebook. No such record now exists.

Frida says everybody had better knock the Trotsky dust off their shoes and get out of here. "Sóli, I have a plan for you," she said, seated at the little wooden desk in her studio. She'd sent Perpetua running down the street with an urgent summons—Frida wants to see you right away. "We have to get you away from here, you're not safe. The police took everything from your room, even your socks. It's because of all those things you wrote. I'm sure they're watching you." The police took many things from many people, but she believes words are the most dangerous. She says maybe Diego was right about "your damn diaries," the confiscated notebooks might put their author in jeopardy.

But she has a plan. She needs to send eight paintings to the Museum of Modern Art in New York, for a show: *Twenty Centuries of Mexican Art.* And after that another show is planned, *Twentieth-Century Portraits.* Frida has become a fixture of her century. The Levy Gallery may be interested as well. She needs a consignment marshal. "Or whatever the hell you call it in English," she said; she'll look it up for the documents. *Pastor de consignación* is what she called it, a "shipping shepherd," a legally authorized agent to accompany the paintings on the train all the way to New York. "Your passport is already fixed up. You were ready to go with Lev last fall, for that hearing."

"Frida, the police won't allow an emigration. Not with a murder investigation still open."

"Who says you're emigrating? I already talked with them about this. Leaving the country for a short time is okay, as long as you're not a suspect. I told them you're my consignment marshal."

"You already talked with the police?"

"Sure. I told them you have to oversee this delivery because I can't trust anybody else to do it," she said, tapping her pencil against the wooden desk. This plan had no complications at all, in her mind, beyond selecting which portraits to send for the show.

"And then?"

"No *and then.* You'll have to carry all these customs forms, one for each painting. You show them at the border, and get each one stamped. Declarations of value and all that. You have to be really careful to hold on to all the receipts from the lockup."

"The lockup?"

"Don't worry, you're not going to jail." Her hair has grown back, just barely long enough to coronate herself again, with the help of plenty of ribbons. When did she cut it off? The conversation of that morning is gone, that notebook is gone. Every time it hits like a rock. In Frida's studio, in front of the window, exactly where Van used to sit for dictation, she now had a half-finished portrait on her easel: Frida in a man's suit, cutting off her hair. *Keeping your damn diaries,* but these paintings are her own version of it.

Today she rattled like a gourd full of seeds, talking and fidgeting with the things on her desk. "Okay, the porter captain on the train will make the guys bring the crates to a special part of the baggage car, where they have a cage. You follow him in there to see him do it. He'll lock the crates inside and give you a receipt for getting them back. So you don't want to lose that."

"A cage?"

"Not the kind of cage for lions. Well, maybe they would put lions in there if they were expensive ones." She seemed desperate to be cheerful. She picked up tubes of paint, like big silver cigars with brown paper labels around their middles, then fingered the brushes standing together in a cup. She was afraid. It took a while to understand that this was the problem: fear. Not for herself but for her friend, whom she had thrown to the lions many times before. This time she wants him saved.

"Oh. So the paintings won't just be in a big suitcase or something?"

"Oh my God, wait till you see. They build a traveling crate for each one. Diego has a man who does this, he's very expert. He wraps them in layers and layers of kraft paper like a mummy and then fits each painting in two wooden crates, one inside the other. There's a space in between that's stuffed with straw, to prevent damage during shipping. The crates are huge. You could get inside one yourself."

That was on a Friday, because Perpetua was cooking fish. The day before the funeral? How long did it take to build those crates?

The police returned a few things the following week, but not much, not even clothing. Knowing those pigs, she said, they stole anything useful and burned the rest. Reba had to ask Natalya to open the wardrobe and pass around Lev's shirts, so the possessionless guards could have something to wear. His shirts were so familiar. It was startling to see them from the back, walking through the garden. Of all of us, they fit Alejandro best: small devout Alejandro, no one would guess they were the same size. Lev was so much larger than his body.

One day (which?), Frida said she went to the police station and screamed until they returned a few more items. Probably the officers locked the doors in terror, and threw things out the windows. So she had a small suitcase of items to hand over, along with the documents, for the trip to New York. That was yesterday. In the dining room of the Blue House, after one last look round the place, those mad blue walls and yellow wicker chairs. That glorious kitchen. Embraces from Belén and Perpetua.

"The police already had destroyed a lot of your things," Frida said flatly when she produced the suitcase. "This is what you'll need for the trip, and the rest you wouldn't want. There were some really old clothes and things, but you won't need that junk right away. I had it packed up and stored in a trunk at Cristina's."

"Anything else? Papers?"

"Only some books I think you borrowed from Lev, so I gave them to Natalya. Your room was all in a big metal box marked 'C,' maybe the third one they tore apart. I could tell because it was your clothes. There was hardly anything else, just some old magazines. We can send you the trunk after you get an address in Gringolandia. Sóli, jump! You're going to be a gringo!"

"This is all?"

She had packed the suitcase herself. It was hard to look inside: the unbearable persistence of hope. Of course there were no notebooks, no manuscript. Only shirts and trousers. A lot of woolen sweaters; Frida believes the sky of New York flings down snow at all times, even August. Also milk of magnesia, aspro gargle, and Horlick's powder for nerves, furthering Frida's vision of Gringolandia. Toothbrush, razor. She says it's not a good idea to bring more than this. A large trunk would draw suspicion.

"Remember, this is not an emigration."

But her embrace was like a child's farewell, dramatic and desperate. She didn't want to let go. "Look, okay. I brought you two presents. One is from Diego. He doesn't know yet. But I'm sure he would want you to have this. For Sóli, the drifter between two houses, to commemorate your journey. Look, it's the codex!"

It was the codex. The ancient book of the Azteca, a long tableau in pictures on accordion-folded paper, describing their journey from the land of the ancients, wandering until they found home. It was a copy, of course, not the original. But probably worth some money. Diego might not be pleased about this. It can always be returned.

Her face brightened. "The other one is from me. I made a painting for you!"

Frida only gives paintings to people she has loved. It was unexpectedly hard to keep from crying as she fetched the crate from the other room and lugged it in. It must be a small portrait; the outer crate is only the size of a suitcase, easily managed with regular baggage. But heavy as lead, for its size. She must have put a lot of paint on that canvas.

"Unfortunately you can't see it, I've already packed it up to go. I hope you'll like it. Write and tell me what you think. But you have to wait until you arrive in your new life. This is very important, okay? You mustn't peek. This is my gift, so don't defy me. Don't open this damn thing until you get to your father's house, or wherever you end up. Okay, promise?"

"Of course. Who would defy you, Frida?"

"And don't get it mixed up with the others. Look, I had the man print your name on the outside of the crate to be sure. You have papers in the folder to get it through customs, the same as the others. But don't give it to the museum by accident."

"Are you crazy? I won't forget."

"Yes, I am crazy, I thought you knew." She stared at the crate. "Look at that, it's an omen. You and I came into life through the same doorway, and now you are supposed to go through this one for me. It's your destiny."

"What makes you think so?"

"Your name. For me you're just Sóli, I forgot you're Shepherd. You were meant to be the *pastor de consignación.*" The shepherd of the shipment.

Eight paintings, a suitcase of Viyella socks and milk of magnesia. And two gifts, from people whose faces already slide backward from memory as the train climbs north.

Oh, the little stolen man. Forgotten until just now. Even he is left behind, the police must have taken him in the sweep, with everything. It's a pity. This train might be just the thing he was looking for, those thousands of years. A long, narrow channel through darkness, a tunnel through the earth and time. *Take me away to another world.*

More memories bubble up every day. The sea cave in Isla Pixol, cold water on prickly boy-skin. Images, conversations, warnings. The first time seeing Frida in the market with Candelaria: What was she wearing? Mother in the little apartment on the alley off of Insurgentes. Billy Boorzai. The first days in Mexico City. Isla Pixol, the names of villages and of trees. Recipes and rules for life from Leandro: What were they? Whom did Mother love, and what made her so happy that day in the rainstorm? The reef full of fishes, what were their colors? What lay at the bottom of the cave? How long did it take, exactly, to swim through it without drowning?

The notebooks are gone. It must have been like this for Lev at the end, with his past entirely stolen. A lifetime of people, unconfirmed by their living presences, or photographs or descriptions in a notebook, can only skulk in the corners like ghosts. They shift like chimeras. Careful words of warning reverse themselves like truth and newspaper stories, becoming their own opposites. An imperfectly remembered life is a useless treachery. Every day, more fragments of the past roll around heavily in the chambers of an empty brain, shedding bits of color, a sentence or a fragrance, something that changes and then disappears. It drops like a stone to the bottom of the cave.

There will not be another notebook after this one. No need. No more pages piling up. Oh, the childish hope of that. As if a stack of pages could someday grow high enough that a boy could stand on top of it and be as tall as Jack London or Dos Passos. That is the sorest embarrassment: those hopeful hours of typing through the night shift while Lorenzo's boots tapped overhead on the roof, all of our hearts bursting with the certainty of our own purposes. No more of that, never another typewriter. Accumulating words is a charlatan's career. How important is anything that could burn to ash in a few minutes? Stuffed into an incineration barrel at the police station, set on fire on a chilly August evening—maybe an officer warmed his hands, and that is the use of that. Better to roam free like a chicken with no future and no past. Searching only to satisfy the hunger of the present: a beetle or lizard snapped up, or perhaps one day, a snake.

Harrison W. Shepherd leaves Mexico with his pockets full of ash. An emancipated traveler.

PART 4

Asheville, North Carolina

1941–1947

(VB)

My name is Violet Brown. *Was,* I will say. When you read this I'll not be living. I will explain that directly.

If I sound colorful, I am not. It's nought but a pair of names, stamped on me by two people who never met. First, my mother. She was fond of romantic novels with "Violets" in them. She was tubercular and passed when I was young. The second name was from my husband Freddy Brown, who came and went quickly through his time also: lost in the great flood of 1916. The swell of the French Broad River wrecked most of Asheville that time, including the Rees Sons Tannery, where he worked. I was widowed the same year as married, yet still am known to this day as Mrs. Brown. A woman can be marked by others: *embossed* is a good word for it, one of a great many taught me by Mr. Shepherd. He remarked once that I had been embossed with names like an address on a package, by people who didn't know the contents but still got to decide how it would be sent.

Mother pined to see me married before she passed, and it happened soon after, when I was fifteen. Now I am older than she ever did get to be, and can see other paths are worthy. I've lived a maiden's life and found happiness, including being helpmeet to a man. I served greatness. I don't wish for more. That is the beginning and end of what needs be said about me. The purpose of this is to make known the life of Mr. Shepherd. When this book lies open he is dead, and so be I. Our argument at rest, if such it was.

He was given to a secretive temperament, and it gained the better of him when he fled Mexico. He stopped keeping his journals and became hopeless of the written word and its consequence. He told me that, later on. Every scrap of his writings lost, things he'd kept track of since boyhood. He let go the hope of becoming a man of letters. I can attest. We were acquainted at that time, and if pressed to say what this young man might become, I'd think first of the kitchen, or any profession that suits one who keeps to himself. But a well-known writer of books? No. He read them. But most did, in those days.

He never went back to his notebooks exactly as before, probably due to the change in situation. He kept carbon copies of his letters, and filed the clippings of news that attracted him. And still did write personal things, on any day that stirred him. I've seen him go in his study and type out memory of a whole event, in a kind of a fury. I expect if he'd been married he would have ranted the tale to his wife. But he didn't have any wife, so his typewriter did the listening. Often it was whole conversations he'd had. His memory for conversation was shocking, I suppose due to his years of taking dictation from impatient men. But he must have had a knack for it, before. Then he'd file it in one of his leather folders and be done with it. You could call it a letter to himself, or God. He had that saying, God speaks for the silent man. That must have been the One he was talking to.

Mr. Shepherd seldom let me see the personal writings. He knew how to file something himself. If a man can cook, he can file. He was the most bashful person I ever did meet, very pained to speak forthrightly of his feelings.

We met soon after the travel mentioned, from Mexico to the United States. The murder unsettled and wrenched something in him badly, I know that much. He never wanted to talk about that time in his life. He spent a few months in the city of New York, I only know because it was winter that he came on south and settled here. I haven't any record of what he did in New York, save for one exception. He visited the father of Sheldon Harte, the boy that was killed in the raid, to give condolence and tell that man about his son's last days, since no other soul ever would. The newspaper reports had been awful, young Sheldon accused of being an accomplice in the "staged attack." That he had turned on his friends and run off, that kind of thing.

It troubled Mr. Shepherd that there were no photographs of Sheldon Harte in Mexico, to give to the father. He mentioned that, more times than you'd think. The boy always would take the camera in his own hand and urge others into the photograph. Now I've pondered why that was troubling to Mr. Shepherd, because he used his notebooks in like fashion, always portraying others, not himself. At the end of all this, when I struggled with my conscience over Mr. Shepherd's wishes, I used his sentiments on Sheldon Harte to help guide my hand. He was sad that Sheldon had perished without being in any photographs. It struck him as wrong that a man should disappear.

His task in New York was delivering important paintings to the galleries, and this he did in a perfectly satisfactory way. Probably he stayed to see the paintings hung so he could make reports to Mrs. Kahlo Rivera. His friendship with her remained an anchor for a time, yet she herself had a great many friends and may have felt anchored elsewhere. That is an opinion. She and Mr. Rivera remarried that same year, returned to Mexico, and resumed life as before. To my knowledge she never offered Mr. Shepherd encouragement to return to Mexico. His only shred of a plan, arriving here in '40, was to go to Washington, D.C., with the address of a lawyer's office in hand and ask where his father was living.

The office happened to be on the same street where he'd ducked the tear gas in the riots, years before. He said he took it as no portent. The father had written he would be moving soon to a new place, and for that reason gave a lawyer's address. The son went with expectations of making some peace, this being all the family he had left. If all went well, he could find a place nearby and perhaps look after the father in old age.

Well, what a surprise he found at the lawyer's office. His father had moved, to the sweet hereafter. The illness mentioned offhandedly in his letter was in truth a malignancy of the intestines he failed to survive. The lawyer explained how the man had come to him to put earthly matters in order, so he knew. He'd left a small sum and the keys to a car, the same he had written his son about. A Chevrolet Roadster, the very model Mr. Shepherd learned to drive in Mexico, white. He kept that car ten years. I knew it well.

So, there he was. If he took any of this as a sign, it was one that said: "Drive!" He got in the automobile and he drove. The streets of Washington, D.C., were overrun with automobiles in those days, this was before the war, when the gasoline ran like water. Mr. Shepherd followed the signs pointing out of town, heading toward Mexico for want of a better direction. Twenty-four years old, with nought in this world to count as friend and no place to call his home. What he found was a Blue Ridge Parkway. He got on that and followed to its end. He thought the Blue Ridges sounded good. He had recollections, for his family had lived in the valley west of Washington in the brief time his mother and father were wed. He hoped to see blue mountains rolling away to the sky, something like the ocean in a child's eye, as he remembered it. But in this instance, he drove hundreds of miles and never saw one blue thing at all. Gray skies only, and brown mountains covered with leafless trees, and then of a sudden, no more parkway. It was a public works project, and the government ran shy of money. That is how he came here to Asheville. It would have been November. He hadn't any gumption to think what to do next. Here he stayed.

THE LACUNA ❋ 267

It is not a bad place to wind up, Asheville. Our town lies in the elbow of the Great Smoky Mountains, circled by high peaks and the oldest forests of the land. The Swannanoa and French Broad Rivers twine together in the valley, and that is how the city came to be put here. Mr. George Vanderbilt found it rewarding to haul trees and coal out of the mountains and float it all out on barges, or carry it off in his railroads in due time. He made himself a fortune, and a good deal of it can still be viewed in his house, the Biltmore mansion. If you want to pay fifty cents to go look at a million dollars, you can do it any day of the week except Sundays. They have paintings of countless worth, a library, forty bedrooms, and Napoleon's chess table. Later during the war, Mr. Shepherd was to have his important duties there at the mansion, but he never did go back in as a visitor.

Our city has had its pioneers and scoundrels like anywhere. When the Central Bank and Trust failed in November of 1930, the city's own funds were in it. That was bad. Those of us on the city rolls went without pay for months. I was a typist for the city clerk's office then, making little enough to begin with, yet we still came to work. For no one offered to pay us for idlement, either. Others had lost much more. Foreclosed houses stood empty in the nicest parts of town: Grove Park, Beaucatcher Mountain, even the stately homes in the woods along the Tunnel Road where it winds down from the Blue Ridge.

It was this road that brought Mr. Shepherd to town, when his parkway ended without further ado. After driving day and night through high-mountain vistas, he would have found himself in the long tunnel through Swannanoa Gap, then spit out from darkness into the valley. He stopped at one of the large houses on the Tunnel Road that had been made a boardinghouse. That was Mrs. Bittle's, a widow lady with children all grown who found herself betwixt the rock and the rail in '34, so began to take in boarders. I was her first one. She had a sign made to put out in the yard whenever she had a vacancy: "Clean To Let With Meals $10 Week, Only Good People Here." Somehow the wording of it struck Mr. Shepherd. Those words changed his course, brought his long drive to an end.

Mrs. Bittle took to him and allowed the Roadster parked in her garage for no extra. He kept that automobile under high polish for many years, though its destiny for the next while was to stay parked, it goes without saying. No new automobile could be had in the war years, nor gasoline for an old one if you had it. Chrysler set their plants to making tanks, Ford built Cyclone engines for the bombers, and they all quit making cars entirely. The railroad moved men and matériel instead of Mr. Vanderbilt's lumber, and the Asheville-Hendersonville airport was taken over by the armed forces. The nice homes that had stood empty since the crash now filled up with the families of government workers, thought to be safer here than in the capital, after the Japanese attacked the refineries at Los Angeles. The Nazis were sinking our tankers right off the Carolina coast, day in and day out. The thinking was that our marble halls might be next. For that reason, the National Gallery sent many trainloads of its national treasures to the Biltmore House, for safekeeping.

We were proud to hold on to treasure. Our city had never been asked to do anything important before. We were ready in a jig. Everything was rationed then: girdles, shoes, bobby pins, yet we did not complain. The Army Corps took over our shopping arcade downtown, and that was fine too, since there was nothing to sell in the shops. We heard they were keeping high-ranking Axis prisoners up at the Grove Park Inn. We reckoned it was Mussolini himself up there under lock and key, soaking in those grand old tubs and sitting on the Roycroft chairs, waiting with heavy heart to receive his comeuppance.

They had the USO dances at the Woodfin House, I didn't go. I turned forty the year before Pearl Harbor, too old for carrying on with soldiers. But the war made each and all feel young in a certain way. The town ripped up the trolley tracks to send off in the scrap-metal drives, and next they tore the iron cells from the old jail building! No American would commit a crime during wartime, was our thinking. Everyone went a little touched.

Mr. Shepherd did nought to call attention to himself. The question did come up in the roominghouse, as to what the arrangement might be between Mr. Shepherd and the Selective Service. The rest of us living there were women without family, or men who couldn't serve, for one reason or another. We thought Mr. Shepherd might have been found unfit for service, like so many his age. His slightly odd and solitary ways gave that impression, and his extremely slim build. He hardly had a scrap of meat on him. Many were the boys who had it so bad in the Depression, ten years later when called up for the draft, they failed the examination. Something inside them, the heart or teeth or legs, would be a little soft from so much hunger in the formative years. It was not just a few, either. It was thirty-nine percent of the young men called. I happen to know, for I was in secretarial service at the enlistment office. I saw all kinds, and for all I knew Mr. Shepherd was one of them. He was later called up to serve in the Civilian Public Service, but I will get to that.

To help pay his board at Mrs. Bittle's he cooked for the other boarders, six in all, including Mrs. Bittle. Every breakfast and supper, and noonday dinner on Sunday. That came about after the war started. He had a knack for making the ration-stamp books spread over the whole ration period. Mrs. Bittle was raised on silver spoons, hopeless at any kind of budget. She would collect the stamp books from all the boarders to get what she needed, yet by Saturday would be down to a jar of mustard and a box of Ralston cereal. She never could understand how it worked, though we tried to explain. She confused the one-point tokens with the ten-point stamps. Mr. Shepherd offered his help, and he was a whiz. He would take our A, B, and C stamps downtown on Mondays, adding everyone's meat points and so forth to get the best items first. Then sail through the week entire, with food to spare.

His trick was the fruits and vegetables. These weren't rationed, it was mainly the packaged goods, soups and canned meats and all such things they needed to send overseas. If the truth be known, Mrs. Bittle probably thought peas grew ready-frozen on the vine and cheese came from the Wej-Cut package, not a cow. But Mr. Shepherd said in Mexico every cook knew how to make from scratch. He could put a passel of red tomatoes into sauce as fast as Mrs. Bittle could have worked open a tin. In spring he planted greens, impinging on Mrs. Bittle's dahlias. She was queasy about that. The rest of us felt it a good bargain.

He looked like a scarecrow out there digging. One of the other boarders, Reg Borden, pointed out the window one time and said that. The boy was just so tall and thin, you'd have to say gaunt. And inside him, some kind of dread that went past the bashfulness. Not a workaday fear, no. He would rush in to clap a bowl over a mouse in the pantry, and once chased a sparrow from the house when it had Mrs. Bittle up on a chair. He would move a dresser any time you asked, manly in all such ways. But certain sudden things struck him dumb. He was shy of the sight of blood, and a loud sound unexpected would set his hand to trembling. A knife dropped on the floor could put such a haint over him, you would look all about for what ghost he'd seen. In summer months especially, he took spells of hardly leaving his room. Mrs. Bittle would suffer the cooking, and we all endured, saying, "Poor Mr. Shepherd has taken the grippe again." But knew very well it was no germ that had brought it on him. This is the truth, it could be anything or nothing, or just Reg Borden standing in the door with his raincoat on. There appeared to be no rhyme or reason.

Yet on most days he was like any broad-shouldered lad you'd ever known, with his manners and a sweet laugh. So fine for speaking, you asked him things just to hear what words he'd pick out in answer, for they'd be not the ones you expected. His face was pretty as a girl's, especially around the eyes. He had delicate hands despite the kitchen work, what people call "piano hands," though Mrs. Bittle had a piano and he didn't play a note.

Miss McKellar was sweet on him I believe, but all her offers to press his collars got her hands upon nothing but his shirts, so far as I know. Reg Borden was overly curious about his failure to serve. Reginald's own excuse was a glass eye. And Mr. Judd, of course too old. That poor man remained confused about which war was presently on the go. They needled Mr. Shepherd about not serving, and a foreigner in the house was something they frowned on behind his back, but Mrs. Bittle maintained he was not the bad type of foreigner, Jap or Italian. Germans she was queasy on, they ought to be bad she said, but of course they owned the hardware downtown, and no one saying you couldn't buy a ten-penny nail. In all, the men and Mrs. Bittle liked the cooking, and that swayed them.

They did press him on the lack of a fiancée, given his youth and vigor. Mr. Borden would raise this at supper, to Mr. Shepherd's mortification. I defended against the charge. I had been unwed all but one year of my life entire, and I informed the gentleman I could see the advantages. Miss McKellar had her theories: a broken heart or a girl back in Old Mexico. All we really knew of this young man was that he had a prior life in that country, and cooking was his talent, second only to making himself unseen.

To earn pocket money he taught Spanish lessons at the Asheville Teachers College, an establishment of good reputation where I also worked, up until the war. I was secretary to the administrator and recommended Mr. Shepherd to her as a person of decent character, which was all I knew. Spanish was a less fashionable language than French, so he only came to teach two days each week. He made no impression on the office staff.

His third talent was well hidden. For three years we all resided in the same house, passed in the upstairs hallway to use the bath, sat in matched parlor chairs on Monday evenings to hear *The Voice of Firestone* over NBC. And we never once saw him draw ink into a fountain pen. If he owned a typewriter I never heard it, and it's not a sound that gets past my ear. I know a Royal from a Smith-Corona from the next room. He wrote nothing in those years. This I know, for he later told me. He was dispirited of his past and stopped keeping the journals after everything was lost.

He'd brought up from Mexico a crate for a painting given him by Mrs. Kahlo, but hadn't opened it. That might seem strange to others. Not to me. He wasn't susceptible to suspense the way most are. If you gave him a package and said, Don't open that till Christmas, he wouldn't shake it. Something in his nature just did not expect good things in store. He set the crate in his wardrobe closet, leaving Mrs. Bittle to run the duster around it on her weekly rounds. There was no use in any of us having paintings. Mrs. Bittle wouldn't let us pound any nails. All pictures in the house were hers, the deceased Mr. Bittle fond of landscapes. So Mr. Shepherd's sat in the dark. I have asked him if he thought much about it. He said if ever he did, he pictured something alive in the crate, and once out, he dreaded he wouldn't have the heart to shut it back in the dark.

At the end of '43 he moved to his own house. A great event. Miss McKellar and I hung up crepe paper in the parlor and pooled our stamps to get him a set of sheets. What had happened prior, to make this possible, was that Mr. Shepherd got called up to do a war job. No, he never saw gunfire. He had the safest war job of the war, he said, which was: to oversee moving many shipments of famous pictures from the museum in Washington, D.C., to the Biltmore House. The Axis powers were having no end of amusement sinking ships and firing upon our coasts. Safety of our national treasures was the concern.

Mr. Shepherd was unsure how Uncle Sam had found him out for the task. When he'd applied at the Teachers College and was asked about previous employments, he listed "Consignment Marshal, moving art pieces to museums." He thought it more reputable than "cook" and a decent cause for traveling from Mexico. (He feared they'd think him a bandit.) Some way the word passed. The War Board knew everything about us in those days. The officers called up the galleries in New York and were surely impressed to learn his association with Mr. and Mrs. Rivera, highly famous. So Shepherd was their man. It took months to see it all through. They kept him on with the CPS for the duration but he rarely had to travel far, nor to any place more dangerous than a room of naked statues.

The job gave him means to set a payment on a two-story bungalow on Montford Avenue that had stood empty for years. It was close by the stop he took for the in-town bus to the library and he'd often taken little walks up that street, for it had a cemetery up at the end and a mental hospital with nice grounds. The empty house struck him in particular. He thought it had an aching look about it, and for that reason chose it. Up until then he'd felt underfoot in every house he ever lived in. Peace and quiet was his only wish.

Soon after moving, he pried the nails off the crate from Mrs. Kahlo to see his gift. Pandora's box you might say now, given everything that happened. The canvas itself was only some sketch she had snatched up from her bin, to carry out her plan. The gift was around the painting. There were the two crates, one inside the other, and the space between not stuffed with straw but paper, all the notebooks and typed pages taken from his room in Mexico after the murder. Hundreds of crumpled pages in all, needing to be smoothed and sorted out. But mostly all there.

Unbeknownst, Mr. Shepherd had been writing a book for years. He believed it had gone up in ash. But Mrs. Kahlo made the police not to destroy it. She was a powerful person evidently. Then hid the pages this way, not telling the author himself what he carried. Was it a trick on her friend, or did she only want to keep him safe? I can't say. But she was first to see what the world soon would, after he'd fixed it up, filled in the missing parts, written and rewritten and stewed over it until he could stew no more. In due time it came to the Stratford and Sons publishing house in New York. That was *Vassals of Majesty*. It came out in '45, before Christmas. That part is common knowledge, or ought to be.

So he was right about something alive in the crate, wanting out. Mrs. Kahlo did that for him. He'd about given up on life as a whole, going away on a train to the next world. If he didn't take one other thing, she wanted him carrying his words.

—VB

October 8, 1943
Asheville, North Carolina
Gringolandia

Dear Frida,
What you have done is a miracle. But how can any thanks be
enough? Just words, brought here and heaped at your feet like a
pile of cold mice with gnawed ears fetched in by a cat. You have
restored a life. You will see.

This morning a white cat appeared here on the back step,
and it seemed you must have sent her too. She didn't cry but
stood quietly, as if waiting for a well-known outcome. The
wind tugged fingers through the creature's coat, trying to un-
button the shaggy garment and pull it off. Think of how you
would paint this cat: with her insides exposed, the delicate rib
cage curved like a ring's setting around a bloody gem of car-
nivorous love. This is how she seemed. When the door opened
just a crack she slipped in, curling immediately on the hearth,
declaring with her eyes: "Ha, you thought I was helpless! I own
you now." Of course she is Frida.

But her name will be Chispa. She is a muse, the spark you
once accused me of having, now glowing quietly on this hearth.
Otherwise the house is still, keeping secrets. The floors are made
of the long, narrow hearts of trees brought down from mountain
slopes, the chimneys are stones rolled round as biscuits in the
Swannanoa River. The windows have interlaced panes like the
ones in your father's house, cracked here and there but holding.

The mitered oak doorsills are like deep wooden picture frames, each holding a perfect view of the next room, where walls are touched with light, and life could be waiting. The grain of the wood tells a story of years in the mountains, all the rains and droughts leading to the beginning of my life, when these trees were felled. The house was built the same year as my birth.

So we're well-matched companions, sheltering roof and solitary soul, crouched in a domestic forest of elms and maples. The other houses along this leafy street are also bungalows with gabled roofs and trussed eaves, an architecture that is here known as Arts and Crafts. It's the opposite in every way from Diego's beloved Functionalismo, nothing modern or shocking. Probably you would both find it boring. But now your mind's eye can see your old friend where he lives: making tamales in a kitchen of his own, with shining white tiles and green-painted trim. Picture him in stocking feet padding happily through golden rooms where bookcases reside directly in the walls, and amber lamps hang on chains from the ceiling. Then, picture him upstairs with your treasure glowing before his eyes, as in a storybook when the child lifts the lid of the magical trunk.

It is a good place, Carolina, built of mountains and river valleys. Did you receive the postcard? The tall buildings you see in it are full of banks and bakeries, the usual things. But look carefully at the background of the picture: mountains. They stand behind every view, like a mother offering a blanket in which to wrap everyday life and shelter it from useless dreads. In June they are walls of white rhododendron blossom. In autumn the forests set themselves aflame with color. Even winter has its icy charms. This you will refuse to believe. But you might like the changeable nature of this place, and its people, who have the modesty of Mexican villagers. The backyards here are divided by slim wire fences like tiny farm fields, and the women tending them shout across fence lines, "hollering" they call it, to

comment on the weather. They pin dungarees to clotheslines
and speak in a dialect that sounds like the plays of Shakespeare.
It isn't the Gringolandia you remember. You might not find it
as despicable as New York.

Congratulations on your successes there, especially the exhibition at Miss Guggenheim's. For you to be chosen among the
thirty-one most important women painters in the century must
make Diego proud, and you, jealous of the other thirty. The
man who wrote about you in *Vogue* was an idiot—of course
you don't have inferiority complexes or blood-obsession or anything like that. That man spent fifteen minutes looking at your
paintings. Could you drive a car for fifteen minutes, then write
a psychological analysis of Henry Ford? All right then, don't
think of it any more.

Have you agreed now to be a Surrealist? Because, as it happens, the French Relief Society intends to sponsor your paintings in their program on surrealism. Do you wonder how this
news reached your friend's ears? Who is the mysterious one
now, and how long will he make you burn with suspense? Not
very long. Here is the news: your former Shipping Shepherd
now holds the same post for the Civilian Corps, a wartime position overseeing movements of art treasures and government-
sponsored exhibits. The wage is forty dollars a week, every one
of them welcome. So you see it's only thanks to you: this job,
this house. These debts mount, all to you.

The real purpose of this letter is to acknowledge the debt
most infinite: for saving my notebooks and papers. Frida, you
always said the most important thing about any person is what
you don't know. Likewise, then, the most important part of any
story is the missing piece. What you gave me is everything. A
self, the simple *yo soy*, I am. I am saved. I drowned, it seemed,
and then came the light. Here I am.

I discovered it four days ago. I've only now opened the crate, for the first time. You must have wondered that I said nothing about it in the telegrams from New York. I remember mentioning the painting you gave me, thanking you in some duplicitous way. I'm sorry. You must think I had no curiosity about your gift. If you've already sent me to hell, it's fair enough, but you sent me for the wrong reasons. Disinterest in your work is not my crime; your paintings are thrilling. My faults lie elsewhere.

The truth of what you did, and what I now possess as a result (have possessed for three years without knowing) is slow to dawn. The last three mornings I've wakened to sense it arriving like a marvelous visitor coming on the train. I get dressed, I pace. I can't imagine how you bribed the police. I wonder how much of the manuscript you had time to read, and what you thought of it. But I ask for no more than what you've done already. You held faith in me as an artist. Not as a child, or servant, but as your peer. My pulse rushes, to think I will now have to earn that faith.

Here is the first step: I have got myself a typewriter. I own almost nothing else, due to the war shortages. My furniture is a few sad handprints of a foreclosed family: children's beds stripped of all but the narrow mattresses, an avuncular parlor chair with holes in its elbows. An electric stove, a wooden icebox that goes hungry for ice. (I'm told we'll get it in winter.) But my lair is the little upstairs room overlooking the street from beneath the gabled eave. My writing table is the bathroom door, taken off its hinges and set across two defunct radio cabinets I found in the alley. (Eviscerated in the last wire-and-copper drive.) And my prize: a typewriter gleaned from the rummage room at the school where I teach Spanish lessons. Probably the last such machine in the city, what with all the old ones melted down for bullets, or else urgently needed in North Africa and the Coral Sea, evidently, along with all sugar, cellulose tape, and ethyl gasoline. My relic lacks only a few of its keys, and with its help I plan to finish the book whose life you spared. It's the story we talked about, Cortés in the empire of the Azteca. The scandals of the ancients will be known.

Thank you also for the small stone figurine. I first found him lying on the bank, the day we had our picknick at Teotihuacán, while you napped. Please don't report my larceny to Dr. Gamio, or to Diego, who might be nationalistic on the subject of stolen art. (It would not bring me favor in my new employment.) This little fellow begged to be taken to a new world, after waiting two thousand years facedown in dirt. You abetted his wish. He sends his gratitude, mingled with mine, from where he now sits on my desk near the window, surveying the surprising scenery of Carolina.

Your astonished and grateful friend,

INSÓLITO

November 2, 1943

Dear Frida,

A glittering shower falls at a slant across my window. Some form of god has come to visit our dark autumn tunnel, like Zeus making himself a beam of light to impregnate Danae. In this case, it is not really glittering light but beech leaves. You've never seen anything as dramatic as these American trees, dying their thousand deaths. The giant beech next door intends to shiver off every hair of its pelt. The world strips and goes naked, the full year of arboreal effort piling on the sidewalks in flat, damp strata. The earth smells of smoke and rainstorms, calling everything to come back, lie down, submit to a quiet, moldy return to the cradle of origins. This is how we celebrate the Day of the Dead in America: by turning up our collars against the scent of earthworms calling us home.

Mexico rules my kitchen, as you know. The *pan de muerto* is rising there now, filling the house with a yellow scent, reminding me how you shaped yours like skulls sprinkled with sugar. My neighbors wouldn't care to see such things delivered on a plate. They celebrate the Day of the Dead very strangely here: they make pumpkins into heads with flaming eyes, and the children run about the neighborhood asking for cookies. But these urchins showed up two days early! Now that the cookies are made, the children seem finished with the whole thing. They have smashed the pumpkin-heads to orange gruel on the sidewalks. The cat may have to help eat the *pan de muerto*. In remembering the dead, one more this year: your father. Old Guillermo, how could he not still be there? Walking slowly around your house, blinking his huge eyes as he enters each room, not seeing the furniture but the angles of light on the floor.

Your grief is reasonable, but it's no good to hear you're a wreck from head to toe. Tuberculosis of the bones makes me shiver. It's like the season's last tomato that sat in a bowl in the kitchen this week, and when taken up to be sliced, collapsed to a limp sac of foul juice—its beautiful plump skin was hiding rot. Frida, you must feel tricked this way by your body. Even your cures sound like diseases, electricity and calcium therapy. But your doctors are good men, especially Dr. E. in San Francisco, who sounds kind. These surgeries are sure to be successful. You will have many more days like this one for remembering, and without number, *abrazos* from your friend,

SÓLI

May 21, 1944

Dear Frida,

This Sunday morning bright images of you keep nudging into my solitary confinement, urging me to write after the long silence. Here is a strange beetle, trapped inside the window near the desk. He bombs his head continually against the glass, distracting the revision of an unwieldy chapter: "The garrison stormed, heads all smashed!" This little bombardier wears a stunning uniform, emerald green with copper-colored linings to his wings, and a respectable proboscis. Words do the thing no justice. You would do better, if you saw it. You could put it in a painting.

And next: every young girl passing by on the sidewalk to catch the Haywood bus, another distraction. They're all Fridas! Since the weather turned warm they all wear peasant clothes, colorful skirts and blouses with ruffled shoulders. They don't wear their skirts long as you do because it's unlawful here, punishable by a fine. I vow it's true, fabric-conservation order. Not enough uniforms to cover all the boys at the front. The War Production Board announced also last week, no blouse may have more than one ruffle per sleeve. I thought you might like to know that, as you sit somewhere in your thousand ruffles reading this, flashing gold teeth—metal that could be used in some alloy for artillery casings, come to think of it. You can't come here, you would be confiscated.

Your despair over the war is understandable. I undertake this letter to cheer you with another view of things. The gringos are embracing the antifascist fight with whole hearts, and that surely must be good, even if it's many years late in the opinion of your friends who first went to fight fascism in Spain. But you should see the Yanks now, swearing unity with people from across borders just as you and Diego used to do, raising your glasses, singing "The Internationale" while we tried to clear the plates. I keep wondering what Lev would make of these times. He would abhor Roosevelt's friendly partnership with Marshal Stalin as our two countries lean shoulder-to-shoulder in battle. But wouldn't he agree with the president, that sacrifice must be made toward the ideal? Our GIs have genuinely rescued the Soviet State, scurrying tons of supplies across the Persian desert to save the starving Russians. And now Stalin's army returns the favor, beating back Hitler on the Eastern Front. A year ago all seemed lost, the Axis was unstoppable in Europe or the Pacific. Now some say this war could be won.

If so, then the victory will belong to housewives as well as soldiers, because every one here is part of the fight. To you the war is useless destruction, a match played out over the wireless, but here it is the organizing principle of our days. If cloth is in short supply, the girls will wear only one ruffle per sleeve, no more, and no fuss. If the Axis sank eight million tons of warships last year, so be it, these ladies will hand over what appears to be eight million tons of hairpins, let the tresses fall where they may. The neighbor children use rocks to bang old hinges from gates for the metal drives, war brides turn in their silver, grandfathers their bronze-tipped canes. Sacrifice is a sacrament. How we all cheered when Howard Hughes's new factory turned out a battleship just twenty-four days after laying its keel! This man Hughes drew my mother to her death, years ago when his stunt flight landed in Mexico City. But however I may miss her, I harbor no grudge as I watch him now, welding together the *John Fitch* from pieces of my neighborhood. All as one, with hairpins and paper clips, we vanquish Hirohito and his Mitsubishi warship factory.

The war is on every page of every magazine. Even in the advertisements, which strangely don't encourage buying now, but the opposite. Manufacturers fly the "E" flag to show their whole production is needed for war use. Buy nothing but war bonds, give your blood to the Red Cross. "Follow doctor's advice to the letter and keep appointments brief," my magazine warns, because half our doctors are in the forces, leaving the home-front men with twice as many to care for. Travel for emergencies only. After victory is won, they promise us the world: a new model of radio, automobiles with synthetic rubber tires, things yet unseen by civilian eye. But for now, don't ask even for a Dot fastener, and good luck finding butter or cheese with your ration stamps. Bacon has vanished from our land. So have new cars, not one this year for civilians, and if you already have one it wears an "A" stamp on its windscreen, for "Almost Empty"—gasoline is rationed. Horse droppings have made a bold comeback on Pack Square. One old cog on my street has roused his Stanley Steamer. He came through yesterday and a neighbor lady fainted, thinking it was an air attack. The new American motto is, "We make do with nothing new," no wristwatches, new shirts, or bedsheets, it's about the same plan as the church: endure your suffering to win a golden hereafter.

You would not believe how cheerfully the people accept this deprivation. It makes them feel brave and important. Rich or poor, the banker's wife and the secretary bring the same ration book to market and leave with the same goods. It isn't the bourgeois Gringolandia you knew, women throwing parties while homeless men starved outside. Now they all agree with your Rosa Luxemburg, "The highest idealism in the interests of the whole." Women here consent to strict rations even on food and shoes for their children. The neighbor family has seven boys, named Romulus, Virgil, and the like, running about in cloth shoes and making toys from roadside litter. Yet their mother calls out to me every day, "Mr. Shepherd, is it not a bless-ed morning?" Another neighbor brought me an "apple pie" made from crackers (she fears a bachelor will starve), and explained how we are to make up our beds: turn the bottom hem to the top every other week to distribute wear and make the sheets last. We can win the war while we sleep!

This way of thinking can be bracing. They view the future as a house they can build with hammers and planks, rather than a ripening fruit that might go rotten due to unexpected natural forces. You warned me not to let Mexican writers make my heart go cold, do you remember? In the hospital. We were speaking of *Los de Abajo*, the scene comparing the revolutionary fight to a rock rolling downhill, moved only by senseless gravity. You said, if I threw a party to cheer myself up, not to invite any writers.

But Americans crave a different story: they believe the rock could roll uphill instead of down. Probably you won't listen to this, but it's not such a bad way of thinking. A writer here could finish a whole book without wanting to drink poison. Even the story of Cortés has its invigorating theme of self-made destiny. People are much in the mood these days for soaring hearts and the clash of battle.

Here in the house of my father, as you called this country, I watch carefully, wondering if this might be a home at last. The land of the square deal and the working stiff, said my old dad. So I square up the corners of my desires, and work at pounding keys until my fingers are stiff as wooden splinters. Frida, someone here may want what I can give. See how that pronoun now stands in the lines I write, tall and square-shouldered. I strive for the stout American declarative, so entirely unaccustomed: I am.

My packet of contraband pages has nearly become a book. The old typewriter grinds its metal jaws, the battle is nearly over. Cortés took the city in the end, I'm sorry to say. I was tempted to revise history, give Mexico City back to the Azteca. But without these four hundred years of oppression, what would Diego paint on his murals? I decided to salvage, mainly for your sakes, the eventual necessity of the Mexican Revolution.

Now I ask your advice. I wonder whether you or Diego may know someone in New York who would look at this poor manuscript, once it has been wrestled to its death. It will need to go somewhere. The mess of papers can't be kept here much longer, spreading like a pox across the floors, terrifying the cat. I must exercise vigilance, or one book might even become two.

I send affection to you and Diego, and also Perpetua, if she does perpetuate. If you have any news of Natalya and Seva, it would be welcome.

Your friend,

INSÓLITO

June 30, 1944

Dear Frida,

Thank you for the name of your friend in New York. Mr. Morrison will someday regret your indiscretion, as he is sure to hear from me. Diego's miseries are worrisome; the struggle to build his rock temple-museum in the Pedregal sounds more surreal than anything in your French exhibit. Nothing he does will ever be small. Your failure to mention your own health I will take as good news, and assume the surgeries in California were successful. I'm sorry Natalya hasn't communicated, but there could be many reasons for it, given the wrecked state of everything in France, and no direct post between France and Mexico. But even so, the movement for socialist democracy seems to be rising from the ashes, with labor now on the march against Vichy in Paris, if the news of this can be trusted. Lev would find some way to be hopeful, even for poor France.

The time with Lev and Natalya seems so distant, I'm startled when any traces of it surface. In the magazine photograph enclosed, look and you'll see two of the New York boys who worked as guards for Lev. Charlie and Jake, you remember them. I practically jumped when I spotted them, right across the page from Mary Martin holding her Calox tooth powder. The picture is a peace meeting at the Carnegie Music Hall where a few hundred gathered to demand armistice. The article I haven't enclosed, but you know the kind of thing: "in attendance were Trotskyites, Teamsters, Socialist professors and old-line Quakers, the crackpot fringes of public opinion, hoping to arouse draft resistance while praying for an easy way out." In other words, the kind of thing you and your friends do on a normal Friday noon, without the praying. People here are the same as in Mexico, their passions bristle in every direction. And the presses are the same also. No reporter worth his buttons will let the facts intrude on a good story.

The newsreels that frightened you in California were of the same ilk, I'm sure. The aim is to terrify us. Not to be outdone by a giant ape climbing a skyscraper, they'll have the quiet Japanese fellow next door harboring clandestine treachery. If you saw a movie star telling about the gardener putting poison on her vegetables, it was only an entertainment set ahead of the main feature. Like Diego eating flesh. You know these howlers. You've had their noise in your ears since the day you married a famous man, and still you do as you please. Don't listen to nonsense, Frida. The idea of putting American Japanese in concentration camps is fantastical. You shouldn't worry so much.

Have faith in our Mr. Roosevelt, who has everyone bucked up. People here salute him as the flag, since most have only ever seen the one flag, or the one president. He came to office when I was only a boy at the Academy, imagine it. In those days his name was a schoolboy joke, scented with roses, but now he is our own kind of Lenin, charting the new American Revolution. Even the Communists here supported him in the last election. No one can argue against guarantees of useful work and protection from old-age hardship. Now he has even imposed a tax on businesses so they can't profit from the war, and he regulates food prices so everyone gets a fair share. We subordinate ourselves to the national good!

Your old friend,

INSÓLITO

Los Angeles Herald and Express, *June 1, 1943*

Nips Still Roam the Coast

Special to Hearst News

Former fruit-and-vegetable stands sit empty, their piles rotted away, but a contamination is not yet scoured from our city. The Dies Committee today released a report noting 40,000 dangerous persons are still at large, more than a year after Order 9066 of the Western Defense Command routed foreign- and American-born Japs to detention centers in the central states. The report contains evidence of espionage rings in which many, if not all, Japanese "fishermen" and "truck farmers" used their merchant status in our country as a cloak for approaching strategic facilities.

Military command keeps watch on more than 100,000 evacuees now residing in detention camps, where observers have noted the detainees care little whether this country or Japan wins the war. Yet the Justice Department is still considering an appeal to release certain detainees professing "loyalty" into non-war jobs. Our Western States oppose the move with a single voice. Senator Hiram Johnson vowed yesterday the

War Department will not allow resettlement of one single Jap in coastal states, pointing out that most residents here would have them shipped to Tojo after the war ends.

No Californian need be reminded of the incendiary bombs dropped on Ft. Stevens and the Pacific forests last year, or the shelling of the Goleta refinery whose flames engulfed our city in terror. The warships of Dai Nippon lurk in plain view off our coast, with pilots ready to fly on the "kamikaze wind" to meet their targets, heinously exchanging life itself for a promise of immortality. But few realize the number of such inimical persons still hiding in the Pacific states under civilian guise.

In a statement to Hearst News today, General John L. DeWitt declared, "We ignore the Dies Committee report at our peril." Describing the adversary's nefarious character he said, "Racial affinities are not severed by migration. The Japanese are an enemy race, and while many of those born on U.S. soil have become 'Americanized,' the racial strains are undiluted." In a recent conference with the Secretary of War, DeWitt cited undisclosed indications of a Nip conspiracy prepared for action. The fact that no violent outburst has yet taken place, he explained, is a confirming indication of such actions soon to be taken.

Whether of alien or American birth, Japs remain banned from our coast until the final surrender. The rightful place of all such persons is detention in the desolate interior. Responding to rumors of release, the Governor's office promised full security for our citizens. "We afford no quarter to those whose presence is inimical to the public safety. Our tolerance of their kind is revoked. Their property has been dispensed, their business contracts cancelled and bank accounts forfeited. FBI agents stand ready to conduct search and seizure raids on homes or businesses suspected of harboring aliens."

To US citizens this comes as welcome news. While Americans face death from fascist bullets overseas, the Justice Department has leaned over backward to preserve the right of free speech in wartime, opening the gates to those who would spread lies and propaganda behind the lines at home.

This report has been submitted for clearance by the Army and Navy.

The New York Times, December 13, 1941

2,541 Axis Aliens Now in Custody

Biddle Says List Includes 1,370 Japanese, 1,002 Germans and 169 Italians

Special to The New York Times

WASHINGTON, Dec. 12—Up to Thursday night the Justice Department had arrested 2,541 German, Japanese and Italian citizens in the roundup of dangerous aliens which got under way with the outbreak of war between Japan and the United States, Attorney General Francis Biddle said tonight. Of these 1,002 are Germans, 1,370 Japanese, and 169 Italians.

Mr. Biddle emphasized that although they were regarded as "dangerous to the peace and safety of the nation," Axis subjects under arrest "represented only a small fraction of the more than 1,100,000 Axis nationals residing in the United States."

"Arrests were limited to persons whose activities have been under investigation by the FBI for some time," said Mr. Biddle.

Aides declared that none of the prisoners would be interned throughout the war except where there is "strong reason to fear for the internal security of the United States."

The Justice Department issued a warning that any Japanese, German or Italian citizen found in possession of a camera, regardless of the use to which it was put, faced loss of his equipment and possible detention. Axis citizens already had been ordered not to make airplane flights of any kind.

26 More Aliens Taken Here

The round-up of potential saboteurs, spies and enemy aliens here brought in twenty-six more prisoners yesterday. Sixteen were German, six Japanese and five Italian. Those arrested yesterday also were taken to Ellis Island and turned over to agents of the Bureau of Immigration and Naturalization. As usual, Federal Bureau of Investigation officials refused to comment.

William H. Marshall, assistant director of emigration and naturalization, said that 553 enemy aliens have been rounded up since Sunday. The figures included those seized in places adjacent to New York City. All enemy aliens were barred by the Civil Aeronautics Authority from riding in commercial, government or private airplanes.

The State Labor Department pointed out that enemy aliens were not entitled to receive unemployment insurance, as the law provides that the payments can be made only to persons "available for work."

The large plaque in front of the Italian Building, 626 Fifth Avenue, was covered yesterday.

September 12, 1944

Dear Frida,
Thank you for sending the clippings. Forgive me for doubting you, this is terrifying news and not well known in these parts. If nothing on earth is new, these howlers are the proof. People will be made afraid at any cost.

Your Insólito remains a muddled assembly of two nations, settled for now in the house of his father, puzzling over its construction. By day we whistle "The Internationale" and reach right across the world to our comrades. My neighbor knits stockings for the orphans of Moscow. But by night the neighborhood bolts its doors and looks beneath the beds for an alien menace. Yet I stake a claim, I am here, for I must be somewhere. But only as a child it seems, struggling to understand what every wife and gentleman passing on the street seems to know by rote. Whom to love, whom to castigate.

The only certainty in my own household is: the novel is finished. I feel a peculiar sadness, like missing a lively, quarrelsome friend who has ended his long visit. These days I purse my lips at the mirror and wonder how it is that other men find first-class reasons to shave, change out of pajamas, and leave the house, practically every day.

Your friend Mr. Morrison recommended an editor who sheds a glimmer of interest in looking at the thing. His response has forced me outdoors three days in a row, blinking like an owl, in search of an envelope or packaging to carry the manuscript to New York. This effort may take longer than writing the book. Stationer's stores no longer have even enough paper for the standard sign declaring their product has gone to the front. The editor may be spared his trouble, due to the paper shortage. Probably the manuscript itself should be heaved over in the next paper drive, as ballast for a warship.

I send you two clippings in return, from earlier in the summer. Our town's newspaper is rationed to twice-weekly editions, but this article merited precious fiber—note the date, our shared birthday. You'll remember I wrote you about this beetle. The other page I tore from a respectable magazine (*Life*, how comprehensive!), enclosed mainly for its spectacular photograph. Like Cortés, I report back to my Queen on a new world wondrous strange. *Feliz cumpleaños*, my friend, from America where we make do with nothing new.

Abrazos,

SÓLI

Life Magazine, *July 17, 1944*

Japanese Beetle:
Voracious, Libidinous, Prolific

by Anthony Standen

Japanese beetles, unlike the Japanese, are without guile. There are, however, many parallels between the two. Both are small but very numerous and prolific, as well as voracious, greedy and devouring. Both have single-track minds. Both are inscrutable, the beetles particularly, for no one can say why they should be attracted by yellow when most of their food is green, nor why they rush avidly to geraniums—the smell of geraniums is used to bait the traps—when geraniums are poisonous to them. The beetles, however, are firmly settled on our middle Atlantic coast, where they chew up apples, peaches, grapes, roses, pasture grass and other useful or agreeable vegetable matter to the tune of $7,000,000 every year, and threaten to become rampant over the greater part of the entire country. Long ago we declared war on them, and though we have little chance of total victory—which would mean exterminating every single beetle on our shores—we may hope to achieve a more limited success, with the insects so harassed and persecuted that their numbers would be kept within decency's limit, although their character would never be changed.

The Asheville Trumpet, *July 6, 1944*

Kamikaze Peril Reaches Asheville

by Carl Nicholas

They are small, crafty, and breed unceasingly. They are driven to fly viciously into their targets, creating immense destruction. The Japanese Beetle has moved down our coast and arrived at our very door. These odd-looking green insects pose a threat to plant life and domestic tranquility alike.

"They fly all over my washing," said Mrs. Jimmy Hyder, a housewife recently sighted on Charlotte Street mounting her offensive. Sons Harold and Alter led the infantry with badminton rackets, and Mrs. Hyder followed with the pump-atomizer, dousing the battlefield with insecticide. Weekly sprayings may tip the balance against the enemy, but Mrs. Hyder complains, "They'll keep on flying into you for no good reason, down to the last one." She warned other Victory Gardeners to expect heavy losses from the enemy this year, especially in the tomatoes and runner beans.

Scientists call the greedy beast "Popillia japonica." The Agriculture Department believes they first sneaked into the country near New Jersey, some years prior to Pearl Harbor, concealed in a crate of fruit. The sly grubs hide under ground in winter, emerging famished and keen to ply their destruction in the warmer months. Their fiendish campaign has now reached the Western Carolinas, spoiling orchards worth many thousand dollars.

Wives and gardeners beware. Though badminton rackets fly on Charlotte Street, Mr. Wick Bentsen of the County Extension Service says no weapons yet devised have been found to stop this Japanese invasion.

———

Mr. Lincoln Barnes, Editor
Stratford and Sons Publishers, New York
December 11, 1944

Dear Mr. Barnes,
The sum you have proposed is overwhelmingly generous.

The changes you suggest in the story will render it much improved. However, I'm not able to consult the pages you mentioned, as the book rests entirely in your hands. You have the only copy. (The envelope also may be the sole issue of its litter.) Paper remains scarce here. Any shortages in supply lines at the

German Bulge were not due to failure of enthusiasm for the paper and scrap drives in Asheville, North Carolina. Thus, it would be useful to have the manuscript returned for corrections, at your convenience.

Your letter made reference to my secretary-typist, to whom you plan to forward more notations. Be assured, the secretary-typist will be in intimate contact with the author, the telephone receptionist, cook, and housekeeper, as we all presently inhabit the same four-dollar shoes. With clothing-ration coupons as they are, it's a useful arrangement.

Gratefully,

HARRISON W. SHEPHERD

December 21

Stalin sixty-five years old today. A panting reporter on the radio said he is the Russian Tom Paine rolled together with Paul Bunyan. Lev would now be sixty-four, but isn't. Revolutions are constantly reborn, he used to say, and men like Stalin never die.

February 1

Tonight's news: the Allies broke open the dikes along the Netherlands coast, letting in the sea and drowning thousands of German soldiers in the flood. Like the Azteca opening dikes to drown Cortés and his men on the shores of Lake Tenochtitlan. But fiction is nonsense, the war is real. Tomorrow the farmers of Walcheren will wake to see a tide standing over their crops, the floating corpses of their cattle, every tree in the land scalded dead by the salt on its roots. The glory of war is so frequently disappointing.

Too much solitude here, pent up with ghosts, and nowhere to go to escape them. The man in the street selling ice from a truck today had a pick, nearly like the one that murdered Lev. This was the month he dreaded most. Its visitations.

February 10
A better day, the manuscript set aside awhile in favor of honest work, as Lev would call it. Painted the dining room, the wainscot between the battens, war surplus paint but a decent color, flannel gray. The neighbor kindly donated an old dining table she doesn't use, and a son's Saturday help for the painting. A regular Tom Sawyer. Paid him two bits, but suspect he'd rather have had the dead rat and string to swing it with.

April 5, 1945

Dear Frida,
Your letter was welcome, even if it didn't carry much good news. It is so much better to think of you stomping down the street with skirts roiling, not in a wheelchair. This is a hateful revision. You and Diego should be marching with banners in Paseo de la Reforma this week, protesting the compromises of the Chapultepec Conference.

We are much less in the news here than Mexico City, but our headlines may entertain: Production lines at Asheville Casket Company have gone idle today (dead silent!) as workers go on strike, flouting their war duties, pending negotiations between management and the Upholsterers Union.

Next: the writer William Sidney Porter, or what is left of him, may be dug up from the cemetery in this very neighborhood, for relocation to Greensboro. The city of Asheville has leveled a protest, believing Mr. Porter to be comfortable where he is. The courts will decide. One hopes that no reupholstering will be required at this time.

Admiral Halsey came to the Grove Park for some sport-hunting: finally, a story involving no death. And fashion is alive: Lilly Daché has worked out how to make civilian Easter bonnets from 76,000 WAC hats discarded by the army in favor of the cloth overseas cap. Much on display here last Sunday. You would like gringo Easter: every woman, even the grayest little pigeon, finds the courage to be a Frida for the day.

Not much personal news. The wisteria vines that climb the sides of my house and twine from the eaves are in full purple bloom, the color of jacaranda. Do you ever hear from Van? A question asked, but truly no answer is wanted. A French instructor here at the Teachers College, a particular Miss Attwood, has lately kept up a long campaign to be taken to the movies. With all presentable men at the front, she feels that a fellow should accept his duty to take a girl to see *The Picture of Dorian Gray*. The idea of a crowded theater makes me shudder. Sometimes leaving the house at all becomes a frightful thing, I carry an inexplicable dread inside that never completely abates. But Miss Attwood would not be refused. Hurd Hatfield made a gratifying Dorian, despite his treachery toward Sibyl Vane and Gladys Hallward. Duty seems fulfilled, all quiet on the Attwood front this week.

At the end of term the Teachers College will close. Your language will cease to be maligned by the Carolina tongue. Its only advocate in Asheville will happily stay home in his vine-covered cottage, as his former pupils turn to parachute-packing and the like. These girls are so much like Mother, with their gum-cracking confidence and feral vocabularies. *Holy Joe! Oh nausea! He's oolie droolie!* But Mother would be old by now, nearly fifty. How she would wail over that, if she were still here. Probably it's a charity that she is not.

Last item: the book is to be published late this year by Stratford and Sons Publishers, New York. The editor, Mr. Barnes, confirmed it today. He wants it titled *Vassals of Majesty*, which is silly, as the characters are vassals of cupiditas and greed. The original title was meant to be *Ten Leagues from Where We Sleep*, as it's about men who find themselves always marching short of their own and everyone else's expectation, including the reader's. But Mr. Barnes says that title has too many words in it. No matter. Stratford has mailed a check for two hundred dollars, an advance payment upon royalties to be received, and if they can find the paper they mean to print up copies by the thousand. A terrifying miracle. These words were all written in dark, quiet rooms. How can they face the bright, noisy world?

You must know. You open your skin and pour yourself on a canvas. And then let the curators drape your intestines all around the halls, for the ruckus of society gossips. Can it be survived?

Your friend,

SÓLI

April 13, 1945
Roosevelt is dead. The end came out of a clear sky. Pen in his hand one moment, then dropped to the floor as his secretary watched—it must have been like seeing Lev's bright light go out. Truly, this is like the death of Lenin: a personality fused with the national purpose, struck down by a cerebral stroke, leaving his nation's purpose standing in its shirtsleeves, wondering what under heaven to do.

All last night in south Asheville a crowd stood along the tracks in the cold, hoping to see the catafalque and coffin inside the lighted car when the cortege passed through. The president could only get to Washington from Warm Springs, they thought, by passing through our valley. But no train came. The news extra this morning said the route was through Greeneville. But some still wait, mostly women with children. In a valley east of Oteen they say a hundred Negro women clearing tobacco ground have been kneeling since yesterday with hands outstretched toward the railroad track. They won't go home.

And now Harry Truman has taken the oath, in his polka-dot tie. He hardly looks the part of Man Fused with the National Purpose. He told the newsmen, "Did you ever have a bull or a load of hay fall on you? If you ever did, you know how I felt last night."

Sometimes history cleaves and for one helpless moment stands still, like the pause when the ax splits a log and the two halves rest on end, waiting to fall. Lev used to say that. So it was after Lenin died, Lev riding his train toward the Caucasus, unaware the ax had fallen on his friend. That Stalin was mounting the funeral platform to capture the panicked crowds. This may be one of those times again, when history moves toward darkness or light. Which face in the newsprint photographs now conceals treachery? Are tyrants working behind blackout shades, sending a false cable to someone on a train, conniving to keep reason at a distance while power makes its move? People are sore afraid, ready to believe anything.

May 8, 1945

The world did not end. Or if so, for the Germans only. Everyone came outside to hear the fire-siren blow at 6:01 signaling midnight in Germany, official end to the firing of weapons. Women in front yards drying their hands on aprons, telling the boys to stop shooting one another with sticks and be still. On Haywood Street the clerks and grocers closing up shop all stood perfectly still through that moment, the length of the siren, looking up at the sky. The reflected sunset blazed in the glass storefronts behind them. Some put hands over their hearts, and all of them faced east. Toward Europe.

No one knows what to do with this peace. When the horns went quiet, every person on Haywood, without a word spoken, turned to look the other way. Japan.

❀

The neighbor boy, whose name is not Tom Sawyer but the even more improbable Romulus, picked a strange flower from the Montford Hill woods and brought it here for identification. He says his mother believed it was a bad animal part that should not be touched. But the father said it's a plant, ask the fellow next door. They suspect me of having an education. We mounted a Library Expeditionary Force and struck out boldly. Victory was ours, Bartram's *Flora of the Carolinas* had full color plates of the specimen in question. It is a "Pink Lady's Slipper." Romulus was gravely disappointed to hear it.

August 20, 1945

Five years this day. Since Lev last saw sunlight. Or said the words *my son*, the only one ever to do so. His look of mischief, when handing over a newly discovered novel. The last fleeting plea over his shoulder before going in with Jacson, *Save me from this lad!* The white cuffs soaked like bandages, drops of blood falling on white paper, these images have receded, mostly gone. But then one appears, startling as a stranger standing in the corner of a room where you'd thought yourself alone. Memories do not always soften with time; some grow edges like knives. He should still be living. Murder has the weight of an unpaid debt, death as unfinished business.

No room in the house was safe today, the radio no distraction, obscenely it reported a brutal murder in the south of the city, at one of the tanneries. The teakettle screaming in the kitchen was Natalya saying his name. A sound can transform itself exactly in the brain.

The library seemed it might be a safer place, but it was not. Upstairs in the newspaper room, the curled edges of papers lay in deep layers on tables stacked with books. His desk, all those unfinished sentences. The wax cylinders that still hold his voice, somewhere. His desk calendar, if it is there, lies open to August 20, the page he last turned over, with life's full and ordinary expectation. The thought of that brought a crumpling grief, kneeling in the upstairs stacks waiting for something inside to burst and flood the maple floorboards. Blood seeping darkly between the cracks.

Hell is falling from the skies. A reporter for the *Times* rode in the plane as a witness, wondering at zero hour whether he should feel sad for "the poor devils about to die." He decided no, it was a fair exchange for Pearl Harbor. The army's plan was to drop this bomb on a different Japanese city that morning, a different set of men and dogs and schoolchildren and mothers, but the thick clouds over that city refused to part. Growing tired of circling and waiting, the bomber pilots flew southward down the channel and chose Nagasaki, thanks to its clear skies.

For want of a nail the shoe was lost, for want of a cloud, the world was lost.

Your blood for mine. If not these, then those. War is the supreme mathematics problem. It strains our skulls, yet we work out the sums, believing we have pressed the most monstrous quantities into a balanced equation.

September 2, 1945

V-J Day. If a typewriter did not have these two letters, today it would have been a useless object. The newspaper headlines could only have been larger if they'd found a way to write "JAPS SURRENDER" down the page lengthwise instead of across the top. Hallelujah, Hirohito has fallen on his knees.

During one of the many church victory picnics, a little girl drowned in the Swannanoa. Romulus came over this evening to sit on the porch swing and tell about it, for he was there: the girl in white hair ribbons gone missing, the hours of searching, then finding her on the river's sandy bottom, where the water was not very deep. He told it all and then was quiet. We could hear music of some celebration still going, all the way from Pack Square. Romulus said he couldn't tell whether it was a good day or a bad one.

MacArthur says the great tragedy has ended. We turned on the wireless, and the assured voices seemed to bring the boy back around. This man MacArthur rode horses once, cheered on by a pack of boys not much older than Romulus. Sometimes playing polo behind the academy, other times commanding bayonets into the breasts of the Bonus Marchers. "The skies no longer rain death," he said now. "Men walk upright in the sunlight and the entire world lies quietly at peace." MacArthur claimed he spoke for thousands of silent lips, forever stilled among the jungles and in the deep waters of the ocean. But how could he speak for so many silent lips lying blue beneath the water? Little fish are surely pecking at them now, nourished by worlds of misfortune.

November 19

Dear Frida,

Here is a small gift, my book, just arrived from New York. Mr. Barnes says it will begin turning up in the bookshops by Friday week, but he sent me two with a note: "A spare copy for your Mother and Dad!" The cover art is quite something, as you'll see, with the twin temples of Tlaloc and Huitzilopochtli in the distance. The flames and thinly clad women running from the conquering army should make up for any archaeological inexactness. This format, I was told, worked well for *Gone With the Wind*.

No one here knows of my impending status as a published author. The neighbor ladies find me suspiciously lacking in ambition or family. Miss Attwood still rings up; few soldiers are home yet, so she makes do with nothing new. Last week we went to a restaurant called Buck's, opened recently to wild enthusiasm, which wraps up your meal like parcel post and sends it out to the gravel car park while you wait. The idea is to picnic inside your auto, staring at other strangers with catsup on their chins and napkins draped on the steering wheels. You would bawl. It is called a drive-in. Now we can buy gasoline, food, and soon we'll have new autos too. Why not make use of all at once?

The war's end has left America with loads of get-up-and-go, and no place to send it. Also war-bond cash saved and nothing to spend it on. Unless we need hollow-lead tubing and field-combat boots, as that's what the factories are geared for making. We still use ration stamps for almost everything. Truman is trying to keep price controls on until shortages abate, but the manufacturers can smell hoarded cash. They're parading ad men through Congress to convince the lawmakers that Free Market is the way to go, and that Harry Truman is in league with Karl Marx. The neighbor ladies here are firm on the side of Harry and Karl Marx, they know price controls are the only thing standing between ourselves and the twenty-dollar steak. I confess to an unpatriotic yearning to buy a refrigerator, but if a Philco showed up in town now without its OPA ration tag, it would go to Mrs. Vanderbilt for the cost of my mortgage.

Meanwhile, the husbands concoct a black market with more plot twists than the Codex Boturini. Romulus, my young informant, reports his dad went to the car dealer's to finagle a new Ford, not yet legally for sale. He was told if he bought the salesman's dog for eight hundred dollars, they would give him a free car to drive the pup home. Romulus cheered. But he was in it for the dog.

One thing can be had without a stamp, though, and that's my book. Please feel no moral duty to read it, you've done enough. Only look for the dedication page, where you'll see a familiar name. I apologize for the title. Mr. Barnes says *Vassals of Majesty* sounds like a book people want to read, and it's his business to know. What would you do? If a museum curator said your paintings should be hung on both sides with pink organdy curtains? Oh yes, I remember, you would poke him in the eye with a paintbrush and tell him to hang organdy curtains over his dog's-ass face.

Lacking your courage, I avoid disagreements with the company that buys my bread and butter, and possibly a Philco. I am getting on fine, with no complaints at all about my new country except that it has no olives worth eating and no peppers fit for adults. This package holds the proof of my incomprehensible good fortune. Use it at the bottom of your door to stop a draft, and know that I am—
Your grateful friend,

H. W. SHEPHERD, *author*

December 5
The first snow of the season fell today on two hundred women standing in a queue on Haywood Street, after an announcement that nylon stockings would be available one-per-customer at Raye's Department Store.

One block down at the bookshop, a single copy of *Vassals of Majesty* was handled by several different customers in the course of the morning. Each conducted a close inspection of the Indian maids fleeing through flames on the dust jacket. No lines formed on the sidewalk, no Philco this year.

Kingsport News, *January 12, 1946*

Book Review

by United Press

The modern reader complains that theatrics have all gone to the movies. Where is the old-fashioned barnburner to carry us away? Here is one to fit the bill. Harrison Shepherd's *Vassals of Majesty* (Stratford and Sons, $2.39) tells of a golden age when Spanish Conquistadors fought for the New World. Cortez plays out as a winning villain, lining his pockets in the name of Church and Queen while paying no heed to the trials endured by his men. The weak-minded Emperor Montezuma makes hardly a better impression, doting on his captive birds while his bloodthirsty chiefs do their worst.

The princes in this story are the common soldiers, pushed to the limits but revealing true humanity. The story's droll assertion: heroes may be less than heroic, while the common man saves the day.

The Evening Post, *January 18, 1946*

"Books for Thought," by Sam Hall Mitchell

Gee, but I Want to Go Home

If you're weary of the military tribunals of Goering and Hess, their grisly details dragging on, try this one on for size: chieftains who cut out the hearts of war-prisoners while still beating! The year is 1520. The place, a glittering city on a lake where the last Aztec emperor meets his mortal enemy Cortés. The book is *Vassals of Majesty*, a plush first effort from author Harrison Shepherd. Swords clash on every page in this clever retelling of the conquest of Mexico's richest empire.

Greed and vengeance drive the action, but the novel's tender theme is a longing for home. The Spanish Royalty cry out for gold, but the young men forced into battle only wish for better shoes in a prickling desert, and something better to cook than cactus pads on a campfire. These soldiers might as well be singing the song every GI knows by heart: *The coffee that they give us, they say is mighty fine, it's good for cuts and bruises and it tastes like iodine!* While leaders plot the fate of golden cities, these soldiers worry they'll lose the wife to another fellow while they're far from home. In a nation of returning soldiers and war-weary civilians, this book will make a huge emotional mark.

The Asheville Trumpet, *February 3, 1946*

Asheville Writer Is Story of the Year

by Carl Nicholas

"Vassals of Majesty" by local wordsmith Harrison Shepherd proves nothing short of sheer fascination. It might seem only stuffed shirts and long-haired professors would clamor to read of men living hundreds of years ago. Not so! Every heart will pound as conqueror Cortez pitches battle against his foe. This book has it all: blood-curdling treachery, and even heart interest. The female pulse will race for handsome Indian prince Cuautla. With the speed of a locomotive the story hurtles to its epic conclusion. Mrs. Jack Cates, owner of Cates Bookshop, confirms she cannot keep it on the shelves.

Asheville's very own Harrison Shepherd is a young man of only thirty holding the secrets of the ages in his pen. Calls to the home confirmed he resides in Montford Hills. Young ladies take note, our sources say he's a bachelor.

The New York Weekly Review, *February 2, 1946*

Vassals of Majesty, BY HARRISON W. SHEPHERD

Stratford and Sons, New York

Never Far from Home

by Michael Reed

In the literary season of Anna's beleaguered King of Siam and Teddy Roosevelt's "Unterrified" grab of Panama, a nation at peace seems keen for tales of exotic foreign conflict. Readers will find rich fodder in this novel of shrewd ambition in the bloody Spanish conquest of Mexico.

Narrating the tale are Cuautla, an heir to the Aztec empire, and Lieutenant Remedios, who must execute the commands of notorious empire-builder Hernando Cortés. History buffs are warned, scarcely a hero in this tale survives with reputation intact. Cortés shows a weakness for Mexican liquor, and cares more about his page in history than for the men who give their lives to write it for him. And the sweet-natured, delusional Emperor Mucteczuma leaves most of the decisions to a ruthless cadre whose protocol for handling war prisoners may cause the reader a night of lost sleep.

From its snappy title onward, this is a potboiler with no real aspirations to literary importance. The exaggerated setting of blood-stained temples and battlements seems to flutter with the tags of a Hollywood film set. But the characters threaten to burst from their archetypes. The humblest have a winning way of striving for honor in duty, while the powerful fall prey to familiar political failures, revealing themselves as ordinary men all, not so different from the modern-day elected official or office clerk. The author suggests no disagreement among men is ever entirely foreign, after all.

(A sample of reviews sent by the publisher's clipping service, twelve in all, Jan.–Feb. 1946)

March 10, 1946

Dear Frida,

Thank you for the box of chiles, a spectacular surprise. I've strung them in a red *ristra* for the kitchen alongside the onions I plait and hang near the stove. The neighbor boy suspects me of "harboring spells," but Perpetua would approve of my kitchen. I will ration these *pasillas de Oaxaca* like anything, dearer than gasoline.

Our Carolina shows signs of spring: crocuses appear in front lawns, long wool underwear vanishes from clotheslines in the back. Yesterday I bought a frozen lamb shank from the butcher's and set it in the flowerbox outside the window to keep it chilled overnight. This morning it had completely thawed. Today I will rub it with garlic for an impromptu feast. The cat Chispa spreads the word of my erratic cooking extravagances around the neighborhood, and now another scoundrel has followed her home. I call him Chisme, for the gossip that brought him. Black as the devil and fond of lamb.

Soon my shanks may get to visit an authentic Philco. The publisher's accountants are preparing a royalty check for the first 50,000 copies of the book. You can't imagine what you set loose on the world, with one quick job of paper-smuggling. I have to run a gauntlet when leaving the house. Two young ladies are out there now, lollygagging on the front walk in saddle shoes and rolled-up dungarees. Reporters for a school newspaper from the look of them, or just autograph hounds, sucked in by the bizarre and rampant rumors that I am a person of interest. Even my neighbors brought over a book for autograph—it was wrapped up as if they meant to give it a state burial, or else cure it for a ham. Romulus says he spotted some girls slipping around to the back to steal my shirts off the clothesline, and chased them off by "whooping and hollering."

I am abashed by this admiration, for it seems directed at some other person. How these girls would hoot if they saw me as I really am, cowering indoors on washdays, festooning the bathroom with my damp balbriggans so they won't be stolen or made the subject of a theme paper in Senior English. My new life. No one has said I eat human flesh in a tortilla, but I'm getting an idea how your lives have been disfigured all these years by gossip. I can't answer the telephone, for it's sure to be a newspaper man asking questions: place of birth, status of bowels. I don't know what to do with this havoc.

I learned today by mail about the publisher's check. Mr. Barnes tried all week to reach me, unaware I was hiding from the telephone. Soon I'll have to do something about the mail; the box fills daily with notes from readers. Seven proposals of marriage, so far. Such a query requires a gentle response, but I'll confess I'm flummoxed. I've had no practice in the skills of being admired. Frida, sometimes an acid panic rises in my throat; people want something, and I am not the thing at all. As I've mentioned, girls are desperate, with the fellows still over there patching up the potholes in France. Poor England and France. Their great kingdoms nothing now but fairy tales.

Did *El Diario* mention Churchill's speech last week in Missouri? The European leaders seem terrified by the new landscape, flattened at the middle with Truman still on his feet at one end, and Stalin at the other. You could see why Mr. Churchill wants to keep them from shaking hands—if Harry and Comrade Joe reach across that mess, these two could make a new empire on which the sun never sets. Mr. Churchill sounded like a child goading his parents into an argument, he was absurdly dramatic: "A shadow has fallen upon the scene. . . . Nobody knows what Soviet Russia intends to do," etcetera. Next he will probably go to Moscow and say the same about us.

How strange, that this is the wide-open moment Lev spent

his life hoping for. With America brimming with brotherly love for the Soviets, our own laborers on the march, and Russia with everything to gain, it seems the right time to support them in tossing out Stalin's bureaucrats and finishing the democratic socialist revolution as Lenin intended. Or, it could go the other way, our two nations falling apart like split kindling. Mr. Churchill seems to want that. "From the Baltic to the Adriatic, an iron curtain has descended across the Continent." He sweetened the pot later with goodwill for the valiant Russians and comrade Stalin. But the howlers went right to work as soon as they heard of this strange new curtain of metal. They are thrilled with the image. The cartoonists draw the poor Russians slamming their heads against an anvil. Probably in a fortnight they'll have forgotten it, but for now it's a sensation. Two words put together, *curtain* and *iron*, have worked alchemy on a kettle of tepid minds and anxious hearts.

The power of words is awful, Frida. Sometimes I want to bury my typewriter in a box of quilts. The radio makes everything worse, because of the knack for amplifying dull sounds. Any two words spoken in haste might become law of the land. But you never know which two. You see why I won't talk to the newsmen.

My dread is sometimes inexplicable. How do you bear up under so many eyes? And what ludicrous worries I have, compared with yours. I hope the bone-graft operation you mention will make your life worth living again. I worry for your weariness, but trust in your strength, and often see your paintings in my dreams.

Your friend,

H. W. SHEPHERD

P.S. I enclose a review, to clear up any mistaken notions you may have about my novel.

The Echo, *February 28, 1946*

This one is flying off the bookstore shelves from coast to coast: *Vassals of Majesty* by Harrison W. Shepherd, with 50,000 sold the first month after publication. Its pageant of noble heroes and dastardly villains plays out on the golden shores of ancient Rome. When you've had enough of the "heart and soul of the common man" exalted by the late FDR, here are uncommon men with derring-do, sweeping the reader into the Success Dream that drives them. Ladies and gentlemen, but definitely. Harry Shepherd cranks out a darn good read. And watch out, girls: he's single!

March 13, 1946

Dear Shepherd,

What's steamin, demon? Remember me, from civilian service? (Nobody forgets this Tom-cat.) Hope you're all the aces since last we soldiered together for Art and Country. Everywhere I go now, some guy is just home from Europe telling how he dodged the lead pill or brought in his bomber on a wing and a prayer. Does anybody want to hear a hair-raising tale of Army SNAFU in the National Gallery? You and me buddy, a couple of Civvy cream puffs, it's a void coupon ain't it? If only my old chum Shepherd were here, we could tell some war stories, sure. How you and I drank so much joe on the train, we almost dropped a marble Rodin on its head in the Asheville station.

Man, you could have had me for soup when I saw your name in the Book Review. *Is that you, or some other Harrison Shepherd? I didn't have you figured for the Shakespeare type. But who knows? If it's really you, drop a line.*

Plant you now, dig you later,

TOM CUDDY

March 29, 1946

Dear Shepherd,

Holy Joe, it's really you. Thanks for the buzz. Cat, you know how to percolate.

With everything you are currently hipped to, this will probably sound like cake and coffee, but a proposition has come up and I figure I'll give it a sock. The Department of State is getting into the art business. It's not enough that chumps like us packed off America's treasures to the Vanderbilt Mansion and back, to keep them safe from Tojo. Now the idea is to pack up a fresh load of paintings on Uncle Sam's ticket, and parade them around the museums of Europe. A special show of American painters to send overseas, to show those Parisians we're not a bunch of rubes. Somebody spilled the beans to the Department of State that the Europeans hate us. Surprise, Jean-Pierre thinks GI Joe is a slob with chocolate on his face! Between you and me, I doubt the Parisians care, as long as we keep putting the bricks back in their castles. But the Congress cares, they are convoying this ship and aim to blitz it.

Here's where you and I come in. They recruited my old boss for the job, Leroy Davidson from the Walker. He only got 50 thousand clams to work with but he's done a killer job, Leroy chose everything himself. He's fed up with the Europeans sniggering about heart-throbbing landscapes and the American Scene, so he decided to give them an eyeful. Seventy-nine paintings, mostly Modern Art: Stuart Davis, Marsden Hartley, Georgia O'Keeffe, it's a killer. Even Goodrich at the Whitney says so. We're hanging it here in New York for the summer and then it moves to the National for a few weeks. Leroy says Congress needs to see what American Art looks like, before we send it off.

That's the story, morning glory. You'd come to D.C. in October. You're already on the State Department's cleared list, Leroy says we can hire you in a tick to help with the crating and get this show ready for transatlantic. If you want, you can even come along for the ride. The war's over, pal, this time we would go first class, not steerage. No more riding on top of our wooden crates in the train car, which really was not half a bad place to lob around,

as it turned out. (Like Hope says, Thanks for the memories!) But think of it,
man, you and me in Europe. Goose-feather beds. What a gasser.

Sounds like you might be cooking with gas already in your present
situation. But give me a buzz if you are ready to take Paris.
So long chum,

TOM CUDDY

April 3, 1946

Dear Frida,

Your letter arrived yesterday and now lies open on the desk,
a spectre, burning at its edges. This damage is not yours, you
aren't the cause. It's a normal and ordinary request, for a friend
to come and visit in New York when you are there for the bone-
graft surgery. A friend who owes you everything, and might
now smuggle *rellenos* into the hospital to speed your recovery,
who should do this. But no sleep came last night, only thoughts
in a nightlong darkness of the summer coming, a ride on the
train, the penetrating glare of strangers. Imposing on your fashionable friends in New York, these Americans who understand
everything. All of it envisioned in a cold panic.

This is a despicable confession. But one telephone call yesterday to the train station to ask about a ticket was enough to
drag a stomach inside out, *dejado de la mano de dios*, left alone
by god, this feeling. Abandoned by reason or safety. Perched
on the side of the bathtub rocking like a child, hopeless, wishing for the invisibility of childhood. August of each year brings
thoughts of dying. But bad days come in any month. Eyes can
pierce a skull. Travel to New York is unthinkable, when even
at the corner market, a stranger's stare can paralyze. This terror
hasn't any name. This running home, feeling like a scorched
muslin curtain that blew too near the candle.

Forgive this cowardice. If you have the strength to lift your head as you travel down Fifth Avenue, look for one book in the shop windows there, standing in as a substitute for your once and future friend,

SÓLI

The Asheville Trumpet, April 28, 1946

Woman's Club Sponsors Book Review Night

by Edwina Boudreaux

The Asheville Woman's Club sponsored its annual Book Review Night on Thursday at 6 p.m. in the Lee H. Edwards High School Auditorium. Tickets sold for twenty-five cents each, raising $45 dollars for the Asheville Library. The theme of the evening was, "Mexico Old and New."

Mrs. Herb Lutheridge, President, opened the program with the Pledge of Allegiance and introduction of speakers. Miss Harriet Boudreaux began the festivities with her review of "The Peacock Sheds His Tail" by Alice Hobart. The book concerns the love story of a Mexican girl and American diplomat in the turbulence of unrest in modern-day Mexico City. For her presentation Miss Boudreaux wore native dress of embroidered blouse and skirt brought from the Mexican continent by her aunt, who traveled there as a bride.

The second presenter was welcomed by many excited young ladies in attendance, Mrs. Violet Brown reviewing "Vassals of Majesty" by Harrison Shepherd. The novel tells the exciting conquest of Ancient Mexico by the Spanish Army. Events came alive under Mrs. Brown's retelling, followed by a lively discussion. Numerous questions arose concerning the author, an Ashevillean residing in the Montford neighborhood, which the speaker demurred at, claiming familiarity with the book itself, not its progenitor. In her forty-five minute presentation

Mrs. Brown brought to the fore many themes that might be missed by the average reader, such as Man Against Nature and Man Against Himself.

Mrs. Alberta Blake, librarian, closed the evening by thanking the audience on behalf the Library Committee, noting all money raised would purchase several new volumes. She assured all those in attendance that duplicate copies of the two books presented will soon be on the shelves.

April 30, 1946

Mrs. Violet Brown
4145 Tunnel Road, Bittle House
Rural Free Delivery, Asheville North Carolina

Dear Mrs. Brown,

This message may startle you, please forgive a bolt from the blue. A telephone call to Mrs. Bittle yesterday confirmed that the former guild of lodgers remains intact, minus myself. (She may thus think it improved vis-à-vis her advertisement of "Only Good People Here.") And that you could therefore be reached by this address.

The purpose of this letter is to plant a request: against all odds, a man who can perform every secretarial duty himself from A to Z, including changing the typewriter ribbon, now seems to be in need of a secretary.

A startling ship of fortune has docked in this harbor on Montford Avenue, towing an unwieldy barge of correspondence, telephone calls, and attention from young ladies. It is a wonder, how others who become so blessed still manage to go forward with their lives. Mr. Sinatra receives five thousand letters a week, according to the *Echo*, and he still looks the picture of high spirits. Only a hundred or so come here each week, but they fall like mounds of autumn leaves, leaving the spirits damp and crawling with nervous beetles. What is to be done? An old friend who recently telephoned, a fellow who also worked at the National Gallery during the war, proposed: "Lace up your boots, jive cat, and requisition yourself a canary to be your stenographer." After translating this advice into my own tongue, the question remained: Where does one requisition such a canary?

Then on Sunday your name rose up boldly, Mrs. Brown, in the *Asheville Trumpet*. There you stood with my book in hand, facing down a riotous crowd at the Woman's Club gala. Applying the same calm efficiency you used for handling Mrs. Bittle and her everlasting muddles. Keeping your steady hand on the tiller, you guided the Book Night toward the deep waters of literary theme, quieting the commotion of Miss Boudreaux in her getup from the "Mexican Continent." The ladies pressed for details of the Author Himself, but you professed no knowledge of such person! Imagine the fracas, if you had revealed the truth: that you and the author had once lived under the same roof, with a landlady who sometimes mixed our laundry together.

Mrs. Brown, dear lady, your discretion is prodigious. You resisted the siren song of tattle. The seams of your character must be sewn with steel thread. If this letter delivers only my everlasting gratitude, that is a greater weight than three cents postage should allow. But it also contains an earnest query. Your conduct in the battle of Mexico Old and New has led me to think you may be just the amanuensis who could put a life to rights, and also help with typing a second book, now underway.

Naturally, you may have a different opinion. Let me sum up a few details and be finished, so you can consider the offer. Weighing in my favor, I hope: I am likely in a position to exceed your present salary. A drawback: my workplace is here where I live. Some ladies might find it awkward to work in the home of an unmarried gentleman. In this letter I have already used the terms cat and canary, not because I could ever think of a secretary in those terms, but because others do, evidently. Mrs. Brown, I have an odd impairment: the world paints its prejudices boldly across banners, and somehow I walk through them without seeing. It's a particular fault of mine, a blindness. I carry on walking down the street, dazed as a calf, with shreds of paper hanging everywhere. I hope in this case to be less naive.

A third point in my favor: I spent years as a stenographer myself, as I already hinted. In Mexico I worked for two different men, both greater than I will ever be. Oddly, the experience did not prepare me for public attention. But I understand the role of professional helpmeet, perhaps better than most men. I am not disposed to tyranny.

If anything about this request strikes you as unseemly, please ignore it and accept my high regard for our previous acquaintance. But if my suggestion holds interest for you, I would gladly schedule an interview at a date and time you suggest.

Sincerely,

HARRISON W. SHEPHERD

May 4, 1946

Dear Mr. Shepherd,
Your letter was what you said. A bolt from the blue. But not the first. At the Lending Library I saw your name on a book cover in January. My thought was, well sir, it's a coincidence there be two Harrison Shepherds in this world. Next, an article in the paper discussed the book, its author reputed to be living in Montford. The subject of Mexico I knew to be your familiar. Curiosity killed the cat for Mrs. Bittle, her niece said she'd spied on the fellow, reporting him tall as a tree and thin as a rail. Who else?
Imagine our surprise. For years we sat here like bumps on a log eating the

cooking of a man who would shortly come to fame. Now old Mr. Judd says, "I had no idee what that young fellow was cooking!" (You remember his drear jokes.) Miss McKellar notes that "still waters run deep." Reg Borden still refuses to believe it's you, but wants to read the book anyway. He's had a long wait. The library has but one copy. I had to wait weeks myself, and I have an "In" with Mrs. Lutheridge since I joined the Library Committee, mainly to set the card files to rights, which were a disgrace.

    Your book is good. This town hasn't had such a sensation since Tommy Wolfe came out with Look Homeward, Angel. *And that sensation was not pleasing to most. Some in Asheville were disgruntled to be left out of the story, and all others dismayed to be left in, thus the scandal was entire. The library refused to carry it. I was already in the Woman's Club (recording secretary), and our meeting convened the week that book came out. I doubt if so many salts of ammonia have ever been used in our city, before or since. You had only to open the door of the meeting hall to get a mighty dose.*

    I couldn't guess how to write a book. But here is my opinion: people love to read of sins and errors, just not their own. You were wise to put your characters far from here, instead of so-called "Altamont" as Mr. Wolfe did. That "Dixieland" is his mother's boardinghouse on Spruce Street, and all here know it. Few were spared the jabs of Wolfe's pen, even his own father whom I myself can remember teetering into the S & W Cafeteria reeking of spirits before noon of a Monday. Many feel there was no need to bring that kind of thing to the lime-light, especially by a family member.

    This all pertains to the subject of your letter. Thank you for saying I am sewn up with steel thread, but I call it plain sense. Some writers get away with murder, using nice words and a mannerly story to bring misery on real folk. You did the other way, writing of murderous things but behaving as a gentleman in the civic sense. That's how I came to speak as I did at Book Review Night. Those girls were apoplectic to make your book into another hometown yarn. We've had that kind of yarn here, and it got itself wound up in a gorm of knots. Mr. Shepherd, you put your story in Mexico. Why not keep it there? That was my thinking.

I know you as a gentleman. Using your home as a place of employment is not unseemly. A lady in the working world all her life knows that tender manners have their place, sometimes less useful than a good cup of coffee. During the war secretaries sometimes emptied bedpans, and certain men will ask worse, even in peacetime. But knowing you as I do from Mrs. Bittle's, I've seen you show more kindness than most, even toward a hen you're fixing to put in the oven.

I will warn, I can be particular. I like a typewriter with an automatic margin and the type bar separate from the carriage. Preferably a Royal or L. C. Smith. These were used at the Selective Service office, and I got accustomed. I will come to your house for interviewing at half past six on Thursday. The neighborhood of your address is a short ride on the bus from my present employer. I'll go directly, after work.
Sincerely,

VIOLET BROWN

May 27

Mother's soul can rest: here is a woman in my life. Mrs. Brown in a pearl-gray snood, age forty-six, sensible as pancake flour. Like characters in a story, our lives were star-crossed but came together. She will rescue the hero, answer his telephone, file the mountains of mail, maybe shake a broom at the laundry thieves. And he can keep his monk's life, the holes in his underwear. Mrs. Brown doesn't care.

At the first interview she laid her failings at my feet, or would have except she hasn't any. Does not smoke cigarettes, take strong drink, go to church or gamble. Has worked for the city, the army, and most daunting of all, the Asheville Woman's Club. Thirty years a widow. She doubts being married would have been much different.

It was strange to speak forthrightly, after living at Mrs. Bittle's those years: exiting the bathroom with downcast eyes, sitting at supper while old Mr. Judd piped up with his yellowed news extras.

Now it seems we shared a kindred silence, restraining our smiles on hearing that Limburger has flown across the Atlantic. But maybe I contrive this, as lovers reconfigure the days *before*, with every glance leading ultimately to union.

In any event here she is, installed in my dining room. I hated to show her the mail, stored in bushel baskets in the empty spare bedroom. She did not flinch. Grasped each bushel by the handles, marched it downstairs, and dumped onto the maple table one mountain for each month. Bravely she dives in, even before we've found her a filing cabinet or acceptable typewriter. (Royal or L. C. Smith.) We shall put the bathroom door back on its hinges, as soon as I've cleared its surface of all piles and chapters, and found a proper desk myself. For now, when one of us needs the WC, the other steps out the back door, pretending to call the cats. This and more, she suffers with perfect composure.

Mrs. Brown is a force: small, unadorned, unapologetic. Her eyebrows arch like a pair of bridges across her wide forehead. Her blouses button to the top, she wears white cotton gloves even on warm days, and she can still any troubled waters with her austere calm and peculiar antique grammar. Each morning on arrival she taps on the front door, puts in her head and calls out, "Mr. Shepherd, where be ye?"

Her words seem scripted by Chaucer. She says "strip-ed" and "learn-ed," making an extra syllable of the past tense. A sack is a "poke." Surveying the piles of letters she declared, "Mr. Shepherd, you get mail by the *passel*." She says "nought" and "nary a one," and the garden greens she brought me were "sallets," the word Shakespeare used. She says "queasy" to mean worried, as did King Lear. When I noted this, she replied, "Well I expect he had a lot to be queasy about. He was a king, wasn't he?"

When pressed about her origins she said her people were "Mountain Whites." She seems reluctant to say more, only that it means Highlanders, people who came through the gap from England ages ago, and reckoned they ought to stay. Remaining on the spot, with idiom intact. She means "reckon" in the British sense, akin to reconnoiter, until knowing a thing for certain, which is to "ken it."

Most shocking was this pronouncement: "My family be there still, living in a cabin home in the hells." This is a kind of bush, evidently, a rhododendron. "They grow thick as can be. If you came to be lost in there, you couldn't push out with a stick. So it's called hells. Pardon if you're offended. It isn't a foul word in that sense."

No offense taken. Her past can stay where it is, lost in the hells, not my business, as my childhood hells are none of hers. We concern ourselves with the future, which we agreed should begin at once, in my dining room, as soon as she could give proper notice. And today here she is, dispatching the mess with carbon paper and a buttoned-up smile.

May 28

Mrs. Brown's advice about the schoolgirls: they won't bite. I took her word on that, and left the house for the first time in a while to wander up to the cemetery. A belated outing for Mother's birthday; it always seems important to go somewhere for her sake. But she is nowhere any longer, least of all the Riverside Cemetery. Even the writer O. Henry might have "up and gone" from here, as Mrs. Brown would say. Tom Wolfe is still in situ, though the town is evidently still put out with him. Many graves bore jars of wilting peonies today, but nary a posy for poor Tom, a man so recently gone, dramatically and in his prime, reeling from the fracas of fame. Maybe Mrs. Brown could have saved him.

A sample of one day's mail, posted forward from Stratford and Sons, received on June 6, 1946, six months after publication of *Vassals of Majesty*. (Spelling sic.) —VB

Dear Mr. Shepherd,

Your book Vassals of Majesty *is tops. I sobbed my heart out hundreds of times, especially at the end when the soldiers burnt up all the King's parrots in the fire. My mother has a Parakeet named Mickey Rooney. My sister never stopped razzing me because I stayed up all night, scared out of my wig on the gory parts. Then she read it, and blew her top. I think Lt. Remedios is a dream boat, but she is all for Cuautla. Which one is supposed to be the best? I am a budding author too. Please send an autograph photo and keep it coming. (My sister says, 2 please!)*
Thanks!

LINDSAY PARKS

Dear Mr. Shepherd,

I am writing about your book in regards to the War in Mexico. Usually I sit on the fence and don't argue with people or try to tell them how it is. The horror of war is part of life since recorded history. But your book showed how men really feel when they are soldiers. I served in the 12th Infantry Regiment, F Company. One of the few that made it out of Berdorf. I read your book in the Van Wyck Army Hospital. About ten other guys on my ward read your book, and most of the others couldn't hold a book or see to read one. Everything about war is bad like you said. Some of us have a bet that you were an Infantry Man yourself.
Yours truly,

GEORGE M. COOK

Dear Mr. Shepherd,

My name is Eleanor White and I reside in Springfield, Missouri. I am currently attending college at Webster Women's College. I myself am not a big reader but I must say, your book made me want to read more, more, more. Now I understand the Mexican Conquistadors through new eyes. I am recommending my History professor to read it. My hat is off to you!
Yours truly,

ELEANOR WHITE

Dear Mr. Harrison,

My name is Gary Duncan and I live in California. My girlfriend was hanging icicles all over me until I read your book Vessels of Majesty. *In a word: "Stimulating." I found your destriptions very thought provoking, even if I didn't think it is the best book ever wrote. But am I going to tell Shelley that?*

I would be tops in her book if you sent a photo. Her birthday is coming up here quick, June 14. Her name is Shelley. And the last name, same as yours, Harrison. Can you top that?

YOUR FRIEND, GARY

Dear Mr. Shepherd,

I would like to say thank you. Your writing is an inspiration to us all, or anyway that is how I feel. Your book hit me when it made me think how the boys on both sides of the war were still human whether Spanish or the Mexicans. Every person is human, even Japs, their mothers must have all cried tears just the same. That gave me something to ponder. Please continue to write more books.

Yours sincerely,

ALICE KENDALL

All correspondence answered with a short note, no photographs or inclusions. —VB

July 6, 1946

Dear Diego,

I trust Frida is still recovering from the surgery in New York. I have no address for her there, but could not let her birthday pass. I expect she is angry with me for failing to visit. Please forward my *saludos,* and tell her I never fail to bake a *rosca* in her honor on this day, whether she is present to eat it or not.

On the eve of your elections I share your thrill and dread, waiting to see what Mexico will declare for herself and her Revolution. The news is sparse, so I welcome any from you. I did read of the National Prize of Arts and Sciences, and so I congratulate you both. Your wife is a National Prize herself, as you know better than anyone.

The news from here is about what you'd expect. You wouldn't care for the food: no *empanadas dulces*, I doubt there is a table-spoon of sugar right now in all Asheville. (My cake today, with molasses and pureed apples, was a sad, dark-brown cousin of its predecessors.) But rations are lifted on nearly everything else. Prices rise like balloons, and we all jump like children under a piñata, reaching for our material passions. Americans believe in water-proof gabardine and Vimm's Vitamin Tablets. The housewives sent their butter to the Front for years, and now require their heavenly reward. To get it all manufactured on schedule, the sacrifice of laborers will have to be made perma-nent, it seems: they toiled like slaves for the war effort and still haven't had a single pay adjustment. You could have heard a wrench drop on Pack Square this spring, when the unions shut down everything. But Truman seized the railroad and drafted the strikers into military service, to command them back to work.

So that is the report you asked for, not entirely good. Our newsmen mostly reviled the "workers' rebellion." Politics here now resemble a pillow fight. Lacking the unifying slogan (Win the War), our opposing parties sling absurd pronouncements back and forth, which everyone pretends carry real weight. How the feathers fly. The newsmen leap on anything, though it's all on the order of, "Four out of five shoppers know this is the better dill pickle," assertions that can't be proven but sway opinion. "Dance for the crowd" is the new order, with news-men leading the politicians like bears on the leash. Real convictions would be a hindrance. The radio is at the root of the evil, their rule is: *No silence, ever.* When anything happens, the commentator has to speak without a moment's pause for gathering wisdom. Falsehood and inanity are preferable to silence. You can't imagine the effect of this. The talkers are rising above the thinkers.

On my own advice, then, I'll close this ramble. But first I have a confession. The day I left Mexico six years ago, Frida gave me your copy of the Codex Boturini. She said it was a gift from you, and gladly I accepted. But I wonder, did she actually ask, or just tell you it was stolen? The culprit herein revealed: the cook. In this parcel I enclose it, rightfully returned. You may remember I was enthralled by this codex, which you showed me in your office one day. I understood it to be a sort of Bible for the homeless. Yet, with its little drawings of people it also resembled the eight-pagers the boys used to have at school, and I'm abashed to admit, your codex had more effect on me than the naked Sally Rand ever did. When Frida put its accordion folds in my hand, I couldn't refuse. I should have asked her whether you'd been informed of your generosity. But I wanted it badly, and took it, for this reason: in my experience, penitence is more attainable than permission.

I hope you'll be pleased to know I made good use of it. My second novel, now complete, is the story of the Mexica people's journey to their new home in the promised valley "Where the Eagle Tears the Snake" (my tentative title). Plot and dramatic interest all came directly from the codex: all those severed heads on stakes, fur-covered enemies, and eagles flying down to carry weapons to the rescue. I hardly needed to invent a thing. It was much like working as your typist: I only had to stay awake to a luminous presence, and make a good transcription.

So I'm in debt to you, not to mention the original author of the codex, attributed to Huitzilopotchli himself. I will soon send the manuscript to my publisher and receive a check for royalties-on-advance. If the Feather-Headed God expects his share, he had better get in contact right away.

With regards to all in your household,

H. SHEPHERD

July 8, 1946

The manuscript sailed off today. Mrs. Brown took it to the post office. Before going out the door she turned back and held out the bulky brown-paper package of it, resting flat on her white-gloved hands. "Look here, Mr. Shepherd, a little raft with all your hopes upon it, sailing for New York. Ye know not how light it feels in my hands."

This afternoon she discovered my birth date had just passed. She is filing old documents, the birth certificate applications and so forth, now that the flurry of typing is done. She seemed hurt. "A man turns thirty years, that's important," she scolded, "and to think I sat here and knew nought of it, all the day long."

I didn't say what Frida would have. That you can't really know the person standing before you, because always there is some missing piece: the birthday like an invisible piñata hanging great and silent over his head, as he stands in his slippers boiling the water for coffee. The scarred, shrunken leg hidden under a green silk dress. A wife and son back in France. Something you never knew. That is the heart of the story.

August 27

Murderous dreams come even in daytime, memories that occlude vision. How can a friend's blood be willed from the mind? Other men do it. They come home from a war, kiss the ground, and go forward, as easily as taking the Haywood bus to the library. Without meeting this rising panic and humiliation. Running out of the library bookless and hatless, rather than end up crumpled behind the newspaper stacks again, watching blood spread across the maple floor boards.

Last week, on the day itself, even the bedroom was too uncertain a place, its shifting walls and window's glare, letting in the clouded sky. Mrs. Brown thought it must be the grippe. She brought tea and toast upstairs on a tray.

Today, one hundred ten paces to the corner market, step by counted step. An automobile passed slowly on the street: a Buick. Two women at the newsstand professed themselves as admirers. One had just come from the market and carried a bouquet of gladiolus wrapped in a paper cone. She meant no harm at all, she was only a young wife going home to some celebration. Not Jacson Mornard stalking Frida in Paris, arms loaded with flowers, any fool could know the difference. But anyone who rises, any greatness, attracts those who would cut it down at the root. Any fool knows that also.

Every day it seems possible to walk to the door. This time, step out. But the sidewalk leads to a bridge across a precipice. There is Mother up ahead slipping off her sling-back shoes, stepping out onto the planks above the rushing ravine. Don't come. You wait here. The red-bellied spider pulls itself into a hole in the plank. Every hole could have something like that inside.

Mrs. Brown might know more than she says. Today she looked up from the table, peering over her glasses to size up her wretched, captive chief, who stands at the door looking out. "They won't bite," she said. But it isn't the girls in saddle oxfords. It is the things that have already begun, proceeding now toward their finish, the supplicant who should have been turned away, and was not. The man at the door with hat in hand and the pickax under his raincoat.

September 2

No word from Frida, still angry. Nor from Diego, not even a curse over his stolen codex, though that's also to be expected. He couldn't remember to write letters even as Chairman General of Lev's Correspondence Committee. The world is a train moving forward, with people like Diego and Frida at the fore and all the rest of us standing back, shuddering at the roar.

Of all those gone away, Frida is the most missed. Not that she ever offered real affection. Only her version of it: a game of cat-and-mouse.

September 3

Well, here is a reason for missing Frida: writing letters. Who else loved my news the way she did? A neighbor named Romulus. Now a sister named Parthenia.

"Don't trouble yourself over it, that's my sister Parthenia Goins," said Mrs. Brown today, hardly even looking up from the page she was typing. "Her husband Ottie is out there too, I see. And some of the nephews."

I'd just told her a band of gypsies had come to the end of their rope on Montford Avenue and were camped on the front yard. Very chagrined, therefore, to learn it was Mrs. Brown's family, come down into town from "the hells." A twice-yearly event, at "Eastertide and the Laboring Day," for the purchase of dry goods and a checkup on the moral progress of Sister Violet. The trip takes them the better part of a day, even though they live only a few miles up toward Mount Mitchell. But the road is "fearsome hateful."

They showed up out there at noon, in a Model T that looked older than God and more likely to drop an axle. The man in the driving seat opened the door to stretch his legs, revealing a beard that reached his belt buckle. Clumped in the back, an old-looking woman and shifting herd of oxlike boys. They sat in the car for hours, until the heat drove them out into the shade of the maple in the front yard. They showed no sign of coming to the door. Mrs. Brown said they likely meant to fetch her back to Mrs. Bittle's, and were waiting for her day's work to end.

"Shouldn't we ask them in?"

"They won't come."

"Well then, you should go."

"I'm not done here. It won't vex them any to wait."

"For *hours*?" I peered out through the curtain. "Couldn't they do some errands and come back, to save their time?"

"Mr. Shepherd, if they had any money or one precious thing, they'd be sure to save it. But time they have aplenty. They like to spend it where they be."

Realizing they might have come to investigate Sister Violet's situation, I did insist on asking them in. Elder Sister accepted, eventually, while the males remained outdoors, all of them smoking pipes. Mrs. Brown introduced us but begged a few minutes more to finish the week's work. The sister, *Parthenia*! What a strange creature, peering about this living room like Columbus among the red men of Hispaniola. She sat in a parlor chair with feet together, hands folded, a black kerchief covering her hair, a lumpish dress covering everything else down to her boots. Not even Frida could have worked this particular peasant style to much advantage. She declined my offer of tea, fiercely, as if accustomed to being poisoned by strangers. We sat facing one another across the shocking silence.

Finally: "Who mought ye all be?"

"I beg your pardon?"

"Who's yer folks?"

"My parents both passed away. I don't have any family."

She took this in slowly, like a snake digesting its catch. Then: "How old be ye?"

"Thirty."

Many other questions stood in line after these, each patiently waiting its turn, each one finally spitting, rubbing its hands, and stepping up to position.

"Violet says ye be from Mexee-co?"

"I lived there. But I was born outside Washington. My mother was Mexican, her father did business with the government here, so that's how she and my father came to meet. She was too young, the family disowned her over the marriage." *Stop.* Filling up a silence with blather, like a radio man. That cannot be what a Parthenia requires.

"Well." A pause. "What brung ye up this air way off the branch?"

A good question. Trying to steer the conversation onto her family proved difficult, but ultimately yielded Parthenia's fascinating diagnosis of Sister Violet's yen for self-improvement: "Our mother read the books. We believe it made her tubercular."

A long pause.

"Violet be the same."

Another pause.

"We was all in our family borned with sense. But Violet be the only one to vex herself on wanting to be learn-ed." *Born-ed, learn-ed,* here was the raw version of Violet's peculiar diction, without the gloss acquired from twenty years of office work. "We was afeared she would turn out like t'other one. The lady doctor that was born-ed here in the town."

"Elizabeth Blackwell?"

"That one. Violet readen a book on her. Mother was afeared of her going away to be learned for the doctoring."

"That would have been an interesting career for your sister."

"Not hardly, sir. T'would of put her in a hazard of hell's fire."

"Medical school?"

"To be learn-ed for the science, yessir. Them men casting aspersion on our Lord's hand in the Creation."

In the dining room, visible through the archway, Sister Violet's lip remained buttoned but her eyebrows nearly reached her widow's peak by the time she finished filing the day's mail. Parthenia took her away then, evidently satisfied the new employer would not threaten her sister's virtue or encourage any interest in the sciences. It explains a good deal about Mrs. Brown: her aloneness in the world, as far from home in this town as any boy from Mexico. Probably farther, given the scalding disapproval of anything "learn-ed." And yet she does carry her origins with her, revealed in the rhythms of speech, the talent for keeping counsel. The unusual respect for silence. Parthenia's silences outlasted her sentences every time, and carried greater weight. How will their tongue survive in a modern world, where the talkers rush to trample every pause?

September 14
Mr. Lincoln Barnes, my Mr. Lincoln. He means well. A second novel makes me "a novelist," says he, and therefore duty-bound to meet my editor in New York. He can't know how entirely it's out of the question. He should invite me to dance with angels on the head of a pin, I'd sooner try, if I could do it from home. But my failure will mean conceding every battle. Beginning with my title, *Where the Eagle Eats the Snake.*

"Wrong," he pronounced yesterday on the telephone. "People hate snakes."

Well then, wouldn't they be happy to see an eagle tearing one to pieces, sitting on a cactus plant? The dust-jacket art seems ready made.

He is keen to call it *Pilgrims of Chapultepec.*

Americans take "pilgrim" to mean the fellow in buckled shoes with hands folded in prayer. And the unpronounceable remainder, as dubious as Brand X soap.

Mrs. Brown suggests that for the next one I ought to turn in the manuscript with a title I despise. That way, she says, they're apt to change it to something you favor. A trick she learned while working for the U.S. Army.

September 26
The exhibit, *Advancing American Art*, is advancing at this very moment toward the National Gallery, packed up on the train with Tom Cuddy as its Shipping Shepherd. And still I have no answer for him. Tommy the golden boy, with the good looks of Van Heijenoort and

a better idea how to use them—it's possible he has never been turned down before. On the telephone, he coaxes. Says I have to be there in D.C., he's desperate for backup, certain there is trouble afoot. Congress has called a special hearing to discuss the exhibit after they've had a look at it. And what Tommy said about the Hearst Press is true, Mrs. Brown brought in one of their magazine ads today, a reproduction of one of the "ugly" paintings with the caption "Your Money Bought This!" They suggest a foregone conclusion among soap-buying housewives: your money would be better spent on soap. But with Mrs. Brown their propaganda failed: she is now intently curious about the show.

Paris with Tommy, dear Lord what a vision. (He was dazzling enough in a dim boxcar.) But surely he'll understand there is too much to do here, revisions and galley proofs still ahead. He'll be less willing to understand why Washington is out of the question. To have a look at those modernists, have a drink with old Tom, help him ship out the paintings. Patiently Mrs. Brown waits to send an answer: yes or no. Probably she has already drafted both letters and only needs the word. Such is her efficiency.

We discussed it again this afternoon, or rather I talked. Justifying my absurd fear of travel and exposure, despising it all the while. My face must have been the Picture of Dorian Gray. At the end, when he goes to pieces.

She used the quiet voice she seems to draw up from a different time, the childhood in mountain hells, I suppose.

"What do ye fear will happen?"

There was no sound but the clock in the hall: *tick, tick*.

"Mr. Shepherd, ye cannot stop a bad thought from coming into your head. But ye need not pull up a chair and bide it sit down."

October 2

The matter is settled, the letter sent. Mrs. Brown provided the solution: herself. She will go along on the trip, make all arrangements, reserve the hotel rooms for both of us in names no one could recognize. No girls in short socks will gather in the halls. We will take the Roadster, she'll carry the money-purse and purchase the gasoline, no strangers need be addressed on the journey. Only Tom, once we arrive at the gallery.

Indispensable Mrs. Brown. She has known all along the problem is not the grippe. But couldn't know how her firm hand on my arm could make many things possible, including walking out the door onto that swaying bridge.

"It appeared you needed steadying," was her diagnosis.

October 12
Poor Tom. And also the forty-odd artists who will suffer from this, but somehow I worry most for Tom. He believed in *Advancing American Art*, and not just the free ride to Europe. Now he has to hang his head, call Paris and Prague, and explain the show isn't coming. They will dismantle it, sell off these treasures to the first low bid so the Department of State can recover the taxpayers' cash. The boss will make Tommy do the worst of it. The O'Keeffe already went for fifty dollars he said, salt in the wound.

Mrs. Brown and I were more than ready to put miles between ourselves and that debacle. But the journey home was long. The mountain parkway is a strange passage from city into wilderness, hundreds of miles of forest and vale without habitation. Occasionally an apple orchard, fenced by a zigzag of split rails, like a piece of green calico cut with pinking shears. Driving along high ridgetops is like being a bird on the wing, with slopes dropping steeply away from the roadsides, and views opening out to rumpled, hazy horizons. The leaves were crimson, auburn, jade, and gold, lying together in patchwork against the mountainsides. "God's hand bestoweth beauty on the advancing trial of winter," Mrs. Brown quoted. But it looked as if God had turned over the job to a Mexican muralist.

When first I made this drive, the forests were leafless. I told Mrs. Brown about it. Father unexpectedly dead, and then this endless passage into a barren wilderness. I thought I had come to a nation of the interred.

"Then you came to Mrs. Bittle's," she said, "and knew it for certain."

"Old Judd seemed mummified. True enough. But certainly not you or Miss McKellar."

Each time we stopped for gasoline she insisted we take on coffee and sandwiches as well. "Feed the car, feed the driver," was her succinct advice. The gray mass of a storm sat on the mountains to the west, waiting like a predator. In the afternoon it pounced, drenching the view and washing the brilliant leaves into matted sop in the road. The rain on the windscreen was blinding. The wiper had to be cranked every few seconds, and it made for difficult, one-handed driving. Mrs. Brown offered to help turn the wiper lever, but its location overhead above the driver makes that awkward.

"Mr. Ford should have thought to put it over here," she said, "so the passenger could help."

"He knew better. In life's dampest passages, the driver often has to go it alone."

"I ought to know that. Here knitting socks without one child of my own."

"Is *that* what you have there? I thought it was an indigo porcupine."

She had a laugh at that. She has eleven nephews and nieces, I learned, and meant to outfit the tribe on this journey, working through socks from top to toe, all from the same massive hank of blue wool. The coming holiday shall be known as "The Christmas of the Blue Socks from Aunt Violet." She worked on a little frame of four interlocked needles that poked out in every direction as she passed the yarn through its rounds.

"Aren't you afraid you'll hurt yourself with that?"

"Mr. Shepherd, if women feared knitting needles as men do, the world would go bare-naked."

What had happened in Washington was an outrage. Yet life goes forward mostly as an exchange of pleasantries on a narrow bridge that hangs above the chasm of outrage. "There's Grandfather Mountain. See, the shape of it. An old man lying down."

"Is it too cold for you? We could stop and get the lap blanket from the back."

"No. I'm warm-blooded."

"We're lucky it's cold. This Roadster overheats famously on hard inclines."

"You don't say."

Grand white clapboard hotels turned up sparsely along the route, their front porches mostly populated with empty rocking chairs. At dusk they began to be lit by the yellow glow of lamplight. Once, just as we passed an inn, a black-skinned man in a red jacket was lighting the porch lanterns one by one, leaning with difficulty around elegant men who sat idle, smoking cigars. Castes of the nation.

Mrs. Brown finally broached the void. "*Indigo Porcupine*, that could just as well be the name of one of those paintings we saw at the show."

"Yes. *Indigo Porcupine Leaping into the Void*, that might do."

"Well. I couldn't make out what all they were meant to be. Truly I've never seen the like, Mr. Shepherd. But I'm deeply obliged for it."

"I wasn't going to come until you volunteered as escort. So I'm the one obliged."

"For all, I meant. The paintings and our nation's capital. Going right straight in the hall where the Congress meets."

"Had you not been to Washington before?"

"This is my first time out of Buncombe County."

"Really?"

"Yes sir. I've read the *Geographics* since I was a girl. My sisters could tell you, I strained for travel like a horse fresh to the bit. But never thought it would happen."

"Mrs. Brown, you make me ashamed. The whole world knocks at my door, and all I want to do is stay home."

"It's a wonder," she said tactfully, working at a tiny sock.

"Well, you're a worldlier person than most of those congressmen. They want Norman Rockwell and statues of muscular horses and nothing new under the sun."

"Even still. There was no cause to speak so rudely. What peeved them?"

"Fear, maybe. The foreign element, that's what Tom thought. They expected to go in the gallery and see old friends, but instead they met strangers. Gashes of color and surrealism. It made them uneasy."

"They didn't say 'uneasy.' They said 'un-American.' I can't see that. If an American paints it, then it's American, isn't it?"

"Not according to Mr. Rankin and the Congress."

Or Truman: *If that's art, then I'm a Hottentot.* Others said *vulgar, obscene, insane, namby-pamby pacifism.* Or *Stalinist*, a perfect irony, from these congressmen who seem as determined as Stalin to suppress creativity among artists. The show scared them out of their wits. The Special Session was a thrashing.

"We should have taken Tom out of that hearing. It was humiliating."

"Your poor friend, he'd worked so. He'll take it hard, will he not?"

"Oh, believe me. Tom Cuddy feels for those paintings about the way you do for your nieces and nephews. He'd knit socks for Winslow Homer, if he knew how. I've seen that in him ever since the civilian services. Moving paintings and sculptures to safekeeping, that was America the Beautiful, for Tom. That was patriotism."

"Bless his heart."

Bless it indeed. Now he's had to hear Congress declare the whole Western world threatened by some paint and canvas. Our finest painters, a menace. One was specifically damned for having urged Roosevelt to come to the aid of the Soviet Union and Britain, after Hitler attacked Russia. Which in fact, Roosevelt did.

The click of knitting needles, the shush of tires through leafy muck. The lozenge of space inside the automobile felt surprisingly safe, like a small home moving through a tunnel of darkness. Mrs. Brown finished off a sock before speaking again.

"Not all the pictures were hard to cipher. Some were plain. The ones with cemeteries and tenement houses got people the most riled, if you ask me. More than the ones that looked like dribble-drabble."

"The Guglielmi and those."

"Why do you think?"

"Congress has to keep up appearances. The paintings were going around the world. We can't let them know we have racial strife and tenement houses."

"My stars, Mr. Shepherd. Europe is lying in a pile. On the news they said Berlin city just dug two thousand graves for the ones that aim to starve to death before spring."

A car blazed by, two bright eyes in the dark.

"They had to dig the graves before the ground froze," she added.

"I understand."

"And London, no better. I read they're allowed nought but four ounces of knitting wool for the year and two yards of material, to cover each person in a family. They must be about naked. What's the harm in those folks seeing some of our troubles?"

"Well, five years of wartime censorship. Old habits die hard. We've gotten very good at pretending everything is shipshape here. Don't you feel that way?"

"What way?"

"That it's a little dangerous to advertise our weak points. Jerry and Tokyo Rose might be listening. Loose lips sink ships."

"They *were* listening. But the war's ended."

"True. But if it keeps the paintings pretty and all people's whining buttoned up, maybe they'll want a new war every five years."

"Mr. Shepherd, for shame. That is no subject for jest. We can't keep on forever saying the nation entire is perfect. Because between you and me, sir, it is not." The needles clicked in the dark. She must have read the pattern with her fingertips.

"Do you remember the first advice you ever gave me?"

She seemed to think it over. "The pot roast at Mrs. Bittle's?"

"Advice about writing."

"I never."

"Oh, you did. In that first letter. You said Tom Wolfe got himself in hot water exposing the scandals of Asheville, and I was wise to keep my story in Mexico. Here was your advice: people love to read about sins and errors, but not their own."

She considered this. "That's different from putting sins and errors off the map entire. How can it be un-American to paint a picture of sadness?"

"I don't know. But they did not want to see any waves on the domestic waters."

For several minutes she knitted at her sock, evidently struggling not to say any more. At length she lost the battle. "If you're standing in the manure pile, it's somebody's job to mention the stink. Those congressmen are saying we have to call it a meadow of buttercups instead of a cesspool. Even the artists have to."

"Well, but suppose the artist's job is just to keep everyone amused? Maybe get their minds off the stink, by calling it a meadow. Where's the harm?"

"Nobody will climb out of the pile. There's the harm. They'll keep where they are, deep to the knees in dung, trying to outdo each other remarking on the buttercups."

"Well, I write historical romance. I'm sorry to let you down, but any time you're looking for the meadow and buttercups, I'm your man."

"Fiddlesticks, Mr. Shepherd. Do ye think I ken ye not?"

"Do you know me? I suppose you do. Well enough."

"Well enough. You are good to children whose parents are not. You take in the straggliest cats. You are dismayed by the treatment of the Negro. You read more newspapers than Mr. Hearst himself, though it aggravates you to no end. Shiffling through all that claptrap hunting a day's one glory. The rise of the little man somewhere, or the fall of a tyrant."

"Is that everything?"

"About. I believe you stand on the side of the union of labor."

"Well done, Mrs. Brown. You can read me like a book."

Even in the full darkness I could feel her glare, the dangerous force of her. She had those needles.

"Set your photograph on the dustcover, or not, it makes no difference. You are still there, Mr. Shepherd, plain to see. Your first one was about the hatefulness of war, everyone said so. How it fills up the rich men's pockets and grieves the poor ones."

"I see."

"You needn't squirm, Mr. Shepherd. Your words are your own wee bairns. You need not leave them orphaned. You should stand up proud and say, 'Those are mine!'"

Soon we passed through the long tunnel at Little Switzerland, a deeper darkness within the night's blue darkness, like a cave in the sea. Mrs. Brown's knitting stayed in her lap, the strange blue bundle with its armature of needles, like a peculiar pet she could no longer bear to touch. When we reached Mrs. Bittle's she said good-bye, but until then we hardly spoke any more. Both driver and passenger seemed to need all our energies to find the way ahead, staring at the bleakness and the rain.

November 15

A letter from Frida after all this time, opened with trembling hands. Thrill and fear are really the same, inside a body. Her operation a partial success, good news, though she still suffers. The handsome Spaniard she met in New York seems to be good medicine, a sturdy platform from which to forgive. Her grammar was so odd though, barely coherent. The date on the letter was Lev's birthday and the day of the October Revolution, but no mention of either. No more red carnations on the table for old loves, the *viejo* and democratic socialism. Diego has gone over completely to the side of the Stalinists now. And she, perhaps to the side of morphine.

December 24

A gift: knitted gloves of soft gray wool. What a remarkable sensation, to slide them on and feel each finger fit perfectly in its allotted space. "I noticed you have none," she said. "Or wear none. I thought maybe they didn't use them in Mexico."

"I've bought three pair since I moved here and they're all too short in the fingers. I wind up with webbed hands like a duck."

"Well, see, I wondered. Your fingers are about twice what God gave the rest of us."

I held out both gloved hands, stunned by the sight of perfection. "How did you do this? Did you measure me in my sleep?"

She grinned. "A grease stain on one of your letters. You must have leaned on the table to stand up, after eating a bacon sandwich."

"Very impressive."

"I brought in a rule and measured all the fingers."

I turned my hands over, admiring the row of slant stitches across each thumb gusset. "Not blue, though. I thought you specialized in indigo."

"Oh, those socks you mean, out of that cheap handspun. Those were for the children. This is pure merino from Belk's. I can use quality on you, because you're not planning to outgrow these in a year or run holes in them on purpose."

"I'll try not to let you down."

A memory of snow. A hill striped sideways with blue shadows

of trees. Screaming, the thrill of pursuit, some adult lobbing white balls, making the sound of a cannon blast with every volley. Cupping up hard snow that leaves pills of ice clinging to the fuzzy palms. Mittens, red with a snowflake pattern across the knuckles, made by someone. Father's mother? No contact was allowed later on, it was Mother's choice to leave everything: grandmothers, snow. All water-ice returns to the breath of the world. But those cast-off mittens might still be somewhere. Evidence of a boy's existence.

I told Mrs. Brown she'd given me my first Christmas gift in over ten years. In our many days together, she has not betrayed such emotion as that confession invoked. "Ten year! And not one soul to give you a measly giftie?"

"My family is all gone."

"But *people*. In Mexico you worked in homes, did ye not?"

"The last ones were Russian, they didn't pay Christmas any notice. Mr. Trotsky had us work through like any other day."

"He didn't hold with our Lord Jesus?"

"He was a good man. But no, he didn't. He was Jewish, his background."

"He's the one that got killed."

"Yes."

"And the ones before that, all Jews?"

"No. Mrs. Rivera was crazy for Christmas, she always organized feasts. I was the cook."

"So you had to work straight through."

"I did."

"Mr. Shepherd, it pains me to be gone away next week."

"Honestly, I'm glad you asked. You need to go see your family, and I need to be reminded what regular people do at holiday times."

"Well, regular, I wouldn't know. But you. You'll have nought here to tell you it's Christmas. What will you do?"

What will an acorn do when it has lain awhile in the ground and the rain swells its husk? Become a fig? "I have the galley proofs to finish," I said.

"Now Mr. Shepherd, that is a fib. You finished those, and I know it."

"I wanted to have one more look. And then I'll start writing something new."

The eyebrows soared. "What about?"

"I'm not sure."

She gathered up her purse and gloves, preparing to go. A light snow had been falling all day. "All work and no play, Mr. Shepherd. Makes the meat go to gristle."

"Does it? I thought it made Jack a dull boy."

"It would do that as well."

"I'll probably get nothing done at all, thanks to the pile of books you brought from the library. I'll poke up the fire and have Christmas with Mr. Hardy and Mr. Dickens. What could be better? And Tristram Shandy. The cats are hinting that I should cook a leg of lamb, so maybe I will. And I'm sure Eddie Cantor and Nora Martin will sing some carols for me on Wednesday night."

"I hate to tell you, but they're singing for their sponsor. I think it's Sal Hepatica."

"You are cruel, Mrs. Brown. Next you'll tell me all those girls on the Lucky Strike Hit Parade are crooning for Lucky Strike cigarettes, and not me."

She sat with her hands on her pocketbook, waiting.

"You want to say something. Go ahead."

"None of my business, Mr. Shepherd. But a man would have a girl usually. Or attachments. That aren't cats or books."

I took off the gloves and folded them carefully. "Now this is really a case of the skillet calling the kettle black. Thirty years is a long time to stay a widow."

"I did have a runny-go at marriage. The one time."

"Well, don't worry. I've had my runny-goes. Attachments, as you say."

"If you say so. And no Christmas present for ten years. If you get attached to something, seems like it wouldn't come all that far loose."

"No, wait, I forgot. Last Christmas Romulus brought over a jam cake from his mother. Half the cake, actually. He said they'd had enough of it."

"Blessed are the grateful, Mr. Shepherd, but that is no account as a real present. Half a jam cake showing signs of prior use."

Chispa slipped into the room, around the edge of the door and along the wall, flattened to it, as if pulled sideways by a separate order of gravity. Slowly she crossed the bottom of the bookcase in similar manner, into the inglenook by the fireplace. I unfolded the gloves. It was tempting to put them on, wear them until Whitsuntide. "I'm not the sort of person who attracts gifts."

"Mr. Shepherd, do ye think I believe it? I open the mail, with all such things in it as people can let sail. Even little embroidered things."

"Then I should say I'm not a good recipient. When people are no good at relationships, I've noticed they often blame the other people. But I don't."

"I've never heard you blame a soul for anything, Mr. Shepherd. It's one of your qualities. To the extent I sometimes wonder if your mother dropped you on your head."

"No, she probably carried me in a suitcase—she was eternally on the move. Anyone I especially liked was soon gone, household people or friends. It's been like that. Or they've left me on their own initiative. Mostly by dying."

"Well. I am not a one to argue with mortal demise."

"Well said, Mrs. Brown."

"You ought to write it down. About yourself and all those that went away."

"What, write about my life? Like poor old Tristram Shandy trying to remember his whole story helter-skelter?"

"You'd get further," she said. "You've been keeping good notes all along."

"Who would want to read such trivial stuff?"

"Well, why write it down in the first place, then? Because you do. I'm not putting my nose into anything, you do it plain in the open, Mr. Shepherd. Seems to me, if you really wanted shed of your own days, you'd not take such care to put them all down on a page. I see you go so deep in- it, you forget day or night and have breakfast at supper."

"I'm just a writer. It's my way of thinking."

"It's your attachments. That's what it looks like to me. You might do as well to attach to your own self, alongside all these story people you dream up from nowhere."

"But who would want to read that?"

The light outside had gone dusky, and now the wind raised a low keen against the window. Clumps of snow fell out of the trees, shattering across the yard. "You won't want to miss your five-fifteen bus," I said.

She donned a formidable knitted hat and stood to leave, reaching to shake my hand. "I will see you on Monday week. Happy Christmas, Mr. Shepherd."

"Happy Christmas, Mrs. Brown. I thank you for the gift."

She closed the door and stepped out toward Haywood, leaving behind a house as silent as an underworld. Chisme slipped into the room, pulled by the same sidelong gravity across the bottom of the wall into the inglenook. Chispa immediately left it then, according to the inscrutable laws of attraction and indifference. The hall clock divided the scene into measured increments: *Tick, tick.*

Who would want to read all this?

Book Review

by United Press

Picture the lady walking by, a real looker, gold bangles on her arm and a tattoo on her ankle. She's headed out for some shopping, with a basket strapped on her back. For today's menu she may choose iguana roasted on the spit, or perhaps armadillo. For cash, her gal pals trade cocoa beans, or a handy gadget that's the rage with their better halves here in ancient Mexico: a double-edged throwing spear called the *atel-atel*.

That's the opening scene of *Pilgrims of Chapultepec*, a novel by Harrison Shepherd that reads like a joyride. This tribe of ancients will settle down in village life for only so long before it loses its charm to pox, invasion, or bandits—you can count on it. Then they hit the trail again, goaded on by a wild-eyed chief who claims he'll lead them to a promised land. How will they know they've found it? He claims the gods told him to look for an eagle on a cactus, snacking on snake.

Apart from its forehead-wrinkle of a title, this book aims to please: hair-rising battles, narrow escapes, and a heaping portion of adventure, in a tale of hardnosed leaders and men who suffer them.

The Evening Post, *March 8, 1947*

"Books for Thought," by Sam Hall Mitchell

The Quick and the Dead

Author Harrison Shepherd, the diffident but talented prodigy who last year brought us *Vassals of Majesty*, has another winning turn based on historical fact in ancient Mexico. In *Pilgrims of Chapultepec*, the Aztec people are driven from their ancestral home in a journey with more twists than a Chinaman's queue. By its end, the author has tackled some surprising themes, including the atom-bomb question.

These pilgrims hike for decades, pushed by a mad king who always promises happiness is just around the bend. The author's "Studs Lonigan" is an Indian youth named Poatli-cue, watched by the jealous king as he hones his skill in battle. Golden boy Poatlicue was singled out by the gods at thirteen to hurl the first *atl-atl*—a razor-sharp flying weapon put in the hero's hand as he was about to die in his first battle. In a New World *Deus ex machina*, the weapon was carried to the hero by an eagle.

The ruthless king fears an upstart's power to unseat him, and offers a bargain: if Poatlicue maintains his loyalty without a hitch, he'll someday help rule the nation. But "someday" never comes, and Poatlicue grows a cynical stripe, doubting the value of following an unwise leader. On dark nights he wonders if the gods chose him for a reason: to behead the sniveling king, and rule in his place?

Poatlicue even questions the seductive power of his *atl-atl*. His tribesmen revere it as a god, rushing to make replicas of the weapon, worshipping it on an altar, believing it will grant them absolute rule. But Poatlicue notes a worrisome trend: as his tribesmen reproduce the blade's design, so do their enemies. Having perfected it, they fashion harsher weapons. With each battle the death numbers grow higher, the killing tools more precise.

Just as we've lately been warned by Bernard Baruch's somber report to Congress, these pilgrims must choose between the quick and the dead, when fate gives them a dread power without means to stop its baleful use. Baruch argues for disposal of all atom bombs, while author Shepherd only calls the reader to wonder until the final page: has the sacred weapon saved those who wield it, or doomed them?

The Asheville Trumpet, *April 8, 1947*

Asheville Writer a Mystery

by Carl Nicholas

Here where Mountain Air is clearest and Heaven is the Nearest, our most prominent writer gives a taste of faraway places in *Pilgrims of Chaltipica*, a new book flying off the shelves this month of every bookstore in the nation. Mrs. Jack Cates, owner of Cates Bookshop, tells us Harrison Shepherd knows the ropes of his trade and this book will not disappoint. "We had a hubbub the week it came in," she said. "Nobody wants to read anything but. And I'm going to warn you, it's got more bare skin in it than a hot day at Beaver Lake."

The author bases his books on his own experience growing up in Mexico, but has resided in the Montford Hills neighborhood since 1941. Calls from the *Trumpet* have not been returned. Mrs. Cates speculates he may regard his privacy, as "the most eligible bachelor in town, if not North Carolina."

At the Asheville Skating Club next door to the bookstore, 21 comely lasses partook of our survey on the subject, with fifteen saying they are "Hep to Shepherd," but definitely. Six maintained otherwise, "Spooky" and "cold cut" among the reasons given. Nine young ladies say they hold it against him for not serving in the armed forces due to a 4-F status, but the others say it was not his fault due to a perforated eardrum, the condition shared with crooner Frank Sinatra. All wondered how a well-heeled single fellow spends his time, as the author has sold nearly one million copies. As the old Asheville saying goes, Our moonshine is the meanest, our Stories are the keenest, our Sportmen are the gamest and—so it seems—our Bachelors are the Tamest!

The Echo, *April 26, 1947*

Pilgrims of Chapultepec, BY HARRISON W. SHEPHERD
$2.69, Stratford and Sons, New York

Don't look now, but a new chump named Harrison W. Shepherd is more popular than Wendell Wilkie. His *Pilgrims of Chaplutepec* is storming the nation this month and sure to be translated abroad. Don't be surprised one day if you hear they're reading Harrison Shepherd in China.

This one will be snapped up by the movies, so read it now before you see the picture. The glittering backdrop of Mexico spreads across every page, and the young hero is a heart-throb, with good looks and a secret weapon to boot. Ladies, this one will break your heart. Will this author ever give us a happy ending?

Shepherd slathers emotion on the page, yet in real life he is a shy fellow who guards against any showing of his feelings. A friend who's known him since college days revealed this mental reserve goes back to Shepherd's short-pants days, when even at his mother's funeral he remained cool as ice.

However, our source revealed, old friend Harry has one curious quirk: "He cannot look at a beautiful woman without whistling."

April 30

It was the perforated eardrum that put the pepper on Mrs. Brown. And the whistling at girls. "This friend from college days. Is that a person?"

"I don't think so. Given that I didn't go to college. The people of my past are dead and gone, Mrs. Brown, that's a fact." *Billy*

Boorzai's huge hands, both of us suffocating with laughter, trying to keep still. An officer's footsteps outside in the hall. Pounding hearts, scarlet shame.

"Who would reckon. The papers make things up out of the blue sky."

"Or, they find a little rain cloud and help it along."

She hesitated in the doorway, backlit from the upstairs hall in her square-shouldered, putty-colored suit. Platform shoes with ankle straps, oh my, and hair let out of its net today, pinned at the sides and curled at the shoulders, longer than I remembered. She looks like a tiny, earnest Jane Russell. Lately it's crossed my mind to wonder if there is some fellow. She takes a midday break for errands and a bite in one of the luncheonettes on Charlotte. She could be meeting a sailor, for all I know.

"When you see a thing like this in print, Mr. Shepherd, people think it's true. I almost think it myself, and that's me, knowing better. How can they do it?"

"Somehow they manage, every day of the year. Why be surprised, just because this time the victim is me?"

She stayed in the doorway. She doesn't like to come in the study, for fear of disturbing. "Mr. Shepherd, why are ye *not*? A shocking thing ought to shock."

A shocking thing. "The man I worked for in Mexico, I don't even know how to tell you what the newsmen did to him. One night some gunmen broke into the house and attacked him with machine guns, attacked all of us, the staff and his family. His grandson got hurt. We were terrified they'd come back. But the press said Lev had organized this attack himself to get sympathy for his cause. They reported that as fact."

"My stars."

"It didn't help us get police protection, I can tell you. And that's just one thing, a case that comes to mind. The other man I worked for reportedly ate human flesh."

"Well. That's Mexican newspapers. We want to think ours are better here. But I suppose they say the same about us."

"It was all over everywhere, about Trotsky staging the shooting attack. Europe, New York. It starts in one paper, and that's the source. The others pick it up and pass it along. Lev used to say there are two kinds of papers, the ones that lie every day, and the ones that save it for special campaigns, for greater impact."

"But a perforated eardrum. My stars. It's like you said. It starts with one and then it goes. We've not heard the end of that one."

"Like howler monkeys."

"The *Trumpet's* your own hometown. They could have asked."

"If they had called, what would you have said?"

She looked like a model standing for a portrait of misery: shoulders squared, high eyebrows knit, hands tightly folded. "I would do as you ask. Mr. Shepherd has no comment to make on that."

"Thank you."

"But."

"But?"

"When they have nothing, they fill in. If you don't stop them, they fill in more. It's like you've agreed to it. To their way of thinking, saying nothing is the same as agreeing."

"Are you saying it's my responsibility to stop another man from lying?"

"Well. No. It's his to stop himself."

"Dios habla por el que calle."

"Meaning what, Mr. Shepherd?"

"God speaks for the man who keeps quiet."

"If you say so."

"'No comment' means 'no comment.' It does not mean, 'I hate to admit this, but yes, he has a punctured eardrum.'"

"Well, people think that. And taking the Fifth means you're guilty."

"Whatever they may think, it does not. A blank space on a form, the missing page, a void, a hole in your knowledge of someone—it's still some real *thing*. It exists. You don't get to fill it in with whatever you want. I'm staking myself on a principle, Mrs. Brown. This country promises us the presumption of innocence."

"*Presumptions* we have got, Mr. Shepherd. Coming out our ears."

"What would you have me say? Mr. Shepherd does not have a punctured eardrum, he does not have a friend from college days, he *does* look at pretty girls without whistling—oh, that's a trap. Where does it stop?"

She had no answer.

"If the *atl-atl* was meant as a symbol for the atom bomb, can't we let the reader have a chance to decide?"

"Well, I know what you're saying. The reporters would have you put in the grinder and feed you to Baby with a spoon."

"I don't think the reporters really want to know the first thing about me. They fancy themselves artists. They'd rather draw free-hand."

"They do have questions."

"I know. The one fellow wanted to ask me about Truman and the Soviet containment policy, remember? *Collier's*, I think."

"*New York Times. Collier's* said they wouldn't even run a review unless you spoke to them."

"And did they?"

"A little one. It wasn't very good."

"If I talked, I would only end up giving them more blanks to fill in. 'How do you feel about Truman's new anti-Soviet position, Mr. Shepherd?' No comment. 'That Bette Davis is quite a looker, isn't she, Mr. Shepherd?' No comment."

"So, the punctured eardrum. No comment."

"Correct."

"Next they'll be reporting you died."

"Imagine the peace and quiet."

The telephone rang, and she ran to get it. Her stockings had seams down the backs. I tried out a wolf-whistle—a feeble one, but I heard her pause on the stairs.

A sample of the mail received May 15, 1947, seventy-five letters in all. After publication of *Pilgrims of Chapultepec*, Stratford and Sons posted the mail forward in boxes once or twice weekly. —VB

Dear Mr. Shepherd,
At the youthful age of seventy here is one codger who tips my hat to you. For years I have re-read the favorites because the new authors are not up to snuff. But some weeks ago I ran short and went to my corner bookstore for a suggestion. The fellow handed me two by Harrison W. Shepherd, a name unknown to me. I read both without a pause. Of course I blush at scenes of copulation and revelry. But you show that modern times are no different from the old, and people the same everywhere. I was stationed overseas in the first war and never learned to like it, but it did teach me a thing or two. Thank you for adding spunk to my life. I look forward to your other books.
Sincerely,

COLLIN THOMAS

Dear Mr. Shepherd,
Although we have never met I consider you a friend. You touch and inspire me. I read Vassals of Majesty *twice and now the new one. Thank you for putting my own heart into words. I have wanted to show courage the way your characters do. You show that men at the top don't always have any more smarts than the rest of us. I have been thinking of telling my boss to jump in the lake and look for better. (Secretary.) Now I just might achieve my goal.*
With admiration,

LYNNE HILL

Dear Mr. Shepherd,

I had to read your book in history at Lancaster Valley High. I don't read too many books but yours is okay. It gave me a lot to ponder about Poatlicue wanting to be a good citizen, and then ending up wanting to kill the King. Our teacher said to ask you three questions about ancient times of Mexico, for our report. My questions:

1. Is it true the Eagle gave the people their first weapon.

2. What kind of government did they have, Democracy or Dictator?

3. Did you ever really shoot a dear?

Thank you. My report is due May 12.
Yours truly,

WENDELL DIXON

One of 19 letters enclosed in a single packet from Lancaster Valley High School, California. —VB

Dear Mr. Harrison Shepherd
My heart is full of happiness, just knowing you are holding this letter in your hand. Thank you for being an author. You have gotten me through a lot of sad times, when my mother died especially. Sometimes I do everything I can just to get through the day, so I can curl up at night with my favorite book. When life is humdrum or just plain old sad I know you will take me away to the place where troubles are forgotten. When I get a letter back from you my life will be complete. Thank you, thank you.
Yours,

ROXANNE WILLS

All correspondence answered in the same week received, insofar as possible. No photographs or inclusions. —VB

June 6, 1947

Dear Frida,

Diego's telegram has terrified me not a little. He seems to be-lieve the doctors nearly killed you, so I fear for all concerned. But for you, above all. I'm determined today to send a cheerful letter, to give you a little picknick from your worries, as you have done often for me. You'll find in this package your birth-day present. Don't be too disappointed: it's only another book, which I hope will amuse you. If not, blame yourself, you should have left me a cook.

I am trying to begin a new story that will be about the Ma-yans, I think, and the fall of civilizations. Everyone wants a happy ending this time, so this should be just the ticket. But the writing proceeds slowly, when life is filled with such thrilling distractions. Only last week I purchased a packet of clothespins, and a new billfold. (The shopgirl informed me it has a secret pouch.) The Roadster and I "Make a Date to Lubricate" every 30 days at the garage on Coxe Avenue. A new appliance shop has opened down the street! And right now I am spying out my study window into the treetops where a gigantic bird is peck-ing a hole. I wish you could see the creature: its red hair stands straight up, as mine does on Mondays. Goodness, the wood chips fly, this thing is the size of an ox. And you were worried my life was dull.

I never want for company. The neighbor boy Romulus seems to prefer my house to his own, now that summer is here and he is paroled from Grade Six. With hands shoved deep in overall pockets he wanders around the house coveting things, but is not a thief. He asks. He particularly wants the little carved idol from Teotihuacán. I haven't told him it's a stolen object. Instead I gave him a fountain pen and an old fedora and he pretends to be Edward Murrow, using a Doomsday voice to interview the cats. I also offered to give him a cat, the useless black one I call Chisme, but he won't take it.

My stenographer comes Monday through Friday to answer mail and telephone, for over a year now. My wonderful amanuensis. She works at the dining room table. With each fresh day's mail piled high there, we pray: "For what we are about to receive may the Lord make us truly thankful." She is a whiz, I have known her sometimes to get through nearly a hundred letters from readers in a day, typing up a kind little note in answer to each. She hauls it all to the post office in a gigantic leather satchel she found somewhere, such as might have been used by the Pony Express: over her shoulder she slings it, and off she goes, does Violet Brown. I can't help thinking you would appreciate the irony of her name, for she is a dove-gray little bird. And something like the mother I need, commanding me to leave the house for fresh air at least once daily, if only to the corner for cigarettes. Lately she has stepped up the program: I am to undertake some level of social adventure each week. Going to the movies by myself is acceptable (Mrs. Brown is lenient), and not too bad if I slip in after the house has gone dark. The purpose of the outings is to overcome my dread of the world and all things in it. Now the magazines are saying I have a punctured eardrum, which is helpful. If the world howls too loudly, I can pretend I don't hear.

Please send word you are recovering. Diego's telegram was a shocker. He seems extremely angry, not only with your doctors but also the world and Every Damn Gringo in it, myself included. You might let him know, Truman did not consult me before committing to defeat the Communists in Greece and Turkey. Secretary of State Marshall has announced a new plan for European assistance that won't thrill your husband either. Frida, you understand men. How are these leaders different from the boys I used to watch at school, trying to make up their teams for football? Before this war we had six great players on the grass. Now only two are left standing. Naturally those two will be rivals, and try to get the rest to line up on their side. Dimes and candy will help, sure.

I struggle to understand why Diego supports Stalin now, after working so closely with Lev, and even seeing him murdered. What rational motives could cause Diego to make this change? "It's a revolutionary necessity," he said, but how am I to know what that means? Betrayal, as the means to an end? Nearly every day I wake up shocked at how little in this world I comprehend. Perhaps Diego is right, and despite all my years of serving brilliant men I am only a dumb gringo. I shall try to keep to the task I seem to know: writing stories for people who believe if you throw a rock, it could roll uphill. If your husband says I am an idiot on the subject of politics, certainly he should know. So don't ask me about the peaceful atom, or how to raise the birth rate in France.

For your amusement I enclose a newspaper review, a favorite from the last round. I take it as proof I am no literary great, but Mrs. Brown says it proves my books are about Important Things. Diego may take it as written proof that someone here besides myself opposes Truman's shocking turn against the rising proletariat. But mostly it proves nothing. You know reviewers, they are the wind in their own sails. I should like to write my books only for the dear person who lies awake reading in bed until page last, then lets the open book fall gently on her face, to touch her smile or drink her tears.

I'm not brave, as you are. However badly broken, you still stand up. In your Tehuana dresses, in your garden, with the pomegranate trees bending toward you to open their red flowers. No matter what happens, you will still be at the center of the world.
Your friend,

INSÓLITO

The New York Weekly Review, *April 26, 1947*

Author's Second Strike Hits the Mark

by Donald Brewer

Do not mistake Harrison Shepherd for a literary great. His stories are full-to-brimming with lusty, bare-chested youths. The settings are glamorous, the plots chest-heavers. You may not admit it to your friends, but somehow you can't put them down.

Pilgrims of Chapultepec (Stratford and Sons), set in Mexico before the Conquest, recounts a pilgrimage of people cast out from home, doomed to follow a neurotic leader who picks fights with his own shadow. Shepherd makes the case for those who find themselves on the ropes against bad policy, wondering what the Sam Hill their leader could be thinking. The protagonist, a boy named Poatlicue, struggles to be a model citizen but comes to view his nation's long march as a winning game for the king, and the scourge of everyone else.

Author Shepherd combines Leatherstocking action with Chaplinesque pathos, as shown in this symbolic hunting scene: Poatlicue and his friend skin a deer, grousing about the king as they hack their kill into anatomical bits. Their leader has made another outrageous edict, reversing a treaty of friendship with a neighboring clan, deciding now it can't be trusted. The tribe will have to move again, in a season when food is scarce. These youths are rankled. Poatlicue tosses a pair of testicles in the dust, calling them "the buck's last big hopes in sad little bags."

He tells his pal, "Our leader is an empty sack. You could just as well knock him over, put a head with horns on a stick, and follow that. Most of us never choose to believe in the nation, we just come up short on better ideas. It's probably a law: the public imagination may not exceed the size of the leaders' ballocks."

The author may be alluding here to the testimony of Donald Benedict, the New York theological student who refused to register for the draft during the war. "We do not contend that the American people maliciously choose the vicious instrument of war," said Benedict during trial, "but in a perplexing situation they lack the imagination and religious faith to respond in a different manner."

Does Shepherd mean to put himself in the draft-dodger's camp? One could ask many questions of this politically astute novelist, starting with his opinion of a leader who has just set the nation reeling with an abrupt foreign policy reversal, from friendly cooperation to Truman's so-called "containment" of the USSR.

We can only wonder, as Shepherd declines to be interviewed. But this week as we line up behind our man in Washington, shelling up $400 million to fight our friends of yesterday because "Every nation must choose," we might listen for a thump in the dust, and wonder whether the public's big hopes will fit in that small, sad sack.

June 11

She has raised the subject of the memoir yet again. I thought it had died a natural death, but no, she presses. If only to put to rest the perforated eardrum question, I suspect. The first chapter was very good in her opinion, and today she confessed that since the day I gave it to her, she comes to work each morning hoping I'll have the next part of it ready for her to type.

"It's been near six months now since chapter one, Mr. Shepherd. If it takes that long for each, you'll not outlive your own boyhood."

I told her I was very sorry to crush her hopes in coming to work and so forth. But there will be no next part. It was a direly mistaken idea. And anyway, even several months ago when I was entertaining the project, I'd run across a problem, the missing notebook. The very next little diary after the first one. I hadn't yet told her.

"I can't recall that year without it. I should have let you know a while ago. I just hoped you'd forget about it. The memoir fell apart before I'd even gotten started."

"What do you mean, gone?" Her eye went to the shelf. She knows where I keep them. They should all be put to the flame.

"The crucial missing piece of the manuscript. There's a word for that, historians use. A lacuna. So blame it on fate and history, if you want."

"Did you have it before? When you first took all of them out of the crate?"

This is not a set of keys gone missing, I informed her with some irritation. It just didn't come with the rest, when Frida packed up the notebooks and papers. Probably it had burned at the police station, or slipped behind a cabinet. It's small, I know exactly what it looked like—it was a little leather-bound accounts book I stole from the maid. About the size of your hand. And now it's gone. Just forget about the memoir, I'm working on something different now. I should burn up all these notebooks so you'll stop nagging me about it.

Mrs. Brown is no fool. "If you remember what the booklet looked like, you could remember well enough what was in it."

June 23

It was only one letter, but she carried it up the stairs like a sack of bricks.

"I hate to disturb. But it says they need this back by return mail."

"Who is it?"

"J. Parnell Thomas."

"Friend or foe?"

"Chairman, House Committee on Un-American Activities, formerly known as the Dies Committee."

"Rings a bell, Dies. Oh yes, I know these gentlemen." *Committee Diez*, we'd pronounced it, like "ten" in Spanish. They arranged Lev's trip to Washington, the visas all prepared and then canceled at the last minute.

"You do?" She seemed startled.

"I mean, I know what they do. They called up my former employer once, from Mexico. To testify on the treacheries of Stalin. They're still in business?"

She held up the letter. "It's just a form. They say it's gone out to all employees of the Department of State."

"I don't believe I'll be shipping any more art for the government."

"Present or previous, it says. They need you to sign a statement saying you're loyal to the United States government."

"Goodness. Why wouldn't I be?"

She moved her glasses from her head to her nose, and read: "Due to close wartime cooperation between the United States and Russia, certain strategic areas of our government may have been opened to Communist sympathizers. As of March 21, 1947, the President and Congress have undertaken to secure the loyalty of all government workers."

"Very cloak and dagger. Where do I sign?"

She approached the bench. "Are you sure you ought, Mr. Shepherd? If you aren't looking to work for the government again, maybe there isn't need."

"Are you doubting my loyalty?"

She surrendered the letter for signature.

"Mrs. Brown, I don't hate much and I don't love much. I'm a free man. But I love writing books for Americans. Look at those letters, all that sky-blue goodness, this country is the berries. And Joseph Stalin murdered my friend. He would have gotten me too, if I'd stood in the way."

"So you've said, Mr. Shepherd. I know it sets a haint upon you, especially of an August, and no wonder. It's no small thing to see bloody murder."

I signed the letter and handed it back. "I'm inclined in this case to stand out of the way. If I ever had to choose, I might just be a coward and save my own skin."

"That's people," she said. "That's how the Good Lord made us to be."

"No, I've known brave men. Lev saw his children murdered, and never gave in. Even young boys, like Sheldon Harte. I'm told they loved life even more than I do, it's why they became revolutionaries. And ended up bludgeoned, or dead in a lime pit."

She stood waiting. For a happier ending, I suppose.

"What we end up calling history is a kind of knife, slicing down through time. A few people are hard enough to bend its edge. But most won't even stand close to the blade. I'm one of those. We don't bend anything."

"You do, though. Look here, I've got boxes of letters downstairs, as you said yourself. People telling how you've saved their day. Do ye think that's ordinary?"

"I give them a lark. A few hours to forget about a disappointing family, or a boss who's a tyrant. But all that mess is still there, when the book ends. I don't save people."

The corners of her mouth turned down. "Mr. Shepherd, here's your trouble. You don't know your own strength."

July 3

The Pack Square Soda Shoppe could not have been decked out with more flag bunting if it were the president's train car. Romulus was dazzled, mostly by his buffalo-like ice cream sundae. Mrs. Brown was rosy-cheeked, sipping cola through a straw. "You ought be thrilled," she said. "A Hollywood movie."

"You keep saying that. I am thrilled."

"Well, ye barely look it," she said. She had on the blue Kerrybrooke beret (*wear it many ways!*), identifying this as a Social Adventure of the highest order.

"You don't," Romulus agreed.

"You pipe down. We men have to stick together. We don't wear our hearts on our sleeves the way women do."

He glanced at his shoulder, then took a whitecap of cream off his cheek with the back of a hand.

"It's not really settled yet, for one thing. Where am I going to find an agent?"

"Did Mr. Lincoln say you *have* to get one? Or just that it would be helpful? What did he say about that exactly?"

"Find someone to negotiate the contract, for the motion-picture option. He can't do it, this is between Hollywood and me. An agent is customary. Or a lawyer."

"Well, lawyers, I have known a few. Working for the city. Not that they could reckon out a motion-picture contract."

"Mr. Lincoln said brace ourselves for the press. They'll step up the pursuit."

A pea-green Cadillac hunched past like some kind of water animal, the small, split windshield like close-set eyes. They will never make another car to touch the Roadster. Mrs. Brown put us in a corner near the window so I wouldn't be spotted in the shop. But even so, I could hear a couple of girls at the counter saying "*him. It is. Isn't.*"

Mrs. Brown snapped her fingers. "I have a man! I think I have the business card in my jewelry case." For a moment she sounded so modern, a regular Gal Friday.

And she saves the day, once again. Or might have, we will see. It's a gentleman she met last year when he came to inquire about renting a vacant room. They had quite a chat in the parlor while waiting for Mrs. Bittle to return from the hairdresser's. He's from New York City, a lawyer, mostly retired. Moving to Asheville because his wife had died, and the daughter Margaret lived here. Grandchildren. He was not sure how he'd get along in Dixieland, but you can't argue with a daughter named Margaret. Even Harry Truman knows that, ha-ha. They'd had the radio on in the parlor, and Mrs. Brown happened to wonder aloud what the stars looked like. The voices give a certain impression, but the actors might be less attractive than they sound. It was *Duffy's Tavern*. The gentleman told her as a matter of fact the actress playing Duffy's daughter might sound like a girl but she is a mature woman, forty if she's a day.

Shirley Booth. And the other one, Cass Daley, has an overbite like a lizard.

How did he know? He's met them, that's how. It's his line. A radio and television lawyer.

I asked Mrs. Brown why he hadn't taken the room.

"Mrs. Bittle wouldn't let to him. She was sorry. He seemed very nice."

"I see. Only good people here. Was he a Negro?"

"No."

"Just too much of a Yankee?"

She glanced at Romulus, then back at me. "You told me in Mexico you use to work for some . . . that didn't have Christmas."

Even the word *Christmas* didn't jog a glimmer of attention from Romulus. He sat glaze-eyed as a mystic, stirring his bowl of ice-cream soup streaked with a bleeding cherry. I tried to work out the puzzle.

"Oh. This man was a Jew?"

Arthur Gold. The New York Jew in Dixie.

July 22

Poor Mrs. Brown, in trouble with the Woman's Club. She was so distracted today, she had to call Mr. Gold back twice to get instructions about mailing the motion-picture contract. She seems to think these women mean to throw her in a cauldron of bouillon. As one of three members of the Cultural Committee, she was not the lone perpetrator. But it was her idea to involve the children.

Their speaker was a girl named Surya, spending the summer with Asheville relatives, on leave from some school-term cultural exchange in Washington, D.C. It was Genevieve Kohler (neighbor to the relatives) who hatched the plot to have this girl from Russia as their Cultural Evening speaker. The ladies were in a jam; Decorating with the New Plastic Fabrics had canceled on short notice. Mrs. Brown thought of inviting local high-school girls, pointing it up as an inspirational talk. The girl had lived through war. She had overcome long odds to arrive in Carolina in time for a Rhododendron Festival.

Mrs. Brown said she looked as hale as a milkmaid, with brown eyes and dimples, and that the talk was both informative and audible. Little Surya spoke of her school in Russia, the free health program, and the Russian plan for old-age care. She contrasted the governing bodies in her country with the newly elected Communist government of Poland. She made favorable mention of the position of women in modern-day Russia, and equally favorable mention of North Carolina, and Washington, D.C. Mrs. Brown said the girl was so unsophisticated and gracious, she doubted the child would have disparaged a spider, had it walked across her face. Yet she created a sensation. The Woman's Club president, vice president, and sergeant-at-arms stood up as a block, interrupted the speaker to announce their devotion to America, and walked out. Some others followed. Mothers who had brought their girls, responding to the handbill distributed at school, left with daughters in tow, indignant at having been duped.

"We did not mislead," Mrs. Brown insists. "We put on the handbill she was here in the youth foreign exchange from the former St. Petersburg."

"Maybe they thought you meant St. Petersburg, the Republic of Florida. Just across the waters from the Mexican continent, as I recall."

"Mr. Shepherd, this is not a joking matter."

"I'm trying to lighten your mood. It's not the disaster you think."

The Asheville Trumpet, *July 23, 1947*

Crowd Takes Stand Against Reds

by Edwina Boudreaux

"Every nation must choose between alternative ways of life," according to President Truman, and the Woman's Club

Cultural Evening on Monday was no exception. Tickets sold for twenty-five cents each for a Cultural Lecture by Miss Surya Poldava of the U.S.S.R. Mrs. Herb Lutheridge, President, opened with the Pledge of Allegiance. The evening was interrupted by audience disagreement and brought to a hasty conclusion. Pastor Case Mabrey of Coxe First Baptist led the closing prayer. Mrs. Lutheridge had no knowledge of the speaker and apologizes to each and every person in attendance. "The Woman's Club opposes the suppression of personal freedoms and Communistic way of life."

Superintendent of Schools Ron Stanley called a meeting yesterday to discuss an occurrence that "shocked the school system." The nature of this assembly was repugnant to all who work with youth in Buncombe County, said Stanley, who did not attend the lecture. "It runs contrary to the philosophy of education we operate under." The Asheville D.A.R. speaking through Mrs. Talmadge Rich, President-General, not in attendance, also went on record as opposing the lecture.

The Woman's Club will review its guidelines to prevent the unfortunate occurrence in the future. The program was organized by Mrs. Glen Kohler of Haywood and Mrs. Violet Brown of Tunnel Road. Reached by telephone, Mrs. Kohler gave her occupation as housewife and apologized for the turn of events. Mrs. Brown, a secretary for a private firm, maintained the program was informative. "The world has people of all kinds, and I don't see the good of wrapping our children's heads in cotton wool." Brown, age 47, is a childless widow.

The Woman's Club will refund the ticket price to all who attended.

. *August 15, 1947*

Harrison W. Shepherd
30 Montford Avenue
Asheville, North Carolina

Dear Mr. Shepherd,
The Federal Bureau of Investigation has been charged by the Congress of
the United States with the conduct of routine investigations of all persons
presently or previously employed by the federal government, in an effort to
ascertain complete and unswerving loyalty to the United States. For this
purpose we request that you immediately supply in writing the following
information: all former places of residence and former employers, schools
and colleges attended, organizations, associations and groups in which the
employee has been a member.
This investigation is directed by the House Committee on Un-American
Activities (formerly known as Dies Committee) and shall include reference
to Civil Service Commission files, military and naval intelligence records,
Dies Committee hearings of other employees when applicable, and local
law-enforcement files. Any derogatory information will result in a full field
investigation.
The Civil Service Commission maintains a master index covering all
persons who have been subject to loyalty investigations since Sept. 1, 1939.
The Loyalty Review Board of North Carolina shall be furnished the name
of any individual found to have associated with such persons, or with any
organization, movement, or group the Attorney General has designated as
totalitarian, fascist, communist, or subversive, or advocating acts of force
or violence or seeking to alter the form of government of the United States by
unconstitutional means. The Review Board shall also be furnished with any
evidence of sabotage, espionage, treason, sedition, or knowingly associating
with spies. The McCormack Registration Act (Statute 631) requires that
every person who is an agent of a foreign principal shall register with the
Secretary of State. The Voorhis Act (Statute 1201) requires that every

organization subject to foreign control which engages in political activity shall be required to register with the Attorney General.

This Bureau expects your full and prompt cooperation in this investigation.

Sincerely,

J. EDGAR HOOVER, DIRECTOR
FEDERAL BUREAU OF INVESTIGATION

September 2

Arthur Gold in person looks like a Dashiell Hammett private eye: white shirt, rolled-up sleeves, steel blue eyes, necktie five years out of date. He's a regular white-haired Sam Spade, complete with the smoky little office up a narrow flight of stairs in the Woolworth's building on Henry Street. The ever-burning cigarette, the epic slouch. If Violet Brown is the "do be" gal for posture, Mr. Gold is the "don't be." His narrow body describes the shape of an S in his chair, with a meridian running through the head, navel, and shins, with all else slumped to the fore or the aft. It was hard at first to reconcile the slumped posture with the astute voice on the telephone. But within minutes he established himself as the same Mr. Gold, planking out the long sentences that arrive unfailingly at their destination. He could be formidable in court. Except midway between his subject and object, you'd become distracted by the cigarette, wondering when that worm of ash will finally drop on his shirt.

"Congratulations on your distinguished career." He unwound himself to stand, shake hands. "Please, call me Artie. Finally we meet, sit down, please. It's a pleasure doing business with a man who has made so much of himself in a relatively short amount of time in this country, and if I may say so, on this earth. How old are you?"

"Thirty-one."

He squinted, evaluating. "Yeah, okay. You look it."

He studied the letter for only a few seconds before tossing it on his desk. "To make a long story short? You will have to answer this. If you don't, they will send you another. It's a form, they've got millions of them. Please, tell me, what is it about this particular request that worries you?"

"I'm not really worried. There's nothing on that list that applies. Honestly, treason and sedition, violent overthrow. I'm all right until they add smoking in bed."

Artie laughed, bobbing his head from the shoulders.

"I'm just wondering what's behind it, before I answer. I make mistakes sometimes. I seem to be naive about certain things."

"How so?"

"I grew up in Mexico, in the Revolution. Being a Communist was just an ordinary household thing. About like fish on Fridays."

"I grew up in a country like that also. New York in the twenties. You ever hear of Eugene V. Debs?"

"I think so."

"So. Grew up in Mexico, but you are a citizen of the United States, this much I know from working on your film contract. You were born here, moved to Mexico at the age of twelve as I recall, returning when exactly?"

"September of '40. Before that, I was here two years to attend school."

He was making notes. "Where and when?"

"Potomac Academy, Washington, D.C., '32 and '33."

"District of Columbia in '32. The summer of the Bonus Army riots."

"I know. I was in them. I was sick a few weeks from the tear gas."

He looked up. "You were in the Bonus Army riots?"

"By accident. I was trying to make a delivery from the A&P."

"Holy smokes. I will not put this in your dossier."

"I don't think my dossier is going to be problematic."

"Mr. Shepherd. Should I call you Harry?"

"No. Just Shepherd is fine. Without the Mr."

"Shepherd. In seventy-five words or less, how would you describe your dossier?"

"Empty. That's the whole truth. I spent almost all my life until now putting food on other people's plates. Eating their leftovers, if any. So you could say my sentiments lodge in the proletarian quarter. The worker control of industry strikes me as a decent idea. But I'm not a member of anything. Is that seventy-five words?"

"Or less. You are concise."

"I don't even vote. My secretary needles me about that."

"You believe in the class struggle, but you don't vote?"

"This country is a puzzle. In Mexico even the conservatives grant the power of the syndicates. But here, during the strikes, the most liberal politicians called the Mine Workers president a coal-black son of Satan. The conservatives probably just thought he was Satan père. It's a pretty watery broth. Republicans, Democrats."

"This I will not deny."

"In the war they were all friends with Stalin, but now he's also joined the Satan family line. That one I agree with. This letter they've sent me, I only want to understand it. So I won't step in something. I tend to do that, step in things."

He sat staring, the ash end of his cigarette growing long and white. "I see. This letter worries you because you're thinking you may get hit with somebody else's gas on your way to the A&P."

"This letter confounds me. I know what communism is. But a few weeks ago, my secretary was voted out of her Woman's Club because she asked a girl from Russia to give a lecture. Just a schoolgirl."

"Shepherd, my friend. This month, in certain quarters, people are burning the *Graphic Survey* magazine because it contains a picture story on life in Russia. Photographs of farms. Windmills, whatever they have on farms. Russian cows. This incites people to bonfires."

"What do you think is frightening them?"

"Hearst news. If the paper says everyone this season will be wearing a Lilly Daché hat that resembles an armadillo, they will purchase the hat. If Hearst tells them to be afraid of Russia, they will buy that too."

"If the hat is too ridiculous, not everyone buys it."

Artie finally ashed his cigarette, then paused to light a new one from the old, which he left burning in the ashtray, presumably for ambiance. He reorganized his S-shaped body into a thoughtful pose against the desk. "Do you want to know my theory?"

"Of course."

"I think it's the bomb."

"People are afraid of the bomb?"

"Yes, I believe that is the heart of the matter. When that bomb went off over Japan, when we saw that an entire city could be turned to fire and gas, it changed the psychology of this country. And when I say 'psychology,' I mean that very literally. It's the radio, you see. The radio makes everyone feel the same thing at the same time. Instead of millions of various thoughts, one big psychological fixation. The radio commands our gut response. Are you following me?"

"Yes. I've seen that."

"That bomb scared the holy Moses out of us. We became horrified in our hearts that we had used it. Okay, it ended the war, it saved American life and so on and so forth. But everyone feels guilty, deep inside. Little Japanese children turned into flaming gas, we know this. How could we not feel bad?"

"I'm sure we do."

"Okay. We used the bomb. We convince ourselves we are very special people, to get to use this weapon. Ideal scenario, we would like to think it came to us from God, meant for our own use and no one else's." He leaned in, eyes and cigarette blazing. "You wrote a book about this topic, am I right?"

"You've read my books?"

"Of course I've read your books. You're an important client, I've read your books. You of all people understand this. Suddenly we are

God's chosen, we have this bomb, and we better be pretty damn certain no one else is going to get this bomb. We must clean our house thoroughly. Can you imagine what would happen if England also had the bomb, France, Germany, Japan, and the Soviet Union all had this bomb? How could a person go to sleep at night?"

"Those countries hardly have standing armies now, they're sacked. All but the Soviet Union."

"Okay. The Soviet Union. You get it."

"I thought we had nothing to fear but fear itself."

"You see, this is what I'm saying. The radio. It creates for us a psychology. Here's what happened to fear itself. Winston Churchill said, 'iron curtain.' Did you see how they all went crazy over that?"

"Of course."

"Then Truman said, 'Every nation must decide.' You are standing on one side of that curtain, my friend, or else you are on the other. And John Edgar Hoover, my God, this man. John Edgar Hoover says this curtain is what separates us from Satan and perhaps also the disease of leprosy. Did you happen to hear his testimony to Congress?"

"I read some of it."

" 'The mad march of Red fascism in America. Teaching our youth a way of life that will destroy the sanctity of the home and respect for authority. Communism is not a political party but an evil and malignant way of life'—these are his words. A disease condition. A quarantine is necessary to keep it from infecting the nation."

"I read that. But newspapers exaggerate. I couldn't quite believe he said all that."

"You have a point. Maybe he did not. And yet in this case it happens that he did. I acquired a transcript of this testimony because it pertains to certain of my clients."

"Why did he say it? I mean, what are his rational motives?"

"Rational motives are not the scope of this discussion. He is an excitable man. He heads a powerful agency. The newspapers love this kind of thing, as you say. It's a moment of history, my friend. You wonder why you've received this letter. I am attempting to draw you a picture."

"Is that really his signature?"

"No. They have a machine. I read Frank Sinatra has one also, for autographs. Maybe you need one. Okay, do you know anything at all about this Dies Committee?"

"I've heard of it. Years ago they contacted my boss to come and testify. This was in Mexico. The State Department arranged visas for us, but it never happened."

"Your Mexican boss had something to say about un-American activities?"

"He wasn't Mexican, he was in exile there, under threat of death from Stalin. So he had a lot to say about the man. This was before the war, when the U.S. was getting very friendly with Stalin. Trotsky felt the U.S. was being hoodwinked. They needed to know he was treacherous."

"Trotsky."

"Lev Trotsky. He was my boss."

The cigarette ash fell to the floor. For a moment the lawyer himself seemed poised to follow it. He straightened, shook his head slowly, and reached for the letter on the desk. "I am going to give you a piece of advice. Don't mention that you once were employed by the leader of the Bolshevik Revolution."

"I was a cook. And this was Trotsky. He hated Stalin even more than J. Edgar Hoover does. He spent his whole life trying to overthrow the Soviet politburo. The American Communist Party vilified him."

"Let me just say, these subtleties are lost on your secretary's Woman's Club, and they are lost on the Dies Committee. Most of them don't know what communism is, could not pick it out of a lineup. They only know what *anti*communism is. The two are practically unrelated."

"You're telling me anticommunism is unrelated to communism. That doesn't make sense."

"It doesn't make sense to you. You're a man of words, so you think we're speaking here of tuna fish and disliking tuna fish, but we are not. We're talking tuna fish and the Spanish influenza." He reached into the papers on his desk and drew out a pair of spectacles. "All former places of residence and former employers," he read. "Schools and colleges attended, organizations in which you have been a member."

"What should I write?"

"Tell them exactly what they already know. Mexico, they probably know very little. Military service record they know. What was your tour?"

"Civilian service. That's how this came up. I helped move federal property for the Department of State during the war."

"Civilian service, so you were 4F?"

"Something like that."

He waited. The intensity of the man's gaze is extraordinary.

"Blue slip," I said.

"Okay. Disqualified from service on account of sexual indifference to the female of the species. This one I could never figure."

"They offered to put me in a psychiatric hospital, to get me sorted out. But then suddenly my particular talents were needed elsewhere, moving art treasures out of Washington. Both coasts were under attack, so it looked very urgent."

"This was when, '42?"

"The end of summer, right after the Japanese deployed their floatplane bomber from that sub they sent up the Columbia River. It looked like a good time for the country to get our goods under cover."

"You're putting me on. If it weren't for Tojo attacking Fort Stevens . . ."

"That's right. I might be up at Highlands Hospital with Zelda

Fitzgerald. Instead, I'm living down the street from there in a house I bought with Uncle Sam's paycheck."

"Shazam," said Artie. "All's fair in love and war."

"Believe me, I know this. Better than most."

"Well, for better or worse, all this they already know about you. What else? What employment history do they have in your file at the State Department?"

"I'm not sure. I think my name must have come to them through a gallery in New York where I delivered paintings from Mexico. Or the school where I taught Spanish."

"Okay, mention those. And anything you recall listing in your employment records at those establishments. Church membership, this kind of thing, to pad out the résumé. Though you are not a joiner, you've said. So give them primary schools in Mexico, the one in D.C. The name of the painter who sent you to New York."

"Will they really go and talk to instructors at the Potomac Academy?"

"So what, they'll find out you were a schoolboy. I don't want to worry you excessively, but schoolboy shenanigans are not now your biggest concern."

September 3

Today Bull's Eye departed, and all this he took with him: schoolboy shenanigans, promises broken, dormitories and secret assignations. An invisible boy made manifest, seen for once by another's eyes, if only for a short while. A city of memories has gone up in fire and gas, and there can be no remorse.

Mrs. Brown wouldn't tolerate having the notebook burned in the fireplace. But in the end she did the job herself, outside in the barrel where she burns scrap papers. "Potomac Academy 1933" has left the world.

She was opposed at first. "You need your notebooks," she kept insisting. Without the notes she fears I'll make a mess of things, like Tristram Shandy. She still refuses to believe the memoir will not be written. I met her gaze, and leveled.

"Look, Mrs. Brown. You're a practical person. And you know me. So don't ask for impossible things. I'm working on a different book now."

"So you said."

"It was a mistaken idea, the memoir. Dragging my own entrails out for the public. And not my idea to start with, you'll recall. I told you I'd given it up when the little leather-bound diary turned up missing. Really I should get rid of all of them, just so you'll quit nagging me about it. But I'm starting with this one."

She had come a half hour early, today of all days, and caught me red-handed. The broad, canvas-bound notebook in my hand. I'd been wondering how to set that cotton duck to flame; the army tends to manufacture indestructible things. Stamped plainly across the front: "Potomac Academy." She could probably see right through to the naked figures inside, as if catching me with an eight-pager. I may have blushed.

"If you won't let me burn it now, I'll just do it after you leave this evening."

"Do as you please then. This evening." Without another word she went to the dining room, slapped out the work on her table, and said little the whole day. But at five o'clock, crept upstairs to my study door. "Mr. Shepherd, be ye free for a word?"

"All right."

"It's something to grieve you, is it? In that notebook you now want burned."

She has borne so much from her inconstant leader. The panics of the last month, for example. A better August than some, but still she takes the brunt.

"It's nothing special, Mrs. Brown. I'm just ready to be done with school days."

"Anybody would be queasy, with federal men nosing in your business."

She acknowledged the deed would already be done, if she had not by chance caught the earlier bus this morning. "Mr. Shepherd, I've got no business depriving you of your own intents and purposes. Give it over and we'll be done."

She took it out to the backyard. I watched from the upstairs window, wondering if she would have a glance inside; it's possible I was testing her. But she did not look. It was her choice to burn it in the barrel with the day's used envelopes and botched letters, rather than in the living room. "Here now, it's still the dog days," she said. "What might the neighbors think, seeing smoke from your hearth on such a warm day of September?"

She is out there now. The week's rubbish went into the tar barrel, the canvas-bound book flaring vividly in the center, its blackened leaves impossibly thin and intact, curling open before disintegrating. She stepped back from the heat of the barrel, but will remain at her post until everything is vapor. Viewed from above, she is framed by fences on both sides of the strange tableau: Mrs. Brown destroys the evidence. Her hat, a small blue plate, dampening in dark speckles as a light summer rain begins to fall.

Now the job is done.

September 8

Today the appeasement program begins. After a weekend spent drawing together a mess of notes into genuine prose, I have produced evidence of a new book. Not just some vague excuse for avoiding the memoir, but two draft chapters of the novel set in Yucatán, handed over to Mrs. Brown. The setting is giving me trouble, though, as I've never visited the Yucatán. I need to see Chichén Itzá, the stones of those temples.

Mrs. Brown's eyebrows sailed, just to hear the names spoken aloud. You could see the childhood longing still in her. The girl, hiding in some chicken coop from sister Parthenia, dreamily turning pages of the *Geographic*.

I asked her to call the Asheville-Hendersonville air-port and find out how Pennsylvania Central Airlines might connect with Mérida. Mexico City will probably be the best bet. No, not passage for one. For two.

September 22

Harrison W. Shepherd
30 Montford Ave., Asheville, North Carolina

Dear Mr. Shepherd,

Allow me to acquaint you with our services. Aware, Inc. is a private loyalty firm whose programs are independent of any government agency. Our corporation publishes the well-known directory, **Strike Back**, used to assist hiring practices in many entertainment and service-related industries. Employers from coast to coast have learned they can rely upon our research.

We have information we believe to be important to your current federal investigation. We have evidence suggesting your books are being read by Communists in China, and that you have opposed the use of the atom bomb. We have a news story linking you to Charles Chaplin, who is almost certainly a Communist. We do not suggest that you are in fact a Communist. In many cases, our clients find they have been painted as such via the weasel-worded gestures of someone who is, in fact, a Communist. Every day, innocents in our country become pawns in the hands of sinister manipulations for the Communist cause. The extent of their network is sadly under-estimated by most. Attorney General Clark has released to us a list of 90 organizations the Justice Department believes to be Communist Fronts. Almost anyone could have unwittingly crossed paths with a person working under the guise of one of these organizations.

*For a fee of $500 we offer you the invaluable opportunity to clear
your name of several charges, including those listed above. We urge you to
contact us without delay to discuss this opportunity to secure our services.
Sincerely yours,*

LOREN MATUS, DIRECTOR

AWARE, INC.

September 23

"No soap," says Artie Gold. "You tell them that, your attorney says no soap, jump in a lake, bye-bye birdie. This letter you do not even have to answer."

Artie had agreed to an emergency meeting on the condition we invite his twelve-year-old friend Grant. Ha-ha, as he would say. Grant is a blended scotch whisky. We met downtown on Patton Avenue, but en route to the bar he had to tramp through some errands. Coleman's Man Store to pick up a shirt. ("Margaret says if I show up one more time looking like a hobo she will put me in a home. It's the husband's parents, they're snobs.") Next, Reiser's Shoe Hospital, to fetch some resuscitated wing tips that should have gone to Reiser's Crematorium, if there is one. Then Finkelstein's Pawn.

"Is this how you generally impress new clients?"

Artie had handed his ticket through the iron grille, and we were waiting for the retrieval. "Ha! Don't worry, I am not living on Skid Row just yet," he said. "Although I wish the same could be said of all my clients. That ticket was given to me in lieu of payment, a very nice camel overcoat I'm told, to be had for only ten dollars." Artie lowered his voice. "I'm going to give it back to the poor guy when cold weather hits."

The bar was Leo's, a little joint in the odd flatiron building that's wedged into the acute corner of Battery and Wall. "This okay with you? Is it adequate to the purposes of impressing a new client?"

"It's fine. I'm sorry, that was a joke."

"Okay. Not very fancy, Leo's. But a club I am allowed to join." Carefully he folded and stacked his wardrobe on the stool beside him: camel coat, shirt, shoes. The girl at the bar had reached for the bottle of Grant's when he came in the door, and came over with two little glasses hooked on her fingertips like thimbles. Artie seemed distracted, watching her fill the glasses, finishing his cigarette. "That club out at Bent Creek, you know it? I recently had a very high-profile client who moved here from Hollywood, prospective client I should say, I'm not naming names, he wanted to take me to his golf club for dinner, Bent Creek. To celebrate, get acquainted. Mr. Heston, I say to him, have you seen their promotional materials? 'We cater to the better class of gentile clientele. We reserve the right to decline service to anyone we deem to be incompatible.' *Incompatible!*"

"Charlton Heston is your client?"

"As it happens, he is not."

The waitress retreated to the other end of the bar, wiping out glasses with a red chamois cloth, but kept glancing at us. Dark lashes, cheekbones, a red ribbon around her black hair, tied on top. A tall, long-waisted girl, but still there was something of Frida about her. The way she carried those glasses on her fingers. Probably a violation of some hygiene rule, but she gets away with it. Men want their lips on her fingertips.

"Hey, how about that Jackie Robinson?" Artie asked out of nowhere. His mind moves like a train, and he pitches things out its window at an astonishing clip. "Are you a baseball fan, Shepherd?"

"I should apologize now for all the things I don't know about. You might find me as thick-skulled as Mr. Heston. Baseball is a yen one learns from a father, I gather."

He tilted his head, nodded. Though quite a talker, Artie was also a listener.

"I wasn't raised in this country. Wasn't raised, really at all."

Artie exhaled a short laugh, not unsympathetic, and tossed back the shot of Grant's. "If a person is not raised, then what? He grows from a seed?"

The whisky was both stringent and soothing, like cigar smoke. Twelve years waiting for a moment, this gullet. "No. In the scullery kitchens and probably the salt mines of this world, many a child is not so much raised as hammered into shape, Artie. To be of use. Surviving by the grace of utility alone."

"This I know to be true, you are correct. Very well said. In this case, the absence of a father notwithstanding, have you heard of Jackie Robinson?"

"I do read the news. The Negro player they've let in the white leagues."

"I saw the man play at McCormick Field this summer. I was there."

"How was that?"

"Sensational. His second or third game with the Dodgers, and they play him down here in Dixie. The Colored section was packed like the last bus out of Arnhem, and the rest of the stands, empty. Like someone had yelled they were passing out free polio germs to the white people that day. I had a good seat, let me tell you."

"I'll bet."

He unfolded the letter and flattened it on the counter. The earlier one from J. Edgar Hoover he'd barely glanced at, but this one he studied with inordinate care. Nevertheless, his verdict: No soap.

"My secretary wanted to burn it with the trash."

"Good girl. You should give her a raise."

"Well. I'm taking her to Mexico."

"Really." A wise-guy smirk.

"As my assistant, Artie. She's forty-seven, for one thing. And for another, not my type."

"Ah, yes. I recall."

"You're only about the third or fourth person to know that about me, by the way. The Selective Service, God, and you. A few others. But certainly my mother never worked it out."

"Please. Discretion is my business, and I mean that sincerely."

"Mrs. Brown is my right hand. This is a research trip, and I'll need to stay a couple of months. She called you about helping with the passport."

"Right, I recall. Well, her opinion of this letter from quote-unquote Aware Incorporated was absolutely correct."

"It's not a form," I pointed out. "These things are very specific. Charles Chaplin. My books being read by Communists in China. I have to say, I'm flabbergasted."

"That is their intention, to flabbergast. Is this a verb, can I say that?"

"I suppose."

"Their mode is the surprise attack: they flabbergast. You hand over five hundred clams."

"And then the game ends?"

"Not exactly. These publications he mentions are real. They accumulate names of alleged Reds and publish them in directories."

"Who reads them?"

"Executives. Radio producers, Hollywood studios, even grocery chains. It's handy, no muss no fuss. They can assure their advertisers they are taking every available precaution against hiring a Red."

"But before he puts me on the list, he's offering the chance to clear my name, for a fee."

Artie spread his hands wide. "God bless America."

"That's straight blackmail. The employers must know the lists are meaningless."

"So you would think. But this guy Matus has acquired for himself a certain cachet. He used to be a member of the Communist Party. Twenty years ago, when everybody including your Aunt Frances was a member of the Communist Party. Now he comes to the FBI, offers to come clean. Before you know it they've got him in front of the HUAC, the whole works. So far he's remembered hundreds of former associates who now work in government and the media, and for an additional fee he will remember more. Amazing, his memory. The *New York Times* is a major employer of Communists, he says. *Time* and *Life* also. This guy is a star."

"And runs his own business on the side."

"An entrepreneur."

"Nobody could take this seriously."

The girl was still watching us. Down at the opposite end, leaning backward against the bar, fiddling with the cameo on a ribbon around her neck.

Artie sighed. "I have a client. A former president of a prestigious southern college. Served on the War Labor Board. Currently president of the Southern Human Welfare Conference. A very celebrated guy, consulting fees and public speaking provide most of his income. Suddenly, he has no income. He has protestors. This antisegregation outfit over which he presides has turned up on the attorney general's list, one of these ninety so-called Communist front organizations."

"On whose authority? Loren Matus?"

"The HUAC in its infinite wisdom has devised what they call an acid test for revealing an organization's true colors. You want to hear their criteria? Any one of the following is sufficient. Number one: it shows unswerving loyalty to the Soviet Union. Or, two: it has refused to condemn the Soviet Union. Or three: it has gained accolades from the Communist press. Or four: it has displayed an anti-American bias, despite professions of love for America."

"So. If you love America, but you hate the segregation laws . . ."

"Yes. That could arguably be an anti-American bias. Let me ask a rhetorical question. Has the American Poodle Society explicitly condemned the Soviet Union?" He signaled to the waitress, and she came immediately, as if pulled on a string. Refilled our glasses, her eyes carefully down. Then the quick smile, a flash of strong teeth with a tiny center gap. Away she went, after that, unspooling the tether.

"Let me ask you something," Artie said. "A personal question, if I may. When you look at a beautiful girl, do you see beauty?"

"A fair question. When you look at a great painting, do you see beauty? You see color and form, right? Loveliness, allure, magnificence. Maybe even arousal. So tell me, Artie. Do you want to have sex with the painting?"

"I'm sorry, my interest is not prurient. I'm just a curious man. Curiosity killed the cat, my wife used to tell me very often."

"Anyway, this letter. You're advising me to ignore it?"

"I am advising you," he said slowly, "that you are being approached by a snake. You could attempt to reason with the snake, or you could offer it a cash contribution. Most likely the snake is still going to bite."

Grant's twelve-year-old whisky is a potent anesthetic. "Luckily enough, it doesn't matter, because I'm not looking for a job right now. I have the only job I ever wanted."

"Luckily enough. You are a writer, employed by the American imagination. Your publisher does not have to answer to any sponsors, only to your readers."

"*Employed by the American imagination.* I like that very much."

"Are they really reading you in China?"

"Goodness, no. Not even in France. Some reviewer said, 'Don't be surprised if this book shows up in China.' Something like that. They also said I was Chaplinesque."

"Well, many artists are not so lucky as yourself. Mr. Chaplin among them. Film stars, directors, television scriptwriters. They all have to be produced, they require sponsors. It's becoming a lucrative industry for the likes of Aware Incorporated."

Suddenly the girl was back, unsummoned. "You're the writer, aren't you? I'm crazy about your books."

"What writer?"

"Harrison Shepherd?"

"That's so strange. You're the second person to ask me that."

"Oh. Sorry, my mistake." She floated away, an unmoored skiff, and disappeared through a door at the back.

Artie reorganized his sigmoidal curve against the bar, the better to stare at his dimwit companion. "What's wrong with you? She's a sugar pie."

"I know it. I'm grateful. To all these girls, I really am."

"So, you could sign a damn cocktail napkin. It would have made her day."

"That's what I can't see, Artie. What thrilled her was a book—she wants a hero. Not some tin whistle double-gaiter on a barstool."

"So. In a pinch, you stand in."

"Do you know how that feels to me, to pass myself off as important? Exactly like passing counterfeit money. Look at her, she's magnificent. My name, some ink on a napkin. How could that be worth the gold-brick standard of her day?"

Artie swiveled back to face the bar, fished a pack of Old Golds out of his pocket.

"So. Matus the snake has contacted me because a motion-picture option got his attention. That's what you think?"

"You know what they say. God wants to punish you, he answers your prayers."

"Artie, I didn't pray for a motion picture. It makes me uneasy. I don't like attention."

"You have a funny way of choosing your profession, in that case."

"People think that. If a person is famous, he must have wanted to be in the public eye. But to me, writing books is a way to earn a living in my pajamas."

Artie nodded thoughtfully. "I take your point. People think lawyers are a cutthroat gang, and me, I couldn't cut the throat of a fish. Margaret says I should take up fishing. And I think, an old softie like me? What would I do if I caught one? Apologize?"

October 3

Two airplane tickets purchased, air-coach to Mexico and back, at a cost of $191 each. A breathtaking sum, but all in the line of duty; Arthur Gold says it can be worked out for some reduction in the tax later on. He is helping Mrs. Brown with the passport applications. Apartment queries sent to Mérida, and fair warning to Frida, expect a visit, though Diego is sure to be out of the country. Romulus will feed the cats and mind the house, eight weeks, I will have to remember to bring back a smashing present.

Mrs. Brown stands at the ready, her suitcase already packed, though the trip is six weeks away. No price is too high for this joy. Her thrill for adventure is a thing I dearly wish I could learn by example. She makes me wish for the boy who once could swim miles underwater, looking for treasure.

Today I teased her, asking whether I needed to look out for any fellow who might be angry with me for taking her off this way. She blinked, taken aback.

"Well, it's not out of the question," I said. "I'm aware that you're an attractive woman. And I've noticed you're sprucing up, of late."

She honestly blushed. No-nonsense Mrs. Brown. She said not to worry myself, if any man she cared for took an interest, I would be first to know it.

The New York Times, *October 23, 1947*

79 in Hollywood Found Subversive, Inquiry Head Says

Evidence of Communist Spying Will Be Offered Next Week, Thomas Declares

By Samuel A. Tower, *special to the* New York Times

WASHINGTON, OCT. 22—Actors, writers and others in Hollywood were named today as members of the Communist party or as Communist sympathizers. The accusations were by Robert Taylor, screen actor, and by other movie figures as the inquiry of the House Committee on Un-American Activities into the extent of Communist penetration into the film industry went into its third day.

At the same time the movie industry, reacting to a persistent committee criticism that no anti-Communist pictures were being made, charged through its counsel, Paul V. Mc-Nutt, that suggestions concerning films to be made represented "one method of censorship" and did "violence to the principle of free speech."

The committee chairman, Rep. J. Parnell Thomas, asserted that the committee would produce at coming sessions evidence that "at least 79" persons in Hollywood had been engaged in subversive activity. After a noon executive session the committee announced that it would present next week evidence of Communist espionage activities, with a surprise witness, in developing further testimony that confidential data on an Army supersonic plane had fallen into Communist hands through a Hollywood literary agent.

Mr. Taylor, arriving to appear at the afternoon session, was greeted with an audible "ah" by the spectators, mostly women, who filled the hearing chamber. Outside the chamber there was a mob scene as those unable to get in swirled and pushed against Capitol police. In his testimony he declared at one point, "I personally believe the Communist party should be outlawed. If I had my way they'd all be sent back to Russia." When this drew loud applause from the audience, Chairman Thomas reprimanded the spectators and requested no further demonstrations.

Mr. Taylor asserted that there had been "more indications" of Communist activity in Hollywood in the past four or five years, but guarded and qualified his testimony when committee interrogators sought specific data on activities and individuals. He testified that, as a member of the Screen Actors

Guild, he had come to believe that there were actors and ac-
tresses "who, if not Communists, are working awfully hard to
be so" and whose philosophy and tactics seemed closely akin
to the Communist party line. This group constituted what he
called "a disrupting influence." The handsome actor declared
that the film, "Song of Russia," was, in his view, Communist
propaganda and that he had objected "strenuously" to playing
in it. He added, however, that the industry at that time was
producing a number of movies designed to strengthen the feeling of the American people toward Russia. Mr. Taylor asserted
that he had not knowingly worked with a Communist and
would not do so. After twenty-five minutes on the stand the
handsome star made his departure, accompanied by applause
and shouts of "Hurray for Robert Taylor" from a middle-aged
woman wearing a red hat.

Members of the Committee asked M-G-M executive James K.
McGuinness, who is in charge of scripts for the studio: Has
the industry the will to make anti-Communist movies? Why
haven't they been made? Why couldn't the studios produce
such films and circulate them through schools, like the patri-
otic wartime pictures?

Representative Emanuel Celler, D. NY, attacked the inquiry
as an act to make "all true Americans blush with shame." "If
Chairman Thomas sought to strike terror into the minds of
the movie magnates, he succeeded. They were white-livered.
One vital aspect of these antics must be kept in mind. Today it
is the motion pictures. Tomorrow it may be the newspapers or
the radio. The threat to civil liberties is a real one."

October 31

I have learned from experience, make the cookies early. Children will
come to the door dressed as hobgoblins. When the doorbell rang just
after four o'clock, Mrs. Brown carried the plate to the door. But it
was a man, clearly audible. I was in the kitchen mopping up after the
afternoon's baking. Flour covered everything like an early frost.

"No, he can't," she said, in a strained voice. "Mr. Shepherd is indisposed." Her instincts for protecting her boss are unflappable.

"Are you the lady of the house?"

"I'm the stenographer."

The badge startled her, and she can't remember the name. FBI, that much she remembers. He'd come to ask Mr. Shepherd a few questions, but as he was unavailable, Mrs. Brown was duty-bound to answer them herself, insofar as she was able.

After it was all over and he left, she came in the dining room and put her head down on the table. I made a pot of coffee. Then, together, we remembered and wrote it down. To show Artie later.

"How long has he lived in this house?"

(She guessed about five years)

"No," the man said. "Mr. Shepherd purchased this house October of 1943."

"Then, my stars, why ask?"

"Has he got a mortgage?"

"If a person has a house he has got a mortgage. Evidently you have the details."

"Where did he live before?"

"He let a room from Marian Bittle at her boarding house on the Black Mountain Highway. What they call the Tunnel Road."

"And before he came to Asheville?"

"I'm sure I don't know. I don't think I can answer any more questions."

"Well, you'll have to try. Executive Order 9835."

"What's that?"

"It means you have to try. If the FBI is asking, you answer. Where did he get that car? That's a pretty pricey car. Or was, in its day."

"I believe the car belonged to his deceased father."

"I noticed an empty Remy bottle in the trash. Is Mr. Shepherd a drinker?"

"I'm sure I don't know. I think we're finished. Mr. Shepherd's lawyer might be the one to take this farther, if needs be."

"Look, lady, don't get sore. An investigation doesn't necessarily mean he's under suspicion. We're conducting a field investigation."

"Of what?"

"Just the usual."

"You can't tell me what it is you think Mr. Shepherd has done?"

"No, ma'am, we cannot."

"But if he were here, you could tell him."

"No, ma'am, we cannot tell the accused this kind of thing, for security considerations. Do you happen to know his income?"

"For goodness' sake. He's a writer. He couldn't say himself what it's going to be, month to month. Do you know what books people will buy next year?"

"Does he attend any meetings?"

"No."

"Well, the neighbors said he does. They see him take the Haywood bus every Thursday. But on other days, only to the market or the newsstand."

"Mr. Shepherd goes to the library on Thursdays."

"Why so regular?"

"He finds it comforting to keep regular habits."

"Ma'am, do you know what magazines he reads?"

"He buys about everything on the Haywood news stand. You could go down there and make a list, if you like."

"Do you happen to know if he's ever studied up on Karl Marx?"

"Go and see if they sell Karl Marx on the Haywood newsstand."

"Do you know where Mr. Shepherd stands on Abstract Art?"

"Well, if he wanted a good look, I expect he'd stand in front of it."

"Very funny. Can you tell me the name of his cat?"

"Are his cats also under suspicion?"

"The neighbors said they hear him using an obscene word to call the cat."

"I've never heard Mr. Shepherd use obscene language against any person. Certainly not his cats."

"Well, they say that he does. They say he uses a very vulgar word to call the cat. They're concerned for the youngsters. They say the boy comes over here."

"My stars. What do they think he calls his cat?"

"I apologize, ma'am, it's a very vulgar word. They said *Jism*."

"The cat's name is Chisme. It means 'gossip'."

Mérida, Yucatán Peninsula

November 1947
Notes for a novel about the end of empire.

When Cortés's men first arrived here, they asked in Spanish, "What is the name of this place?" From the native Mayans they received the same answer every time: "Yucatán!" In their language that word means: "I do not understand you."

The apartment is decently spacious, the two bedrooms and a good-sized table for working in the main room, with the window overlooking the street. The kitchen and bath are a jumble but there's no need for cooking. It's too easy to walk downstairs to the restaurant in the courtyard, morning or night. The previous residents must have shared this languor, because a long, white sprout of a bean was growing from the drain of the sink when we arrived. I offered to put it in a pot for the balcony and call it our garden.

Mrs. Brown did not smile at the joke. She submits to not one iota of domesticity here, except to make the coffee as she did at home. The inside of her room I have not seen; we simply chose doors at the beginning, and her lair remains a mystery. She emerges each morning in her gloves and Lilly Daché hat, as reliably as the little Mayan women in the market will be wearing their white embroidered blouses and lace-bottomed skirts. The gloves and Lilly Daché are Mrs. Brown's native costume.

A typewriter is installed on the writing table, delivered yesterday, a sure sign of progress. A car and driver for touring the ancient sites may soon surface as well. Mrs. Brown has gamely got her sea legs on, already going to the shops on her own to get small necessities. Each day she manages more of the arrangements, soldiering through the obstacles of a language she cannot speak. My advice (which she did not heed): in answer to any question, say "Yucatán!" *I do not understand.*

A reasonable title for the novel: *The Name of This Place.*

But for now, the name of this place is mud. Or so Mrs. Brown must think, when forced to take her life in her white-gloved hands. She grips the side-arm of the rumble seat with one, the other squashing her hat to her head, as we pummel down the peninsula over shocking roads, navigated by our fearless driver Jesús. After all the time we spent searching for this combination, vehicle and driver both together in one place, I dare not ask whether he is old enough for the job. He is just a boy, despite the authority of his Mayan nose and magnificent profile. It's a shock to realize that, not his youth really but my age, that he must regard me as a man, perhaps his mother's age more or less, not worth any real study. A series of directions to follow, and a wage at the end of the journey.

And yet he's seen something of life already, clearly. His shirt is weathered as thin as a newspaper, and the lower part of one ear is missing. It took a while to notice that. It's his left, away from the passengers' side. He calmly asserted, when asked, that it was bitten off by a jaguar. So he has the imagination, if not the experience, for labor in the service of a novelist. He can lecture on any subject without hesitation. Today en route to Chichén Itzá it was the military history of his people, the Maya: "More courageous than ten armies of Federales," he shouted above the banging axles and backfiring engine of the ramshackle Ford. Or mostly Ford; one door and the front fenders are of a different parentage. Across the land of the mestizo we ride, in a mixed-caste automobile.

"At this place, Valladolid," Jesús announced above the racket, "we view the scene of the last Mayan rebellion. One hundred years ago the Yucateca took our whole peninsula back from the ladinos. We declared independence from Mexico like your Tejas of North America, and nearly made it the nation of the Maya again." Except for Mérida, he confessed, where the Federales lodged throughout the rebellion. But fate was decided at Valladolid. A final victory over the Mexican army was at hand, but just as the Mayan warriors were poised to strike, an old shaman came with urgent news: the ancient calendar said it was time to return to their villages to plant corn. They put down their weapons and went home.

"The Gods speak to my people in their hearts," says the boy called Jesús, beating his breast with one fist as he drives, head tilted back in sloe-eyed tranquillity even as the tires hit another crater in the road and his whole body levitates. The Mayans obeyed the ancient imperatives of survival. They walked away from power, letting the federal army take back the peninsula and return it to Mexican rule.

Somewhere during the lecture he lost his way on the dirt track through jungle, and we found ourselves also called back to his home village, conveniently at lunchtime, as it happened. We were near enough to Chichén Itzá, the temples of one of its outlying towns towered above the treetops, a monument to ancient prosperity throwing its shadow across thatched roofs and the naked children who gathered to see what might emerge from this calamitous machine. We could as well have arrived by flying saucer.

The mother of Jesús, similarly sloe-eyed, bade us sit on a log while she dipped beans from a cauldron that must bubble eternally on the fire outside her hut. Her name: Maria, naturally. Her lath house, like every one in the village, had a tall, peaked roof of thatch, open at each gable end for ventilation. Inside the open doorway a knot of motionless brown limbs, presumably sleeping children, weighted a hammock into a deep V shape, the inverse of the roofline. At the side of the house a scrambled garden grew, but the front was bare dirt, furnished only with the logs on which we perched. Mrs. Brown steadied the tin plate on her knee with a gloved hand, tweed skirt pulled around her knees, eyebrows sailing high, calf leather brogues set carefully together in the dust. Flowering riotously around her were a hundred or more orchids, planted in rusted lard tins. White, pink, yellow, the paired petals hung like butterflies above roots and leaves.

My beauties, Maria called them, leaning forward to brush a speck of ash from her son's worn shirt, then gently boxing his good ear. "The only importance is beauty."

The light here at the window is good, and the view is a satisfying distraction. The street stays busy at all hours, this apartment is only a short walk from the central plaza, the markets and old stone cathedral. It must be the oldest part of Mérida, judging by its charm and conspicuous fortifications.

In the afternoon when the sun lights the stucco buildings across the street, it's possible to count a dozen different colors of paint, all fading together on the highest parts of the wall: yellow, ochre, brick, blood, cobalt, turquoise. The national color of Mexico. And the scent of Mexico is a similar blend: jasmine, dog piss, cilantro, lime. Mexico admits you through an arched stone orifice into the tree-filled courtyard of its heart, where a dog pisses against a wall and a waiter hustles through a curtain of jasmine to bring a bowl of tortilla soup, steaming with cilantro and lime. Cats stalk lizards among the clay pots around the fountain, doves settle into the flowering vines and coo their prayers, thankful for the existence of lizards. The potted plants silently exhale, outgrowing their clay pots. Like Mexico's children they stand pinched and patient in last year's too-small shoes. The pebble thrown into the canyon bumps and tumbles downhill.

Here life is strong-scented, overpowering. Even the words. Just ordering breakfast requires some word like *toronja*, triplet of muscular syllables full of lust and tears, a squirt in the eye. Nothing like the effete "grapefruit," which does not even mean what it says.

Our young lord Jesús today found the right track to Chichén Itzá. What a marvel. The Temple of Warriors, the Ball Court, the tall pyramid called the Castle. Magnificent limestone buildings glare at one another in silence across the grassy plaza. Everything is dazzling white, a timeless architecture of pale limestone. Elegant and remote. Whatever I came here looking for is hiding, holding its breath. No crime and punishment present themselves in bloodstained hallways. Unlike the grisly Azteca with their gods sticking out their tongues, the Maya seem serenely untouchable. What they've left behind is in every measure as grand and elegant as the white marble temples of the Greeks.

In the fringe of forest surrounding the plaza we found more temples crumbling quietly into themselves, sleeping under green blankets of vine. Like the ruin in the forest on Isla Pixol, beside the hole in the water, at the end of the lacuna. That one had a smiling skeleton carved on a stone. Here, footpaths through the trees led away in all directions, to different parts of a partially excavated city: the marketplace with its carved columns. The steam bath in a shady grove, its dark stone chamber like a womb, entered through a tiny triangular doorway. The vault inside was a high, inverted V shape, punctuated at each end with a round hole for venting steam. Maybe the story begins here, lit by a dim, steamy ray of light streaming through that hole: the setting for a love scene, or a murder, better yet. Political intrigue. But the place feels bloodless.

The enormous central pyramid stands high and heroic, dominating the plaza. It seems taller than the Pyramid of the Sun at Teotihuacán, though memory can play tricks in matters of heroism. We felt compelled to climb its immense stone stairs to the very top, just as it was with Frida all those years ago, dragging her miserable leg all the way. But Mrs. Brown managed the climb without sending a single soul to the devil.

Today we drove south through villages of Mayan farmers, most beginning with *X*—pronounced "ish." X-puil, X-mal, Jesús revealed the secret of the Mayan tongue: shhh. *X* does not mark the spot, it marks a hush. The Mayans speak their language everywhere in the countryside, and it sounds like whispered secrets. Women stand together in doorways, muttering: shhh, shhh. Fathers and sons walk along the roadside carrying ancient-looking hoes, quietly making a plan: shhh.

Another day driving, this time to the east. We stopped at a town and walked out an ancient stone roadbed to the mouth of a lacuna. A cenote, it's called here: a deep, round hole with limestone cliffs for its sides and blue water at the bottom. A kingfisher darted through foliage, calling: *Kill him! Kill him!* The view from above was dizzying, down the sheer rock face of the hole to the water far below. No handrail stood at the cliff's edge to prevent our falling in. Or diving in, swimming down deep to see what is there, the devil or the sea.

It is fresh water here, many kilometers from the ocean. The Mayans built their towns and civilization on these cenotes, because no sacred thing is more holy than a water source. The entire Yucatán Peninsula has not a single river or stream running on its surface, only these water caves running below, with round mouths opening here and there to the light above. *Chi-chen* means "mouth of the world," and so it is, these gasping mouths are as old as human dread. The ancients fed them as best they knew how, throwing in jade and onyx, golden goblets, human remains. Without a thought to what they might be doing to their drinking water.

Jesús claimed that many valuable artifacts had been dredged from this cenote, but all had been carried off to Harvard and the Peabody Museum. He actually named those places, so it likely could be true. Colonial ransacking in the scientific age.

On our walk back through the jungle we looked but could find no trace of the ancient farms and villages that must have been here. Thousands of ordinary people were part of this metropolis, but their homes would have been perishable wattle and thatch, stuccoed with lime and mud. Every trace of their living has returned to the earth now, except for the limestone temples of art and worship. The things made of ambition, which rise higher than daily bread.

Our automobile parked in the village had attracted a crowd. The tallest boy introduced himself (Maximiliano), and demanded pay for having guarded the vehicle during our absence. "From whom?" we asked, and Maximiliano pointed to the gang of small thugs he claimed would have damaged or even dismantled it. "They are very crafty," he said in English. His payment, a handful of coins, he instantly distributed among all the vandals, their alliance thus perfected. Even morality is a business of supply and demand.

Some older boys had lurked back, distancing themselves from piracy, but came forward then with woodcarvings to sell. Mrs. Brown took one in hand, turning it carefully. They were figures of ancient warriors in elaborate headdress, very much like my little obsidian fellow. It was striking how the wide, slant faces of the figures resembled the faces of the boys who made them. Mrs. Brown paid the sculptor his price, only a little more than the extortion had cost us. A good day for young men standing on the stone and bones of their ancestors to make their way.

In the plaza near our apartment, people come every evening to stroll around in a circle. Lovers come drifting, connected by entwined fingers. Married couples come at a clip, the children like rafts towed on ropes behind the ship. No one is alone. Even the vendors sitting on stools around the periphery work steadily at connection, nodding at potential buyers, like a sewing machine prodding its needle into the cloth.

"We used to do this in Isla Pixol," I told Mrs. Brown. "My mother always wanted to go walk the circle. As long as she had a new dress."

Mrs. Brown in the jaunty blue beret dissected her fried fish, a late supper after our day on the road. But life in the plaza was just waking up. Two men wheeled a great wooden marimba to a spot near the dining tables and uncloaked it, preparing to play.

She said, "You're home here. That's good to see. It serves ye well."

"I don't know that I'm home anywhere."

"Well, you are a queasy one, I'll grant it." she said. She used her knife to push the fish's crisp head and tail together at one side of the plate. "I always knew you came from Mexico, at Mrs. Bittle's you told us that. But see, we thought you were just bashful. We never thought of a whole country where you could call down a waiter in his language, or say, 'Look, they're going to do the hat dance,' and they would do the hat dance. Now, that sounds silly."

"No, I understand. You thought, 'foreigner,' and not of a particular place."

"I reckon that is it. All along, you have known about these folk here and I've had no inkling. I read the *Geographics*, but you can't think of the people in those stories as having life and breath, and knowing things you don't. But that sounds silly too."

"No, I think most people are the same. Until they've gone somewhere."

"I thank my lucky stars, Mr. Shepherd, and I thank you. I do. That I'm a person who went somewhere." She set her hands in her lap and drew herself fully into looking outward, as people do when settling down in a theater. Vendors had begun to work the dining crowd. You could buy anything if your supper went on long enough: roses, bicycle tires, a shellacked armadillo. A mother and daughter in long skirts and shawls moved from table to table showing their embroidery. I waved them off with a gesture so small Mrs. Brown probably didn't see. She feels obliged to look at every single thing, lest the artisans be offended.

"I have been wondering what your novel will be about," she said. "Apart from the setting."

"I wonder too. I think I want to write about the end of things. How civilizations fall, and what leads up to that. How we're connected to everything in the past."

To my shock she said, "Oh, I wouldn't."

"Mrs. Brown, I declare. That's twice you've told me how to be a writer. You apologized the first time."

"Well. I'm sorry again."

"Why would you say that?"

"I have no business. It just came out. Some of the things that happened back at home have set me to the fret."

"I do step in the pie sometimes, I know that. Go on."

"Should I?"

"Please."

"I think the readers won't like it. We don't like to see ourselves joined hard to the past. We'd as soon take the scissors and cut every ribbon of that."

"Then I am sunk. All I ever write about is history."

"People in gold arm bracelets, though. Nothing that would happen to our own kind. That's how I reckon people take to it so well."

"So I shouldn't try something new? What happened to the writer standing up for himself? Not leaving my words to be orphaned, my little bairns, as you called them."

"I still hold by that. But there's no shame in a clever disguise. To say what you believe and still keep out of trouble. Thus to now, it has done ye well."

"Oh. Then you think it wouldn't go so well if I set my stories, let's say, in a concentration camp in Texas or Georgia. One of those places where we sent our citizen Japs and Germans during the war."

She looked stricken. "No, sir, we would not like to read that. Not even about the other Japanese sinking ships and bombing our coast. That's over, and we'd just as soon be shed of it."

The marimba players struck up "La Llorona," the most cheerful rendition of a song about death. I spied the man with the shellacked armadillo for sale. It was only a matter of time, he comes every night.

"If that's so, then why did Americans make off with the historical artifacts of Mexico to put them, where did he say? In the Peabody Museum?"

"It's the same as your books, Mr. Shepherd. It's somebody else's gold pieces and bad luck. If we fill up our museums with that, we won't have to look at the dead folk lying at the bottom of our own water wells."

"And who is *we*?"

She pondered this, eyebrows lowered. "Just Americans," she said at length. "That's the only kind of person I know how to be. Not like you."

"You'd do that? Take scissors and cut off your past?"

"I did already. My family would tell you I went to the town and got above my raisings. It's what Parthenia calls 'modern.' "

"And what would you call it?"

"American. Like I said. The magazines tell us we're special, not like the ones that birthed us. Brand-new. They paint a picture of some old-country rube with a shawl on her head, and make you fear you'll be like that, unless you buy cake mix and a home freezer."

"But that sounds lonely. Walking around without any ancestors."

"I don't say it's good. It's just how we be. I hate to say it, but that rube in the shawl is my sister, and I don't want to be her. I can't help it."

A man walked among the tables working a marionette, a smiling skeleton of articulated papier-mâché bones. To the delight of a family dining nearby, he made the skeleton sneak along slowly, lifting its bony feet high, then suddenly leap on their table. The children squealed as it stamped on their plates, for the father's coins.

"And history is nothing but a cemetery," I said to Mrs. Brown. The puppeteer was behind her, she'd missed the show.

"That is exactly right. For us to visit when we have a mind, or just not go at all. Let the weeds grow up."

"Here in Mexico there's a holiday just for being with your dead. You go where your family is buried and have a great party, right on the grave."

"You have to? Plumb on top of the graves?" Wide-eyed, she looked like the girl she must have been before she was Mrs. Brown.

"People love it, as much as they love a wedding. Really it is a kind of wedding, to the people in your past. You take a vow they're all still with you. You cook a feast and bring enough food for the dead people too."

"Well, sir, that would not happen in Buncombe County. Probably the police would arrest you."

"You might be right."

She took her glass of limeade and sipped at the straw while holding eye contact. It was unsettling. The puppeteer had moved into her line of view, and her eyes left me to follow that skeleton. When she had drained her glass, she said, "You understand things like that, a wedding in the graveyard. You are from another country."

"But I want to be brand-new too. The land of weightless people and fast automobiles suits me fine. I made myself a writer there."

"You could have stayed here and done the same."

"I don't think so. I've thought about it. I had ghosts to leave behind. Mexican writers struggle with their ghosts, I think. In general. Maybe it's easier to say what you want in America, without those ancestral compromises weighing you down like stones."

"Easier to look down upon others, too."

"Do you mean to say I do that?"

"Mr. Shepherd, you do not. But some do. They look around and say, 'This here is good, and that is evil,' and it's decided. We are America, so that over there must be something else altogether."

Mrs. Brown will never cease to amaze. "That's very insightful. You think that comes of cutting our anchor to the past?"

"I do. Because if you had to go sit on a grave and think hard about it, you couldn't just say 'This is America.' Some Indian would cross your mind, some fellow that shot his arrow on that very spot. Or the man that shot the Indian, or whipped his slaves or hung up some tart woman for a witch. You'd couldn't just say it's all fine and dandy."

"Maybe readers need some of that, then. Connections to the past."

"Fairly warned is fair afeared," she said.

"I thought it was 'forearmed.' Forewarned is forearmed."

She glanced at her forearms, and never did reply.

Today was the village of Hoctún, a town the color of wheat, with a pyramid sitting at its center. It brought to mind the village with the giant stone head in the square, and Mother's shaman. Every turn in the road here runs into memory. Isla Mujeres was almost unbearable, from the ferry on. Mrs. Brown sees all, and it puts her on a fret, as she would say. I imagine her pressed against the fret-board of God's guitar, held against the slender silver bar until she wails her assigned note. She says she came here to do my worrying for me. She does much more: typing up drafted scenes, only to see me throw them away. Arranging things. She's befriended someone English-speaking at the tourist bureau, a journalist who helps her negotiate miracles. Mexico's bureaucracies do not daunt Mrs. Brown. She has worked for the United States Army.

I told her I want to study village life now, up close. We've seen enough of pyramids, I need goats and cookfires. To peer inside a hut and examine that V-shaped vault, after seeing the same architecture in stone temples. Her inspired idea: to return to the village of Maria, mother of Jesús.

✳

The eternal cauldron of beans still bubbled. Maria was animated while serving us lunch, telling about the lumbermen who passed through earlier this morning. They are clearing the forests all around, dragging out the felled giants on the same dirt track that brought us in. All she can do is stand in the road and halt each truck, insisting they let her inspect the fallen timber and pluck the living orchids from its top branches. That explains the flowers growing from tins in the yard: her rescued orphans. These orchids lived all their lives high up in the bright air, unseen by human eyes, until the firmament under their roots suddenly tumbled. It's a precarious place, up there with the howlers. Everyone wants the tallest tree to fall.

But Maria of the Orchids seemed to have no such fears, at home in the forest primeval. "The important thing is beauty," she said once more, reaching a small brown hand toward the treetops. "Even death grants us beauty."

Another visit to Chichén Itzá tomorrow, the last trip. Then we pack it all in. We will need to take the train for Mexico City on Thursday or Friday if we're to be there from Christmas until the new year, as Frida insists. Candelaria is meeting us at the station. Candelaria at the wheel of an automobile seems as probable as Jesus running a guided tour. Or Mrs. Brown in hat and gloves sitting beside the flagrant Frida, drinking tea on a bench painted with lighting bolts. Likely, all these things will come to pass.

Chichén Itzá looked completely different today, probably because of everything else we've seen since the first visit. "Elegant and remote," I jotted in my notes that time, "reluctant to reveal its human history." But today a story came up in relief from every surface, urgent and visible. Every stone was carved with some image: the snarling jaguar, the feathered serpent, a long frieze of swimming goldfish. Emperors stood life-size on stone steles jutting up from the plaza like giant teeth. The Maya carved human figures only in profile: the almond eye, the flattened forehead sloping toward the exquisite arch of nose. They needn't have worried about that profile being forgotten, it's the spitting image of Jesús and ten thousand others, automobile vandals included. Better to carve something else in stone, if you mean to be remembered: "I was cruel to my best friend and got away with it. My favorite meal was squid in ink sauce. My mother never quite liked me as I was."

Traces of paint clung to the surfaces too: red, green, violet. In their time, all these buildings were brightly painted. What a shock to realize that, and how foolish to have been tricked earlier by the serenity of white limestone. Like looking at a skeleton and saying, "How quiet this man was, and how thin." Today Chichén Itzá declared the truth of what it was: garish. Loud and bright, full of piss and jasmine, and why not? It was Mexico. Or rather, Mexico is still what this once was.

For the last time we climbed the tall pyramid, El Castillo. "We don't have to go on, you know," I told Mrs. Brown, halfway up. The day was so bright and hot it almost tasted of gunpowder, and she had left her hat in the car, where Jesús was now napping. She paused on the stone step, shading her eyes with one flat hand, her hair blowing back like the mermaid on the prow of a ship. She had removed her gloves to use both hands for the climb, the steps were that monstrous. "Of course we do," she said, sighing deeply as if to say, "Men do this." And that is a fact, men do, unable to resist the same impulse that built the thing in the first place: senseless ambition.

But the view from the top, we convinced ourselves, was worth the pain. We sat on a ledge looking down on the tourists in the plaza, pitying those little ants because they were not up here, and if they ever meant to be, they would have to pay the price. And there is the full sum of it, senseless ambition reduced to its rudiments. Civilizations are built on that, and a water hole.

"Imagine the place crawling with slaves and kings," I said.

"Ten thousand slaves to every one king, I'd imagine."

And barking dogs. And mothers, wondering if their children have fallen down the well. We stayed a good while, reconstructing the scene. She was curious about how a writer decides where to begin the story. You start with "In the beginning," I told her, but it should be as close to the end as possible. There's the trick.

"How can you know?"

"You just decide. It could be right here. In the first light of dawn, the king in maroon robes and a golden breastplate stood atop his temple, glowering down at the chaos. He understood with dismay that his empire was collapsing. You have to get right into the action, readers are impatient. If you dilly-dally, they'll go turn on the radio and listen to *Duffy's Tavern* instead, because it's all wrapped up in an hour."

"How could the king know his empire is about to collapse?"

"Because everything's in a mess."

"Fiddlesticks," she said. "Everything's always a mess, but people say 'Buck up, we just have to get through this one bad patch.'"

"True enough. But you and I know it was, because we've read about it. Chichén Itzá was the center of a vast and powerful empire, art and architecture that flourished for centuries. And then around 900 after Christ, it mysteriously vanished."

"People don't vanish," she said. "Hitler took his life, but Germany is still there. Just for example. People going to work and having their birthdays and what all."

True enough, and the Mayans who now people this forest surely do not think of themselves as a failed culture. They build their huts of ancient design, make gardens, and sing children to sleep. Rulers and generals change without their notice. In the time since Cortés, the great Spanish empire has collapsed into one small landmass of rock and vineyards, the little right paw of Europe. Its far-flung provinces have been lost, the million shackled subjugates set free. Spain outlawed slavery, built schools and hospitals, and its poets, come to think of it, are practically in a contest now to condemn the Spanish history of conquest. Did Cortés see all that roaring toward him like a steam locomotive? Did England or France? All this earnest forward motion, the marches to the mountain, the murals and outstretched hands: which part of it do we ever call failure?

"A novel needs a good collapse," I maintained. "Success and failure. People read books to escape the uncertainties of life. And they build pyramids to last forever, so we can have something to climb on top of and admire."

"You know best," she said. "But there's no use admiring a thing just because it lasted. My brother once had a boil on his bottom a whole year, and it was nothing you'd want to see in the photogravure."

"Violet Brown, the poet."

She laughed.

"I'll remind you of that boil, next time you try to stop me from burning old notebooks and letters."

She didn't like that. She pulled her thin cotton gloves from under her belt where she'd tucked them. Put them on, smoothed ruffled feathers. "Some things are worth remembering, and some are not. That's all I meant."

"And you can say which is which?"

"No, I can't. But piling rocks on top of rocks might not be the ticket. Maybe we should admire people the most for living in this jungle without leaving one mark on it."

"But how would we know about them a thousand years later?"

"In a thousand years, Mr. Shepherd, the cow can jump over the moon."

That was the end of it, because a rising storm cloud began to turn the day a menacing color, driving us down from our aerie. The heavens let loose as we reached the ground. Children who'd been hawking woodcarvings and embroidery now disappeared into the forest for shelter, while the tourists hurried back to their autos. Behind us the temples stood in the strange yellow light with rain darkening their stone pates, dissolving their limestone one particle at a time, carrying off the day's measure of history.

PART 5

Asheville, North Carolina

1948–1950

(VB)

Star Week, *February 1, 1948*

Southern Star Shines on
Shepherd Romance

Young men in the Land of Sky seem to prefer the taste of old wine. A decade ago in Ashville, North Carolina, young writer Thomas Wolfe rocketed to fame, fleeing Southern scandal for Manhattan's forgiving bohemian scene and the arms of a lady seventeen years his senior. The writer's family tried to squelch the match with comely theater designer Aline Bernstein—that's *Mrs.* Bernstein—and so did Mr. Bernstein, we're guessing. But Wolfe carried the torch to an early grave.

Now Harrison Shepherd is out to prove history repeats. This Ashville writer rode his pen to the heights with *Vassals of Majesty* and last year's *Pilgrims of Chaltepec*, ringing up more sales than Wolfe saw in a lifetime. Thanks to secretive habits and a well-known scorn for press correspondents, Shepherd has nudged over Wolfe as the talk of his town. In a new move plainly inspired by his tutor, Shepherd has now linked up with a lady exactly seventeen years his senior. Married? At least once, say our sources.

Little else is known about the mysterious Violet Brown, but the trim brunette must have some powerful lure for snaring this diffident bachelor and his piles of cash. You could hear the hearts crack on both sides of the Mason-Dixon last month as the couple took a pre-honeymoon tour through Mexico, Shepherd's boyhood home, where his family still resides.

Did Mamacita approve the January–May romance? Do wedding bells toll for Harrison Shepherd? Not just yet, says airport clerk Jack Curtis, who viewed the couple's passports

on their recent return to the Ashville-Hendersonville airport.
Mr. Tall, Dark and Handsome kept a tight hand on his Shrink-
ing Violet, but as of January 26 she is on the books as "widowed." And the bachelor? Curtis reports: "still single."

February 6

When she came in with both arms loaded and dumped the mail
and papers in a heap on the dining room table, my first thoughts
were purely selfish. Alas, this mess. The world comes in. I'd wanted
her to take more days off after our return, craving time upstairs un-
disturbed. To be in my pajamas still at suppertime, the shades still
drawn, reeling out my tale of Lord Itzá and his troubles. A story
needs a good collapse.

She began talking before she'd unbuttoned her coat, plainly out
of sorts. She is not like that, filling up a silence with idle talk, the
goings-on at Mrs. Bittle's while we were away. Then came the report
that Mr. Judd had died, on Christmas Day.

So that was it, I thought. I gave condolences.

"Well, it was his time. Even Marian Bittle thought so, and she is
not one for philosophy. She said the son came right away and took
care of everything, so she could go on with her Christmas. But this
is what floored her. Before the old man was even buried, nine people
read the obituary and came asking to let the room. Some of them had
families, can you imagine? Wanting to bring a wife and children, all
to live in the one room. There's no rooms for let anywhere. It's all the
war marriages, and now these babies nobody thought to expect. Mrs.
Bittle says a man bought a potato field outside town and is putting
up two hundred houses out there, just houses, she says, not a single
shop for them to get their goods. I suppose they'll have to come all
the way into town for that. And the houses all alike, maybe each one
is a little different shade of color, but the same house over and over,
lined up in a row."

"Goodness. It sounds like Moscow. Who would live in a place like that?"

"Well, that's the thing. The plan is for two hundred houses. But seven hundred families are already lined up to buy them."

Then she sat down at the table and began to sob. It has never happened before. The day the agent came to the door she felt faint afterward, and put her head on the table, but this was different. Her shoulders racked. She let out a thin, throbbing wail.

"Now, it can't be as bad as that." I sounded like an actor in a play. Two absurd people in this room, and I had not been introduced to either one. I was still thinking somehow her distress went back to the housing shortage.

She'd seen the first of the stories several days ago, but didn't phone, hoping to spare me embarrassment for a while. Or else, not knowing what to say. All the stories linking us romantically, she has been carrying that alone. Remarks and stares at the library and the market. I know she is often recognized.

I couldn't read much of it. It made me feel too helpless, lost in some landscape of murdered truth. Lev would have been scientific, tracking the trail of this particular prevarication, studying how the branches diverged and where the thing started. Probably in *Star Week* or the *Echo*, though the story also made the reputable papers, and of course the *Trumpet*. It always begins somewhere, one howler waking up the others. They pass it on, embellished, not through any creative drive but only a pure slothful failure to verify a fact. If the reporters made any calls, it would have been for soliciting a denial. Failing that, they run it as truth, upping the ante just enough to put their own byline on it. The lady is "demure" and then "fatally demure" and then has a "tragic past." I am evidently now locked in a battle with an "old-fashioned Mexican family" over my right to pursue the love match.

Only when I made the coffee did I see my hands were shaking.

I have had dreams of being shot, watching the blood pour out, and wondering whether it hurts.

I set a cup near her elbow, but couldn't sit down opposite her, not like a husband facing a wife across a meal. We used to do that at Mrs. Bittle's, of course, when I was the cook and she the worldly secretary. A lot of water under the bridge. I stood.

After a time she sat up, and looked at the coffee strangely, as if it had been delivered by fairies. It struck me like a draught of cold air then, about Mrs. Bittle and the housing shortage. "Is she making you move out because of this?"

"She raised my monthly rate. She said she would have to, if I meant to stay there. Due to the publicity."

"That's ridiculous. You're in a bind, and she's taking advantage. Do you want me to call her?"

"How would that look, Mr. Shepherd? You protecting me."

"I don't know."

"I'll pay it. She knows I couldn't find a single other room in town, with things the way they are."

"Is the shortage really as bad as that?" Of course it is in the papers, everywhere. It just didn't occur that everywhere was here.

"Folks read the obituaries and the homicides now, Mr. Shepherd, to find a room let open. But the police and the undertaker families get those. The rest of us had just as well reckon the next house to open up for us will be the cedar box."

"Mrs. Brown, goodness. This isn't like you." It weighed: these rooms I have, riches undeserved. For a single person who could easily live in little more than a cedar box, and frequently has.

"Anyhow, I've gone years without a hike at Mrs. Bittle's," she said. "The new man is paying twice as much. I'm lucky to have what I have."

"I'll raise your salary to compensate for it."

"You needn't."

"No, I will. If you can find another place suitable, tell me what it costs."

She went to the water closet and ran the water in there, probably washing her face. When she came out she retrieved the letter opener from the drawer where she keeps it, like the woman in a play who draws the revolver from the bureau. Instead of shooting the villain, she sat down and began to sort envelopes into piles. Not glancing up.

"Look. I'll talk to the presses about this, or send out a statement. Denying the romance business. Whatever you want me to do, to defend your name."

"I'm nobody, I don't have any name. It's your own you have to think about."

"Well, in that case there's nothing to be done. This is just more of the usual, we could have expected it. I should have thought, before I asked you to go with me."

She began slitting envelopes open. Her hair was in a net, her wool sweater buttoned to the throat; she looked ten years older than when I'd seen her last.

"At least it can't get any worse now. We're walking away from the wreck," I said. "It's just what happens."

"What happens?" she asked, in a curiously snipped tone.

"*Del árbol caído todos hacen leña.* From the fallen tree everybody makes firewood."

At that she looked up. "Mr. Shepherd, where did we fall?"

February 14

Dear Shep,
What's tickin? Be my valentine? Oops—you're taken! I read all about it in the papers. Well, hats off to you pal, I've thought of bagging an older pigeon for myself. She wouldn't ask for a lot in the boodle department and

it throws everyone else off the scent. But the hell you yell. One of the hearts
you cracked north of the Mason-Dixon was mine. Did I have to read about
it in the Echo?

    When are you coming to New York? The new job at the museum is
steady, mostly sweetening up the top cats for cash. I've got an apartment
in the Lower East Seventies now, very voot. *Kerouac was spotted in the*
neighborhood, and Artie Shaw plays in a joint on the corner. But forget
about bebop, keep your eye out now for a potent lad named Frankie Laine.
Tell him Tom-cat sent you.

    Are you the only news in Asheville these days? Howzabout that old girl
Zelda, think she'd marry me? I hear she resides in one of the white-coat
joints there in your fair city. Did Scott come around on visiting days, when
he was still kicking? You need to cut me in on the juicy stuff. Or are you
riding so high on the rocket to fame, you can't throw your old pal a saludo?
From now on I'll just have to read Star Week *to find out what's oop-*
pop-a-da with Harrison Shepherd.
Dig you later,

TOM CUDDY

March 11, 1948

Dear Tom,

It's strange you asked about Zelda Fitzgerald. She died in a fire
two nights ago. It started in the hospital kitchen and went up
the dumbwaiter shaft into her room, a freak tragedy. There's
no guessing what the national presses will say, but I'm cutting
you in on the scoop as you asked. I heard about the dumbwaiter
from the fire marshal himself, this morning at the tobacco stand
where I get the morning papers. Highland Hospital is just at
the top of my street. Zelda and I have been neighbors for years,
but I haven't given her much thought. Now I feel like a bum. It
could have been any of us in that hospital, Tom.

The rest of my news is not such a bring-down. I am coming along very well on the new book, and have signed a motion-picture package on the last one. Most definitely, I am not married, or involved in any secret romance. Those stories are completely invented. The Violet Brown in question is my stenographer. She wears cotton gloves indoors and unless some terrible accident has deceived us, never has shared a coffee cup that touched my lips. She accompanied me on the research trip to Yucatán, so the gossip-marketers must have learned about it and fallen in love with their fantasies. Believe me, the lady is chaste. This latest run of stories has been very troubling, harder for her than for me. I'm constantly stupefied that anyone believes the nonsense that runs in the papers. And yet they do, time and again. Tommy, you ought to know I am not one for marriage, any more than I was one for the army, back when you and I were ducking bullets for the National Museum. So put your poor cracked heart back together, soldier. I didn't snub you from any wedding list.

I have no plans for New York soon, but you should visit here. Asheville has changed since the war, we are said to be a tourist destination, first rate. Out on the Tunnel Road they have a brand-new contraption that will wash and wax an auto with the driver still in it. We have instant coffee here too, and lady drivers. Are we voot? You shall have to come and see for yourself. Until then I am, as you may have heard,

Still single,

SHEP

March 22

Dear Shep,
My friends are all green that I am hep to Shep, especially when I told them about your movie package. Holy Joe, congrats on that. Could you find a

tiny role for me? I'll be the lad in the loincloth sitting on a rock, smoking a herd of Camels during the battle scene, trying to sneak a gander at Robert Taylor. Lord and Butler, that fellow is cuter than snappers. And pointing the finger at anything pink now, I see in the papers.

Please advise: a friend here seems to be in that kind of hash. He works in radio but has the looks for television—Puerto Rican, a Latin dreamboat type. With brains, even, this boy reads, and very impressed I know you, by the way. Up until last year he was a steaming romeo. Now he can't get hired for anything. He was mixed up with the Communists ages ago, and it's a gestanko scene for those cats now, people are even getting deported. It happened to a Negro lady I knew from the museum, a writer who reviews our shows for the Harlem papers. I didn't even know she was foreign. Evidently her family came from Trinidad in the '20s when she was a tiny tot. So one day this lady is typing her story on Negro artists, then the FBI knocks on her door and she's cooling her heels on Ellis Island, next stop Trinidad. You can see why my Puerto Rican pal is worried. You're a foreigner too. He says to ask if you know some cat in the higher-ups who could help him out.

The hell you yell, Asheville has instant coffee now? I might have to come and review the action myself. The boss sends me out on the trail to beat the gums with the richie riches, so they'll loan out their Picassos for our big shows. Lately he's been scobo for the Vanderbilts. So wipe your feet on the mat, cat, I might be headed for your roost.

Later,

TOM CUDDY

April 23

Dear Mr. Shepherd,

Your news is extremely welcome. All of us at Stratford and Sons are pleased to know your novel is moving forward at a clip. I've read the chapters you sent, and find them in every way up to the standard we expect from our boy

Shepherd. This may be your best to date. This contract explains the terms we discussed by telephone. The late summer completion date you suggest will be very suitable. You'll hear soon from our sales department to discuss the title, dust jacket, and so forth. They are determined to include an author photograph this time, so please give the request a fair consideration. I'm afraid your title, The Name of This Place, *does not strike us as quite the ticket. I believe* Cataclysm of the Empire *has a good ring. But we have time to sort that out.*

Enclosed herein you will find two copies of the contract for your signature. Attached to last page please note the affidavit of anti-Communism, also for signature before a notary public. As you may know, this formality is now requisite in all moving-picture contracts, and is expected soon to be mandatory in publishing, so we are working to get the necessary papers on file.

I send greetings from my Miss Daley, who enjoys her chats with your Mrs. Brown. And cheers from Miss James in the mailing room who says your letters mount up there as always, fragrant with perfume, despite rumors of your engagement. Many will be gratified to know another of your books will soon be available.

Yours sincerely,

LINCOLN BARNES

May 4

Artie proposed breakfast at the Swiss Kitchen, one of his haunts. It seemed to be a tourist place, they had a giant sign out front with a boy in lederhosen (*Food Worth Yodeling About!*) and waitresses dressed as milkmaids. Artie, in his ancient cuffed trousers and faint old-man smell, was unembarrassed by any of it.

"What makes it Swiss food?" I asked, studying the menu.

"A lot of grease. Bratwurst, only here they are going to call it sausage. German food with a strict doctrine of neutrality."

With Artie, irony carries the mailbag right to the door of nonchalance. Nothing seems to excite him. Short of a revelation that one has worked for Lev Trotsky. Through a haze of burning cigarettes he studied the new book contract. "These terms are basically good. I'm sorry about the anticommunism business."

"I'll sign it. I just hope they won't ask me to disavow anything more difficult."

"Such as?"

"Coffee with too much sugar. Mad irritation. Plotting murders I could never go through with. That sort of thing."

"These crimes are very difficult to prosecute. Otherwise, all of us except Eleanor Roosevelt would be in the pokey."

One of the waitresses in blond plaits was making her way toward us, a twin to the one who'd seated us at our window table. "The pokey," I repeated.

"A technical legal term, meaning the hoosegow. You're not much of one for American slang, are you? For a young man of words."

"It has never come naturally to me, no. You must hear a lot of it in your business. Actors and musicians."

"Oh yes. From those clients I hear 'Artie, where is the cabbage?' Clams, dough, moolah, many words for the one thing they don't have these days."

Our milkmaid slipped a pad and pencil from her apron pocket, then dropped the pencil. Deliberately, I could vouch. She knelt to retrieve it, all lowered lashes and ruffled décolletage, the cup runneth over. My stars, as Mrs. Brown would put it. Where do these precious creatures come from, is it Artie who draws them?

"Doll face, tell us your specials. And promise we will see your face again in thirty seconds when you return with coffee. Extra sugar for my friend." Yes, it's Artie.

"You have a manner of speaking," he said when she had gone. "The first time we spoke on the phone, I heard it. Every word is perfect, but there is an accent. Like Gary Cooper. Not quite the regular apple pie."

"They tell me the same thing in Mexico—my Spanish has a faint accent. I am the permanent foreigner."

"Well, don't cure it. Your way with words, I mean. We need the income."

"It's not my mother's fault, she was an ace at slang. Flapper first-class. Today is her birthday, by the way. I always took her to lunch."

"Happy birthday, Mrs. Shepherd. How old?"

"Forever young. She died in '38."

"Condolences. How did it happen?"

"A car accident in Mexico City. She was dating a news correspondent, they were racing to the airport to get a look at Howard Hughes."

"Now that is going out with a bang. I mean no disrespect."

"No, you're right, she was all bang. In death as in life. I miss her."

"Now, you mention plotting murders that you cannot find the heart to execute. Is this anything I ought to know about, as your legal representative?"

"Just the usual. Newspapermen. The rumors have upset my stenographer this spring. People are treating her badly. Even some of her friends have been callous."

"Now that is a subject. Freedom of the presses to destroy a person's life for no good reason." He studied the menu with the same concentration he'd given the book contract, reading all the fine print. When he'd finished he closed it.

"Congratulations on the new book, by the way. As I said, these are excellent terms. A pretty penny. Now, let me ask you something, a little personal. But I ask in a professional capacity, as the guy whose job is to look out for you and promote the general welfare."

"All right, fire away."

"I know that Mrs. Brown is not your type, categorically speaking. You once mentioned I am one of a few who knows about this. The Selective Service being another. What I am asking, and I hope the answer is yes, isn't there *somebody* else who knows?"

"Somebody. No, not for quite a while. An offer does seem to be on the table right now, but. It's not very easy to discuss this, Artie."

He held up a hand, took a sip of his coffee. "My intention is not to make you uncomfortable."

"You're concerned for my safety?"

"That you could be put at risk of, shall we say, exposure. Blackmail can arrive from unexpected quarters. I am not speaking in this case of Aware, Incorporated. I have had clients in your situation."

"Oh. Well, no, I don't think that's a worry. This particular friend would have a great deal to lose. From exposure, as you say."

"Not another Bolshevik? Never mind, pretend I didn't ask."

I laughed. "No, don't worry, this one is all stars and stripes. We worked together in Civilian Services during the war, moving paintings into safe storage here from the National Gallery. There were quite a few of us in that corps, you'd be amazed. The art world may never be the same."

"Really."

"He's working for a museum these days, in New York. Out of touch for years, and suddenly now he's coming to town. It's not easy to contemplate, I'll tell you the truth. I'd settled pretty well on living as a monk."

Artie waved away a cloud of smoke. "Yeah, me too. I would say, 'Since my wife died,' but under oath I would have to say since long before that. Who has the energy?"

"You might be surprised, Artie. Cocktail waitresses seem to hum around you like little bees."

"Entertainment, my friend. Sweet music. In the long run, most of us spend about fifteen minutes total in the entanglements of passion, and the rest of our days looking back on it, humming the tune. Not a bad arrangement."

"So it seems."

He carefully lit a new cigarette from the old one. "Now *love*."

"Yes. Love is another story."

"And this you have in spades, my friend. You are loved by the multitudes. Ladies and gents standing in line down the block, waiting for your every word."

Their opinion of me is approximately the same as for a talking pony. Frida said that. "Yes, I'm very lucky. Employed by the American imagination, as you put it."

"Long may it wave."

"Now I have a question for you, Artie."

"Personal?"

"No. This friend in New York tells me foreigners are being deported there, for suspicion of just about anything. Working for Negro rights and so forth. My friend is dramatic, he can exaggerate."

"Your friend in this case does not exaggerate."

"That's diabolical. To bolster support by deporting the opposition."

"Diabolical is a polite term for this behavior."

"Are they setting their caps mostly for noncitizens?"

"Mr. Hoover and Mr. Watkins at the INS are becoming very enthusiastic with their housecleaning. Some of the deportees have been living in this country since Homer was a pup. A fellow I know of, Williamson, labor secretary of the Communist Party, currently held without bond on Ellis Island. Accused of being an immigrant. He says he was born in San Francisco. Forty-five years of age, he has family, witnesses. But all the birth certificates in that city were lost in the earthquake and fire of '06."

"Goodness."

"Shepherd, you have a birth certificate, do you not?"

"I do. It was some trouble with both parents dead, but I located the hospital. I have both passports, U.S. and Mexican. I had to sort it out during the war, as you'd guess. Called up to work for the Department of State, they like to see credentials."

"Keep that U.S. passport with your guns and liquor. That is my advice."

Breakfast was biscuits and gravy, sausages, and eggs on many heavy white plates. Artie rearranged it all to make room for his ashtray, and continued smoking right through the meal. With so much grease everywhere, I wondered about spontaneous combustion.

"Mrs. Brown does her best to keep me out of trouble," I said. "She claims my ideology is transparent. But no criminal record as yet."

"Who needs crimes? The INS has a stable of witnesses, professionals. Very well paid, very talented, they can produce a testimony for any occasion. If a man is not a Communist, they'll prove he is. If he is, they can get him booked for 'creating confusion and hysteria,' to hold him until CP membership becomes illegal."

"Outlaw a political party? What kind of country does that?"

"The kind in which you reside. The party has disavowed violence, as you know. Last year they also severed all ties with the Information Bureau of the Soviet Union, to be on the safe side. Turns out, there is no safe side. A federal grand jury just declared that Communist Party membership is a threat to the civilian defense. Now Congress is working on the Mundt-Nixon bill, requiring members to enter their names in a registry. So denying CP membership will soon be a crime also. These people are damned if they do, and damned if they do not."

Outside in the parking lot under the restaurant's jolly billboard, that yodeling boy in his lederhosen, a dark-colored auto pulled in and a couple emerged from it, in the throes of a terrible argument. The plate glass window shut out any sound, but their rage was visible. The man kept circling the woman to shout at her face, and she kept turning away, her loose raincoat swinging like a bell, her flat shoes stepping side to side. A child peered from the oval of the auto's rear window, the small doomed fish in the bowl.

"Well. At least I'm no party member."

"Mr. Shepherd, you have a colorful past. Your Mexican friends, do they stay in touch?"

"Frida does. Mrs. Kahlo. Intermittently. She's just joined up again with the Communist Party, after a lapse. She says it's all going strong there."

"So it may be, and legal also, in her locale. But I suggest discretion."

"You're not saying I should simply cut off old friends, for fear of association?"

"No, I am not, and I recognize you, sir, as a man with a spinal column. But you would be amazed at the number of people who do exactly what you've just said."

"I see. My stenographer would say, 'Fairly warned is fair afeared.'"

"That is about the sum of what I can offer you, yes."

"So, keeping old letters and so forth in the house. Maybe not a good idea."

"A man with a spinal column, and a brain. Bravo. Now, what about our friend Agent X, who came calling last October. Does he also keep in touch?"

"Not another peep. He must have discovered what a lackluster stiff I am."

"Maybe. We should all be so lucky. But these men don't care who you are. Not even what you're planning to do, despite what they may say. They're like bloodhounds. What gets them baying is the whiff of where you have already been."

"Well, that can't change. I spent years around Communists, cleaning their dishes while they deliberated the transitional program and formalized party directives. You know something, Artie? They eat what people eat. They paint the dining room yellow, and love their children. I keep wondering, what have people got against Communists?"

"I told you. 'Anticommunism' is not very much concerned with 'communism.'"

"So you said. Tuna fish, and the Spanish influenza. It's hard to believe."

"Think of religion. A virgin birth. Likewise hard to believe. Yet taken by many as evidence that purveyors of indecency are every-where."

The arguing couple outside got back in their car and drove away. A stop on their journey.

"Communism? Most people have no idea what it is," Artie said. "I do not exaggerate. Look around this restaurant, ask any of these fine citizens. 'Excuse me, sir, I've been thinking of an idea, a bunch of working people owning the means of their own production. What do you make of that?' You know, he might be all for it."

"Communism is the same as Stalin, that's what he thinks."

"Correct. And baseball is nine white men and a stick. Seeing is believing. For years the president told us we had no fear. They put up signs to that effect in every post office. 'Tojo doesn't scare us.' Now we have a change of program, they're plastering up a new slogan: 'Run like hell.'"

"I see what you mean."

"According to Elmo Roper's last poll, forty percent of Americans believe the Jews have too much power in this country. Tell me, we have how many Jewish men in the Congress?"

"Not many, I shouldn't think. Maybe none at all?"

"So what is the problem? Foreign-sounding people, not Christian, and not apologetic about it. They may have their own ideas. It sug-gests a challenge to our hard-earned peace and bounty. Making a fuss over Negro segregation would be another example."

"I see that. The issue is not Communism per se."

He leaned forward, his blue eyes watery, feverish looking. He held up both hands as if he meant to clasp my face between them. "You know what the issue is? Do you want to know? It's what these guys have decided to call *America*. They have the audacity to say, '*There*, you sons of bitches, don't lay a finger on it. *That* is a finished prod-uct!'"

"But any country is still in the making. *Always*. That's just history, people have to see that."

He dropped his hands, sat back against the booth. "Pardon my French, but tell it to the goddamn Marines."

"My stenographer said the same thing, more or less. Minus the French."

Artie had finished his breakfast and now stacked up plates, ash-tray on top, recovering himself. "Your Mrs. Brown, a very astute lady. How is she?"

"Astute, as you say. And not mine, for the record. She's all right, I think."

"Good." He ground out his cigarette, smoothed the contract on the table, and folded it into its envelope. "You can sign this. Affidavit and all, if that's what you want. I can't say yes or no. But I'm go-ing to tell you something about history in the making. Remember you heard this first from Artie Gold, over a plate of ground hog and cackle. This is going to get serious. What these men are doing could become permanent."

"What do you mean?"

Suddenly he looked weary. "You force people to stop asking ques-tions, and before you know it they have auctioned off the question mark, or sold it for scrap. No boldness. No good ideas for fixing what's broken in the land. Because if you happen to mention it's bro-ken, you are automatically disqualified."

"Surely that's overstating it," I said. "America runs on extremes. The latest craze and a tank of gas will get you about anywhere. To-day the Kremlin is a messianic movement and you're better dead than red. Tomorrow they'll decide the real mischief is cigarettes and sugar in your coffee. The culture is built on hyperbole." I wanted to see him smile. "Or maybe you really do think this food is worth yodeling about."

He didn't smile. "I'm an old man, I've seen a lot. But what these men are doing is putting poison on the lawn. It kills your crabgrass all right, and then you have a lot of dead stuff out there for a very long time. Maybe forever."

The Asheville Trumpet, *June 18, 1948*

City Slams Doors on Polio Menace

by Carl Nicholas

The City Health Commission this week banned all public gatherings, to stem the tide of infantile paralysis sweeping our state. The quarantine began at 1 am Monday, closing movie houses, skating parlors, swimming pools, and other public sites of infestation. All city churches except the Roman Catholic have sensibly urged their flocks to pray from the safety of home. This city of 50,000 souls is quiet as a grave, as housewives stay home from shopping and our businesses and resorts see profits stolen by the epidemic.

Dr. Ken Malusa, interviewed at the Health Department by telephone, reminded us that even the wisest of medical men can offer no chemical cure for polio. "This germ is crafty, you won't see him with the human eye or even the best microscopes. Many have given it a try, but the sneaky fellow won't show his face. Penicillin doesn't scare him, it's no use at all. My advice is, keep the kiddies away from the crowds where he travels."

That goes for men and ladies too, no one's in the clear. Seven percent of hapless victims die, says Dr. Malusa, and nearly all are crippled. The good doctor said no explanation accounts for the epidemics each year, which occur in summer only. Asheville is presently suffering the worst rate of epidemic in our nation, in a state that already this year has seen more than one thousand victims fall to the polio menace. The national total is nearly six thousand.

The town fathers have composed a letter to Bishop Vernon Reynolds in Raleigh urging him to grant permission to Roman Catholics here to remain away from their rites.

July 6

Dear Frida,

It's two in the morning, and bright as day outside. The paved street has a watery shine, with the trees lined up along both banks like the canals of Xochimilco. The moon is not quite full: perfect down the left side but a little ragged on the right, so waning. C for Cristo means it is dying away. I couldn't sleep tonight so sat up to meet our birthday. But I must have fallen into a dream for a few seconds, because you were here in my room just now, in your wheelchair, your hair all done up. Working at an easel with your back to me. I said, "Frida, look, the streets have turned to rivers. Let's take a boat somewhere." You turned to me with empty eye sockets and said, "You go on, Sóli. I have to stay."

The radio news may have put me off sleep. Stalin's blockade of Berlin is a horror, and not so difficult for us to imagine here. Asheville is also under siege, quarantined because of the polio. Today I walked downtown to put Mrs. Brown's wage in the bank, and I saw not one other living soul on the way. The school playgrounds, empty. The luncheonettes dark, their counters attended by lines of empty chrome stools. The city is a graveyard. My only compatriots today were the plaster models in the store windows, with their smug blind eyes and smart attire. Of course, the bank was closed.

I can imagine you here, Frida, limp-skipping through the streets to have a laugh at all this fear. You've already had the polio, you have your leg to show for it, your billowing woe and passion that can't be chased indoors for anything. It's a gift to survive death, isn't it? It puts us outside the fray. How strange, that I include myself, I wonder now what I mean. What was my childhood disease? Love, I suppose. I was susceptible to contracting great love, suffering the chills and delirium of that pox.

But it seems I am safe now, unlikely to contract it again. The advantages of immunity are plain. People contort themselves around the terror of being alone, making any compromise against that. It's a great freedom to give up on love, and get on with everything else.

Mainly this summer my everything-else is the new book. I believe it will be serious, Frida, and worthy. But at any rate finished soon, in autumn I hope. I proceed at a sluggish pace because I have to do all my own retyping. Mrs. Brown's efficiency has spoiled me, and now she can't come to work because her landlady is hysterical over the epidemic. She threatened the boarders that if they go out in public or ride the buses, they aren't welcome back in the house. Mrs. Brown tolerates the intolerable from that woman. Stalin himself could learn from the Siege of Mrs. Bittle.

I have wondered, Why shouldn't I let Mrs. Brown live here? We already work together, I have an empty bedroom. You see, I am dumb as a calf, trying to divine the rules about such things. In Mexico all manner of people could live in one house, half carrying hearts on their sleeves and the other half carrying side-arms, all rolled in one chalupa. But no, not here. Even a dumb calf gains a dim understanding, after enough blows to the head! We would be hung out as filthy laundry in *Echo* and *Star Week*. Children would be instructed to cross to the opposite side of the street, to pass the house.

Luckily, the mail remains under control. Mrs. Brown organized for it all to come to Mrs. Bittle's, until and unless the landlady realizes the menace of an envelope licked by a stranger. My house is as empty as the luncheonettes, Mrs. Brown's table tidy as she left it, typewriter under a dustcover, telephone standing like a black daffodil blooming from the table, its earpiece dangling. If I want company I can sift through the mail; she forwards it all here in boxes after she has answered it. Those letters continue to astonish, the flow has hardly slowed. Now the girls all beg: Please, Mr. Shepherd, give us a happy ending next time! As if I held sway over anything real, with my invented puppets. These girls have bet on a dark horse. No one should count on me for a happy outcome.

You and I are the same. Do people ask you to erase the bleeding hearts and daggers from your paintings, to make them more jolly? But Mexico is different, I know that. You're allowed your hearts and daggers there.

Our Christmas visit sustains my memories, though it's true what you said, you have become a different person. I won't agree however that you are a bag of bones. Diego is a fool, that skinny lizard Maria Félix should run up a tree and eat ants. But your health does worry me, I'll be honest. One thing that kept me sitting up tonight is the dread that I may not celebrate many more birthdays with you.

More than anything, I regret the cross words during our visit. I understand your temper, that it's a kind of poetry rather than actual truth, and that you and Mrs. Brown were not apt to get along perfectly. You and she are both important women in my life, and too many cooks will put a fire in the kitchen. If any forgiving is to be done, Mrs. Brown and I have already done it. I'm certain she would send her greetings with mine.

Abrazos to Diego, and to Candelaria, Belén, Carmen Alba, Perpetua, Alejandro, and everyone else in your house, where I seem to have more friends than in the entire city where I now live. But most of all to you, *mi querida, feliz cumpleaños.*

SÓLI

July 30

Mrs. Brown called before nine this morning, beside herself. A second letter from the scorpion at the loyalty firm. Loren Matus. An incriminating photograph, he claims, but it makes no sense at all. I made her read that part of the letter twice. "A photo of Harrison Shepherd and his wife at a Communist Party meeting in 1930." I'm to pay him a fee of five hundred dollars for the chance to examine it.

She took a letter, over the phone: Why this photograph could not be what he says. In 1930 Harrison Shepherd was fourteen years of age, attending an elementary school for the mentally damaged in Mexico City. His political leaning was to collect centipedes in a jar and set them loose under Señora Bartolome's desk during the prayers. Since that year he has discovered no reason to marry, nor has anyone signed on for the job, but it might have quite entertained him to have a wife in 1930. A lot of people might pay money to see that. Signed sincerely Harrison Shepherd. HS/VB.

August 11

"Advance the spark," says Tom Cuddy on the phone, "Square-o-lina here I come." He has museum business with the Vanderbilts, will be staying three nights at the Grove Park, proposes we meet there. "An assignation," he calls it. Oh Tom, Tom, vanity's son, expecting me to show up with hat in hand, heart pounding. Knowing, in fact, I will.

The Assignation

Long time no see, says the handsome scoundrel, looking up from his highball. The firm handshake, the chair pulled out. The terrace restaurant at the Grove Park is very grand, white cloths on the tables and candles flickering, but all other chairs were empty. Tom must have been the only guest in the hotel.

"You're brave, letting your boss send you here. Have they not heard about our quarantine, in Manhattan? Or are you all just so dashing, the plague can't catch up?"

"Who's afraid of a little polio germ?" he said. "Builds up the character."

"Tommy, that's no joke."

"What's your poison? This is a sloe gin fizz. Don't let the name throw you, it's a fast ticket. The apron back there at the bar has a heavy foot."

"All right. A ticket on the fast train, please."

Tommy signaled the waiter, who hovered constantly nearby in the dark, either at the patio entrance or over by the wall, sneaking a smoke. I have wondered if waiters will ever become invisible to me, as they seem to be for others. I wanted to help this lad out, go get the drinks myself and later help him carry the plates to the kitchen.

Tommy's cigarette end glowed, constantly in motion. "Oh, come on, look what the polio did for FDR. A gimp leg gets you the sympathy vote, you can be maudlin as anything and they all go dotty for it. *I hate the wah, Eleanor hates the wah, our little dog Fala hates the wah. . . .*"

The drinks appeared, followed by dinner, materializing from the dark just as Tom had, unreal as the image rising in a movie house. Cruelty is just a role he plays, like Hurd Hatfield as Dorian Gray. Tommy has seen some damage in his day. The Modern show he helped curate, ridiculed by Congress, he took that personally. And that's probably the least of it, for a boy who wants so madly to belong, and will not quite.

The truth of Tommy is slow to rise, but he is down there somewhere, underneath the shining surface. The day we first met, sitting on a crate of Rodin in the train, he dropped the clever banter along with his jaw upon hearing the name Rivera. He has studied those murals in photographs. He wanted to know everything: the mixture of plaster, the pigments. And Frida, how she laid the paint on, with brushes or knives? The warm or cool colors first? That unearthly sadness that radiates from her paintings, does she feel it herself, when she's painting? Those were his words, unearthly sadness. Tommy has handled two Kahlos already, in his time at the museum.

Later on in his room, lying on our backs smoking his herd of Camels one after another, shirtless in the dark, it could have been the Potomac Academy, or the tiny barracks at Lev's. But those places couldn't have contained him, Tom Cuddy is a one-man band. His questions don't need answers, it's hard enough just to work out what he's asking. Who would win at arm-wrestling, Frankie Laine or Perry Como? Has Christian Dior gone screwball or hopped on the genius wagon?

"Why, what's Dior done?"

"Took all the padding off the girls' shoulders and stuffed it in their brassieres."

He is thinking of leaving the gallery, the art world altogether. For advertising.

"What, to write jingles? Lucky Strike Means Fine Tobacco?"

"No, you egg. Art direction. Creating the Look of Tomorrow."

"I thought the museum was what you loved. Kandinsky and Edward Hopper. Now you want to be Llewelyn Evans in *The Hucksters*, selling Beautee Soap to unsuspecting housewives?"

"Not soap, glamour. Sex, God and the *Pa*-tri-*ah*." Tommy blew a meticulous smoke ring, watched it rise toward the ceiling. "On the seventh day Tom Cuddy made America. And Tom Cuddy said, *Cat, that is good.*"

"If I were a religious man I'd get off this bed, before lightning strikes it."

"One day you will see, Shepherd my friend. The men campaigning for president are going to hire advertisers."

"Tommy, you've lost your marbles."

"This is no fish. Do you know how many television stations there are now?"

"Six or seven, I guess."

"Twenty."

"How's your friend, by the way? The Latin Romeo with the face for television."

The question shifted Tom's mood, turning him petulant. Ramiro is gone, not to Puerto Rico but out of the city, far from the glamorous spotlight. Maybe selling brushes door to door. It was hard to avoid speculating on the clockwork of Tom Cuddy's universe: Ramiro's setting sun, the rising star of Harrison Shepherd. The long compromise against loneliness. Tom says he'll be back here in a month, and probably more times after that. To Casheville, as he calls it. Regular assignations on expense account at the Grove Park, as long as he continues to happify the Vanderbilts as planned.

"You're lucky you live here," he said.

"What, in Square-o-lina? Under a quarantine."

"Well, here, Shep, or any damned place you want. Writing what you want, with nobody watching over your shoulder. In the city we're like ants under a lens, getting scorched in the sun."

"Scorched ants. That's dramatic." I pushed myself up off the bed. It took some effort, a lot of sloe gin under the bridge, but I needed to pace the little room. Tommy's energy came off his skin like electricity. I stood by the window, a porthole into the dark.

"*I'm* dramatic," he said. "You should hear the real gory. The joes in radio and television. The producers are like those little brutes in grammar school, crowding around to watch the ant fry. Conspiracy indictments, *alien* hearings. Do you know how many New Yorkers are *from* someplace? The city's going to be as empty as this hotel."

In a rare turn of events, he seemed to have run out of words. I could hear the place breathing: the gasp of roof beams, the slow circulation of water through pipes.

Tommy lit another Camel. "They don't even have to indict you. One day you just feel the heat and you know they're up there, kneeling in the circle, watching you writhe. Your name has gone on a list. Everybody stops talking when you come into a room. You think we don't know about the plague?"

"They're only television producers, Tommy. Not heads of state, with secret police at their disposal. Just men who get up in the morning, put on Sears Roebuck suits, and go to an office to decide who gets a pie in the face today. It's hard to feature how they could be so monstrous."

" 'Hard to feature.' " Tom clucked his tongue, whether at a writer's prose or his innocence, who could say. "Little shepherd boy. What am I going to do with you?"

September 2

The stars and planets are right again. Mrs. Brown is back, all this week, cheerful as anything today in a new peplum blouse. The Woman's Club has let her back on the Program Committee, mainly because she kept the club running by telephone and the post during the quarantine. Most of the good ladies were flummoxed by solitude.

We're on track to complete the novel draft by month's end. Mrs. Brown says this one is my best, and she hasn't even seen the ending yet. The title is another go-round, the publisher as usual wants crashing cymbals: *The Mighty Fallen*, or *Ashes of Empire*. I'd hoped for a pinch of metaphor. Mrs. Brown sat at her table looking thoughtful, holding a pencil alongside her cheek, and then offered: "Remember at Chichén Itzá on top of the temple, the last day? Everything looked bright, and then the storm came and put it in a different light. It was the same view, all the same things, but suddenly it went fearsome. That's what you want, isn't it? Is there a name for that?"

"Yes. J. Edgar Hoover."

She's asked permission to leave early tomorrow to see Truman on his whistle-stop for the reelection. He's coming through Asheville, speaking from a platform on the back of the Ferdinand Magellan. It's the same train the people here stood waiting for all night, when it carried Roosevelt home. But it never came.

September 15

The Grove Park is a reassuring place, all that squared-off, heavy Mission furniture with its feet firmly on the ground. The giant stone fireplaces, the carpentered grandfather clocks, even the roof, snub and rounded like the thatch of a fairy-tale cottage, with little eyebrow curves above the windows of the top-floor rooms. Tom likes those best, he feels he's an artist up in a garret. He insists Scott Fitzgerald always took a top-floor room here when he came to visit Zelda. "Just ask the bellhop, I *told* you so, and I'm right. He might have written *Gatsby* in the very room where I'm sleeping tonight."

"More likely *The Crack-Up*. If he was here in town for the reason you say."

Tommy rolled his head in a circle. "Oh, *The Crack-Up*, well done!" He moves like an actor, physically earnest, aware of his better angles. Today he had a better audience: the terrace was jammed, people out enjoying the autumn sun. The tourist trade is back, all those postponed vacations must be had before cold weather hits, it's like a rush on the bank. Tommy was playing dissect-the-guests.

"That one over there has got clocks on his socks. I'll lay a fiver on it. Go over and ask him to raise up his pants leg."

"I don't know what that means. Clocks on his socks."

"It means," he leaned forward, sotto voce, "the car he left with the valet has a *fox tail* attached to the antenna. Hubba hubba. You don't know these college boys. I can see them in the dark." Sloe gin was not fast enough for Tommy today, so we drank "Seabreezes," a concoction he'd explained to the bartender. Complicated instructions for what amounted to gin and orange juice.

"Over there, the couple. Parisians, a jasper and his zazz girl, *très* vout-o-reenee."

"Really." There was no learning Tommy's language, I'd given up on trying.

"In Paris I can always pick out the Americans like anything, *ping, ping!*" One eye closed, he feigned using a pistol. "A Frenchman's like *this*"—he pulled his shoulders toward his ears—"like someone's put ice down his collar. And a Brit's just the opposite, shoulders back. 'I say, a spot of ice down the old neck! Not a problem, by Jove.'"

"And the American?"

Tommy flung himself back in his chair, knees spread wide, hands clasped behind his golden head, vowels flat: 'Ice, what's the big idea? I take mine straight up.'"

And the Mexican: *I carried the ice here on my back, I chopped it with a machete, and probably it still isn't right.* Tommy lifted two fingers to signal the next round.

"No more for me," I said. "I'm nursing a ridiculous hope that I'm still going to get some work done this evening. Coca-Cola, please."

The waiter nodded. Every waiter in the place was dark-skinned, and all the guests white. It felt like an occupied zone after cease-fire, two distinct factions inhabiting the same place: the one tribe relaxed and garrulous, draped unguarded on the chairs in colorful clothes, while the other stood wordless in starched coats, white collars sharp against black skin. In Mexico when we served a table it was normally the guests in starched collars, the servants in floral tapestries.

Tommy informed me that Coca-Cola sells fifty million bottles a day.

"Who are you, Elmo Roper?"

"It's enough to float a battleship. I mean, literally it is, if you think about it. The French National Assembly just voted to nix Coca-Cola, no buy no sell, anywhere in their empire. What's the static?"

"Maybe they don't want it poured down their backs."

"You're going home and working *tonight*?" His eyes are so pale and clear, his whole complexion really, he seems to give off light rather than absorb it. Moths must fly into his flame and perish gladly.

"I can stay the afternoon. But I'm so near the end of the book. It's hard to think of much else."

"Oh, Jack *will* be a dull boy."

"Or my meat will go to gristle, if my stenographer is to be believed."

He leaned forward, pinched the flesh of my upper arm, clucked his tongue. Then fell back in his chair. He had a way of looking tossed around, like one half of a prizefight. "And what's the buzz on your cooper?"

I pondered this. "I give up."

"Your moving picture."

"Oh. I'm not sure. The Hollywood winds blow hot and cold."

"Listen, I could sell it. Make your picture the talk of the season."

"I thought you wanted a look at Robert Taylor. Now you're selling him?"

"Cat, you don't listen to me. I am going to be an ad man. I interviewed with a firm last week."

"I do listen. You're going to sell presidential candidates. You know what, they need you right now. All four of them."

"You said it! Four men running, and not one winner I can see. Lord and butler, spare me that cold cut Tom Dewey and his toothbrush moustache."

"You may not be spared. The newspapers say it's already over. With the Democrats split three ways, Dewey's just waiting to be confirmed. The editorial this morning said Truman's cabinet should resign now and get out of the way."

"It can't *be*. Dewey doesn't even look like a proper Republican. He looks like a magazine salesman."

"Some salesman, he's not even campaigning. 'America the Beautiful' is not exactly a platform. I suppose he doesn't want to lower himself to Truman's level, it would show lack of confidence."

Tommy put his face in his hands. "Not Tom Dewey the toothbrush moustache! *Please* not that mug in all the photos for the next four years."

"Would you rather look at Strom Thurmond for four years?"

"What a drizzle bag."

A stout woman in a scant bandeau and espadrilles minced across the terrace. In Mexico she would have been a beauty of a certain type, but not here, I gathered. Tommy's eyes tracked her too dramatically, like Charlie Chaplin in *The Gold Rush*.

"Maybe Scarlett O'Hara will come out and stump for Strom," I suggested. "And Rhett Butler, whistling Dixiecrat to call out the segregationists."

Tom looked up, eyes wide. "Now *that* is a campaign image. You've got the gift! And on the other team, Henry Wallace as the Pied Piper, with the liberals skipping off behind him."

"Poor Truman, he's got nobody left. I read he's asked a dozen men to run as his vice president, and they all turned him down. Do you think that's true?"

"He can't get reelected, why should they waste the time?"

A young couple slid into the next table, inciting Tom to announce: "Hardware and headlights, call the nabs." The fellow was an Adonis, more or less Tommy in a younger model. The girl wore a tennis dress and diamond bracelets.

"My stenographer went out to see Truman at his whistle stop here, just a couple of weeks ago. She's League of Women Voters. So there's one he can count on."

"Oh, gee. Little man with high voice makes barnyard jokes from back of train."

"She said he turned out quite a crowd."

"Natch. The first thing he's accomplished in the last two years."

"That's not fair. The Republicans kill every one of his bills in Congress. They can't be bothered with the minimum wage or housing starts, they're all crowding into the communism hearings to see Alger Hiss charged with espionage."

Tommy vamped a few bars of "I'm Just Wild About Harry," with jazz hands.

"It's true, Tommy. If you read something besides the *Echo*, you'd know that."

"Fine, down with it. Harry Truman gets *two* votes."

"I don't vote. I never have."

"*Really?* Conk me. I had you down for a Henry Wallace type. The rise of the common man and all that. All the reviewers say so."

"Politics in this country are never quite what they seem. I don't quite feel . . . what? Entitled."

He looked genuinely amazed. "*Entitled*. Cat, this is *America*, they let anybody vote. Crooks, wigs, even cookies like us. Dogs and cats, probably. Don't take Fido to the polls, he might cancel you out."

"Well, that's the thing, it's all too much. Too fast. I need to brood on things."

He cocked his head in a sympathetic pout. "Sad stranger in the happy land."

The New York Times, *September 26, 1948*

Truman Is Linked by Scott to Reds

Special to The New York Times

BOSTON, MASS., SEPT. 25—Hugh D. Scott Jr., chairman of the Republican National Committee, told Massachusetts Republicans today that the Communist party endorsed Mr. Truman for Vice President in 1944, with the result that the President now shows "indifference to Communist penetration at home." Delivering the keynote address at the party's state convention, Mr. Scott assailed the President's reference to spy investigations as a "red herring" and said the explanation for this attitude could be found in history.

"The New York *Daily Worker*, the official Communist organ in the United States, endorsed Mr. Truman cordially in the issue of Aug. 12, 1944," he said. "The endorsement was signed by Eugene Dennis, secretary of the Communist party, who recently was cited for contempt of the House of Representatives for refusing to testify concerning his subversive activities in this country."

Mr. Scott quoted Mr. Dennis as writing, in connection with the Democratic Party's 1944 candidates: "It is a ticket representative not only of the Democratic Party but of important and wider sections of the camp of national unity."

Another link between the President and *The Daily Worker* was claimed by Mr. Scott. This is a letter written on Senate stationery and signed by Harry S. Truman, August 14, 1944. This communication to Samuel Barron, public relations director of *The Daily Worker*, expresses thanks for the copy of an article that appeared in the paper.

Calling for an all-out drive on subversives in Government, Mr. Scott said: "Once the Dewey-Warren administration takes over we will see the greatest housecleaning in Washington since St. Patrick cleaned the snakes out of Ireland."

Senator Henry Cabot Lodge Jr. was chairman of the convention, which adopted a platform making no mention of controversial state referenda on birth control and labor unions.

November 1

This strange day. Early snow, and a visit from the FBI.

The snow fell in huge, leisurely flakes, piling itself carefully on everything, even twigs and telephone wires. Putting white caps on the hydrants, covering the mud puddles and buckled sidewalks. A Benediction for the Day of the Dead. Or perhaps last rites, this weary world with all its faults consenting to lie down with a sigh and be covered up with a sheet. "Holy is the day"—I had just thought those words when he came tramping tiredly up the walk, leaving behind a trail, the impressions of his leather shoes. At the curb he'd hesitated, turning this way and that before coming up my walk. It looked like an Arthur Murray dance diagram.

Myers is the name. I made sure to get it this time, Melvin C. Myers, special agent from the Federal Bureau of Investigation. Not the same man who was here before, right away I knew it was a different voice. This Myers is a man of rank, evidently, but he seemed almost apologetic. Too old for a fight, sorry that life has come to this.

I could hardly let him stand out there getting a snowdrift on his hat. I had a fire on the hearth and coffee made, prepared for a solitary day. Mrs. Brown is kept home by the weather, her bus line canceled. So I brought Myers his coffee on the sofa and poked up the fire, to all appearances entertaining a guest. We joked about the elections coming up, how Truman will soon be looking for a new job. Three magazines lay on the coffee table, the week's editions I'd purchased from the newsstand, all of them with President Dewey on their covers, his bold new plan for the nation outlined inside. Chisme and Chispa weren't fooled by the friendly patter, they rose from their pool of warmth by the hearth, hissed inaudibly, and slunk away. I should have done the same.

He believes I have a very large problem, does Mr. Myers. Things really do not look good regarding my position with the State Department. I'm about to be in the same boat with Truman, he said. Hunting a new job.

"Oh, well, it's too bad. A lot of it going around." I decided to play it contrite, to satisfy this fellow. No need to tell him I hadn't worked for the State Department in years, and had no intention of ever doing so again.

"Except for us gumshoes," he said with a chuckle. "Our job security is A-okay."

"I've heard that. Snakes out of Ireland, and so forth."

He was eager to show me his portfolio of evidence against me, and I was curious, especially about the photograph. Harrison Shepherd and wife, Communist party meeting 1930. It was a puzzling disappointment, not one thing in the picture I could recognize. No person I'd ever known, no place I had been.

"Is this the noose around my neck? I can't even guess which one of those men is supposed to be me. I was fourteen that year, living in Mexico." I handed back the photograph, and he took a great deal of care to put it inside a folder and settle it in the correct compartment of his briefcase.

Then said, "That photograph is a piece of garbage. I realize that."

The man was so shabby and earnest, I almost hated to let him down. Probably people habitually responded this way—shop clerks slipped back his change, the butcher put an extra ounce of chuck on the scales. Probably I'd let him in the door because of some vague sense he was a man of Artie's ilk. A short, bald, gentile Arthur Gold. A widower, judging from his clothes, and the long, scant hair combed over his bald head, no one to tell him that was a bad idea. He had none of Artie's cleverness but seemed to carry the same torch. Searching for an honest man and fed up with the whole shmear.

"I know that you were in Mexico," he said. "We have this information. You worked for a painter in Mexico City, a very well-known Red. I can't recall his name, but it's in the files. I came here today to question you about this. In all of this mess, this kind of weather, in North Carolina. I don't even have chains on the tires." He sighed.

"To question me about working for a painter in Mexico?"

"That's about the extent of it. You could deny it, most of them deny. To begin with. But I'll be honest with you, it doesn't usually help."

"Why would I deny it?"

"This information alone is reason for dismissing you from your government post. That's what happens now, if you choose not to deny the associations. In time there may be more. I think you're probably going to get a McFarland letter."

"Who is McFarland?"

"McFarland is nobody. But this letter is bad news, it would contain the actual charges. The higher-ups have intimated they are accumulating some pretty shocking evidence against you."

"I see. Who is supplying this shocking evidence?"

"Mr. Shepherd, be reasonable. You know we can't tell you that. If we allowed all the accused to confront their accusers, we would have no informants left. It would infringe on our ability to investigate."

"Your ability to investigate. That's the important thing."

"Correct. In this day and age, we have a duty to protect the citizen. It's a precarious business. People have no idea, they should be very grateful. You should be grateful, Mr. Shepherd."

"It's a difficult point you make, Mr. Myers. I felt pretty cozy here today, before you came knocking." I got up to put more wood on the fire, a piece of cedar shingle that sent a little shower of sparks onto the floor. I dusted up the ash, no harm done. But I seemed to have gotten up the dander of Myers, as far as it went.

"The mental world of the Communist is secretive," he said. "The Soviet Fatherland has to be preserved at any cost, and its enemies confounded." He seemed to be quoting a handbook, speaking in the general direction of the bookcase. Maybe he was trying to read titles: *Dickens, Dostoyevsky, Dreiser,* the suspect will alphabetize his books at any cost. Mrs. Brown, largely to blame.

"I wouldn't know," I said. I stayed where I was, feet to the fire. This was some sort of Jacson Mornard who'd arrived at my door, hat in hand, blade beneath the coat. I had let him in, brought the coffee. As Lev always said, you won't see it coming.

He shifted himself around to face me. "The thinking of the Communist is that no one who opposes him can possibly have any merit whatsoever. It's a psychological illness. The Communist cannot adjust himself to logic."

"That's a point of view. But I was thinking of what you said about confronting my accuser. I thought the Constitution gave me the right to know the charges against me. And who was bringing them."

Myers drained his coffee cup and leaned forward with a little grunt to set the cup on the table. We were nearly finished, I could tell.

"Whenever I hear this kind of thing," he said, "a person speaking about constitutional rights, free speech, and so forth, I think, 'How can he be such a sap? Now I can be *sure* that man is a Red.' A word to the wise, Mr. Shepherd. We just do not hear a real American speaking in that manner."

November 2

Mrs. Brown left early to go to the polls. She says the Elementary down the block would be my voting place, if I could be troubled to use it. I have promised her I'll get my voting card before the next go-round. Meanwhile the neighborhood children are having the day off, out fighting their snow wars, building forts and goggle-eyed men. The one in the next yard looks like Agent Myers, rotund and slump-shouldered, a potato for his nose, peering at my window wearing the old fedora I gave Romulus.

November 3

She came in at nine with the mail and daily papers, all claiming Dewey had won the presidency, in the largest typeface imaginable. Poor Tommy: that toothbrush moustache does loom large, above the fold. But Mrs. Brown's eyes were ablaze. She did a little dance stomping the snow off her boots in the doorway, unwinding her scarf. I haven't seen such fire in her since Mexico.

"You look like you've had the canary for breakfast."

"Here it is, Mr. Shepherd. Dewey hasn't won it. Turn on the radio."

At first the news was about airlifts into Berlin, those desperate people now six months under siege. The American flyers are getting in more food than ever, thousands of tons, and now also coal so the Berliners won't freeze. The interview was an air force man who said next month they plan to drop candy and toys from the planes, with little parachutes. "Those German kiddies will have Santa Claus, whether Joe Stalin wants them to or not," he vowed.

"Mr. Shepherd, how be ye?" she asked suddenly. I must have looked unwell.

I blew my nose to preserve dignity. I'd been close to tears, for the most ridiculous reason. "I was thinking of my old boss, Lev Trotsky," I confessed. "He would have loved that report. The triumph of compassion over Stalin's iron fist. The people prevail, with candy and parachutes."

"It's our boys helping them do it," she said, and I said yes, it is, and wanted to dance with Mrs. Brown, stomp my feet at the doorsill. My country 'tis of thee.

At half past, the election news came back. Truman had been awakened and rolled out of bed in Missouri, informed he might not be on vacation yet. He didn't stay up last night to listen to the returns; the Democratic campaign had not rented a suite or organized any party for that. They saw no need. While Dewey's men popped the champagne in New York, Harry put on his pajamas, ate a ham sandwich, and went to bed early.

Now the race was neck and neck, with many states still counting. By mid-morning it was Harry ahead by a nose. We didn't move from the radio.

Shortly before noon they called it. Harry Truman won.

"Oh, Mr. Shepherd, it's a day to remember. Those news men could not make a thing true just by saying so. It's only living makes life."

I knew what she meant. The cold spell on us is deep, but however bitter the day might appear, winter will pass. I made a fire for us in the living room. A neighbor across the way has torn down his old carriage house and piled the scrap wood by the street.

Mrs. Brown rolled up the *Washington Post* like a log and waved it high, her eyes alight with mischief. "Here's something to fuel the flames," she suggested. Before long we'd cast in every one, the magazines too, warming our hands over those trumpeting false prophecies. The magazines with color in them curled in a blue-green blaze. By afternoon the house was so warm Mrs. Brown took off her gloves.

"You can't give up," she kept repeating. "You think you know it's all hopeless but you do not, Mr. Shepherd. You know not."

December 10

The United Nations have adopted the Universal Declaration of Human Rights. It was all on the radio today, and even the howlers achieved a tone of deference. Eighteen articles, establishing every person on earth to be born free and equal, endowed with conscience to act toward every other in a spirit of brotherhood. Maybe Mrs. Brown is right, and we know not where a little raft of hope could carry us.

Article 18 states: All persons have the right to freedom of thought, conscience and religion or belief.

> Mr. Harrison W. Shepherd
> 30 Montford Ave.
> Asheville, North Carolina
>
> Date: December 13, 1948
>
> Dear Mr. Shepherd,
> The evidence indicates that at certain times since ___1930___ you have been a close associate of _____ Mr. Deigo Riveira _____ a person or persons who displayed active and sympathetic interest in the Communist Party. We also have evidence that your name has appeared in Life Magazine, Look Magazine, Echo, Star Week, New York Post, Kingsport News, New York Times, Weekly Review, Chicago Times Book Review, Washington Post, National Review, Kansas City Star, Memphis Star, Raleigh Spectator, Library Review, The Daily Worker, Hollywood Week, Asheville Trumpet making statements to the effect that you believe in the overthrow of the United States government.
>
> The foregoing information indicates that you have been and are a member, close affiliate, or sympathetic associate of the Communist Party, and are therefore permanently dismissed from active employment by the federal government. All pension monies and any portion of salaries unpaid as yet, if any, are hereby claimed as property of the U.S. government. Sincerely,
>
> J. EDGAR HOOVER, DIRECTOR
> FEDERAL BUREAU OF INVESTIGATION

The Raleigh Spectator, *December 16, 1948*

Communist Writer Fired for Misdeeds

The Associated Press

WASHINGTON, D.C.—Writer Harrison Shepherd, nationally known author of books on the topic of Mexico, was fired this week from federal employment for reasons of un-Americanism. The Asheville man had worked for the Department of State since 1943. His role there remains unclear, but Melvin C. Myers, chief investigator on the case, confirmed it could well have given access to sensitive information. The misdeeds came to light through the massive loyalty investigation of federal employees initiated last year, which has so far identified hundreds of cases of un-Americanism but no espionage. Myers cited this as proof the campaign is working to drive out potential spies that may be hidden in government ranks.

December 18

They seem so thrilled to pounce, these press men. Not before, when I was nobody of consequence, only now. Mrs. Brown says envy plays into it. "There are some who'd hardly lift a finger for kindness, but they would haul up a load of rock to dump on some soul they think's been too lucky. They take it as duty, to equal out life's misery."

"They think I've been too *lucky*?"

She sighed. "Mr. Shepherd, it's what you've said a hundred times, they don't know a person's whole story. They think you just sit in your little room making up tales and getting bags of money for it, while they have to go out rain or shine and talk to Mrs. Smith on Charlotte Street about a pie contest. They're put out with you for having an easier life."

"Mrs. Brown, who in this world has an easier life?"

"I wonder that too."

January 26, 1949

An assignation. First of the new year. Tommy's attention seems to be wearing thin. Lying on his back blowing smoke rings, his eyes kept going to the window like a bird trapped indoors, wanting out. Rather than gazing upon the spectacle of me, sitting in the Morris chair all bundled up in my long knitted scarf. Mrs. Brown's Christmas present. If I can keep her long enough I shall be warm as a lamb, head to toe. I thought of getting out last year's gloves and putting those on too; the little room was freezing.

Maybe I'm only imagining Tommy has gone cool. What do I know of hearts in winter? He's tired, I know that much. And disappointed. No job in advertising yet, still a traveling salesman for Art, in Washington all last week before coming here. Something at the National Gallery.

"It must have been a hubbub in D.C., with the inauguration."

"*Hubbub*," he said. "Cat, what language do you speak? My *grandmother* said 'hubbub.' Harry Truman says 'hubbub.' I believe it was the theme of his inaugural speech. 'My fellow Americans, we face a great hubbub.'"

"Actually his theme was the false philosophy of communism. We will roll up our sleeves and defeat it."

"That sounds like a variety of hubbub."

"It's not all that funny, Tommy. Not to me. I was hoping for a new theme."

"Oh, cheer up. You'll never get to move Winslow Homers for the Department again, poor you. Maybe this solid gold little writing hobby will pan out instead."

"Because I still have money, I have no problems. Is that what you think?"

"It will get you through times with no friends, my friend."

"So they say."

Tommy was carefully studying the palm of his hand, for some reason.

"My motion-picture agreement is off, by the way. No reason given. They're getting ever so touchy out there about the color red."

"Stark! There goes my chance to meet Robert Taylor."

"You could probably arrange it. If you wanted to help him testify against someone. The money's fantastic, I hear."

Cold was literally leaking into the room. I could feel it pour in like water around the edges of the window. I had a strange vision of the whole hotel sunk like a ship beneath the sea, entering the world of the fishes.

"Do you know what, Tommy? Next month we should get together at my house. Honestly, it would be nice. I'll make a *lomo adobado*. You've never seen my house."

He raised his eyebrows. "Oh, but what will the neighbors think."

"They'll think I have a friend. One person knocking on my door who's not in the pay of myself or the FBI. You hear about it all the time."

He didn't answer. Finished with the hand inspection, he wound his watch.

"Aren't you sick of hotels?"

"Fed up to the blinkers, if you want to know. Let's go down to the bar."

"We should get dinner. Some nice oxtail soup and Horlick's, that's what you need. You've let yourself get run down."

"Oxtail soup and Horlick's. Cat, you are off the cob."

"Corny, that would mean. Sorry. I guess I'll go."

He rolled himself upright, facing me, black socks on the floor. "Sorry me, chum, I'm just whammed. Sick of hotels, you said it. What is this furniture, all these bars on everything? It gives me the heebies, like I'm in the pen."

"It's a style. Mission."

"*Mission.* Do they send up a preacher with the room service?" He lay back down on the bed, reached overhead to grasp the upright slats on the headboard, and briefly rattled them like a prisoner. "The hotel in D.C. had a lousy bar, the place was gestanko in general. Did I tell you there was a big scene?"

"No."

"Last night. No, night before. I get back to my hotel after a whole day of meetings with the drizzle bags, I'm beat to the socks, and I can't even get to the elevator. There's a scene in the lobby. This huge colored cat, he's got on a nice overcoat, hat, briefcase, everything, but he's flailing. Football with the bellhops. I mean he's down on the floor, they tackled him when he came in I guess. He's a Negro, see. The hotel doesn't have Negro guests."

"What happened?"

"Well, dig this. It turns out he's an ambassador from some African country. Ethiopia, I want to say. They got it sorted out. It's all right because he was foreign, not an American Negro. What do you make of that?"

"Good God. I hate to contemplate. That foreigners aren't even worth the full measure of American contempt?"

"Could be. But he seemed decent. A nice accent, like a Brit. We rode the elevator together, he was on my floor. He said he hoped I didn't mind. He's stayed there loads of times before, and they still make the same mistake."

"Mind what? You said he hoped you didn't mind."

"I'm sure I don't know."

"How did you feel, Tommy?"

He rolled over onto one elbow, narrowing his eyes. "*Feel?*"

"In the elevator, with that poor man."

He fell back again, staring at the ceiling. "I felt I was going up."

February 11

"There was a poke on your mailbox," Mrs. Brown announced this morning as she came in the door. After these years it still takes me by surprise, though I should have known, she stood there holding it. A poke is a sack. A mesh bag in this case, the type the neighbor uses for carrying home her groceries. Today it contained sundry fountain pens, a fedora, things I've given Romulus over several years. Including the rubber *atl-atl* brought from Mexico, his reward for feeding the cats.

"Here's a note," Mrs. Brown said, puzzling over it. "Romulus isn't to visit here any more." *Please keep away from my boy* was the nature of her explanation. Agent Myers had advised her they should not keep any objects given him by a Communist.

"Take a letter, Mrs. Brown. Tell the lady she needs to get in touch with General Eisenhower right away, because he too is in possession of a Communist Object."

Mrs. Brown sat at the typewriter, hands poised, waiting for the cue that my words were going to make some kind of sense. Sometimes she waits all day.

"What did they call it? Oh, yes!" I said, snapping my fingers. My memory is fine, thank you. "The Order of Victory. It was in *Life Magazine* years ago, they had a full-page photo. A platinum star set with diamonds. Stalin gave it to him at Yalta. Tell her the next time Agent Myers comes around, she'd better tell him to go see Eisenhower. Make sure the general puts that thing in a poke and sends it right back to Stalin."

March 4

I grew cross with Mrs. Brown today. It shouldn't have happened, she is as good as gold. She did the shopping for me, I'm losing the nerve for going out, and it's only March. She tolerates, as usual. Returned with change and receipts, plus cheerful news of spring, crocuses in the yards on Montford, tennis shoes on sale. A 12-pack of pencils is now 29 cents. The Zippo lighter went up to $6, so she went against orders and bought matches, more economical. I scolded her for it, telling her matches don't work worth a damn in the bathtub. I've never sworn at her before. It made her go pale and sit down, like a telegram bearing bad news. It took her half an hour to respond.

"You shouldn't be smoking in the bath, Mr. Shepherd."

"Why, because I'll burn down the house?"

This afternoon she brought letters up to my study for signature, and I noticed her nails looked ragged. She is on edge too; we both jump when the telephone rings, like schoolgirls, waiting for Lincoln Barnes to ring up. It's been months that they've had the manuscript, and now the corrected galleys. A title, jacket art, everything you might want to have on hand for a publication. Except a publication date.

"Your stories are all about Mexico," Mrs. Brown posed today, with forceful cheer. "Have you ever thought about writing them for Mexicans?"

"Where in the world did that come from?"

"I only ask."

"I don't write in Spanish. I write in English, about Mexicans. If I wrote in Spanish, I suppose I'd have to write about Americans."

"I know you speak Spanish perfectly well. I've heard you."

"Ordering a plate of fish is not writing a novel. I don't even dream in Spanish. I can't seem to invent anything in that language. Don't expect me to explain."

She should have said *Yes sir*, and turned on her Kerrybrooke heels. That's how Gal Friday does it in the movies. Yet there she stood, wearing that look: Hell or High Water. "You might could learn," she said. "If you stayed there awhile longer."

"Living there from the '20s until 1940 wasn't enough? You think a few more decades of practice might do the trick?"

"I mean living there as a man. A writer. You'd get used to it."

"Is this a suggestion?"

She didn't answer. I laid down my book and glared.

"Look, I don't have the temperament. Mexican writers are all depressives."

She has been hiding mail. Filing it in the boxes for the attic without letting me see it all first, as is the custom. I caught her out and made her show what she'd been holding back. She insists nearly all the mail is the same as ever, it's only a handful that are "not very nice."

"We say onions to H. W. Shepherd!" is the general sentiment. Shepherd the squealing pathetic traitorous free speecher, the Communist.

"You have to forgive hateful people, for what a man hates, he knows not."

"Who said that, Jesus Christ?"

"Mr. Shepherd, there's still a good deal of nice mail here, and some hateful. The good are from people who've read a book of yours or more, and glad of it. And the hateful ones are from people who know nothing of you. That's all I'm saying. Look if you're going to look. See if they mention a word you ever wrote."

She was right, they didn't. They addressed a creature they had learned about through some other means. The news, presumably.

"I can see how you'd get your feelings hurt," she said. "As a man. But not as a writer, for they've not read your books. From the look of it, I'd say they've read nary a book at all."

Still, it was hard to put the things down. Like a gruesome potboiler. You know how it will finish, you know it will turn your stomach, you go on reading. There were a dozen or more. "Your treacherous behavior in the Department of State is nothing but slings and arrows aimed at Old Glory. It is hard for us Americans to know how self-hating Communists can live with your grotesque deeds."

"If the majority felt as you do, we would all be in chains. Freedom is what our country is based on. If you won't stand up for our country, you deserve no freedom."

"I and my friends will certainly do all we can to spread the word about your disgusting hatred for our country, and make you even more a footnote of litery history than already."

"It sickens me to think you and your old haggard wife might raise another America-hating child. I hope she is barren."

"Go back to your own filthy country. When we need Mexican's opinion of America we'll ask."

"I'm proud to say I don't own your book, if I did it would go in the fireplace."

Well, naturally I felt a twinge at that one. After our newspaper-burning party. But Mrs. Brown said fiddlesticks, it's usual to start the fire with a newspaper when it's no longer of any use. "This is something different. It's not civilized. Imagine saying any such things to a human person."

"No, you're right. They're an angry bunch."

She took the pages out of my hands. "Angry is not the word for it. These folk don't even ken you to be a real man. They give you no benefit of a doubt. I expect they'd be kinder to a neighbor's dog that bit them."

"Well, that's true. My neighbor here at least sent a note about Romulus. She said 'please,' and sent the gifts back. I'll give her that."

"They are just so happy to see the mighty fallen," was her verdict. She tore the letters to pieces and threw them in the bin, then sat down to the day's typing. Even from upstairs, her Royal sounded like a Browning machine gun.

April 7

Infuriating telephone conversation with Lincoln Barnes.

Say, did you ever think of doing short pieces? The kind of thing they run in the Popular Fiction Group?

Pulp stories. I asked him why.

"Oh, just wondering."

My opinion of those stories, which I shared with Lincoln Barnes, is that they are all written by one person using a hundred different pseudonyms. Her real name might be Harriet Wheeler. She eats nothing but chocolates and lives in one of the upstairs rooms at the Grove Park.

It should have been a good day. With Tommy coming tomorrow. Not on the Vandy-wagon either, he just wants to visit. Passing through on his way to see some sculpture in Chattanooga. He'll stay here, he wants to see my cave he says, the pork roast is already marinating. Mrs. Brown left early, I was boiling chiles and garlic in water to mix with the vinegar and oregano when the phone rang. Months without a call, waiting for Tommy and for Lincoln Barnes, and now they both turn up.

Barnes didn't want to talk to me directly, I could tell. He'd hoped to leave a message with Mrs. Brown. I usually don't answer in the afternoons. What he seems to be saying is they are uncertain about publishing the book. At all. With the Communist Business starting to tie their hands.

"I could see that, if I were a Communist. Luckily for you, I am not."

"Look, I know you're not a Communist. Everybody here knows that. We know you're loyal to the U.S. Your name doesn't even sound all that Mexican."

I had to go in the kitchen and turn off the pot, it was boiling over.

"What you are," he said when I came back, "is controversial. The fellows running the show here are not very keen on controversial, because it stirs people up. For most readers out there, controversial means exactly the same thing as anti-American."

"Barnes. You're a man of words, they matter to you. Why would you say this? You don't like controversy because it stirs people up. Controversy *means* stirring up."

He didn't respond.

"You could say you don't like an eggshell, because it has egg in it. Why not go ahead and say you don't like eggs?"

He sighed into the phone. "I'm on your side, Shepherd. Believe me. I didn't call you up to play games. The suggestion that has been made here is that we publish the book under a pseudonym."

Good idea. How about Harriet Wheeler? This is madness. The

novel is set in Mexico, written in the same style as two previous books, which have been read by practically everyone in the nation, schoolchildren included. Does he think they'll believe this is some other writer's work?

He said every publisher in New York is now scrambling to publish books set in ancient Mexico.

"Are you serious?"

"Oh, yes. You're going to have fifty imitators soon. Why not get in line? You could be among the first."

The thing was boggling. He mentioned other possibilities. Using a ghostwriter. Not exactly that, but a real person, I would pay him a fee to use his name. In case I am worried about the press uncovering that the book was actually written by me.

Uncovering. My words, me, how could there be any difference?

"You're an editor, Mr. Barnes. Your stock-in-trade is the handi-work of other people. So this could be Stanback Powders we're discussing, or fine leather shoes, as far as you're concerned. I don't know, I'm only guessing. But for me it is different. I am the tongue of the shoe. If you pull me out of it, the whole thing falls apart."

April 8

A day could be perfect. You could forget fear altogether. Or fear might no longer make any difference, because it is the whole ocean and you're in it. You hold your breath, swim for light.

Tommy found it hilarious that Barnes had to be talked into putting my name on my book. Or that he would at least "pitch that idea to marketing." A freaking gasser. Somehow I was persuaded to agree. Tommy is persuasive.

"Oh my *God*, pitch that to marketing. Author's name on the author's book, *what next?*"

God has no better card to play than an April day, a well-tuned car, a world with nothing so wrong in it really, if a *lomo adobado* could still be cooked to such perfection, consumed to excess, distributed thereafter between a working Philco refrigerator and two happy, use-less cats. And all of it left behind, dishes still in the sink. The moun-tain parkway is open to the west now, a skyline viaduct to the Great Smokies, they finished it just for us. Tommy and me. We were quite sure of that. The tunnels are no longer blind, they all go somewhere. You arrive at the other side.

"Mr. Barnes seemed to think he was taking a terrible risk on me. I'm a regular Moriarty, my menace looms large. He said, 'I just hope I won't be sorry about this.'"

"Oh, you devil," Tommy said. "Wanting your name on your book. Next thing you know they'll be calling a spade a spade."

"Calling a rake a rake," I proposed, opening the Roadster full throttle on the parkway, letting the curves pull us, feeling their out-bound gravity. The world blurred, the April trees lit up with pale green flames, scenes flashed by, falling water, swinging bridges strung across rocky ravines. Windows wide open, the full breath of spring of dirt of new life stirring in the breast of whatever was left for dead, all that rushed at us now. Tommy's hair shuddered golden in the wind. He is a rake, a rake, the blinding shine of him reflected in the windscreen, Tommy's glint and glory. Tommy's hand laid here and there as if it hardly mattered, making me want to wreck the car. To find speed, drive myself deep into it.

"You and me, cat, this is the life," he said, and with Tommy that's as near as it gets to the terms of affection. "This is the life and you know it."

Loose pages, Montford

June 1949–January 1950

(VB)

When the FBI called on Mrs. Brown, that was the alarm bell gone off. That was the waking up. How stupid I have been. I'd failed to expect it, the FBI going to see her at Mrs. Bittle's. So I knew then, burn everything. It was May 10 or 11, the burning. They'd come on the evening of May 4, she said, not a forgettable date, and she went a week without telling me. I didn't expect that either. It wasn't Myers but two other men, looking for anything she could think of. Not only during our acquaintance, they told her, but anything she might know about my past. Tax avoidance, girlfriend troubles.

Well, I hope you told them. I have the worst trouble finding any girl-friends.

She would not let me make it into a joke. They offered to give her money if she thought of something. They mentioned five thousand dollars. She asked if I had any idea what kind of money that is. I said, "Do you think I don't?" We were sitting at the green table in the kitchen, it was after we'd taken to eating lunch there together because she doesn't like going to the luncheonettes now. I fixed her a pork sandwich that day. It was raining. No, not raining, because later she would be out in the back, that fire roaring.

What I remember plainly is how she bit the sandwich, set it down, chewed, bit again. Nearly choking, the whole time. I was sorry I'd made the sandwich, she was obviously not hungry but now would feel obligated to eat. In Mexico she looked at every piece of embroidery that any barefoot mother held up to her. Not just pretending, really examining the stitches with full appreciation. She can't dissemble to save her life.

That is why, when I asked why she wasn't hungry, she told me the reason. She really had not wanted to bother me about the FBI men who came to see her at Mrs. Bittle's. Not to worry me. *Five thousand dollars.* For the first time I began to understand what a danger I pose to her. I have been so thick, so naive.

She said she felt covered with dirt with those two men there. Mrs. Bittle dusting every sill in the parlor, trying to hear. I could picture that, and Mrs. Brown telling them I was a fine citizen, standing up for me, which I told her she should not do anymore. The less said to those men, the better.

"Maybe you're wrong," she said. "Maybe we need to give them what for."

"Why? What does it matter if I go on their list as a Communist?"

"For one thing, it proves their so-called informing man was reliable. Whoever is making things up about you. Now these agents will look on their Communist list and see you're on it. Then they'll look to see who accused you, and they'll say, 'Well, good, that fellow was reliable. We'll use him again.'"

That is true. She was right. Her acuity humbled me.

She had more to say, about using gossip as its own evidence. The Woman's Club now has a committee to check the schoolbooks for Americanism. In Mrs. Brown's opinion things have gone too far, it's time somebody showed some intestinal fortitude. Her words. She was holding back tears. What I held back, that would be harder to name. Chispa strolled in with her tail high, indifferent to the crisis. Checked the half-filled food dish next to the Philco, snubbed it, left the kitchen. Life proceeds, it enrages. The untouched ones spend their luck without a thought, believing they deserve it.

I told Mrs. Brown she should consider looking for a different job. Her eyes flew wide, the sandwich in both hands. She looked like an advertisement.

"You firing me, Mr. Shepherd? For what I just said?"

I told her that wasn't it. That I was very worried about causing her more trouble than I already had. She drank half a glass of water and went to look for a handkerchief in the other room. I heard her rummaging in the big leather mail pouch. I cleared the plates, put that sandwich out of sight so it wouldn't be the end of her. Some waterworks in the dining room, I think. All dried up when she returned, but the eyes were puffy.

"Mr. Shepherd, don't you read the papers? They've already had me as your secret wife, the whore of Babylon, crime partner, and I don't know what. Your bee keeper, for all I know. Who else would have me now? My stars, I might yet learn to keep bees."

That is what she said, bee keeper. I wanted to give her a bear hug. It would have involved lifting her off her feet, she's so small, I really could see the whole thing. Probably we both did, facing one another in a white-tiled kitchen, hands open at our sides, the embrace playing out between us like a motion-picture scene that makes you whistle and throw popcorn. We elected just to stand and watch it.

We made the agreement then. I would keep her hired, on certain conditions. A lot of things had to be taken care of: all the rest of the old notebooks. All those names and dates. I have done nothing wrong, she knows this and I know it, and still we both understand the position she is in. They could get a warrant, use something in those notebooks as evidence and make her a party to it.

I told her it's time, I kept saying that. It is time. I'd been piddling at it, trying for more than a year since we pitched Billy Boorzai into the flames. Better dead than read, I told her. Expecting a fight, but strangely, no fight came. Not even from Violet the defiant, who always insists, *Those are your words so claim them, leave your bairns not to be orphaned, you wrote those*. She too is defeated. She wanted to do the job herself. Stood at the door watching while I cleared the whole shelf, all the way back to the beginning. She seemed as eager as I was to get it over with, taking our medicine.

She went downstairs with the first armload, and I ransacked my desk drawers. Sometimes I'll type up a day and forget to file it with the others. And letters. I'd long since done away with Frida's—they were hardly mine to begin with—but the carbons of my own were harder to part with. I scooped up all that now, and odd little clippings I'd kept, oh, I was on a tear. By the time she had the fire going in the tar bucket outdoors, I was making a mad sack of the house to see if there were any notebooks I'd missed, hidden from myself like a drunk's gin bottle tucked in the chandelier. It feels that way sometimes, that desperate.

I went a day. Spent that evening standing at the window lighting one cigarette off the last, after she'd gone, to keep myself from sitting and writing out the scene as freshly recalled. One week, thirty packs of cigarettes. Weeks. Without spooling out more of a tale, creating more to burn, knitting away at the front of the long knotted scarf that will have to be unraveled at the back. How helpless I feel before this flood of words, how ridiculous. A hundred times trying to shut off the flow. Under orders from Mother. From Frida and Diego, arms crossed, feet tapping, stop it. In the name of the law. Stop writing down everything, it makes me nervous. And something inside the boy cries out, *Those are the only two choices: read, or dead.*

This only feels like madness; really now it's just the usual thing, summer and polio. Going mad inside a house. The wisteria vines have blocked up the windows. No matter where I try to look out, it's those palmate leaves, green hands shoved against my eyes. The neighbor used to bring over his pruners and do the job as a favor, but Myers likely advised him against pruning Communist vines. He hasn't done his own either, I notice. The house looks like it's cowering behind its own shrubbery. Every bungalow on the block is the same, curtained, folded shut. Quarantine. The siege of Berlin ended May 12, the barricades finally came down. But here they seem high as ever.

Tommy can't risk the plague—Keep cool, he says. Nor can Mrs. Brown, but she would if she could, I'm sure of that.

Lincoln Barnes says, Don't get excited. Arthur Gold has informed him that breach of contract can be costly, and they would be wise to release this book on the schedule previously agreed upon by all parties. He must have been persuasive. Barnes said if we don't make any waves they'll put the book out quietly, buried in their list of summer reading.

America has had a change of management. It's as plain as anything in the magazine advertisements. All the July issues came this week, and where are the square-shouldered gals pouring Ovaltine for their children, the mother who knows what's best? Who smiles ruefully and shakes her finger at that husband who used the wrong hair tonic? She's fired. They've got scientists in now, white laboratory coats and reports showing that the ordinary doesn't measure up to our brand. Goodness, they can prove anything: skin softness, quicker relief. I miss the mothers. If you didn't like the taste of Ovaltine, you might have wheedled. With these new authorities, you've got no chance.

"Summer Reading" is upon us, but so far not one review of *The Unforetold*. Sales nil, reports Barnes; the bookstores have not really picked it up so much as others on the list. A whisper campaign, he was afraid of that. *I just hope we won't be sorry about this.*

He needs to hire some of those scientists. Our studies show Harrison Shepherd provides a happier reader, 14 percent faster to achieve the racing pulse. This morning I found an advertisement for a condensed-book series: regular books with all the unnecessary parts cut out, to get it over faster. "Dr. George Gallup recently revealed in his polls, an astonishingly high percentage of the nation's university graduates *no longer read books.* The reason is obvious: because of their educational advantages, they occupy positions where they are busy, busy, busy always!"

I'll tell Barnes that must be it. Not a whisper campaign, no Communist longhairs or fairies about, everyone's just too busy.

❋

The library has opened two days a week now. Evidently the polio germ takes a rest on Mondays and Fridays. Well, three cheers for the brave ladies who volunteered to preside over the crypt. Not a soul in the place, the perfect opportunity to walk about openly carrying *Look Homeward, Angel* and *Tropic of Cancer* without raising an eyebrow. All of Henry Miller in fact, I'll take the whole pile, and Kinsey too.

How extraordinary he is, the good Dr. Kinsey. Another man in a white coat, with proof. Everything we ever dared think about men and sex turns out to be true. One hundred percent of men are homosexual for 4 percent of their lives (the Billy Boorzais), and 4 percent are homosexual for 100 percent of their lives (the Tommy Cuddys). Strangest of all, Dr. Kinsey's book has not been checked out of the library before. Not even once: the slip in the jacket hasn't a single name on it. Yet the spine was well cracked, every page of the book dog-eared and bent.

The news all looks the same now. The National Educators Association routs communism at its national convention in Boston. "The Communist is not suitable as a teacher." Nor as butcher, baker, candlestick maker, beggar man, or thief, as far as that goes. The Negro singer Paul Robeson they have taken to calling the Black Stalin.

Has the world stopped on its axis? It doesn't seem to be so, as the wheels of Mexico creak forward on their slow revolution. Europe raises herself from the ash and holds out a hand to her poor and damaged. But if Truman calls for any change, education improvements, or Social Security, a chorus shouts him down: welfare state, collectivism, conspiracy. What an extraordinary state of things, we are the finished product. A rock thrown in the canyon rolls neither uphill or down, it's frozen in place.

August 5

Nationalist China falls to Mao's armies. Or fell already. Acheson disclosed the collapse. The chorus is now at full howl, Truman presides over the Party of Treason, he and his Democrat cronies have thrown China into the mouth of the Communist dogs, didn't everyone say he should send more gunpowder to help Chiang Kai-shek? *I just hope we won't be sorry about this, and now we are, now you pay.*

September 23
Russia has the bomb. Every evening radio program was stopped for this: the crooners in front of microphones quietly folded their sheet music, the wise guys laughing it up at Duffy's Tavern set their steins slowly on the counter, their jaws dropped, they gaped. The fine fabric of our nation, ripped open to reveal a naked vulnerability. An atomic explosion has occurred in the USSR. Truman said the thing in as few words as possible. Two nations now have the bomb.

A man is shot dead this morning in Oteen. A panic on this land, the crowds toting pitchforks. Someone gave the Russians that bomb, they didn't make it on their own, they don't have the brains the drive the science, it had to be Alger Hiss but it could have been any of them, Paul Robeson, Harrison Shepherd, they all stick together it's what they do.

It feels out of the question to go outdoors, to walk about in the open. With anger running this high, it finds targets. The man in Oteen was killed by someone living right on the same street, a warehouse security guard. At the end of a brooding night shift, instead of going home he walked through an unlatched screen door, screaming, "Dirty Russians!" and shot a neighbor in his undershirt. The wife and children watching.

They are Slavs, judging from the name, probably emigrated to escape Stalin. The gunman knew of the family through his son. The children go to school together.

The terrible concert in Peekskill, that was Robeson. Workingman's songs and Negro spirituals and concertgoers beaten bloody afterward. Just one road leading out of the place—how trapped those families must have felt, with throngs of armed police and citizens waiting at the roadsides to hurl rocks at their buses. Hands pressed flat against the windows, automobiles overturned, families dragged out and beaten, no matter their color. It's here in *Life Magazine*, photo and caption: *"In scheduling the concert the party-liners had hoped for just such a chance to become propaganda martyrs, so there was a tendency to conclude that 'they asked for it.' The Communists got more help from the hoodlums who stoned the buses than they did from their own fellow travelers."*

It's the same as the Mexican press after we were attacked at Lev's. We asked for those blazing guns and fire bombs and screaming panic and Seva shot, Trotsky organized it all himself. We are doing this to ourselves.

The Evening Post, *October 6, 1949*

"Books for Thought," by Sam Hall Mitchell

An End Foretold

Harrison W. Shepherd is that twentieth-century phenomenon—the international Communist. He has vehemently shunned publicity, but thanks to a persistent campaign of public exposure his ties with Mexican Communists have lately come to light. His life has been obscure but hardly small, as thousands of Americans were drawn into his message, particularly the young and impressionable as his writings pressed their way even into children's schoolrooms.

Now his latest arrives as the most insidious of the lot. *The Unforetold* is the story of an ancient empire crumbling through its final days, while those in power remain insensible to their nation's impending collapse. This book takes a dismal view of humanity indeed, leaving no room for wise leadership or energetic patriotism. We should expect nothing else from Harrison Shepherd, who was quoted two years ago in the *New York Weekly Review* (March '47) as follows: "Our leader is an empty sack. You could just as well knock him over, put a head with horns on a stick, and follow that. Most of us never choose to believe in the nation, we just come up short on better ideas."

Earlier this year Shepherd was dismissed from a government position for Communist activity. The public cannot now be blamed for wishing to second the motion with a single mind, dismissing the rogue scribe from our libraries, bookstores and homes.

Mrs. Brown is on a war path. "Mr. Shepherd, it's a character in your book that said that. Would they hang Charles Dickens for a thief because he made up the old fellow Fagin that told boys to go pick pockets?" Given the current climate, I told her, Charles Dickens is wise to be dead already. Which did not please her.

Intestinal fortitude, Mrs. Brown has got. Marching in here to work despite Mrs. Bittle's ban, the concern no longer being polio but other contaminations. Mrs. Brown says if the lady evicts her, she will go live with a niece. One of Parthenia's daughters "up and married a towner" and they get on well, the niece and aunt. The couple's house is small as a pin, but she could sleep on a chaise, care for the baby, and try to be a help.

We waited for the telephone to ring off its handle. Other newspapers are sure to pick this up, as it's too thrilling to keep under a hat. She stood near the telephone, arms crossed, ready to knock me cold if I tried to overrule her. "You can go on about your business now and leave me be, Mr. Shepherd, any man who calls here to confirm that quote will have me to talk to, and he shall hear what's what."

I agreed, we seem to have no choice this time. We can set the record straight: these are words spoken by a character in a novel, Poatlicue by name, disgruntled with a deranged Aztec king.

We looked it up, to verify the passage. It's from *Pilgrims of Chapultepec*, we both recognized that—a scene about midway through, the fourth forced exodus, the two boys talking while they skin out the deer. Sure enough, he's got it word for word, this Sam Hall Mitchell, but why that line, attributed to an interview? Mrs. Brown looked through the files and found he did take it from the *Review*, as he says, a piece about the book that quoted that excerpt. She had several copies in the files, and I may have sent one to Frida—we'd liked this reviewer. He was thoughtful on many subjects, including Soviet containment, a new doctrine at that time. Poor man, they'll now be after him too. The last line he'd quoted from my book, Mr. Mitchell has dropped in his exposé, for better or for worse. Wherein Poatlicue says, "It's probably a law: the public imagination may not exceed the size of the leaders' ballocks."

Not a call came about it. A strange, quiet day, the telephone did not ring once.

October 19

Of all things unexpected, this is the largest. Harrison Shepherd fires the shot heard 'round the world. That quote has gone everywhere, even overseas to the armed services, they've run it in *Stars and Stripes*. *Here's what one spineless fellow thinks back home, and you can bet Harrison Shepherd did not serve active duty: "Our leader is an empty sack, let's knock him over, put some horns on a stick and follow that. Most of us never choose to believe in our country, we just come up short on better ideas."*

Republic Digest, "Words from the Nation's Most Dangerous." Harrison Shepherd has gone to the top of their list, above Alger Hiss and the Hollywood Ten. The clip service at the publisher's counted sixty-one newspapers and magazines running the quote so far, and the monthlies are yet to come. These words seem to be driving some form of madness that gets in the head like a nursery rhyme. Leader is an empty sack, empty sack, empty sack! Head with horns upon a stick, follow that!

It's hard to guess why the publisher needed to call Mrs. Brown with that stunning figure from the clip service. Can it be they are pleased? Because they are rid of me now? The receptionists at Stratford's are star-eyed at the measure of my infamy; they have no capacity to resist it. The reach of the quote has gone far beyond any readership of mine, by a hundredfold, bringing joy to people with no prior knowledge of my prowess. It's bracing in these times. A man you can love to despise.

Mrs. Brown is so distracted she can't type a letter. Most of the morning she sat in a chair near the front window, knitting a baby shawl. She keeps dropping stitches, finding mistakes, tearing it all out to begin again. Her eyes go out to the street. I've never seen her so frightened. More dangerous than Alger Hiss. Who is well on his way now to conviction for treason.

Most of us never choose to believe in our country, we just come up short on better ideas. The most widely printed words ever written by Harrison Shepherd.

The Echo, *October 21, 1949*

Spy Secrets Between Hard Covers

Author Harrison Shepherd has covered a long career of Communist tricks under the guise of mild-mannered writer, producing facile novels that appeal mainly to intellectuals and longhairs. But he has thrown off his cover with the latest round of arrogance, declaring openly in print, "Our leader is an empty sack. You could just as well knock him over, put a head with horns on a stick and follow that."

Threatening violent overthrow is a matter for public outrage. What's at the bottom of this twisted mind? His family life tells it all. Born in Lychgate, Virginia, Shepherd was a child of divorce. The father worked as an accountant in the Hoover administration, while the mother was an impecunious Mata Hari, changing her name repeatedly to get close to men in government on both sides of the Mexico border. New York psychiatrist Nathan Leonard, asked to weigh in on the disturbing case, said, "The shattering psychological effects of a maternal example like this cannot be escaped."

The son dropped out of school to become a Communist sympathizer, working in the households of leading Stalinist functionaries in Mexico City. From there he moved on to a life of such intrigue it would confound most men: art smuggler, womanizer, State Department courier, using at least two pseudonyms on two continents. All this he accomplished despite a physical appearance so repellent, photographers have shunned him for a lifetime. Such remarkable feats of philandering and espionage carried out by a homely man may arouse false hopes in the Walter Mittys among us. But Harrison Shepherd is not cut from the ordinary cloth.

Among the latest charges: he supplied secrets to the Communist Chinese revolt against Chiang Kai-shek. Like all enemies of America, he adheres to the plan of giving aid and comfort to our enemies. A year ago he told the *Evening Post* he agreed with Bernard Baruch that our atomic bombs should all be thrown in the drink. Now he's found a better way to throw us on the mercy of the Communists: experts confirm a copy of his book has been found with certain passages underlined, possibly a coded blueprint for the atom bomb. Fortunately this country has a cure for such troubled minds. It is known as the electric chair.

According to the United Press, the Committee on Un-American Activities has already documented countless plans to smuggle bomb secrets to Russia and China. In a 384-page report released last week after five years of investigation, the committee detailed techniques used by American Communists for sending coded secrets to Moscow. "Devices for concealing such messages include necklaces, boxes containing matches cut at various lengths, dental plates, a notching of postage stamps, engraved cigarette cases, embroidered handkerchiefs, special book-bindings and tiny compartments in phonograph records." A copy of George Bernard Shaw's *Devil's Disciple*, the report disclosed, was found to carry a Russian code message by means of having certain of its words underlined in invisible ink.

Now another Devil's Disciple, in the guise of writer Harrison Shepherd, has released his latest tome, *The Unforetold*. To such a chilling title we need only add a small footnote: buyer beware.

November 7

Mrs. Brown went to the bookstore to have a look. She did not want to go, and did not want to tell me about it when she came back. So help me God, I pressed her into spying for me. They've made a "Ban Harrison Shepherd" window display. I'm not alone; they've found a pile of other books written by Communists.

The sign asks, "Would you buy a book if you knew your money was going to the Communist Party?" Under the question were two boxes marked "Yes" and "No," with a cup of pencils handy for the plebiscite.

What more can they take from me? I asked Mrs. Brown, what do they want? About what anyone wants, was her best guess: safety. That and grace. They know not what they do. Probably they were all aimed at heaven at one time, and lost their way.

What is that, *grace*?

She says, believing you are special and saved from harm. Kissed by God.

Well, that's how thick I am, I never knew how to want what everyone wants. I only thought to look for a home, some place to be taken in. Handing over a crumpled heart, seeing it dropped in the wastepaper basket every time. Here, though. Americans sent love letters in return.

December 22, 1949

Dear Shepherd,

All right pal, keep your hair on. Probably this is not going to be the salutations you've been waiting for. Merry Xmas and all that. Things have changed here, it can't be helped. I collared a job in ads. No fish! Me myself, in an office full of neck ties, and let me tell you, these cats are steaming. I don't want to be the jerk that can't keep up.

Listen, I sure was hung up to see what you wrote about our country. Sorry you feel that way, I guess I never really knew you so well. Cats joke around, but I for one still believe in the Patria and I'm just sorry you can't say the same. I guess coming from another country, you have your reasons.

Don't be a dog about this, right? Nice knowing you but things change. Best for both of us if we shove off and no more correspondence. No one in my present situ knows of our acquaintance.

So long,

TOM CUDDY

1950, January

The newspapers slump under the weight of their end-of-the-world headlines. ALGER HISS VERDICT: SPY AND LIAR. Larger type even than used for V-J Day; evidently the new enemies are worse than the Japanese. Phony liberals who sell their souls along with the secrets that safeguard our nation. Stalinist tuning forks. Slobbering on the shoes of their Muscovite masters. Henry Wallace is under fire now too, testifying before the Un-American Committee. Henry Wallace, vice president under Roosevelt, the Liberal Democrat candidate in the last election, now faces Trial by Headline. WALLACE DENIES SENDING URANIUM TO RUSSIANS. May God protect him, today he lashed out against the press: "King Solomon should add to his list of things beyond the wisdom of men: why the newspapers print what they do!"

Mrs. Brown noted that Wallace has been reading aloud from his diary in the hearings, as evidence of what was said in the uranium meetings now under scrutiny. "Good thing he kept that diary," she says, standing in my doorway in a red-and-white-checked tailored shirt. With her, there's no knowing, it could be the latest fashion or something she made from a tablecloth—or both. Mrs. Brown proves stylish gals can still be thrifty in 'fifty.

She believes I'm taking things too personally. She brings the articles on Wallace, Robeson, Trumbo, those Hollywood writers, the union men, teachers, accountants, office workers, the butcher, the baker, and in the end neither of us is consoled. It's not just you, she says. People driven out of work, children taunted at school. The children whose father was shot, over in Oteen. What can any child be learning now, she asks, but to fear the wide world and all that's in it?

"Mr. Shepherd, they have to grow up in this. How will they all be?"

The Asheville Trumpet, February 12, 1950

Asheville Writer Faces Tough Questions

by Carl Nicholas

In a letter received this week from Federal Investigator Melvin C. Myers, the *Asheville Trumpet* has learned local writer Harrison Shepherd faces numerous charges related to his Communism. Foremost among them is misrepresentation of qualifications in signing an affidavit that he had never been a Communist. He is further charged with falsifying qualifications to serve as an educator. The press release from Myers stated a subpoena will soon be sent to Shepherd with arrangements to follow regarding a hearing before the House Un-American Activities Committee in Washington, D.C.

Fellow citizens of Asheville cannot say we wish him well. It is no source of pride that our town is called home by one of the many Communists now known to have infiltrated government, as revealed this week by Senator Joseph McCarthy at a meeting of the Ohio County Woman's Club of Wheeling, West Virginia.

Mrs. Herb Lutheridge, President, Asheville Woman's Club, confirms the Senator's speech was intended here when the freshman Senator first contacted the Program Committee, hoping to make our city the first stop on his re-election campaign crusade through the South and West. Mrs. Lutheridge says honorarium discussion was under way when the Senator's office notified her of plans to kick off the tour instead in W. Virginia. Mrs. Lutheridge regrets the mixup but stated, "The main thing is, we are proud of this young man going to Washington to ferret out all those with Soviet leanings."

The information release concerning Shepherd states that House Un-American Activities Committee has full authority to subpoena a suspect and ask questions based on substantive researches, for the public record. If the hearing warrants, criminal charges will follow. The subcommittee is charged to investigate communism in many guises including "education," which pertains to Harrison Shepherd as many schoolchildren read his books about the Mexican civilizations. In closing, the letter states, "Through a simple exercise of question and answer, the witness may prove his innocence or be seen to hide behind the Fifth Amendment."

The *New York Times* reported this month that Communist parties worldwide now have a record membership of 26 million persons.

The Wheeling Intelligencer, *February 10, 1950*

M'Carthy Charges Reds Hold U.S. Jobs

Wisconsin Senator Tells Lincoln Fete Here 'Chips Down'

by Frank Desmond of the Intelligencer *Staff*

Joseph McCarthy, junior U.S. Senator from Wisconsin, was given a rousing ovation last night when, as guest of the Ohio County Republican Women's Club, he declared bluntly that the fate of the world rests with the clash between the atheism of Moscow and the Christian spirit throughout other parts of the world.

More than 275 representative Republican men and women were on hand to attend the colorful Lincoln Day dinner of the valley women which was held in the Collonnade room of the McLure hotel.

Disdaining any oratorical fireworks, McCarthy's talk was of an intimate, homey nature, punctuated at times with humor. But on the serious side, he launched many barbs at the present setup of the State Department, at President Truman's reluctance to press investigation of "traitors from within," and other pertinent matters. . . . However, he added: "The morals of our people have not been destroyed. They still exist and this cloak of numbness and apathy needs only a spark to rekindle them."

Referring directly to the State Department, he declared: "While I cannot take the time to name all of the men in the State Department who have been named as members of the Communist Party and members of a spy ring, I have here in my hand a list of 205 that were known to the Secretary of State as being members of the Communist Party and who, nevertheless, are still working and shaping the policy in the State Department."

The speaker dwelt at length on the Alger Hiss case and mentioned the names of several others who, during the not so many years, were found to entertain subversive ideas but were still given positions of high trust in the government. "As you hear of this story of high treason," he said, "I know that you are saying to yourself well, why doesn't Congress do something about it?

"Actually, ladies and gentlemen, the reason for the graft, the corruption, the disloyalty, the treason in high government positions, the reason this continues is because of a lack of moral uprising on the part of the 140 million American people. In the light of history, however, this is not hard to explain. It is the result of an emotional hangover and a temporary moral lapse which follows every war. It is the apathy to evil which people who have been subjected to the tremendous evils of war feel.

"As the people of the world see mass murder, the destruction of defenseless and innocent people and all of the crime and lack of morals which go with war, they become numb and apathetic. It has always been thus after war."

At another time, he declared: "Today, we are engaged in a final all-out battle between Communistic atheism and Christianity. The modern champions of Communism have selected this as the time and, ladies and gentlemen, the chips are down they are truly down."

In an informal quiz with his audience, the Senator answered a number of questions dealing mostly with the plan of Secretary of Agriculture Brannan to destroy millions of tons of potatoes, eggs, butter, and fruits; he gave forthright views on the old age and social security problems and a number of other topics. . . .

Mrs. A. E. Eberhard, president of the Women's Group, presided. State Senator William Hannig led the group singing. The invocation was delivered by the Rev. Philip Goertz, pastor of the Second Presbyterian church, and the benediction was pronounced by the Rev. W. Carroll Thorn, of St. Luke's Episcopal Church.

(undated page, HWS journal)

Universal declaration of rights of the howlers:
Article 1. All human beings are endowed with the god-given right to make firewood from the fallen tree. Article 2. Any tree will do. If it is tall, it should be cut down. The quality of wood is no matter, the tree asked for it by growing tall. A decent public will cheer to see it toppled. Article 3. Rules of normal kindness do not extend to the celebrated person. Article 4. All persons may hope to become celebrated. Article 5. It is more important to speak than to think. The only danger is silence. Article 6. A howler must choose one course or the other: lie routinely, or do so only on important occasions, to be more convincing. (The Trotsky tenet.)

UNITED STATES HOUSE OF REPRESENTATIVES,
SPECIAL SUBCOMMITTEE OF THE COMMITTEE
ON UN-AMERICAN ACTIVITIES
PUBLIC HEARING, TUESDAY, MARCH 7, 1950

TRANSCRIPT: UNITED STATES GOVERNMENT PRINTING OFFICE

COMMITTEE ON UN-AMERICAN ACTIVITIES,
UNITED STATES HOUSE OF REPRESENTATIVES:
JOHN S. WOOD, *Georgia, Chairman*;
FRANCIS E. WALTER, *Pennsylvania*; RICHARD M. NIXON,
California; BURR P. HARRISON, *Virginia*; FRANCIS CASE, *South
Dakota*; JOHN MCSWEENEY, *Ohio*; HAROLD H. VELDE, *Illinois*;
MORGAN M. MOULDER, *Missouri*; BERNARD W. KEARNEY, *New York*

FRANK L. RAVENNER, COUNSEL
MELVIN C. MYERS, SENIOR INVESTIGATOR

The subcommittee of the Committee on Un-American Activities met in a public session, pursuant to notice, at 9:35 a.m. in room 226, Old House Office Building, Hon. John S. Wood (chairman) presiding. Committee members present: Representatives John S. Wood (chairman), Francis E. Walter, John McSweeney, Richard M. Nixon (arriving as indicated) and Harold H. Velde. Staff members present: Frank L. Ravenner, counsel; Melvin C. Myers, chief investigator.

MR. WOOD: The record will show this is the Committee on Un-American Activities sitting now in the city of Washington, District of Columbia. Those present in addition to Committee and Staff members are the recording secretary and visitors from the press corps in the back gallery of the room. Mr. Harrison Shepherd sits here before us accompanied by two persons. The committee will be in order.

Mr. Shepherd, will you hold up your right hand, please, and take the oath. Do you solemnly swear the testimony you shall give this committee will be the truth, the whole truth and nothing but the truth, so help you God?

MR. SHEPHERD: Yes.

MR. WOOD: Will you state your full name?

MR. SHEPHERD: Harrison William Shepherd.

MR. WOOD: When and where were you born?

MR. SHEPHERD: Lychgate, Virginia, July 6, 1916.

MR. WOOD: Have you any objection to the photographers making pictures?

MR. SHEPHERD: I would be happier if they didn't.

MR. WOOD: Well, gentlemen, you've heard him. Follow your conscience as usual.

(Murmuring and laughter from the gallery and photographs flashed.)

MR. RAVENNER: Honorable Chairman, before we begin questioning, may I ask to have Mr. Shepherd's friends or counsel identified?

MR. SHEPHERD: This is Mr. Arthur Gold, who is a lawyer, and Mrs. Violet Brown, who is my stenographer.

MR. WOOD: Mr. Shepherd, the committee retains a recording secretary to make a very thorough transcript of these proceedings. Mrs. Ward, would you please identify yourself.

(So identified.)

MR. SHEPHERD: Sir, Mrs. Brown and Mr. Gold are here in the capacity of friends.

MR. RAVENNER: Fine, then. Mr. Shepherd, the purpose of this meeting is for the Committee to determine the truth or falsity of certain statements you have made, regarding membership or association with the Communist Party. Do you understand?

MR. SHEPHERD: Yes.

MR. RAVENNER: All right. This will not take all day, gentlemen, we should be out of here in time for lunch. Mr. Shepherd, would you please tell us where you now reside, and your present occupation.

MR. SHEPHERD: I live in Asheville, North Carolina, and am an author of books.

MR. RAVENNER: How long have you lived there, and what employment have you held in that time?

MR. SHEPHERD: Since 1940. I haven't had very much work in Asheville, other than the writing. During the war I taught some Spanish lessons at a Teachers College.

MR. RAVENNER: While teaching foreign languages at the College, did you ever succeed in recruiting students to a Communist way of thinking?

MR. SHEPHERD: Goodness, I doubt it. I couldn't recruit them to put their bubble gum in the wastepaper basket before standing up to do conjugations. Sometimes it fell out of their mouths on the third-person plurals.

(Laughter in the gallery.)

MR. RAVENNER: Now will you answer the question? Did any of your students join up with the Communist Party?

MR. SHEPHERD: I honestly don't know what they did after the class.

MR. RAVENNER: Were you also in the Armed Services during those years, as a young man obviously fit for service?

THE LACUNA ❦ 483

MR. SHEPHERD: Unfortunately I was not found fit for service. I was called up instead for special work with the National Gallery of Art in Washington, D.C.

MR. RAVENNER: You were found unfit for service on what grounds, Mr. Shepherd?

MR. SHEPHERD: Psychological grounds.

MR. RAVENNER: You were determined unfit for reasons of mental and sexual deviance, is that correct?

MR. SHEPHERD: I was found only sane enough for the Civilian Services, sir. My mental capacities were deemed adequate for handling the country's most important national treasures. That was the determination of the Selective Service board.

(Mr. Nixon here entered the hearing and was seated near Mr. Velde. Brief discussion between Mr. Nixon and Mr. Velde.)

MR. RAVENNER: Did you or did you not at that time believe membership in the Communist Party was inimical to the interests of the United States?

MR. SHEPHERD: To be honest, sir, I didn't think one way or another about it. I never met any Communist Party members in this country.

MR. RAVENNER: Can you give me an answer 'Yes' or 'No'?

MR. SHEPHERD: Does a citizen have a right to be uncertain until further informed?

MR. RAVENNER: Let me inform you. A member of the Communist Party is a person who seeks the overthrow of the government of the United States by force and violence in this country. Is that something you approve of?

MR. SHEPHERD: I've never sought to overthrow the United States. Is that an answer?

MR. RAVENNER: It is a form of answer. Now, I understand that you were born in the United States, but chose to spend most of your life in another country. Is that correct?

MR. SHEPHERD: My mother was Mexican. We moved back there when I was twelve. She threatened to leave me by the tracks if I put up a fuss. So yes sir, I chose to go.

MR. RAVENNER: And after many years, what made you want to live here again?

MR. SHEPHERD: That's a complicated question you ask. It would take me a good while to answer, and you said you wanted to get this over quickly.

MR. RAVENNER: Well, then, let me ask an easier question. Did you associate with Communists while living in Mexico?

(A long hesitation from the witness, prior to answering.)

MR. SHEPHERD: That is not an easier question. Again, it could take some explanation.

MR. RAVENNER: Then let me make it easier still. We have papers here that show you were granted travel documents to come here in November 1939, as a travel companion and assistant to a man called to testify before this same committee. The Dies Committee, as it was called then. Our documents say a Harrison Shepherd, born 1916 in Lychgate, Virginia, was a member of the party that was granted a travel visa. Are you that person?

MR. SHEPHERD: I am.

MR. RAVENNER: Then we may assume these documents refer to you. That you were then living in the Mexican headquarters of the well-known Communist leader of Stalin's Bolshevik revolution, Leonadovich Trotsky.

MR. SHEPHERD: I beg your pardon?

MR. RAVENNER: Answer the question.

MR. SHEPHERD: I only want to clarify. Do you mean Lev Davidovich Trotsky, who led a worldwide movement to oppose Stalin? He was called by your Committee as a friendly witness, sir.

MR. RAVENNER: Just answer the question. Did you work for this Trotsky?

MR. SHEPHERD: Yes.

MR. RAVENNER: In what capacity?

MR. SHEPHERD: As his cook, his secretary-typist, and sometimes cleaner of rabbit cages. But usually the Commissar
preferred handling the manure himself.

MR. WOOD: Here, I'll have order!

MR. RAVENNER: You say you were his secretary. Do you
mean to say you helped prepare documents whose purpose
was to arouse a Communist insurrection?

(The witness did not answer.)

MR. VELDE: Mr. Shepherd, you may take the Fifth Amendment if you wish.

MR. SHEPHERD: I don't know how to answer, when you say
'helped prepare documents.' I was a typist. Sometimes I
could hardly understand the words in those documents. I
don't have any expertise in politics.

MR. NIXON: Is the welder of a bomb casing innocent of the
destruction it causes, just because he doesn't understand
physics?

MR. SHEPHERD: It's a very good question. Our munitions
plants make arms we sell to almost every country. Are we
now on both sides of all the wars?

MR. RAVENNER: Mr. Shepherd, you are instructed to answer
'yes' or 'no' to all further questions. One more outburst
will land you in contempt of Congress. Did you help prepare Communist documents for this Trotsky, a leader of
the Bolshevik revolution?

MR. SHEPHERD: Yes.

MR. RAVENNER: And are you still in contact with Comrade
Trotsky?

(Very long pause.)

MR. SHEPHERD: No.

MR. RAVENNER: Did you come to the United States directly from his employ?

(Pause.)

MR. RAVENNER: Yes or no?

MR. SHEPHERD: Sorry. Could you clarify the question?

MR. RAVENNER: Yes or no. Your last place of residence, prior to entering the United States in September, 1940, was the Trotskyite World Revolutionary Headquarters on Morelos Street, Coyoacán, outside of Mexico City.

MR. SHEPHERD: Yes.

MR. RAVENNER: Is it true that in that same place, several extreme acts of espionage and violence were committed, all directly linked with the Secret Police of Joseph Stalin?

MR. SHEPHERD: Yes. Committed against us.

MR. RAVENNER: You say you have no head for politics, so try to focus your powers, if you will, on one simple question. From that headquarters, did you come here on a program of overthrowing the United States government, however poorly you may have understood it? I want to hear one word, sir. Yes, or no.

MR. SHEPHERD: No.

MR. RAVENNER:: For what purpose, then, did you come to the United States?

MR. SHEPHERD: (Pause.) Yes or no?

MR. RAVENNER: You may elaborate in this instance.

MR. SHEPHERD: I came to deliver paintings to museums in New York City.

MR. NIXON: Well, that's some delivery job if he's still here after ten years. Even Sears Roebuck doesn't generally take that long.

(Laughter in the gallery.)

MR. RAVENNER: Tell me, what was the nature of these paintings?

MR. SHEPHERD: Oil-based paint applied to canvas.

(Laughter in the gallery.)

MR. WOOD: Mr. Shepherd, we are not fools. We can see you're attempting to mock this hearing. This is the last time I will warn you to answer the question as directly as you can. What sort of paintings did you smuggle into the United States?

MR. SHEPHERD: Surrealist. All transported with legal customs documents. The papers are still on file at the museums, I expect.

MR. RAVENNER: And were these paintings by the Mexican painter Diego Rivera, who is well known as a dangerous Communist agitator?

MR. SHEPHERD: No.

MR. RAVENNER: No?

MR. WOOD: Remember, Mr. Shepherd, that you have sworn an oath.

MR. SHEPHERD: Not Mr. Rivera's paintings, no.

(Congressmen Wood and Verne spent some moments conferring with Mr. Ravenner and looking through documents.)

MR. RAVENNER: Were these paintings from the household of Diego Rivera, or his possessions? Answer the question fully.

MR. SHEPHERD: They were painted by his wife, the artist Frida Kahlo.

MR. RAVENNER: Then you admit, you knowingly associated with the Communist militants, Mr. and Mrs. Diego Rivera?

MR. SHEPHERD: Yes.

MR. RAVENNER:: For what purpose?

MR. SHEPHERD: In the instance you mention, to oversee the transport of her paintings to galleries in New York.

MR. RAVENNER: They hired you to carry crates across the border into the United States. Where you have now remained nearly ten years. My documents say there were eight crates altogether, some of them too large for a man to lift by himself.

MR. SHEPHERD: That's right. We used hand trucks to get them off the trains.

MR. RAVENNER: Did you know precisely what you were transporting? Did you pack these crates yourself?

MR. SHEPHERD: No. I had a roster with the names of the paintings.

MR. RAVENNER: You smuggled large crates of unknown content into this country? From the headquarters of some of the most dangerous Communists in any country touching our borders. Is that correct?

(The defendant conferred briefly with the identified friend, Arthur Gold.)

MR. SHEPHERD: Congressmen, nothing exploded.

MR. WOOD: What say?

MR. SHEPHERD: I delivered artworks. You're hinting at a crime that was not committed.

MR. WOOD: Mr. Shepherd, I will put to you then a different question. Could this so-called artwork also be called Communist propaganda?

MR. SHEPHERD: In my opinion, sir? Art takes its meaning in the eye of the beholder.

MR. RAVENNER: Could you state an answer in plain English? What was the purpose of the concealed objects you transported into this country?

MR. SHEPHERD: May I answer freely?

MR. RAVENNER: In your own words, yes. All right.

MR. SHEPHERD: The purpose of art is to elevate the spirit, or pay a surgeon's bill. Or both, really. It can help a person remember or forget. If your house doesn't have many windows in it, you can hang up a painting and have a view. Of a whole different country, if you want. If your spouse is homely, you can gaze at a lovely face and not get in trouble for it.

(Laughter in the gallery.)

It can be painted on a public wall or locked in a mansion. The first paintings Mrs. Kahlo ever sold went to one of your famous film stars, Edward G. Robinson. Art is one thing I do know about. A book has all the same uses I mentioned, especially for the house without enough windows. Art by itself is nothing, until it comes into that house. People here wanted Mrs. Kahlo's art, and I carried it.

(Silence in the gallery.)

You asked me why I've stayed here so long. I can try to say. People have a lot of color and songs in Mexico, more art than they have hopes, it often seemed to me. Here, I found people bursting with hope but not many songs. They didn't sing, they turned on the radio. They wanted stories, like anything. So I decided to try my hand at making art for the hopeful. Because I wasn't any good at the other thing, manufacturing hopes for the artful. America was the most hopeful place I'd ever imagined. My neighbors were giving over their hairpins and door hinges to melt down for building the good ship America. I wanted to give her things too. So I stayed here.

(Quiet in the gallery for some time. Of an unusual kind, the type to hear a pin drop.)

MR. RAVENNER: You say that Edward G. Robinson is an associate of Communists?

MR. SHEPHERD: I'm sorry, I might have made a mistake. It was a long time ago. It might have been J. Edgar Hoover who bought the paintings.

(Considerable laughter in the gallery.)

MR. WOOD: Order!

MR. RAVENNER: Now see here, if you continue to mock this hearing we will hold you in contempt of Congress. I am going to ask you a series of questions to which you will answer Yes or No. One word beyond that will get you removed to the jail house. Do you understand me?

MR. SHEPHERD: Yes.

MR. RAVENNER: Do you now, or did you ever, work for Communists in Mexico?

MR. SHEPHERD: Yes.

MR. RAVENNER: Have you yourself written works about foreign people, men disloyal to their leaders, with the intention of distributing these tracts widely in the United States?

(Pause.)

MR. SHEPHERD: Yes.

MR. RAVENNER: Have you been in contact with Communist revolutionaries since coming to the United States?

MR. SHEPHERD: Yes.

MR. RAVENNER: I have here a good deal of evidence, *in print*, news articles and so forth, to the effect your books are being read in Communist China. That you opposed the use of the atomic bomb. I have evidence you made the following statement. I want you to listen carefully, and then confirm or deny it. And here I quote Mr. Shepherd: "Our leader is an empty sack. You could just as well knock him over, put a head with horns on a stick, and follow that. Most of us never choose to believe in the nation, we just come up short on better ideas." Mr. Shepherd, are these your words?

MR. SHEPHERD: A few among many, yes. In a story.

MR. RAVENNER: Mr. Shepherd, I am asking a simple question. Did you write these words? You are asked only to confirm or deny.

MR. SHEPHERD: Yes. Those are my words.

MR. RAVENNER: Mr. Wood, gentlemen, that is all I have. This hearing is finished.

Afterward, 1959

by Violet Brown

The Asheville Trumpet, *July 16, 1951*

Obituary

Harrison Shepherd, 34, perished June 29 while swimming in the ocean near Mexico City. A resident of Asheville, the deceased had traveled to Mexico under an assumed name while under investigation for crimes including dismissal from the Department of State for treasonous actions, misrepresentation of qualifications and fraud. He wrote two books, had no record of military service and was well known as a Communist. Authorities cite no evidence of foul play and believe he took his life. Reared in a broken home, Shepherd leaves no survivors. No services are planned.

The most important part of a story is the piece of it you don't know. He said that plenty. It would be no surprise if he asks for that put on his gravestone, if there is to be one. There you see. Hangs the tale, and still yet more to find out.

You believe a thing is hopeless. You believe a book burned, yet the words persist. In this case twice, first in Mexico, his notes and drafts all taken by police after the murder, meant for destruction but precariously rescued. Then later on given to me for burning, and not burned. You believe a life ended, but the newsmen can't make that true by saying so, even saying it many times. It's dying makes a death, and living makes life.

The salvation of all, the life or the tale either one, I'll come to directly. First the notebooks. For you see I hadn't burned them, the day I was asked. He said I could only stay on working with him if we disposed of every word, his life entire if you asked me. I saw what he meant to do that day, and why. He took those writings to be evidence for his hanging. But I believed it could be otherwise, evidence for the good in him. I had no idea what his notes contained, but I knew the man.

I took what he pulled off his shelves that day, and while he was upstairs looking for more, I stuffed it all in the big leather mail pouch. My heart cantered, I have no nerve for crime. But that day, found some. By the time he was watching me out the upstairs window, I was half done. You should see what all I threw in that tar barrel: wastepaper, advertising supplements, the whole trash basket under my table, and more. Quite a few ugly letters I'd set aside. Things that deserved to be gone.

His notebooks went home with me to Mrs. Bittle's, and there they stayed in a box in my wardrobe, hidden under some knitting wool. Let those men come and search the place, was my thought, for they'd not have a second look at a box of knitting wool and needles. Most will run from the sight. I thought I would only keep it there until Mr. Shepherd changed his mind. Or until such time as needed, to prove he'd done no wrong. No such time came, as far as I could see, though I still had no idea what he'd written in a natural lifetime of little books. A nerve for that sort of crime I did not have, to poke my nose in a living man's diary.

I didn't do that until coming back from Mexico. At first, a glance was all I could endure, looking for certain dates and such, to make a proper obituary. But of course that did not come to pass, they ran their own little useless piece, so my researching wasn't any excuse for long. But still I went on glancing, a page here and thither. Time and again I took up his notebooks knowing they were not meant for my eyes, yet my eyes went on looking, many were the reasons. Some of them plain by now, I surely think.

Going to Mexico, that had been my idea. I didn't like to say so afterward, due to events. But at the time I proposed it, things had come to a point. After the hearing he'd stopped writing, for good he said. Instead he bought a television set and let its nonsense rule his days. *Mook the Moon Man* comes on at four, and so on. I still came to his house twice a week, but the mail was not worth answering. My concern wasn't to take his money, I'd found another job. I could have left him alone, but feared to do it.

One day he sat staring at the advertisements and declared he hated what America looked like now. Sofas and chairs with little pointy legs. Like a woman in high heels, he said, walking around smiling with a bad backache. And those metal funnel-hat lamps on poles, they look like they want to electrocute you. He missed beauty.

I asked him, why not go to Mexico then, I reckon it is prettier there. He said he couldn't unless I went with him. Thinking that would be that. But I said, "All right, I will call the air-port right now." What possessed me? I can't say.

He was so changed by then, even his looks. Whatever used to show up for its workaday there inside him, it had shut off the lights and gone on home. He was fagged out in the chair as usual, in his old gray flannels, smoking, never taking his eyes off the set. *Captain Video* was on, some underwater band of thieves fighting. They had Al Hodge by the neck, fixing to drown him. I asked him whether we ought to go back to Mérida, because he'd seemed to like it there. He said no, let's go to Isla Pixol so he could dive in the ocean, because that was all that made him happy as a boy. That was a grave moment, I see that now. Full of all that was to come, and me with no inkling. But I believe he did. Have an inkling.

That was in April, a year and some past the hearing. A Monday or Thursday, for those were the afternoons I still came. A joyful month if there ever was one, you'd think. Even a feather duster will lay an egg in April. But such generous feeling had gone from the land. No real work remained for me at Mr. Shepherd's after the hearing, and I'd commenced looking for another income, disliking to be any burden. I was floored to find the city wouldn't hire me. Not at the clerk's office, though I'd once kept that whole place afloat. Not at the library where I'd volunteered. I can't be a government employee due to previous association with the wrong element, they told me, it is all in print, and nothing to be done about it. It was the same at the Teachers College. After some months of asking, a hateful thing in itself, an acquaintance from the Woman's Club consented to recommend me as a bookkeeper at Raye's Department Store. It was a low position, mornings only, and I had to work in a basement office. They could take no chance on a customer seeing my face.

Hard times are nothing new to me. My father used to say a man can get used to anything except hanging by the neck. I believe that. But Mr. Shepherd could not. He had a well of hopelessness inside him, and it bubbled out to flood his days and his sights for the future if any. He said if readers found him so despicable, he wouldn't trouble them with more books. It was hard to argue, as the trinkle of mail that still came was dreadful. Why does a person spend money on a stamp, to spout bile at a stranger? "Now our boys are going to Korea to be killed and mutilated by the Communists. So if one of them named Harrison Shepherd is starving, that delights me immeasurably."

He'd been called names before, and borne it. But when a man's words are taken from him and poisoned, it's the same as poisoning the man. He could not speak, for how his own tongue would be fouled. Words were his all. I felt I'd witnessed a murder, just as he'd seen his friend murdered in Mexico. Only this time they left the body living.

His books weren't banned anymore, just gone. They said he'd defrauded the publisher with the loyalty affidavit, so the advance money had to be returned and the book dropped. Not many options remained to Harrison Shepherd, watching a Moon Man in his living room being one of the few. He said Artie Gold had predicted it. That sometimes you really can see the empire is falling, and Mr. Gold saw it coming, all the green grass of our land killed for good. I said fiddlesticks, grass will grow right up through a sidewalk and the Lord loves what He cannot kill.

But that was false cheer, I knew better. Nothing was coming up by then, no gumption rising anywhere without a resolution promptly passed to cut it down. The Woman's Club had become a drear business, their sole concern to oppose waywardness: a City Council man or a school history book. Harriet Tubman and Frederick Douglass no good for children, they set a bad example. It's the same everywhere now, look at faces. In the luncheonettes on Charlotte you'll see people lined up with a haint upon them, sore afraid of not being as American as the next one. What's the matter, sir, you look as though you've seen a Communist! The word itself could get a child's mouth washed with soap. It used to be in the *Geographics*, I learned the word as a child, "Every-Day Life in the Ukraine" and so forth. But the newspapers and magazines have had their mouths washed with soap too. Even today, years after Mr. Shepherd's hearing. It would still proceed just about as it did then. People have no more vinegar in them. You can resign from the Woman's Club, but the world is all, you can't just stop attending.

Around the first part of May, then, after we'd discussed it, I went and had a talk with Arthur Gold about going to Mexico. Mr. Gold encouraged it. He said the drives were stepping up. Now that they had what they called evidence on Mr. Shepherd from the hearing, it was paperwork and only that, before criminal charges came. With an indictment the federal men would take his passport. Really Mr. Gold was unsure why they hadn't done so already. He said Mr. Shepherd should go now, while he still could.

I hated to ask it, but inquired whether it would be wise for him just to go on down to Mexico and stay put. Mr. Gold allowed that he and Mr. Shepherd had discussed this already, some time ago. It wouldn't do any good. The federal investigators can pull him right back here, once they have indicted. Mr. Gold said there were many examples. A man escaped from Ellis Island by stowing away on a ship, and they tracked him down all the way to France. They'll go to the ends of the earth to haul back people they've declared unfit to be Americans. It makes no sense. Like hateful letters from people declaring they'll never read Mr. Shepherd's books. Why not leave the book where it is and get on with the day? I didn't see how they could take another pound of flesh from this poor man, when all he'd done in life was work at making others content. Mr. Gold said with due respect, a lot of men without one mean bone in them are currently sitting in Sing Sing prison. And now the Congress was voting to make treason laws bind in cold war as they do in a shooting war. Meaning, some would hang.

Well, that lit a fire under me. I went on and booked the tickets and made the plans. Mr. Gold advised reserving the tickets under a different name, the film stars do that regularly. Then simply give the right name when you show up. I chose Ben Franklin and Betsy Ross. Mr. Shepherd was tickled with that. He began to take interest. He stopped smoking all the time and went outside more. They opened the swimming pool in Montford after two summers closed for the polio, and he started to go there often. He'd loved swimming as a boy. I would walk to the pool with him sometimes just to sit and watch, for he was changed in the water, shiny as soap, and could hold his breath like I don't know what. I want to say a fish, but that isn't right. He'd go the whole pool, one end to the other not coming up. I asked him about it, and he said his childhood was that exciting: he learned to hold his breath for entertainment.

The flight was on the Compañia Mexicana de Aviación. In Mexico City, on the way to the train station, we got caught up in an awful traffic jam. Suitcases between us in the taxicab and the sweat rolling down, for we had to keep the windows closed, the city entire smelled of tear gas. The driver told Mr. Shepherd a riot had been going for days, working men, and police trying to break it up. Mr. Shepherd said good, they've still got fight in them here, and while we sat stuck there he told a story of long ago, his school years in Washington. The homeless veterans making a riot for their war pay. He said it smelled like this. The army used gas and guns against people living in tents, Americans. And those folks still yet bold enough to give it heck, fight back or die trying.

We took the train to Veracruz, then a bus, and a ferry. Like the sailors with Columbus, I felt we'd soon come to the edge and plop off. Mr. Shepherd said his mother used to complain Isla Pixol was so far from anything, you had to yell three times before Jesus would hear you. That I believed. The hotel in town was old as Moses, its elevator nothing but a cage on a chain. The boy that carried our suitcases into it claimed it was the oldest in all the New World, and I believed that too.

First off, Mr. Shepherd hired a car to take us out to the old hacienda where he had lived. The old place lay in ruins, but he didn't seem disappointed. He went back many more times, often alone. I found my way around the little town and shopped for trinkets to bring my niece and the babies. One day Mr. Shepherd came back with a man who had supper with us, the two of them slapping one another's shoulders, saying "brother" and "the devil." Each unable to believe the other was still alive. Leandro was his name. There were others in the village, evidently, who remembered the boy with no inkling he now walked the earth as a man of repute, or even as a man.

All Mr. Shepherd wanted to do was dive in the water. I wanted no part of that, but to hear him tell it, the ocean was heaven and all the fish angels. He had a diving mask he'd bought in town, and needed nothing else, he'd stay out the day entire and come back sunburned. I thought he would grow some gills. More and more he returned to the fishes, leaving the world of people, it seemed. One evening he came to dinner with a calendar and showed me a day he'd circled, some two weeks off. He wanted to stay until then. Well, that meant changing our return, no small thing. I wasn't very pleased. I'd begged time off unpaid from Raye's, and they would be happy to replace me. I asked if he meant to change it again after that. Like a child putting off the bedtime. He said no, that was the day, after the full moon. That meant something to him.

On our last day, he got himself set to go out to his beach and wanted me to come. I didn't mind sitting on the shore with a book. I'd done so before. But once there, he began to act peculiar. A slew of little boys came by, and he told them in Spanish he'd pay them money to come watch him dive, just to see how long he could stay under. These fellows looked like they'd take his coin to watch him whistle Dixie if that's what he wanted, so off we all did troop down a path through the bushes.

The place he meant to go diving was a little cove with cliffs behind it and a strip of shore growing smaller by the minute, as the tide came up. The morning was getting on, and he seemed impatient to go in the water. The tide was still low but coming in right fast, eating up that little beach as it came. I wondered how long he'd expect me to stay there. I don't know what he said before wading in. I paid no heed. Probably I was a little put out with him. I had my book. But after a while I looked out at the water and didn't see him. I waited. Then counted to fifty, then one hundred. I didn't see any way he could have left the cove. And it struck me: he's drowned. Those little boys knew it too, standing in their group, for they were not looking at the water anymore, but at me. They seemed to think it was up to me now, to fix what had gone wrong.

Did I scream? That isn't my way, so I don't think so. I'm sure I stood up, threw down the book, and moved about. I remember thinking I couldn't go in the water because it would wreck my shoes. So it hadn't soaked in yet, that life had set down here before me a far worse thing than wrecked shoes. Or anything else I'd thus far known. It's true I lost a husband in the flood of the French Broad River in '16, Freddy Brown, and that broke a young girl's heart. But this was worse. My heart had grown older, with more in it to break. I can't put words to that afternoon. He would know words for the feelings I bore, but I only knew the feelings.

I told those boys as best I could, to run get some kind of help. A group of men came out from the village and searched the cove. One was the friend, Leandro. Later the police came along too. By nightfall a hundred people must have been in that cove as the tide went out, every hour giving back more beach for the crowd that came to stand on it. It never really went dark, for the moon rose big and full, just as the sun went down. Most of those people were merely curious to see a body, I expect. Yet all went away that night without satisfaction, there was no body. He was just gone.

I remember parts of that day, not all. I can't say how I came back to the hotel. Police had to search his room for some clue or a note, thinking Mr. Shepherd might have done away with himself on purpose. I knew better, and yet I really didn't. I stood at the door while they turned out suitcases and drawers, and me thinking, "Here it is again, the police ransacking for evidence, and the man they will not find." I spied one peculiar thing—the little stone man he liked to carry in his pocket. He'd left his room tidy, every last thing put away, but that little man was out on the table grinning at me! Or rather it howled, that round mouth open like a hole in the head. It made me want to howl too, and not much does. I could tell it had been set there for a reason, and I was the reason. But what he meant to tell me, I knew not.

Once back home, I took care of things as best I knew how, which was not very well. I could only think one thing at a time, starting with: get up. Arthur Gold was a great help, also torn up about it, but less surprised. He had done the will, you see. Mr. Shepherd left all to me, his house and proceeds from the books, if any. The cats. The money was no fortune, but more than a widow's mite. Curiously, he had wired some money to a bank in Mexico City, addressed to Mrs. Kahlo. He did that shortly before our trip. He hadn't mentioned it, but I decided it was no great surprise. That lady was ever in need of cash.

With his legal testament was a letter he'd written to me. It contained certain instructions about his books, and personal things, appreciation for the years. Most of it need not be told here. But he said two things that shocked: first, that we'd had a great love. So he said, in those words. No one had been more important to him. And he said not to grieve. His sole regret was the stain his life and ways had put upon mine, and he wanted me to be shed of all such worry. He said this is the happy ending everyone wanted. Well, I was furious at that. For him to quit on life, and call that happiness.

I moved into his house, farewell to Mrs. Bittle at last, I won't dwell on that. The part-time at Raye's gave me afternoons free for setting things to rights in his house and answering what mail still came. My first chore was an obituary for the Asheville paper. I can't begin to tell what care I took, keening over each word and many unwritten. I delivered it to the office and spoke with a man, and was barely out the door I expect when he threw it in his ashcan. They ran their own little piece instead. They had no wish to tell what a man has done with his life. That would require honest witness. The simpler thing is to state what he has been called.

In 1954 came the death of his friend, Mrs. Kahlo. The family must have gone through some upheaval, the usual business of sorting the clutter of the deceased, for they sent a trunk of Mr. Shepherd's things. A young man's clothes many years out of date, a few photographs, and not much else to speak of. But inside the trunk was a letter from Mrs. Kahlo, addressed to me. I thought that very strange. We'd only met the once. But there was my name, so this trunk was not some mere forgotten thing, she'd meant to have it sent to me. She planned that before she died.

The letter was so peculiar. A drawing of a pyramid sketched out in drab purple and brown, and on its top a yellow eye with lines like rays from the sun. Across the eye she'd written "soli" to mean the sun, I gathered. And scribbled at the top of the page in a hand like a child's: "Violet Brown, Your American friend is dead. Someone else is here." It was in English. But I could no more understand it than the man in the moon.

The photographs I put away, and the clothes I meant to give the Salvation Army, for who knows what a person will wear if he's cold enough. They would have to be washed first, and it sat for some weeks before I could get around to that. It was only by luck I went through the trouser pockets. That makes my heart race now, for how easily this could have gone another way. But it happened as it did. I found the little notebook.

I knew what it was. I'll say that. I opened the little leather booklet and saw a penciled hand, the boy with his laments about Mother and so forth. Oh, I cried. I felt I'd found my own lost child. I sat and read it through on the bedroom floor where I'd been sorting the clothes. My heart pounding, because of that cave he found under the water. And his business with the moon, learning to wait for a day the tide would help push him through to the other side, without his drowning first. That was him all over. That patient study.

I read all of it. The happy ending, as he called it. Because that is what he did, right under my nose while I sat reading on the beach. He swam in that cave, to rest with the bones or else come out the other side, and walk himself into life as some other man who is not dead.

Fight or die was his choice. I know which it was. Mrs. Kahlo would have hidden him when he got that far, and helped him make a new start. She thrived on that kind of thing. He had wired the money. "Someone else is here," she'd written, plain as daylight, and also the name she used to call him, long forgotten. It was his idea to make her send a message, to put me at rest. I feel I know that too.

I had to get out all his notebooks then, and look again. Three years earlier I'd read most of it through eyes half-shut with grief, then packed it away, forgetting what all I could. Now, out came the box. Papers covered the dining table, a mess like times of yore. With that one little booklet put back in place, it came as a different story. Because of that burrow through rock and water—lacuna, he called it. This time I read with a different heart, understanding the hero would still be standing at journey's end. Or at least, live or die, he'd known of a chance and aimed to take it. What you don't know can't hurt you, they say. Yet it can. So much hangs upon it.

What I have done with these writings he could have done himself. Set down his life as he chose, for others to read. He began the one chapter, then stopped, claiming he couldn't go forward for want of the booklet that was lost. I could say, "Now it is found, so Mr. Shepherd would want to go on with his story." Which is fiddlesticks, and I know it. He wanted to put his boyhood away and keep still about it. God speaks for the silent man, oh, that I have heard. I've struggled with my conscience, it has cost me dear. It does so still.

Yet one day I decided to go on with it. I was here in Montford, for he gave me the place and only could have meant for me to live in it. I use a different bedroom to sleep in, of course, and his study room under the gable eave is a place I don't go. But it had to be his own bathroom mirror I faced each morning, the very place where he shaved and answered his Lord and conscience. Now it was a lady looking back from the glass, and one bright morn I told her: Listen here. If God speaks for the man who keeps quiet, then Violet Brown may be His instrument.

I don't say it was swift or sure. It took considering. Typing up a manuscript, that I can do. His hand was legible, and errors were few. Putting all in order was no easy trick, but no worse than some card files I've seen at the Asheville library. I left nothing out but the things that had no business, a market list or telephone numbers, certain letters. Of his story I have told all, even when it pained me to do it, or passed my understanding. But the question stood everlasting at my shoulder: Was it mine to tell?

This day the telephone could ring and my heart would squeeze, for the thought it might be him, and the answer no. Even as I am a person of the world, and eight years now gone by since I saw him in it. Years do not erase a bereavement. Mr. Shepherd, where be ye? I could still ask. And here is an answer: in those little books. I always could find him there. So this might be nothing very different from the pining girls singing for lost love on the radio. Maybe I turned to typing it for the pleasure of being his daily helpmeet again. Even if that's so, in the middle of all, the story worked itself ahead of the man. I will say Mr. Shepherd persuaded me, against his own will.

Not in so many words. I did hope for that, some instruction in his text to guide my hand. Well, my stars, the thing was like the Bible—look hard enough in its pages, and you'll find what you seek. Love your neighbor, or slay him with the jawbone of an ass.

It's the same herein. He plainly said, Burn these words. He said a mute people will leave behind good stout architecture, and not their squalid lives of trial. Those who come after will be struck by the majesty. He meant to leave behind only the monuments of his books. As he lived and breathed, I saw his wish and I held to that. And then saw the monuments tumble. In this strange, cold time that has settled on us, people did what they could to bury the man and throw everything he'd ever made into the hole they'd dug for him. Like a mummy in Egypt.

His life was a marvel, whether he knew that or didn't. His way of seeing a cat in a cold wind, or skeletons pressed flat in the dust. A dead fish thrown in the kitchen slop pail. He could cry for about anything and give it a decent burial. He was so afraid of living, yet live he did. That's a monument. He wrote about those who came before, giving flesh to their cares. He was driven to it.

Now I do the same for him. Even knowing, as I do, how everyone makes firewood from the fallen tree. The professors like to hunt out some sin of Shakespeare himself, and pass that off as the golden store of the learned. I couldn't bear this to touch Mr. Shepherd, or his loved ones or even children, if such a thing has now come to pass. I want time for him. All the paint washed off, bare limestone revealed.

That is my reason for having it locked up and held. Mr. Gold knew how to fix that up. People at a bank do this very thing, holding documents for a set number of years before hauling it out of the vault for the newspapers or what have you. I told him fifty. I had to choose, and that is a sturdy number. Long enough to be sure we are gone. Yet not so long that I couldn't imagine people still walking about in shoes, rather than flying on clouds. People who might want to look back on those who labored and birthed the times they have inherited. But maybe that's wrong, and already we'll be a graveyard of weeds they won't want to visit. You, I mean to say. The times you have inherited. I wonder that: Who be ye?

I dread to do what I do now, commending a man's life into the bleak passage to some other place, be it filled with light or darkness. This is my small raft. I know not what waits on the other side.

ABOUT THE AUTHOR

Barbara Kingsolver is the author of seven works of fiction, including the novels *The Poisonwood Bible*, *Animal Dreams*, and *The Bean Trees*, as well as books of poetry, essays, and creative nonfiction. Her most recent book is the enormously influential bestseller *Animal, Vegetable, Miracle: A Year of Food Life*. Kingsolver's work has been translated into more than twenty languages and has earned literary awards and a devoted readership at home and abroad. In 2000, she was awarded the National Humanities Medal, our country's highest honor for service through the arts. She lives with her family on a farm in southern Appalachia.